W9-BRP-709

THE ATLAS SIX

Olivie Blake

ALSO *by*
OLIVIE BLAKE:

Masters of Death
Lovely Tangled Vices
One For My Enemy
La Petite Mort
Fairytales of the Macabre (Fairytale Collections, Vol. I)
Midsummer Night Dreams (Fairytale Collections, Vol. II)
The Lovers Grim (Fairytale Collections, Vol. III)

By OLIVIE BLAKE *and*
LITTLE CHMURA:

Alpha
Alpha, Vol. II: Rising

to my physicist boy
and my starry-eyed girl

and to LORD OLIVER,
for all the punches.

Copyright © 2020 by Olivie Blake.
Illustrations by Little Chmura. Cover design by Olivie Blake.

All rights reserved. This book or any portion thereof
may not be reproduced or used in any manner whatsoever
without the express written permission of the author.

BEGINNING.

PERHAPS IT WAS A TIRED THING, all the references the world had already
made to the Ptolemaic Royal Library of Alexandria. History had proven
it endlessly fascinating as a subject, either because the obsession with what
it might have contained was bounded only by the imagination or because
humanity typically longs for things most ardently as a collective. All men can
love a forbidden thing, generally speaking, and in most cases knowledge is
precisely that; lost knowledge even more so. Tired or not, there is something
for everyone to long for when it comes to the Library of Alexandria, and
we have always been a species highly susceptible to the call of the distant
unknown.

Before it was destroyed, the library was said to contain over four
hundred thousand papyrus scrolls on history, mathematics, science,
engineering, and also magic, which advanced in scope and progress as much
as any other topic of study. Many people incorrectly assume time to be a
steady incline, a measured arc of growth and progress, but when history is
written by the victors the narrative can often misrepresent that shape. In
reality, time as we experience it is merely an ebb and flow, more circular
than it is direct. Social trends and stigmas change, and the direction is not
always forward. Magic is no different.

The little-known truth of the matter is that the Library of Alexandria
burned down to save itself. It died to rise again, in something less
metaphorically phoenix-like and more strategically Sherlockian. When
Julius Caesar rose to power, it became obvious to the ancient Caretakers
that an empire could only sit successfully upon a chair of three legs:
subjugation, desperation, and ignorance. They knew, too, that the world
would forever be besieged by similar pursuits of despotism, and therefore

determined that such a valuable archive of wisdom would have to be carefully hidden in order to survive.

It was an old trick, really, death and disappearance so to start again, which depended entirely on the library's ability to keep its own secret. The medeians, the most learned among the magical population, were permitted to use the pieces they squirreled away so long as they accepted an equal obligation to care for them. In the society that grew from the library's remains, privileges for its members were as unmatched as their responsibilities. All the knowledge the world possessed existed at their fingertips, and all they had to do in return was continue to nurture it, to make it grow.

As the world spread—expanding beyond the libraries of Babylon, Carthage, Constantinople to the collections of Islamic and Asian libraries lost to imperialism and empire—so did the Alexandrian archives, and as their influence expanded, so did the so-called Society itself. Every ten years a new class of potential initiates was chosen. The candidates spent one year in training, learning the functions of the archives and what would eventually become a lifelong craft. It was, in many ways, comparable to a doctorate or a fellowship. For one year, each individual selected for the Society lived, ate, slept, and breathed the archives and their contents, with five of the six potential candidates being inducted at the end of the year. Following that, the new initiates rigorously pursued their course of study for an additional year before being presented with the opportunity to stay and continue their work, or, more likely, to accept a new offer of employment. Alexandrians typically went on to be political leaders, patrons, CEOs and laureates. The truly curious would remain behind and vie for positions as Caretakers. What awaited an Alexandrian after initiation was wealth, power, prestige, and knowledge beyond their wildest dreams, and thus, to be chosen to sit for initiation was the first in a lifetime of endless possibility.

This was what Dalton Ellery relayed to the most recent class of initiates, none of whom had been informed why they were there or what they would be competing for. Likely they did not yet grasp that by virtue of standing in that room, Dalton Ellery was himself a uniquely skilled medeian, the likes of which they would not encounter again for generations, who had chosen this path over the many others he might have taken. He, like them, had once discarded the person he might have been and the life he might have lived—which would have been ordinary by comparison, most likely. He would

have had a profession of some sort, perhaps even a lucrative one, folding
into the mortal economy in some useful way, but witnessing nothing like
what he'd seen by virtue of his acceptance. He might have done exceptional
magic, but would have fallen shy of extraordinary himself. Inevitably he
would have succumbed to mundanity, to struggle, to boredom, as all humans
eventually did—but now, because of this, he wouldn't. The pittances of a
shrunken existence would count among the many things he would never again
encounter from the moment he'd taken his seat in this room.

He looked out at their faces and imagined again the life he might have
lived; the lives they *all* might have lived had they never been offered such…
riches. Eternal glory. Unparalleled wisdom. Here they would unlock the
secrets the world had kept from itself for centuries, for millennia. Things
no ordinary eyes would ever see, and which no lesser minds could possibly
understand.

Here, their lives would change. Here their former selves would be
destroyed, like the library itself, only to be built back up again and hidden in
the shadows, never to be seen except by the Caretakers, by the Alexandrians,
and by the ghost of lives uncrossed and paths untaken.

Greatness isn't easy, Dalton didn't say, nor did he add that greatness was
never offered to anyone who couldn't stand to bear it. He merely told them
of the library, of their paths to initiation, and of what stood within reach—if
they only had the courage to reach out and grasp it.

They were entranced, as well they should be. Dalton was a very good
at breathing life into things, ideas, objects. It was a subtle skill. Optically his
skills were less magical and more professional finesse, which made him an
exceptional academic. In fact, it made him the perfect face for the new class
of Alexandrians.

He knew before he started talking that they would all accept the offer. It
was a formality, really. Nobody turned down the Alexandrian Society. Even
those pretending at disinterest would be unable to resist. They would fight, he
knew, tooth and nail, to survive the next year of their lives, and if they were
as steadfast and talented as the Society presumed them to be, most of them
would.

Most of them.

THE MORAL OF THE STORY IS THIS:
Beware the man who faces you unarmed.
If in his eyes you are not the target,
then you can be sure you are the weapon.

I: WEAPONS

LIBBY

Five Hours Ago

THE DAY LIBBY RHODES met Nicolás Ferrer de Varona was coincidentally also the day she discovered that *incensed*, a word she had previously had no use for, was now the only conceivable way to describe the sensation of being near him. That had been the day Libby accidentally set fire to the lining of several centuries-old drapes in the office of Professor Breckenridge, Dean of Students, clinching both Libby's admission to New York University of Magical Arts as well as her undying hatred for Nico in a single incident. All the days since that one had been a futile exercise in restraint.

Incandescence aside, this was to be a very different sort of day, as it was finally going to be the last of them. Barring any accidental encounters, which Libby was certain they'd both furiously ignore—Manhattan was a big place, after all, with plenty of people ravenously avoiding each other—she and Nico were finally going their separate ways. She'd practically burst into song over it that morning, which her boyfriend Ezra presumed to be the consequence of the occasion's more immediate matters: graduating top of her class (tied with Nico, but there was no use focusing on that), or delivering the NYUMA valedictory speech. Neither accolade was anything to scoff at, obviously, but the more enticing prospect was the newness of the era approaching.

It was the last day Libby Rhodes would ever set eyes on Nico de Varona, and she couldn't have been more exuberant about the dawn of a simpler, superior, less Nico-infested life.

"Rhodes," he acknowledged upon taking his seat beside her on the commencement stage. He slid her surname around like a marble on his tongue before sniffing the air, facetious as always. "Hm. Do you smell smoke, Rhodes?"

Very funny. *Hilarious.*

"Careful, Varona. You know this auditorium's on a fault line, don't you?"

"Of course. Have to, seeing as I'll be working on it next year, won't I?" he mused, and then peered into the crowd, half a tick of laughter tugging at the corner of his mouth. "Ah, Fowler's here too, I see."

Libby bristled at the mention of Ezra. "Why wouldn't he be here?"

"Oh, no reason. Just thought you might've leveled up by now, Rhodes."

Do not engage, do not engage, do not engage—

"Ezra's just been promoted, actually," she said coolly.

"From mediocrity to competence?"

"No, from—"

Libby broke off, tightening one fist and counting silently to three.

"He's a project manager now."

"My goodness," Nico said drily, "how *impressive.*"

She shot him a glare, and he smiled.

"Your tie's crooked," she informed him, giving her voice a lilt of impassivity as his hand reflexively rose to straighten it. "Did Gideon not fix it for you on your way in?"

"He did, but—" Nico broke off, catching himself, while Libby silently congratulated her success. "Very funny, Rhodes."

"What's funny?"

"Gideon's my nanny, hilarious. Something new and different."

"What, like mocking Ezra is suddenly revolutionary?"

"It's not my fault the subject of Fowler's inadequacy is evergreen," Nico replied, and were it not for the fact that they were in front of all of their classmates and a great number of their faculty and staff as well, Libby would not have paused for an additional centering breath and instead entertained whatever her abilities compelled her to do.

Unfortunately, setting fire to Nico de Varona's undergarments was considered unacceptable behavior.

Last day, Libby reminded herself. *Last day of Nico.*

He could say whatever he liked, then, and it meant nothing.

"How's your speech?" Nico asked, and she rolled her eyes.

"Like I'd discuss it with you."

"Why on earth not? I know you get stage fright."

"I do not get—" Another breath. Two breaths, for good measure. "I do not get stage fright," she managed, more evenly this time, "and even if I did, what exactly would you do to help me?"

"Oh, did you think I was offering to help?" Nico asked. "Apologies, I was not."

"Still disappointed you weren't the one elected to deliver it?"

"Please," Nico scoffed under his breath, "you and I both know nobody wasted any time voting on something as idiotic as who should give the commencement speech. Half the people here are already drunk," he pointed out, and while she knew he was more right than she'd ever admit to him being, she also knew it was a sore subject. He could pretend at nonchalance as much as he liked, but she knew he never enjoyed losing to her, whether he considered it a subject of importance or not.

She knew it because in his position she would have felt exactly the same way.

"Oh?" she prompted, amused. "If nobody cared, then how did I win?"

"Because you're the only one who *voted*, Rhodes, it's like you're not even listening to me—"

"Rhodes," cautioned Breckenridge, breezing by their seats on the commencement stage as the processions around them continued. "Varona. Is it too much to ask you to be civil for the next hour?"

"Professor," they both replied in acknowledgement, forcing twin smiles as Nico once again fussed impulsively with his tie.

"No trouble at all," Libby assured the Dean, knowing that even Nico would not be so idiotic as to disagree. "Everything's fine."

Breckenridge arched a brow. "Morning going well, then?"

"Swimmingly," said Nico, flashing her one of his charming smiles. It was the worst thing about him, really, that he could be such a non-headache with everyone who wasn't Libby. Nico de Varona was every teacher's favorite; when it came to their peers, everyone wanted to be him or date him, or at the very least befriend him.

In some highly distant, *extremely* generous sense, Libby could see how that was understandable. Nico was enormously likable, unfairly so, and no matter how clever or talented Libby was, students and faculty alike preferred Nico to her. Whatever gift it was he had, it was like Midas; the effortless turning of nonsense to gold, more a reflex than a skill, and Libby, a gifted academic, had never been able to learn it. Nico's brand of easy charm had no metric for study, no identifiable markers of finesse.

He also had a monstrous capacity to fool people into thinking he knew what he was talking about, which he resolutely did not. Sometimes, maybe. But certainly not always.

Worse than anything Nico happened to be as a person was what he *had*, which was the job Libby had really wanted—not that she'd ever admit that. Sure, being hired at the best magical venture capitalist firm in Manhattan was no small thing. She'd be providing funding to innovative medeian technology, able to choose from a portfolio of exciting ideas with massive potential for growth and social capital. Now was the time to act; the world was overpopulated, resources drained and overused, alternative energy sources more imperative than ever. Down the line, she could change the very structure of medeian advancements—could choose this start-up or that to alter the progression of the entire global economy—and she'd be paid well to do it, too. But she'd *wanted* the research fellowship at NYUMA, and that, of course, had gone straight to Nico.

As Breckenridge took her seat and Nico decided to pretend at reasonability, Libby pondered what it would be like in her blissful future where things didn't always come down to the two of them competing. For four years Nico had been an inescapable feature of her life, like some sort of bothersome vestigial organ. Physical medeians with their mastery of the elements were rare; so rare, in fact, that they had been the only two. For four long, torturous years, they'd been shoved into every class together without respite, the extent of their prowess matched only by the force of their mutual antipathy.

For Nico, who was used to getting his way, Libby was purely an annoyance. She'd found him smug and arrogant from the moment they met and hadn't hesitated to tell him so, and there was nothing Nico de Varona hated more than someone who didn't adore him on sight. It was probably the first trauma he'd ever suffered; knowing him, the idea that a woman could exist who didn't worship at his feet must have kept him up at night. For Libby, however, things were far more complex. For all that their personalities clashed, Nico was something far worse than just an average asshole. He was also an obnoxious, classist reminder of everything Libby failed to possess.

Nico came from a family of prominent medeians, and had trained privately from his opulent palace (she assumed) in Havana since he was a child. Libby, a Pittsburgh native whose suburban lineage had no medeians or even witches to speak of, had planned to go to Columbia until NYUMA, via Breckenridge, intervened. She had known nothing of basic medeian principles, starting off behind in every aspect of magical theory, and had worked twice as hard as everyone else—only for that effort to be dismissed in favor of *yes, that's very good, Libby… and now Nico, how about you try?*

Nico de Varona would never know what that felt like, Libby thought again, as she had countless times. Nico was handsome, clever, charming, rich. Libby was… powerful, yes, equally as powerful and likely to become more so over time given her sense of discipline, but with four years of Nico de Varona as a yardstick for magical achievement, Libby found herself unfairly measured. If not for him she might have breezed through her studies, perhaps even found them dull. She would not have had a rival, nor even a peer. After all, without Nico, who could even hold a candle to what she could do?

No one. She'd never met anyone with anything even close to hers or Nico's proficiency with physical magic. The little tremors from the slightest flaring of his temper would take a lesser medeian four hours and herculean effort to create from nothing, the same way a mere spark from Libby had been enough to secure a full scholarship to NYUMA and lucrative full-time employment after that. That sort of power would have been revered, even exalted, if either of them had been singularities—which, for the first time, they would be. Without Nico for comparison beside her, Libby would finally be free to excel without having to push herself half to death to stand out.

It was a strange thought, actually, and strangely lonely. But still, thrilling all the same.

She felt a little rumble under her feet and glanced over, noting that Nico looked lost in thought.

"Hey," she said, nudging him. "Stop."

He gave her a bored glance. "It's not always me, Rhodes. I don't go around blaming you for forest fires."

She rolled her eyes. "I know the difference between an earthquake and a Varona tantrum."

"Careful," he cautioned, gaze flicking to where Ezra sat beside her parents. "Don't want Fowler to see us having another row, do we? Might get the wrong impression."

Honestly, this again. "You do realize your obsession with my boyfriend is childish, don't you, Varona? It's beneath you."

"I didn't realize you thought anything was beneath me," Nico replied lazily.

Across the stage, Breckenridge shot them a warning glance.

"Just get over it," Libby muttered. Nico and Ezra had loathed each other during the two years they'd all been at NYUMA together before Ezra graduated, which happened to be a separate matter from Nico's opposition to her. "You never have to see each other again. *We*," she amended belatedly, "never have to see each other again."

"Don't make it sound so tragic, Rhodes."

She shot him a glare, and he turned his head, half-smiling at her.

"Where there's smoke," he murmured, and she felt another rush of loathing.

"Varona, can you just—"

"—pleased to introduce your co-valedictorian, Elizabeth Rhodes!" came the voice of the commencement announcer, as Libby glanced up, realizing that their entire audience was now staring expectantly at her, Ezra giving her a little frown from the crowd that suggested he had observed her bickering with Nico yet again.

She forced a smile, rising to her feet, and gave Nico's ankle a kick as she went.

"Try not to touch your hair," was Nico's parting benediction, muttered under his breath and of course intended to make her fixate on her bangs, which for the entire two minutes of her prepared speech threatened to fall into her eyes. One of his lesser magics, getting under her skin, and by the time she finished, she wanted very badly to kick him again, falling into her seat and reminding herself how marvelous life was going to be in approximately twenty minutes, when she would be free of him forever.

"Well done, you two," Breckenridge said wryly, shaking their hands as they departed the stage. "An entire commencement ceremony, impressive."

"Yes, we are very impressive," Nico agreed, in a tone that Libby would have slapped him for, only Breckenridge gave a low chuckle of amusement and shook her head fondly, departing in the opposite direction as Libby and Nico made their way down the stairs.

Libby paused to conjure something terrible; a final, devastating parting malediction. Something to haunt him while she walked away.

But then instead, she held a hand out to him, deciding to be an adult.

Civil.

Et cetera.

"Have, you know. A good life," she said, and Nico glanced skeptically at her palm.

"*That's* the line you're going with, Rhodes?" he asked, pursing his lips. "Come on, you can do better. I know you must have rehearsed it in the shower."

God, he was infuriating. "Forget it," she said, retracting her hand and pivoting away. "See you never, Varona."

"Better," he called after her, pairing it with careless applause. "Bra-*va*, Elizabeth—"

She whipped around, curling a fist. "What was *your* line, then?"

"Well, why bother telling you now?" he asked, with a grin that was more like a self-satisfied smirk. "Maybe I'll just let you ponder it. You know," he added, taking a step towards her, "when you need something to occupy your mind over the course of your monotonous life with Fowler."

"You're a real piece of work, you know that?" she snapped. "Pigtail-pulling isn't sexy, Varona. In ten years you'll still be alone with no one but Gideon to pick out your ties for you, and believe me, I won't spare you a single thought."

"Whereas in ten years *you'll* be saddled with three baby Fowlers," Nico retorted, "wondering what the fuck happened to your career while your patently unremarkable husband asks you where dinner is."

There it was again:

Incensed.

"If I never see you again, Varona," Libby fumed quietly, "it'll still be *too soon*—"

"Pardon me," came the voice of a man beside them, and Nico and Libby both rounded on him.

"What?" they demanded in unison, and he, whoever he was, smiled.

He was dark-skinned, his head shaved and slightly gleaming, appearing somewhere in his forties. He was also exceedingly British, from mannerisms to dress (tweed; very much tweed, with an accent of tartan), and quite tall.

Also, enormously unwelcome.

"Nicolás Ferrer de Varona and Elizabeth Rhodes?" the man asked. "I wonder if I might make you an offer."

"We have jobs," Libby informed him irritably, not wanting to wait for Nico's inevitably patrician response, "and more importantly, we're in the middle of something."

"Yes, I see that," the man replied, looking amused. "However, I am on something of a tight schedule, and I'm afraid when it comes to my offer, I really must have the best."

"And which of us would that be, exactly?" Nico asked, holding Libby's glare for a gratuitous moment of conceit before smoothly turning towards the man who stood waiting, an umbrella hooked onto his left arm. "Unless, of course, the best is—"

"It's both of you," the man confirmed, as Nico and Libby exchanged a heated glance akin to *of course it is*, "or, perhaps, one." He shrugged, and Libby, despite her disinterest, frowned slightly. "Which of you succeeds is up to you, not me."

"Succeeds?" she asked, before she quite realized she was speaking. "What does that mean?"

"There's only room for five," the man said. "Six are chosen. The best in the world," he added.

"The *world*?" Libby echoed doubtfully. "Sounds fairly hyperbolic."

The man inclined his head.

"Well, since you asked, I'm happy to verify our parameters. There are nearly ten billion people in the world at present, correct?" he prompted, and Libby and Nico, both a bit bewildered, nodded warily. "Nine and a half billion, to be more specific, of which only a portion are magical. Five million, give or take, who can be classified as witches. Of those, only six percent are identified as medeian-caliber magicians, eligible for training at the university level at institutions sprinkled across the globe. Only ten percent of those will qualify for the best universities, like this one," he said, gesturing around to the NYUMA banners. "Of those, only a fraction—one percent or less—are considered by our selection committee; the vast majority will be cut without a second glance. That leaves three hundred people. Of those, another ten percent *might* have the requisite qualifications; specialties, academic performance, personality traits, et cetera."

Thirty people. Nico gave Libby a smug look like he knew she was doing the math, and she shot back a contemptuous one like she knew he wasn't.

"Then comes the fun part, of course—the *real* selectivity," the man continued. "Which students have the rarest magic? The most inquisitive minds? The vast majority of your most talented classmates will go on to serve the magical economy as accountants, investors, magical lawyers," he informed them. "Maybe the rare few will create something truly special. But only thirty people in total are good enough to be considered extraordinary, and of those, only six are rare enough to be invited through the door."

The man smiled slightly. "By the end of the year, of course, only five will walk back out of it. But that's a matter for future consideration."

Libby, who was still a little taken aback by the selection parameters, allowed Nico to speak first.

"You think there are four people better than Rhodes or me?"

"I think there are six people of equally remarkable talent," the man corrected with an air of repetition, as if that much had already been established, "of which you may be qualified or may not."

"So you want us to compete against each other, then," Libby observed sourly, flicking a glance at Nico, "again."

"And four others," the man agreed, holding out a card for them both. "Atlas Blakely," he informed them, as Libby glanced down, eyeing the card. *Atlas Blakely, Caretaker.* "As I said, I would like to make you an offer."

"Caretaker of what?" Nico asked, and the man, Atlas, gave him a genial smile.

"Better that I enlighten all of you at once," he said. "Forgive me, but it is quite a lengthy explanation, and the offer does expire in a matter of hours."

Libby, who was never particularly impulsive, remained warily opposed. "You're not even going to tell us what your offer is?" she asked him, finding his recruitment tactics needlessly furtive. "Why on earth would we ever agree to accept it?"

"Well, that part's really not up to me, is it?" Atlas prompted, shrugging. "Anyway, as I said, I do have quite a pressing schedule," he informed them, tucking his umbrella onto his arm again. "Time zones are a tricky business. Which of you may I expect?" he asked, glancing pointedly between them, and Libby frowned.

"I thought you said that was up to us?"

"Oh, it is, of course, eventually," Atlas said with a nod. "I merely presumed, given how eager you both seemed to be to go your separate ways, that only one of you would accept my invitation."

Her glance collided with Nico's, both of them bristling.

"Well, Rhodes?" Nico said, in his softly mocking tone. "Do you want to tell him I'm better, or should I?"

"Libs," came Ezra's voice, jogging up to her from behind. "Ready to go? Your mom's waiting outs-"

"Oh, *hello*, Fowler," Nico said, turning to Ezra with a disdainful smile. "Project manager, hm?"

Libby inwardly flinched. Of course he'd said it like an insult. It was a prestigious position for any medeian, but Nico de Varona wasn't just any medeian. He would go onto be something big, something... *remarkable*.

He was one of the six best in the world.

In the *world*.

And so was she.

For what, though?

Libby blinked, startling herself out of her thoughts, when she realized Nico was still talking.

"—in the middle of something, Fowler. Perhaps you could give us a moment?"

Ezra slid a wary gaze to Libby, frowning. "Are you...?"

"I'm fine," she assured him. "Just... wait one second, okay? Just one second," she repeated, nudging him away and turning back to Atlas before realizing, belatedly, that Ezra hadn't given any indication he'd noticed anyone else standing there.

"Well, Nicolás?" Atlas was asking Nico, looking expectant.

"Oh, it's Nico, please." Nico slipped Atlas' card into his pocket, giving Libby a look of pompous satisfaction as he offered his right hand to be shaken. "When should I expect to meet with you, Mr. Blakely?"

Oh no.

Oh *no*.

"You're welcome to call me Atlas, Nico. You may use the card for transport this afternoon," Atlas replied, turning to Libby. "And as for you, Miss Rhodes, I must say I'm disappointed," he said, as her mind raced in opposition, "but in any case, it's been a pleas-"

"I'll be there," Libby blurted hastily, and to her fury, Nico's mouth twitched with expectation, obviously both entertained and unsurprised by her decision. "It's just an offer, right?" she prompted, approximately half to Nico, half to Atlas, and a sliver of whatever remained to herself. "I can choose to accept or reject it after you explain what it is, can't I?"

"Certainly," Atlas confirmed, inclining his head. "I'll see you both this evening, then."

"Just one thing," Libby said, pausing him after a quick glance at Ezra, who was observing them from a distance through narrowed eyes. "My boyfriend can't see you, can he?" To Atlas' head shake in confirmation, she asked hesitantly, "Then what does he think we're doing right now, exactly?"

"Oh, I believe he's filling in the blanks with something his mind considers reasonable," Atlas said, and Libby felt herself pale a little, not overly enthralled about what that might be. "Until this afternoon, then," Atlas added, before disappearing from sight, leaving Nico to shake with silent laughter in his wake.

"What are you snickering at?" Libby hissed, glaring at him, and after a moment to compose himself Nico managed a shrug, winking over her shoulder at Ezra.

"Guess you'll find out. See you later, Rhodes," he said, and departed with an ostentatious bow, leaving Libby to wonder if she didn't, in fact, smell smoke.

REINA

Four Hours Ago

THE DAY REINA MORI WAS BORN there had been a fire blazing nearby. For an urban environment, particularly one so unaccustomed to flame, there was a heightened sense of mortality that day. Fire was so primitive, so archaic a problem; for Tokyo, an epicenter of advancements in both magical and mortal technologies, to suffer something as backwards as the unsophistication of boundless flame was troublingly biblical. Sometimes, when Reina slept, the smell of it crept into her nose and she woke up coughing, retching a little over the side of her bed until the memory of smoke had cleared from her lungs.

The doctors knew she possessed power of the highest medeian caliber right away, exceeding even the trinkets of normal magic, which were rare enough on their own. There wasn't a lot of natural life to speak of in the high-rise of the hospital, but what *did* exist—the occasional decorative plants sitting idly in the corners, handfuls of cut-flowers in vases meant for sympathy— had crept towards her infant form like nervous little children, anxious and yearning and fearful of dying.

Reina's grandmother called her birth a miracle, saying that when Reina took her first breath, the rest of the world sighed back in relief, clinging to the bounty of life she gave them. Reina, on the other hand, considered her first breath to be the beginning of a lifetime's set of chores.

The truth was that being labeled a naturalist shouldn't have been such a drain on her as it was. There were other medeian naturalists, many who were born in rural areas of the country, who typically opted to enlist with large agricultural companies; there, they could be paid handsomely for their services in increasing rice production or purifying water. That Reina was considered to be one of them, or that she would be called a naturalist at all, was something of a misnomer. Other medeians asked things of nature, and if they beckoned sweetly or worthily or powerfully enough, nature gave. In Reina's case, nature was like an irritating sibling, or possibly an incurable addict who happened to be a relative, always popping up to make unreasonable demands.

There was no reason to go to school in Osaka, really, except to get out of Tokyo. Tokyo's magical university was plenty good, if not perhaps a bit better, but Reina had never been overly thrilled by the prospect of living in the same place into perpetuity. She had searched and searched for experiences like hers—something that was less *look what a savior you are* and more *look what a burden it is to care for so many things*—and had found it in mythology, mostly. There, witches, or gods who were perceived to be witches, bore experiences Reina found intensely relatable and, in some cases, desirable: Exile to islands. Six months in the Underworld. The compulsive turning of one's enemies to something which couldn't speak. Her teachers encouraged her to practice her naturalism, to take botany and herbology and focus her studies on the minutiae of plants, but Reina wanted the classics. She wanted literature, and more importantly, the freedom it brought to think of something which did not gaze at her with the blank neediness of chlorophyll. When Tokyo pressed a scholarship into her hands, imploring her to study with their leading naturalists, she took up Osaka's freer curriculum instead.

A small escape, but it was one, still.

She graduated from the Osaka Institute of Magic and got a job as a waitress in a cafe and tearoom near the magical epicenter of the city. The best part about being a waitress where magic did most of the legwork? Plenty of time to read. And write. Reina, who'd had countless agricultural firms ready to pounce the moment she'd graduated (several of them for rival companies from China and the United States as well as Japan), had done everything she could to steer clear of working amid the vastness of planting fields, where both the earth and its inhabitants would drain her for their purposes. The cafe contained no plants, certainly no animals, and while from time to time the wooden furniture would warp under her hands, going so far as to longingly spelling her name in the exposed rings, it was easy enough to ignore.

Which wasn't to say people had ceased to come looking for her. Today, it was a tall, dark-skinned man in a Burberry trench coat.

To his credit, he didn't look like the usual capitalist villain. He looked a bit like Sherlock Holmes, in fact. He came in, sat at a table, and placed three small seedlings on its surface, waiting until Reina had risen to her feet with a sigh.

There was nobody else in the cafe; she assumed he'd taken care of that.

"Make them grow," he suggested, apropos of nothing.

He said it in a restrained Tokyo dialect rather than a typical Osaka one, which made two things very clear: One, he knew precisely who she was, or at least where she was from. Two, this was obviously not his first language.

Reina gave the man a dull look. "I don't make them grow," she said in English. "They just do it."

He looked unfazed in a smug sort of way, as if he'd guessed she might say that, answering in an accented English that was intensely, poshly British. "You think that has nothing to do with you?"

She knew what he expected her to say. Today, like all days, he would not get it.

"You want something from me," Reina observed, adding tonelessly, "Everyone does."

"I do," the man agreed. "I'd like a coffee, please."

"Great." She waved a hand over her shoulder. "It'll be out in two minutes. Anything else?"

"Yes," he said. "Does it work better when you're angry? When you're sad?"

So, not coffee then. "I don't know what you're talking about."

"There are other naturalists." He fixed her with a long, searching glance. "Why should I choose you?"

"You shouldn't," she said. "I'm a waitress, not a naturalist."

One of the seedlings split open and dug into the wood of the table.

"There are gifts and there are talents," the man said. "What would you say this is?"

"Neither." The second seedling cracked. "A curse, maybe."

"Hm." The man glanced down at the seeds, then up at Reina. "What are you reading?"

She'd forgotten she still had the book tucked under her arm. "A translation of a manuscript by Circe, the Greek witch."

His mouth twitched. "That manuscript is long lost, isn't it?"

"People read it," Reina said. "They wrote down what it contained."

"About as reliable as the New Testament, then," the man said.

Reina shrugged. "It's what I have."

"What if I said you could have the real thing?"

The third seedling shot up, colliding with the ceiling, and when it fell, it dug into the grains of the floor.

For a few seconds, neither of them moved.

"It doesn't exist," Reina said, clearing her throat. "You just said so."

"No, I specifically said it was long-lost," the man said. "Not everyone gets to see it."

Reina felt her mouth tighten. It was a strange bribe, but she'd been offered things before. Everything came with a price. "So what would I have to do, then?" she asked, irritated. "Promise you eight years of harvest in exchange? Make up a percentage of your annual profits? No, thank you."

She turned and something cracked beneath her feet. Little green roots sprouted from the floor and crept out like tendrils, like tentacles, reaching for her ankles and tapping at the base of her shoes.

"How about," the man posed neutrally, "in exchange for three answers?"

Reina turned sharply, and the man didn't hesitate. Clearly he'd had some practice leveraging people before. "What makes it happen?" he asked. His first question, and certainly not the one Reina would have gone with if she'd been the one given the choice.

"I don't know." He arched a brow, waiting, and she sighed. "Fine, it… uses me. Uses my energy, my thoughts, my emotions. If there's more energy to give, then it takes more of it. Most of the time I'm restraining it, but if I let my mind go—"

"What happens to you in those moments? No, wait, let me clarify," he amended, apparently sticking to his promise of three answers. "Does it drain you?"

She set her jaw. "It gives a little back, sometimes. But normally, yes."

"I see. Last question," he said. "What happens if you try to use it?"

"I told you," she said, "I don't use it."

He sat back, gesturing to the two seedlings still remaining on the table, one half-heartedly growing roots while the other lay split open and bare.

The implication there was clear: *Try it and see.*

She weighed the outcomes, running the calculations.

"Who are you?" Reina asked, tearing her attention from the seedling.

"Atlas Blakely, Caretaker," replied the man.

"And what is it you care for?"

"I'd be happy to tell you," he said, "but the truth is it's a bit exclusive. I can't technically invite you yet, as you're still tied for sixth on our list."

She frowned. "What does that mean?"

"It means only six can be invited," Atlas said plainly. "Your professors at the Osaka Institute seem to think you will refuse my offer, which means your spot is somewhat…" He trailed off. "Well, I'll be frank. It's not unanimous, Miss Mori. I have exactly twenty minutes to convince the rest of the council that you should be our sixth choice."

"Who says I want to be chosen?"

He shrugged. "Maybe you don't," he permitted. "If that's the case, I will alert the other candidate the slot is theirs. A traveler," he clarified. "A young man, very intelligent, well-trained. Perhaps better trained than you." A pause to let that sink in. "It's a very rare gift he possesses," Atlas conceded, "but he has, in my view, a considerably less useful ability than yours."

She said nothing. The plant, which had curled around her ankle, gave a malcontented sigh, wilting slightly at her apprehension.

"Very well," Atlas said, rising to his feet, and Reina flinched.

"Wait." She swallowed. "Show me the manuscript."

Atlas arched a brow.

"You said three answers were all I had to give," Reina reminded him, and the corners of his mouth quirked up, approving.

"So I did, didn't I?"

He waved a hand, producing a handwoven book, and levitated it in the air between them. The cover slid open carefully, revealing contents of tiny, scrawled handwriting that appeared to be a mix of ancient Greek and pseudo-hieroglyphic runes.

"What spell were you reading?" he asked as she reached for it, hand already half-extended. "Apologies," Atlas said, waving the book back from her a few inches, "I can't let you touch it. It already shouldn't be out of the archives, but again, I'm hoping you will prove my efforts worthwhile. What spell were you reading?"

"I, um. The cloaking spell." Reina stared at the pages, only understanding about half of it. Osaka's program for rune-reading had been somewhat elementary; Tokyo's would have been better, but again, it had come with strings. "The one she used to mask the appearance of the island."

Atlas nodded, the pages turning of their own accord, and there, on the page, was a crude drawing of Aiaia, part of the writing stripped away from age. It was a crude, unfinished illusion spell, which was something Reina had not been able to study at all beyond basic medeian theory. Illusion courses at the Osaka Institute were for illusionists, which she was not.

"Oh," she said.

Atlas smiled.

"Fifteen minutes," he reminded her, and then he vanished the book.

So this, too, came with strings. That was obvious. Reina had never liked this sort of persuasion, but there was a logical piece of her that understood people would never stop asking. She was a well of power, a vault with a heavy door, and people would either find ways to break in or she would have to simply open them on occasion. Only for a worthy purchaser.

She closed her eyes.

Can we? asked the seeds in their little seed language, which felt mostly like tiny pricks against her skin. Like children's voices, *pleasepleaseplease Mother may we?*

She sighed.

Grow, she told them in their language. She had never known what it felt like to them, but it seemed they understood her well enough. *Have what you need from me,* she added grumpily, *just do it.*

The relief was a slither from inside her bones: *Yessssssssssssssssss.*

When she opened her eyes, the seedling on the ground had blossomed into a thin series of branches, stretching from her feet up to the ceiling and then sprawling over it, spreading across it like a rash. The one embedded in the table had cracked the wood in half, sprouting upwards from it like moss over a barren tree trunk. The last, the broken one, quivered and burst in a ripe stretch of color, taking the form of vines which then proceeded to bear fruit, each one ripening at an astronomical rate while they watched.

When the apples were round and heavy and temptingly ready to be plucked, Reina exhaled, releasing the ache in her shoulders, and glanced expectantly at her visitor.

"Ah," Atlas said, shifting in his seat. The plants had left little room for him to sit comfortably, and he no longer had space for his legs. "So it's both a gift and a talent, then."

Reina knew her own worth well enough not to comment. "What other books do you have?"

"I haven't extended an offer yet, Miss Mori," Atlas replied.

"You'll want me," she said, lifting her chin. "Nobody can do what I can do."

"True, but you don't know the other candidates on the list," he pointed out. "We have two of the finest physicists the world has seen for generations, a uniquely gifted illusionist, a telepath the likes of which are incomparable, an empath capable of luring a crowd of thousands—"

"It doesn't matter who else you have." Reina set her jaw. "You'll still want me."

Atlas considered her a moment.

"Yes," he said. "Yes, that's quite true, isn't it?"

Ha ha ha, laughed the plants. *Ha ha, Mother wins, we win.*

"Stop it," Reina whispered to the branches that had swept down to brush the top of her head with approval, and Atlas rose to his feet with a chuckle, extending a hand which contained a single slip of cardstock.

"Take this," he said, "and in about four hours, you'll be transported for orientation."

"For what?" Reina asked, and he shrugged.

"Better I not have to repeat myself," he replied. "Best of luck to you, Reina Mori. This will not be your final test."

Then he was gone, and Reina scowled.

The last thing she needed was a cafe full of plants, and now his coffee sat forgotten on the counter, already going cold.

TRISTAN

Three Hours Ago

"No," Tristan said when the door opened. "Not again. Not now."

"Mate," groaned Rupesh, "you've been in here for ages."

"Yes," Tristan agreed. "Doing my job. Incredible, isn't it?"

"Hardly," Rupesh muttered, falling into the vacant chair across from Tristan's desk. "You're the future son and heir, Tris. Hardly makes sense for you to work so hard when you'll only inherit it by default."

"First of all, this company isn't the monarchy," Tristan muttered, not looking up from the figures he'd been working on. He waved a hand, rearranging them. His valuation was slightly off and he adjusted the discount rate, knowing the risk-averse board of investors would want to see a broader range of percentages. "Even if it were, I'm not the heir, I'm just—"

"Just engaged to the boss's daughter," Rupesh supplied for him, raising a brow. "You should set the date, you know. It's been a couple of months, hasn't it? I'm sure Eden's getting impatient."

She was, and she'd been growing less subtle about it by the day. "I've been busy," Tristan said stiffly. "And anyway, this is precisely what I said I didn't have time for. Out," he said, gesturing to the door. "I have at least three more valuations to finish before I can leave."

It was the annual Wessex family holiday and Tristan would be Eden's escort, as always. This would be Tristan's fourth year coming along as the eldest Wessex daughter's plus one, and needless to say, it was not his favorite activity. Watching his step, holding his tongue, all of it was exhausting—but still, it was worth it. It was worth it to be here, to be considered an heir by someone whose name was not the one belonging to his biological father.

Tristan wondered if he could talk Eden into letting him take *her* name; assuming, that is, that he could summon the final step necessary to seal his fate.

"You're going on *holiday* with them," Rupesh pointed out, crooking a single dark brow. "You're already part of the family."

"No, I'm not." Not yet. Tristan rubbed his temple, glancing over the figures again. The capital required to make this deal work was steep, not to mention that the existing magical infrastructure was riddled with problems. Still, the potential to cash in was higher for this portfolio than it was for any of the thirteen other medeian projects he'd valued that day. James would like it, even if the rest of the board didn't, and the name on the building wasn't his for nothing.

Tristan filed the project under *maybe*, adding, "I'm not just going to inherit this company, Rup. If I want it, I have to work for it. You might consider doing the same," he advised, looking up to adjust his glasses, and Rupesh rolled his eyes.

"Just finish, then," Rupesh suggested. "Eden's been posting pictures of her get-ready routine all morning."

Eden Wessex, daughter of billionaire investor James Wessex, was a pretty heiress and therefore a ready-built product, capable of making capital out of intangibles like beauty and influence alone. It had been Tristan himself who'd advised the Wessex board to consider investing in *Lightning*, the magical version of a mortal social media app. Eden had been the face of the company ever since.

"Right, thanks," Tristan said, clearing his throat. He was probably missing messages from her as they spoke. "I'll be done soon. Is that all?"

"You know I can't leave until you do, mate." Rupesh winked at him. "Can't very well leave before the golden boy, can I?"

"Right, well, you're doing yourself no favors, then," Tristan said, gesturing to the door. Two more, he thought, glancing at the paperwork. Well, one. One of them was clearly unsuitable. "Run along, Rup. And do something about that coffee stain."

"What?" Rupesh asked, glancing down, and Tristan looked up from the file.

"Been letting your illusions get stale," he noted, pointing to the mark at the bottom of Rupesh's tie. "You can't spend five hundred quid on a designer belt and then rummage your stain spells out of a bin." Though, even as he said it, Tristan knew it was a very Rupesh quality to do precisely that. Some people cared only about what others could see, and Rupesh in particular was unaware of the extent to which Tristan saw through him.

"God, you're a pain, you know that?" Rupesh said, rolling his eyes. "No one else is paying attention to whether my charms have worn through or not."

"That you know of." For Tristan, there was little else to pay attention to.

"Just another reason to loathe you, mate," Rupesh said, grinning. "Anyway, finish up, Tris. Do us all a favor and go be picturesque by the sea so the rest of us can take it easy for a few days, would you?"

"Trying," Tristan assured him, and then the door shut, leaving him alone at last.

He tossed one pitch aside, picking up the promising one. The figures looked reliable. Not a lot of capital required upfront, which meant—

The door opened, and Tristan groaned.

"For the last time, Rupesh—"

"Not quite Rupesh," came a deep voice in reply, and Tristan looked up, eyeing the stranger in the room. He was a tall, dark-skinned man in a nondescript tweed suit, and he was glancing around at the vaulted ceilings of Tristan's office.

"Well," the man observed, letting the door fall shut as he meandered inside. "This is a far cry from where you started, isn't it?"

Anyone who knew where Tristan had started was trouble, and he braced himself, souring.

"If you're a—" He bit down on the word *friend*, grinding it between his teeth. "An *associate* of my father's—"

"Not quite that," the man assured him. "Though we all know about Adrian Caine in some capacity, don't we?"

We. Tristan fought a grimace.

"I'm not a Caine here," he said. It was still the name on his desk, but people here would likely never make the connection. The wealthy cared little for the filth underfoot if it was cleaned up from time to time and mostly left out of sight. "There's nothing I can do for you."

"I'm not asking for anything," the man said, pausing for a moment. "Though, I do have to wonder how you came upon this particular path. After all, you were heir to your own empire of sorts, weren't you?" he asked, and Tristan said nothing. "I'm not sure how the only Caine son came to play for the Wessex fortune."

"Some things aren't about money," Tristan muttered. "And if you don't mind—"

"What's it about, then?" the man asked, and Tristan sighed loudly.

"Look, I don't know who let you in, but—"

"You can do more than this." The man fixed him with a solemn stare. "You and I both know this won't satisfy you for long."

"You don't actually know me," Tristan pointed out. "Knowing my name is only a very small piece, and not a particularly persuasive one."

"I know you're rarer than you think you are," the man countered. "Your father may think your gifts a waste, but I know better. Anyone could be an illusionist. Anyone can be a thug. Anyone can be Adrian Caine." His lips thinned. "What you have, no one can do."

"What exactly do I have?" Tristan asked drily. "And don't say potential."

"Potential? Hardly. Certainly not here." The man waved a hand around the palatial office. "It's a very nice cage, but a cage nonetheless."

"Who are you?" Tristan asked him, which was probably delayed, though in his defense, he'd been working for several hours. He wasn't at his sharpest. "If you're not a friend of my father's and you're not a friend of James Wessex—and I'm assuming you're not here to pitch me your latest medeian software service," he muttered, throwing down the inadequate proposal as the man's mouth twitched with confirmation, "I can't imagine there's a reason for you to be here at all."

"Is it so difficult to believe I might be here for you, Tristan?" the man asked, looking vaguely entertained. "I was once in your position, you know."

Tristan leaned back, gesturing to his corner office. "I doubt that."

"True, I was never poised to marry into the most powerful medeian family in London, I'll give you that," the stranger replied with a chuckle. "But I was once very set on a particular path. One I thought was my only option for success, until one day, someone made me an offer."

He leaned forward, setting a slim card on Tristan's desk. It read only *Atlas Blakely, Caretaker*, and shimmered slightly from an illusion.

Tristan frowned at it. A transportation charm.

"Where does it go?" he asked neutrally, and the man, Atlas Blakely, smiled.

"You can see the charm, then?"

"Given the circumstances, safer to assume it has one." Tristan rubbed his forehead, wary. From his desk drawer, his phone buzzed loudly; Eden would be looking for him. "I'm not stupid enough to touch something like this. I have places to be, and whatever this is—"

"You can see through illusions," Atlas said, prompting him to tense with apprehension. Not just anyone was allowed to know that about him. Not that Tristan cared for any details about him to be known, but his talent was most effective when others were left unaware. "You can see value, and better yet, you can see *falseness*. You can see truth. That is what makes you special, Tristan. You can work every day of your life to expand James Wessex's business, or you can be what you are. *Who* you are." Atlas fixed him with a firm glance. "How long do you think you can do this before James figures out the truth about where you come from? The accent is a nice touch, but I can hear the East End underneath. The echo of a working-class witch," Atlas hinted softly, "that lives in your working-class tongue."

Tristan curled a hand under his desk, bristling.

"Is this blackmail?"

"No," said Atlas. "It's an offer. An opportunity."

"I have plenty of opportunities."

"You deserve better ones," Atlas said. "Better than James Wessex. Certainly better than Eden Wessex, and miles better than Adrian Caine."

Tristan's phone buzzed again. Likely Eden was sending him pictures of her tits. Four years of dating and she never tired of showing off the augmentation charm she didn't know he could see through.

"You don't know what you're talking about," Tristan said.

"Don't I?" Atlas countered, gesturing to the card. "You have a couple of hours to decide."

"Decide what?" Tristan asked brusquely, defensive with nerves, but Atlas had already risen to his feet, shrugging.

"I'm happy to answer your questions," Atlas said, "but not here. Not now. If you're going to continue living this life, Tristan, then there's no point having any conversation at all, is there? But there's much more available to you than you think, if you care to take it." He glanced sideways at Tristan. "More than where you came from, and certainly more than where you are."

Easy for him to say, Tristan thought. Whoever Atlas Blakely was, *his* father wasn't a bullish tyrant who considered his biggest disappointment in life to be his only son. *He* wasn't the one who'd zeroed in on Eden Wessex five years ago at a party when he'd been tending bar and decided that she was the best way; the easiest way; the *only* way out.

Though, he also wasn't the one whose best friend in the office thought he was getting away with fucking her, unaware the shoddy contraception charm left on his prick regularly made itself clear from across the room.

"What is it?" Tristan asked. "This…" He let the word curl up on his tongue. "Opportunity."

"Once in a lifetime," Atlas said, which wasn't an answer. "You will know as much when you see it."

That was nearly always true. There was little Tristan Caine couldn't see.

"I have places to be," Tristan said.

A life to live. A future to curate.

Atlas nodded.

"Choose wisely," he advised, and slipped from the room, pulling the door shut behind him.

CALLUM
Two Hours Ago

CALLUM NOVA WAS VERY ACCUSTOMED to getting what he wanted. He had
a magical specialty so effective that if he kept it to himself, which he generally
did, he would get top marks in every class without effort. It was a hypnosis
of sorts. Some of his exes called it a hallucinogenic effect in retrospect, like
coming down from a drug. If they weren't on their guard at all times, he could
talk them into anything. It made things easy for him. Too easy? Sometimes,
yes.

That didn't mean Callum didn't like a challenge.

Since Callum had graduated university and returned from Athens six
years ago he'd been up to very little indeed, which wasn't his favorite fact
about himself. He worked for his family business, of course, as plenty of
postgraduate medeians did. A magical media conglomerate, the Nova family's
primary business was beauty. It was grandeur. It was also all an illusion, every
single bit of it, and Callum was the falsest illusion of all. He handled the
commodity of vanity, and he was good at it. Better than good.

It was boring, though, convincing people of things they already believed.
Callum had a distinctly rare specialty as a so-called manipulist, and rarer still
was his talent; far exceeding the common capacity of any witch who could
cast at a basic level. He was smart to begin with, which meant convincing
people to do precisely as he wanted for purposes of magical exercise had to
be considerably challenging to really break a sweat. He was also eternally in
search of entertainment, and therefore the man at the door had to say very
little for Callum to be convinced.

"Caretaker," Callum read aloud, scrutinizing the card with his feet
propped up on his desk. He'd come in four hours late to work and neither the
managing partner (his sister) nor the owner (his father) had anything to say

about the meeting he'd missed. He would make up for it that afternoon, when he would sit down for two minutes (could be done in ninety seconds, but he'd stay long enough to finish the espresso) with the client the Novas needed in order to secure a full portfolio of high-ranking illusionists for London Fashion Week. "I hope it's something interesting you care for, Atlas Blakely."

"It is," said Atlas, rising to his feet. "Shall I presume to see you, then?"

"Presumptions are dangerous," Callum said, feeling out the edges of Atlas' interests. They were blurred and rough, not easily infected. He guessed that Atlas Blakely, whoever he was, had been warned about Callum's particular skills, which meant he must have dug deep to even discover its true nature. Anyone willing to do the dirty work was worth a few minutes of time, in Callum's view. "Who else is involved?"

"Five others."

A good number, Callum thought. Exclusive enough, but statistically speaking he could bring himself to like one in five people.

"Who's the most interesting?"

"Interesting is subjective," Atlas said.

"So, me, then," Callum guessed.

Atlas gave a humorless smile. "You're not uninteresting, Mr. Nova, though I suspect this will be the first time you encounter a room full of people as rare as yourself."

"Intriguing," Callum said, removing his feet from the desk to lean forward. "Still, I'd like to know more about them."

Atlas arched a brow. "You have no interest in knowing about the opportunity itself, Mr. Nova?"

"If I want it, it's mine," Callum said, shrugging. "I can always wait and make that decision later. More interesting than the game is always the players, you know. Well, I suppose more accurately," he amended, "the game is different depending on the players."

Atlas' mouth twisted slightly.

"Nico de Varona," he said.

"Never heard of him," Callum said. "What's he do?"

"He's a physicist," Atlas said. "He can compel forces of physicality to adjust to his demands, just as you do with intent."

"Boring." Callum leaned back. "But I suppose I'll give him a try. Who else?"

"Libby Rhodes is also a physicist," Atlas continued. "Her influence over her surroundings is unlike anything I've ever seen. Reina Mori, likewise, is a naturalist for whom the earth personally offers fruit."

"Naturalists are easy to come by," Callum said, though admittedly, he was curious now. "Who else?"

"Tristan Caine. He can see through illusions."

Rare. Very rare. Not particularly useful, though. "And?"

"Parisa Kamali." That name was said with hesitation. "Her specialty is better left unsaid, I suspect."

"Oh?" Callum asked, arching a brow. "And did you tell them about mine?"

"They didn't ask about you," Atlas said.

Callum cleared his throat.

"Do you make a habit of psychologically profiling everyone you meet?" he asked neutrally, and Atlas didn't answer. "Though," Callum mused, "I suppose people less inclined to notice when they're being influenced are unlikely to call you on it, aren't they?"

"I suppose in some ways we are opposites, Mr. Nova," Atlas said. "I know what people want to hear. You make them want to hear what you know."

"Suppose I'm just naturally interesting?" Callum suggested blithely, and Atlas made a low, laughing sound of concession.

"You know, for someone who knows his own value so distinctly, perhaps you forget that beneath your natural talent lies someone very, very uninspired," Atlas said, and Callum blinked, caught off guard. "Which is not to say there's a vacancy, but—"

"A vacancy?" Callum echoed, bristling. "What is this, negging?"

"Not a vacancy," Atlas repeated, "but certainly something unfinished." He rose to his feet. "Thank you very much for your time, Mr. Nova," he said, "as I imagine you could have done a great number of things during the period we spoke. How long would it have taken you to start a war, do you think? Or to end one?" He paused, and Callum said nothing. "Five minutes? Perhaps ten? How long would it have taken you to kill someone? To save a life? I admire what you have not done," Atlas acknowledged, tilting his head with something of a beckoning glance, "but I do have to question why you haven't done it."

"Because I'd drive myself mad interfering with the world," said Callum impatiently. "It requires a certain level of restraint to be what I am."

"Restraint," Atlas said, "or perhaps a lack of imagination."

Callum was far too secure to gape, so he didn't.

Instead, Callum said: "This had better be worth my time."

He did not say: Four minutes, thirty-nine seconds. That's how long it would take.

He had the feeling Atlas Blakely, Caretaker, was baiting him, and he also had the distinct feeling he shouldn't bother trying not to be caught.

"I could say the same for you," Atlas said, and tipped his hat politely in farewell.

PARISA

One Hour Ago

SHE'D BEEN SITTING IN THE BAR in her favorite black dress, sipping a martini. She always came to do this alone. For a time she'd been in the habit of having girlfriends around, but ultimately determined they were too noisy. Disruptive. Often jealous, too, which Parisa couldn't abide. She'd had one or two female friends at school in Paris and had once been close to her siblings in Tehran, but since then she'd determined she was better as a singular object. That made sense to her, ultimately. People who lined up to see the *Mona Lisa* typically couldn't name the paintings hanging nearby, and there was nothing wrong with that.

There were quite a lot of words for what Parisa was, which was something she supposed most people would not approve. Perhaps it went without saying that Parisa didn't put a lot of stock in approval. She was talented and smart, but above that—at least according to everyone who'd ever looked at her—she was beautiful, and being gifted approval for something that had been handed to her by some fortuitous arrangement of DNA instead of earned by her own two hands wasn't something she felt necessary to either idolize or condemn. She didn't rail against her looks; didn't give thanks for them, either. She simply used them like any other tool, like a hammer or a shovel or whatever else was necessary to complete the requisite task. Besides, disapproval was nothing worth thinking about. The same women who might have disapproved were quick to fawn over her diamonds, her shoes, her breasts—all of which were natural, never synthetic, not even illusioned. Whatever they wanted to call Parisa, at least she was authentic. She was real, even if she made a living on false promises.

Really, there was nothing more dangerous than a woman who knew her own worth.

Parisa watched the older men in the corner, the ones in the expensive suits, who were having a business meeting. She'd listened for a few minutes to the subject of conversation—after all, not everything was sex; sometimes insider trading was the easier option, and she was smart enough to serve multiple threats—but ultimately lost interest, as the business concept was fundamentally unsound. The men themselves, however, remained intriguing. One of them was toying with his wedding ring and fussing internally about his wife. Boring. One of the others was clearly harboring some sort of unresolved sexual angst about the boring fussy one, which was more interesting, albeit unhelpful for her purposes. The last one was handsome, probably rich, a tan where his wedding ring should have been. Parisa shifted in her chair, crossing one leg delicately over the other.

The man looked up, catching a glimpse of her thigh.

Well. He was certainly willing. That much was clear.

She looked elsewhere, not sure the man would be ending his business meeting anytime soon. In the meantime, she'd occupy her thoughts with someone else's. Maybe the wealthy woman in the back corner who looked likely to cry any minute. No, too depressing. There was always the bartender, who certainly knew how to use his hands. He'd pictured them on her already, traveling over a fairly accurate mental illustration of her hips, only she wouldn't get anything out of that. An orgasm, surely, but what good was that? An orgasm she could have on her own without becoming the girl who fucks bartenders. If anyone was going to be involved in Parisa's life, they were going to bring money, power, or magic. Nothing else would do.

She angled herself towards the dark-skinned man at the end of the bar, contemplating the silence that came from his head. She hadn't seen him come in, which was unusual. A medeian, then, or at least a witch. That was interesting. She watched him toy with a slim card, tapping it against the bar, and frowned at the words. *Atlas Blakely, Caretaker.* Caretaker of what?

The problem with being a smart girl was being naturally curious. Parisa turned away from the business meeting, aiming herself instead towards Atlas Blakely and fiddling with their respective positions in the room, turning the volume up.

She focused in on his mind and saw… six people. No, five. Five people, without faces. Extraordinary magic. Ah, yes, he was definitely a medeian, and so were they, it seemed. He felt a kinship with one of the five. One of them was a prize; something the man, Atlas, had recently won. He felt a bit smug over it. Two of them were a set, they came together. They didn't like being shoved in like twins in a too-small womb but too bad, that's what they were. One was a vacancy, a question, the edge of a narrow cliff. Another was… the answer, like an echo, though she couldn't quite see why. She tried to see their faces clearly but couldn't; they warped in and out of view, beckoning her closer.

Parisa peered around, pacing a little inside his thoughts. They seemed curated, a bit like a museum, as if they'd been intended for her to view in a particular order. A long process of selection, then a mirror. Five frames with hazy portraits, and then a mirror. Parisa looked at her own face and felt a jolt, startled.

At the end of the bar, the man rose to his feet, placing the card in front of her, and without him detailing anything aloud, she already knew why he'd given it to her. She'd spent long enough in his mind to understand it, and she realized now that he'd willingly let her in. In one hour, his thoughts said, the card would take her somewhere. Somewhere important. It was obviously the most important place in the world to this man, whoever he was. That bit Parisa suspected was her interpretation, as it was slightly fuzzier. She knew instinctively that whatever it was, it would be more worthwhile than the man having the business meeting. *That* man had recently repaired stitching in his suit. It had been refitted; it wasn't new. A man wore a new suit to a business meeting like this if he could afford it, and that man couldn't.

Parisa sighed in resignation, picking up the card from the bar.

An hour later, she sat in a room with Atlas Blakely and the five people she'd seen hazily represented in his mind without either of them speaking a word to each other, friendly or otherwise. She watched the handsome Latin boy—definitely a boy; he was obsessed with the girl sitting next to Parisa, who was tinted with inexperience—decide she was beautiful and she smiled to herself, knowing perfectly well she could eat that boy alive and he'd let her. He'd be fun for a day or so, maybe, but this seemed bigger than that. This seemed much more important.

The blond South African was interesting. He was eyeing the Englishman, Tristan, with extreme curiosity, possibly even something ravenous. Good, Parisa thought, pleased. She didn't like men like him. He'd want her to shout his name, to scream about his dick, to say things like 'oh baby yes how do you

do it how do you make me feel like this?' and that was a chore; it rarely ended
in anything worthwhile. Rich people like him typically held tight to their
wallets, and experience had taught her that did her no good.

Besides, the six of them were equals here. He had nothing to offer her,
except perhaps loyalty, but he wasn't the type to give it easily. He was used
to getting his way, which she could see from observing the functions of his
thoughts was something he did with at least some level of intention. Parisa
Kamali had never wanted to be under anyone's thumb, and she certainly
wouldn't start now.

The boy, too, was probably useless, which was disappointing. He was
obviously wealthy and certainly not unattractive (*Nicolás*, she thought with
satisfaction, rolling his name around in her head like she might have done
with him, whispering it to the inch of skin just below the lobe of his ear) but
he obviously tired quickly of things that were too easily won. Not Parisa's
style. The girl he was fixated on was equally easy to discard, though Parisa
had been with girls before and rarely ruled them out. She'd spent the better
portion of last month, in fact, with a wealthy mortal heiress who'd bought
Parisa this outfit, these boots, this purse. People were all the same, really, when
you got to the core of them, and Parisa always did. It was Parisa's business,
seeing things she wasn't supposed to see. In this case, though, this particular
girl was unequivocally hopeless. She had a boyfriend she seemed to actually
like. She had *good intentions*, too, which were the most unfortunate. Always
indicative of someone not easily put to use. The girl, Libby, was so good she
was no good at all. Parisa moved on from her quickly.

Reina, the naturalist with the nose ring, was easily the most threatening
presence in the room. She radiated raw power, which in Parisa's experience
was the mark of someone who shouldn't be messed with. Parisa put her in a
mental box marked 'Do Not Disturb' and resolved to stay out of her way.

Then there was Tristan, the Englishman, whom Parisa liked within
moments of slipping unobtrusively into his thoughts. There was a festering
anger in his head, beating dully like a tribal drum. It was obvious he didn't
know why he was here, but now that he was he wanted to punish everyone
in the room, himself included. Parisa liked that. She found it interesting,
or at least relatable. She watched Tristan notice everything that was off in
the room—all the illusions everyone else had used to hide various parts of
themselves, which varied from Libby's little spot of concealer on a stress

blemish hidden by her fringe to the false golden-flecked tips of Callum's hair—and marveled a little at his instant dismissal.

He was unimpressed.

He'd change his mind, Parisa thought, if she decided she wanted him to.

Which wasn't to say she did, necessarily. Again, there was nothing in it for her to pursue someone who provided no leverage. Perhaps the most beneficial connection was in fact the Caretaker, Atlas. Parisa was already calculating how much work it would take to win Atlas Blakely's interests when the door opened behind them, and she and the others turned.

"Ah, Dalton," said Atlas. A narrow-hipped, elegantly lean man—perhaps a few years older than Parisa and dressed in a clean, starched Oxford with lines as precise as the sleek part of his raven-black hair—nodded in reply.

"Atlas," he said with a low voice, his gaze falling on Parisa.

Yes, Parisa thought. *Yes, you.*

He thought she was beautiful. Easy, everyone did. He tried not to look at her breasts. It wasn't really working. She smiled at him and his thoughts raced, then went blank. He was momentarily silent, and then Atlas cleared his throat.

"Everyone, Dalton Ellery," Atlas said, and Dalton nodded curtly, looking over Parisa's head to glance with a somewhat forced smile at the others in the room.

"Welcome," he said. "Congratulations on being tapped for entry to the Alexandrian Society." His voice was smooth and buttery despite his posture being slightly stiff, his broad shoulders—the result of considerable craftsmanship, for which Parisa was certain his shirts were specially tailored—appearing to lock uncomfortably in place. He was clean-shaven, meticulous. He looked fanatical about cleanliness and she wanted to press her tongue to the nape of his artfully tapered neck. "I'm sure you all understand by now what an honor it is to be here."

"Dalton is a member of our most recently initiated class," Atlas said. "He'll be guiding you through the process, helping you transition into your new positions."

Parisa could think of a few positions she'd need no assistance with whatsoever. She slid into Dalton's subconscious, probing around. Would he want a chase? Or would she prefer her to be the aggressor? He was blocking something from her, from everyone, and Parisa frowned, surprised. It wasn't unheard of to practice some method of defense against telepathy, but it was an effort, even for a medeian with a considerable amount of talent. Was there someone else in the room Dalton was expecting could read his mind?

She caught a flicker of a smile from Atlas, who arched a brow at her, and blinked.

Oh, she thought, and his smile broadened.

Perhaps now you know what it's like for other people, Atlas said, and then added carefully, *and I would advise you to stay away from Dalton. I will be advising him to do the same.*

Does he usually follow your instructions? Parisa asked.

His smile was unerring. *Yes. As should you.*

And the others?

I can't prevent you from doing whatever it is you'll do over the course of the year. But even so, there are boundaries, Miss Kamali.

She smiled in concession, wiping her mind clean. Defense, offense, she was equally skilled, and in response, Atlas nodded once.

"Well," he said. "Shall we discuss the details of your initiation, then?"

II: TRUTH

NICO

NICO WAS FIDGETING. He was very often fidgeting; he was the sort of person who required motion, unable to sit still. People usually didn't mind it because he was perfectly likely to smile, to laugh, to fill up a room with the buoyancy of his personality, but it cost him quite a bit of energy, resulting in a somewhat pointless burn. Traces of magic were known to spill, too, if he wasn't paying attention, and his presence already had a tendency to reshape the landscape around him, sometimes forcing things out of the way.

Libby shot him a warning look as the ground beneath them rumbled, slate eyes reproachful beneath what he could see of her furrowed brow beneath her fussy bangs.

"What's going *on* with you?" she muttered to him after they were released, referring with spectacular lack of subtlety to what she probably considered an irresponsible disruption.

It was always such a marvelous thing how habitually she remarked on his tremors of agitation; no one else would have identified such an insubstantial change to their environment, of course, but then there was darling Elizabeth, who never failed to bring it to Nico's attention. It was like having an ugly scar, something he couldn't hide, even if she was the only one who saw it. He remained uncertain whether her delight in reminding him was a result of her insufferable personality, her alarmingly too-similar powers, or their longstanding history of forced coexistence, but he assumed it was some magical combination of all three, making it at least 33% her fault.

"It's a big decision, that's all," Nico said, though it wasn't. He'd already made it.

They'd each been given a twenty-four hour waiting period to decide whether they would accept the offer to compete for initiation to the Alexandrian Society, but rather than being transported directly via charm as they had been for their arrival, they were deposited through their respective portals of public transit. Unfortunately, living in Manhattan a mere matter of blocks from Libby Rhodes meant that she and Nico had the same transit point, and were now moments away from arriving at Grand Central's magical port of entry (near the oyster bar).

He glanced at her, conceding to ask in a mostly inoffensive tone, "What are you thinking?"

She slid him a sidelong glance in exchange, then flicked her grey-green eyes to the pulse of his thumb against his thigh. "I'm thinking I really should have gotten that fellowship," she muttered, and because buoyancy came naturally to him, Nico smiled, letting the shape of it stretch broadly across his lips.

"I knew it," he said triumphantly. "I *knew* you wanted it. You're so full of shit, Rhodes."

"Jesus." She rolled her eyes, fussing again with her bangs. "I don't know why I bother."

"Just answer the question."

"No." She turned to him with a scowl. "I thought we agreed never to speak to each other again after graduation?"

"Well, clearly that's not happening."

He beat his thumb against his thigh a few more times at the precise moment she remarked to nobody, "I love this song," which was another customary difference between them. He had felt the presence of the rhythm first; she had heard the melody sooner and identified it more quickly.

Again, there was no telling whether they had always been this way, or if they had learned it over the course of their unwilling inseparability. If not for her, Nico might not have noticed most of the things he did, and probably vice versa. A uniquely upsetting curse, really, how little he knew how to exist when she wasn't there; his only mode of pleasure was in knowing she probably felt the same whenever she could bring herself to stomach the admission.

"Gideon probably says hi," Nico said, which was an offering of sorts.

"I know. He said hi when I saw him this morning."

A pause, and then, "He and Max both love me, you know, even if you don't."

"Yes, I know. And rightfully, I hate it."

Their shoes tapped along the floor and they emerged on the sidewalk, where they were free to transport themselves magically if they wanted; conversation over.

Or, possibly, not. "The other candidates are older than we are," Libby noted aloud. "They've all been working already, you know? They're so… sophisticated-looking."

"Looks aren't everything," Nico said. "Though that Parisa girl is extremely hot."

"God, don't be a pig." She half-smiled, mostly-smirked. "You have absolutely no chance with her."

"Whatever, Rhodes."

Nico slid a hand through his hair, gesturing down the block. "This way?"

"Yeah."

Necessity required that they entertain certain détentes in their unending war for supremacy. They paused for the usual half-second to be sure no taxicabs were flying through the intersection before crossing the street, engaging the brisk walk-run that New York City taught its residents by virtue of experience.

"You're going to do it, aren't you?" Libby asked him. All her usual flare-ups of anxiety were on full display; she twirled her hair with one hand, chewing her lip absently.

"Yeah, probably." Definitely. "Aren't you?"

"Well—" She hesitated. "I mean yes, of course, I'm not stupid. I can't pass this up, it's even better than the NYUMA fellowship. But…" She trailed off. "I suppose it's a bit intimidating."

Liar. She already knew she was good; she was filling the social role of modesty she knew he wouldn't deign to play. "You've really got to work on your self-esteem, Rhodes. Self-deprecation went out as a fashionable personality trait at least five years ago."

"You're such a dick, Varona." She was chewing her thumbnail now. Stupid habit, though he detested the hair-twirling far more. "I hate you," she added. A gratuitous conversational tic established between them, akin to an 'um' or a thoughtful pause.

"Yeah, yeah, understood. So you're going to do it?"

She finally abandoned a spare inch of pretense, rolling her eyes. "Of course. Assuming Ezra's fine with it."

"Jesus. You can't be serious."

Every now and then, Libby achieved a look that successfully withered his balls, and this was one of those instances. It was the kind of look that reminded him she'd set him on fire the first time she'd met him without even batting an eye.

He'd like her more if she did it more often.

"I live with him, Varona," Libby reminded him, as if Nico could possibly forget her absurd selection of Ezra Fowler, their former R.A. and human wet blanket. "I think I should probably tell him if I'm planning to jet off to Alexandria for a year. Or even longer, I guess. Assuming I get initiated, that is," she said, with an air of unsaid *and I will be.*

They exchanged a look of agreement that required no translation.

"I mean, you *are* going to talk about it with Max and Gideon, aren't you?" Libby prompted him, arching a brow that disappeared once again beneath her bangs. "You guys haven't been apart for longer than an hour since freshman year."

"You say that like we're surgically attached. We have our own lives," Nico reminded her.

Libby's brow remained annoyingly lost to the span of her forehead.

"We *do*," Nico snapped, and her lips twisted up, doubtful. "And anyway, they're not up to anything. Max is independently wealthy and Gideon—" He broke off. "Well, you know Gideon."

She softened at that. "Yeah. Well, um."

She toyed with her hair. It occurred to Nico, not for the first time, that he should really start playing Libby Rhodes anxiety-habit bingo.

"See you tomorrow," he said, pausing as they arrived at her block. "Right?"

"Hm? Yeah." She was thinking about something. "Right, and—"

"Rhodes," he sighed, and she looked up, frowning. "Look, just don't... you know. Don't get all Rhodes about it."

"That's not a thing, Varona," she grumbled.

"It's absolutely a thing," he assured her. "Just don't Rhodes out on this."

"*What* the—"

"You know," he cut in. "Don't spend all this time like, fretting or whatever. It's exhausting."

She set her jaw. "So I'm exhausting now?"

She really was, and how she didn't already know it remained an eternal mystery. "You're good, Rhodes," he reminded her, leaping to cut her off before she got needlessly defensive. "You're good, okay? Just accept that I wouldn't bother hating you if you weren't."

"Varona, that presumes I care *at all* what you think."

"You care what everyone thinks, Rhodes. Especially me."

"Oh, *especially* you, really?"

"Yes." Clearly. "No point denying it."

She was agitated now, but at least that was an improvement on weak and insecure. "Look, whatever," she muttered. "Just… see you. Tomorrow, I guess." She pivoted away, heading up the block.

"Tell Ezra I say 'sup,'" he called after her. She flipped him off over her shoulder.

All was well, then, or at least the same as it always was.

Nico managed the handful of blocks on foot before waving himself up the stairs of his building, fiddling with the wards and barging in without a key to find Gideon seated on the cramped sofa beside a dozing, outstretched black lab.

"Nicolás," Gideon said, glancing up at his entry with a smile. "Como estas?"

"Ah, bien, más o menos. Ça va?"

"Oui, ça va," Gideon replied, giving the dog a nudge. "Max, wake up."

After a moment's pause, the dog slid groggily from the sofa, stretching out with a heavy-lidded look of annoyance. Then, in a blink, he was back to his usual form, scratching idly at his buzz cut to glare over his shoulder at Gideon.

"I was comfortable, you massive fuck," announced the man who was sometimes Maximilian Viridian Wolfe (barely domesticated under the best of circumstances) and sometimes not.

"Well, I wasn't," Gideon said in his usual measured tone before setting himself on his feet, tossing aside the newspaper he'd been reading. "Should we go out? Get dinner?"

"Nah, I'll cook," Nico said. He was really the only one who could, seeing as Max was mostly uninterested in picking up practical skills, preferring instead to sleep on the couch and ponder his existence, while Gideon… had other problems. Right now Gideon was shirtless, stretching his hands overhead past the usual wayward glints from his sandy hair, and if not for the bruising below his eyes, he would have looked almost perfectly normal.

He wasn't, of course, but deceptive normalcy was all part of Gideon's charm.

Eternal sluggishness aside, Nico had certainly seen Gideon in poorer states than this one. Hastily avoiding his mother, for instance, who had a tendency to show up in public toilets or the occasional gutter of rainwater, or skirting his foster family, who were less a family than a bunch of bloodsucking Nova Scotian leeches. Gideon's condition had been worse than usual in recent weeks, but Nico was pretty sure that was the inevitable result of graduating NYUMA. For four years Gideon had gotten to have a mostly normal life, but now he was back to…

Well, whatever life became, Nico supposed, when you had nowhere to go and a serious case of something a less-informed person might call chronic narcolepsy.

"Ropa vieja?" Nico suggested, saying nothing of what he was thinking.

"*Yes*." Max smashed a fist into the side of Gideon's arm, heading into the bathroom. He was, as he always was when he shifted, completely nude. Nico rolled his eyes and Max winked, not bothering to cover himself as he strode past.

"Libby texted me," Gideon remarked to Nico in Max's absence. "Says you were your usual dickish self."

"Is that all she said?" Nico prompted, hoping it was.

Ah, but of course not. "Said you guys got some sort of mysterious job offer."

"Mysterious?" Damn it.

"In that she wouldn't tell me what it was, yes."

They had been warned not to, but still.

"I can't believe she told you already," Nico grumbled, disgusted anew. "Seriously, how?"

"Messaged me just before you got here. I like that she keeps me informed." Gideon reached up, scratching the back of his neck. "How long would it have taken you to tell us if she hadn't?"

That sneaky little monstress. This was Nico's punishment, then. Forced communication with people who mattered to him, which she knew he loathed, all for implying that her boyfriend was precisely what he was.

"Ropa vieja takes a while," Nico demurred, retreating hastily to the kitchen. "Has to braise."

"Not a good answer, Nico," Gideon called after him, and regrettably Nico stopped, sighing.

"I," he began, and pivoted back to Gideon. "I… can't tell you what it is. Not yet."

With a pleading glance Nico enacted the faultless trust built on their four years of shared history, and after a moment, Gideon shrugged.

"Okay," he conceded. "But you still have to tell us things, you know. You've been on eggshells with me lately, it's weird." He paused. "You know, maybe you shouldn't come this time."

"Why not?" Nico demanded.

"Because you're babying him," came Max's drawl as he emerged from his room, clipping Nico's shoulder with his. He had deigned to put on an incongruous mix of sweatpants and a cashmere sweater, which was at least an improvement on the apartment's state of sanitation. "You're fussing, Nicky. Nobody likes a fusser."

"I'm not," Nico began, but at Gideon's look of skepticism, he sighed. "Fine, I am. But in my defense, I make it look very appealing."

"When did you even have time to grow maternal instincts?" Max asked him, sniffing the air as Nico began sifting through food in the kitchen.

"Probably during some class you didn't attend," Gideon told Max before turning back to Nico. "Hey," he cautioned in a low voice, nudging him. "I'm serious. If you're going somewhere, I'd like to know about it."

"You won't even notice I'm gone," Nico said with a sidelong glance.

"Why, because you expect me to come visit?"

Nico reached over, backhanding Gideon to remove him from the path to the fridge. "Yes," he said, pretending not to see that his answer had left Gideon with some relief. "In fact you could come, actually. Could put you in a nice drawer somewhere, you know? Stand you upright in my closet."

"No, thanks." Gideon sank to the ground to lean against the cabinets, yawning. "Do you have more of that—"

"Yes." Nico dug through one of the kitchen drawers, tossing Gideon a vial that was caught with one hand. "But you're not using it," Nico warned with a spatula, "unless I'm allowed to come tonight."

"I can't decide if that's a reflection on your concern for me or just your massive fear that something exciting will happen without you present," Gideon muttered, draining the contents of the vial. "But yeah, sure, fine."

"Hey, you need me. That stuff doesn't come easily," Nico reminded him, though in truth he would never tell Gideon just how easily it didn't come. He'd had to do a lot of things he didn't want to say aloud just to make sure the third year alchemical had left her mind blank enough for him to steal the formula. That he'd even managed *that* skill—which had taken nearly the entire four years at NYUMA to learn and had depleted him so thoroughly that for four days Libby Rhodes thought he was either dying or trying to trick her into *hoping* he was dying—was already more than he'd do for anyone else.

The trouble with having Gideon for a friend was the constant possibility of losing him. People like Gideon, who was not technically a person, were not, by most laws of nature, supposed to exist. Gideon's parents, an irresponsible finfolk and an even more irresponsible equidae (a mermaid and satyr respectively, by colloquial terms), had always possessed the 25% chance their offspring would look perfectly human, which Gideon did. They, of course, had not cared that their human-looking child would not be technically anything at all that could be registered, and that while he would have medeian abilities, he would not be afforded the class of species to which all medeians were required by law to belong. Gideon wasn't entitled to any social services, couldn't be legally employed, and unfortunately couldn't spin straw into gold without considerable effort. That Gideon had been educated at all was mostly an accident, along with an instance of wide scale institutional fraud.

It all basically came down to one thing: the opportunity to study a subspecies like Gideon was not something NYUMA had been prepared to pass up, but now that he was no longer enrolled as a student, he was back to being nothing.

Just a man who could walk through dreams, and Nico's best friend.

"I'm sorry," Nico said, and Gideon glanced up. "I was going to tell you, I just…"

Felt guilty.

"I keep telling you," Gideon said. "You don't need to."

If Libby Rhodes mocked that Nico and Gideon were attached at the hip, it was only so that Nico could personally assure Gideon's survival. Libby would not understand that, of course; she was one of the spare few who knew that Gideon was not what he seemed, but she didn't know what it meant. She didn't know how often Gideon ended up in harm's way, unable to secure himself corporeally in a single realm, or how often he got swallowed up inside his own head, lost to the intangible spaces of thought and subconsciousness, and couldn't find his way back. She didn't know that Gideon had enemies, or that those who knew what he was and intended to use him for it were most dangerous, above all.

Libby didn't know, either, that while Nico didn't underestimate her, she relentlessly underestimated him. He had perfected skills in multiple specialties outside his own, all of which had cost him greatly. He could change his shape to follow the other two into the environment of dreams (animals had fewer restrictions on their boundaries than humans), but only after learning to manipulate each element of his own molecular structure; something he only did once a month, because it meant a full day's recovery afterwards. He could brew something to bind Gideon's physical form more permanently to the reality he currently stood in, but only after backbreaking effort that left Nico throbbing and sore for a week.

There had been no way Nico was turning down the Society's offer. Power? He needed it. An obscure cure? He needed that, too. Money, prestige, connections? He needed all of it, and Gideon would be better for his access. Two years away was hardly too much to ask.

"I never expected you to put your life on hold for me, Nico," Gideon said.

No, he didn't, and that was the only reason Nico had done it to begin with; or thought he had no choice but to do it, anyway, until today.

"Look, the moment you became my friend, you became my problem," Nico told him, and then, realizing what he'd said, he amended, "Or, you know, mine. Or whatever."

Gideon rose to his feet with a sigh. "Nico—"

"Can you guys stop whispering?" Max yelled from the sofa. "It's hard to hear you from here."

Nico and Gideon exchanged a glance.

"You heard him," Nico said, figuring it wasn't worth continuing the argument.

Gideon, who had obviously decided the same, plucked some carrots from the produce drawer for a side dish, nudging Nico aside with a motion of his hip.

"Shall I grate?"

"You're grating already," Nico grumbled, but he caught the evidence of a smile on Gideon's face, deciding the rest of the conversation could stand to wait.

TRISTAN

THE PROBLEM WITH SEEING THROUGH THINGS SO READILY was the development of a certain degree of natural cynicism. Some people could be promised knowledge and power without a compulsion to uncover the caveats implied, but Tristan was not one of them.

"I need to talk to you," he said, remaining behind the other five candidates and approaching the Caretaker who'd so evasively insisted on recruiting him.

Atlas looked up from muted conversation with whoever the man was who'd come in to drone on at length about the Society; Dalton something-or-other, who'd been effusing quite a lot of magic while he spoke. That was partially why Tristan had not made an effort to listen. If he were going to be convinced to abandon the life he'd already set up so meticulously for himself, he wasn't going to be illusioned or manipulated into it. It would be his choice, based on uncompromisable facts, and Atlas would give them to him or Tristan would leave. Simple as that.

Atlas seemed to have gathered as much from a glance and nodded, dismissing Dalton.

"Ask," Atlas beckoned, neither patiently nor impatiently, and Tristan's mouth tightened.

"You know as well as I do that my abilities are rare, but not useful. You can't possibly expect me to believe I have one of the six most valuable magical specialties in the world."

Atlas leaned against the table, considering Tristan for a moment in silence.

"So why would I have chosen you, then, if I didn't believe it?"

"That's precisely what I want to know," Tristan said staunchly. "If this has anything to do with my father—"

"It doesn't," Atlas said, dismissing Tristan's concerns with a wave of a hand. "Your father is a witch, Mr Caine. Skilled enough, but commonplace."

Of course Atlas would want him to believe that. It wasn't the first time someone had tried to magnify Tristan's abilities in order to reach or infiltrate his father's gang. "My father is the head of a magical crime syndicate," Tristan said, bristling, "and even if he were not, I am—"

"You," Atlas cut in, "don't even understand what you are, I'd wager. What was your specialty? And I do not mean your abilities," he clarified. "I mean to ask which credential you received from the London School of Magic as a medeian."

Tristan scrutinized him warily. "I thought you already knew everything about everyone in that room."

"I do," Atlas said with a shrug, "but I'm a rather busy and important man with many things on my mind, so I would prefer you to tell me anyway."

Fine. No sense dragging this out. "I studied in the college of illusion."

"But you are not an illusionist," Atlas pointed out.

"No," Tristan said gruffly, "but as I can see *through* illusions—"

"No," Atlas corrected, startling him. "You can do more than see through illusions."

He rose to his feet with sudden immediacy, beckoning Tristan after him. "Walk with me," he said, and though Tristan did not remotely want to listen, he conceded to follow, allowing Atlas to lead him through a narrow hallway that wound into a wider corridor.

"Here," Atlas determined, pausing abruptly before a painting. "What is this a painting of?"

Disappointing. This, as far as Tristan could tell, was predictable cultish recruitment. Evade and flatter, mystify and conceal.

"I don't have time," Tristan snapped, "to play games. I assure you, I was diagnosed by every medeian at the London School, and I know the extent to which my abilities are—"

"In the moment I asked," Atlas interrupted, "you identified this painting as a portrait of the artist's lover." He gestured again to the painting behind him. "You saw a number of things, of course—far more than I was able to distinguish from my brief foray into your observations—but you looked at this nondescript portrait of a nineteenth century Society benefactor and interpreted the details which led you to conclude what you were looking at, which no one but you would have seen."

Atlas pointed to the title on the plaque, which read simply: *Viscount Welles, 1816.*

"You ascertained that the light coming in through the window came not from a typical portrait studio, but a location both the artist and the subject found comfortable. You noted his presentation was informal and the marks of his rank were added hastily afterward. You came to a reasonable conclusion not on what was presented to you, but on what you deduced. This is because you see components," Atlas pointed out, and Tristan, always wary of a hidden agenda, assumed a guarded suspension of disbelief. "In mortal terms that would make you a savant. You also see magical components, which is why you were identified for medeian classification. But you are correct," he conceded, "to suspect that our interest in you exceeds the magic you have exhibited deliberately up to this point."

Atlas saddled Tristan with a look of immense and troubling expectation.

"You are more than rare," Atlas said, pronouncing it with finality. "You cannot begin to imagine your capabilities, Tristan, because no one has ever known what to do with you, and thus you have never encountered a reason to know. Have you ever studied space? Time? Thought?"

To Tristan's momentary furrow of bemusement, Atlas said, "Precisely. You were educated alongside a group of illusionists, intending only to profit from marketable sleight of hand."

Tristan bristled. "Is that what you think I am?"

"Obviously not, Tristan, or I would not be standing here trying to convince you otherwise."

Tristan considered that a moment.

"You make it sound like the game is rigged in my favor," he observed, still guarded, and Atlas shook his head.

"Not at all. I know how useful you are; it's your turn to convince the others. The promise of your talents is nothing compared to whatever you ultimately prove to be."

At that point, Atlas gave Tristan a curt, inattentive smile, expressing wordlessly that he wished to conclude the conversation.

"I can promise you nothing," Atlas said. "I will, in fact, promise you nothing, and whatever you take from this, do not be misled; nothing I have told you is a guarantee of anything at all. Unlike the others of your initiate class, your power remains largely untested. Your potential is almost entirely unreached, and however unmatched I believe it to be, it will have to be you who brings it to fruition. I'm afraid, Mr Caine, that you will simply have to take the gamble if you wish to see it through to the reward."

Tristan wasn't entirely risk averse; he had been known to cast his lot in venturesome ways before. In fact, the majority of his current life had been a gamble, and while it had been paying off as he intended thus far, he hadn't been aware at first how unsatisfactory that return would be. Based on his previous decisions, Tristan would be married to an heiress in a matter of months, the inheritor to a massive player in the magical economy, finally dismantled from his father's criminal enterprise and probably equally likely to jump off a bridge as he was to 'accidentally' poison Rupesh's favorite detoxifying kombuchas.

Some gamble.

"Shall I see you to the lifts?" Atlas prompted.

"No, thank you," said Tristan, who figured he ought to start learning the building. "I can find them myself."

PARISA

FOLLOWING DALTON ELLERY'S PATH was not a particularly trying task. The building was mildly sentient, possessing enough layers of enchantment that it had a basic primordial sense of thought, and so it was a simple enough effort to identify the motion of his footsteps along the vertebrae of its corridors. Parisa stepped daintily in his trajectory, hardly breaking a sweat.

To her relief, he was still handsome upon second glance. It wasn't a face he had put on for them at the meeting; typically, masking charms of any kind were too strenuous to hold at unnecessary moments, like this one.

She felt, though, the little catch of an unseen mechanism when he spotted her; his defenses flying up.

"You don't seem like the power-seeking type," Parisa ventured, deciding to guess aloud what sort of man Dalton Ellery was. The assertion was so accurate as to be unremarkable; he had a studious look to him, and a solemnity that didn't lend itself to the hypermale braggadocio of politicians and businessmen.

Her more pressing estimation—the more reckless guess—had been that candor might alternatively unnerve or embolden him. Either way would be enough to secure herself a place in his thoughts, in which case it would be like leaving the door open a crack behind her. She would more easily find her way back to his thoughts if she had been inside his head to begin with.

"Miss Kamali," said Dalton, his tone evenly measured despite his initial surprise. "I cannot imagine I seem like much at all, given the inconsequence of our meeting."

That was insufficiently informative, to say the least; neither unnerved nor emboldened, but merely factual.

She tried again, attempting, "I wouldn't describe anything that just happened as inconsequential."

"No?" He shrugged, inclining his head to dismiss himself. "Well, perhaps you're right. If you'll excuse me—"

That wouldn't do. "Dalton," she said, and he glanced at her, giving her a look of intensely restrained politeness. "Surely it's reasonable that I still have questions, despite your illuminating presentation."

"Questions about…?"

"Everything. This Society, among other things."

"Well, Miss Kamali, I'm afraid I can't give you many answers beyond the ones I have already provided."

If Parisa hadn't already been aware how little men cared for evidence of female frustration, she might have grimaced. His indifference was deeply unhelpful.

"You," she attempted, venturing a more effective topic. "You chose to do this once yourself, did you not?"

"Yes," Dalton said, with an unspoken *obviously*.

"You chose this after one meeting?" she prompted. "Tapped by Atlas Blakely, sat in a room with strangers just as we were… and you simply agreed, no questions asked?"

Finally, a hitch of hesitation. "Yes. It is, as I'm sure you know, a compelling offer."

"But then," she pointed out, "you chose to stay beyond your initiation period."

His brow twitched; another promising sign. "Does that surprise you?"

"Of course," she said, relieved to see he was finally taking a more active role in the conversation. "Your pitch to us in that room was about power, wasn't it? Returning to the world after initiation to take advantage of the resources allotted to the Society's members," she clarified, "and yet, given the opportunity to do so, you chose to remain here." As a cleric, essentially. Some intermediary between the Alexandrian divine and their chosen flock.

"Someone once told me I don't seem like the power-seeking type," Dalton said.

She smiled. He didn't know it yet, but she had found her footing.

"Well, I suppose I have little reason *not* to join," Parisa replied with a shrug. Nothing, after all, was keeping her. "Only that I am not particularly enamored with teamwork."

"You will be glad to have a team," Dalton assured her. "The specialties are chosen to complement each other, in part. Three of you specialize in physicalities, while the other three—"

"So you know my specialty, then."

He smiled grimly. "Yes, Miss Kamali."

"So I suppose you don't trust me?"

"Habitually, I refrain from trusting people like you," said Dalton.

That, Parisa thought, was rather telling.

"I imagine you suspect me of using you, then," she said.

His response was a wry half-smile with a clear enough translation: *I know better than to answer that.*

"Well," she said. "Then I suppose I'll have to prove you wrong."

He gave her another curt nod. "Best of luck to you, Miss Kamali," he said. "I have very high hopes for you."

He turned, about to head for the corridor, when Parisa reached for his arm, catching him unawares just long enough to draw herself up on her toes, bracing her palms on his chest.

There would be the slightest pulse of contemplation here—the hardest work was managed in the moments before a thing was accomplished. The promise of her breath on his lips; the angle at which he viewed her, her dark eyes overlarge, and the way he would gradually become conscious of her warmth. He would smell her perfume now and catch hints of it again later, wondering if she had rounded a nearby corner or recently been in a room. He would catalogue the sensation of her smallness in the same incongruous moment he registered the pressure of her presence; the immediacy of her, the nearness, would momentarily unsettle him, and in that moment, lacking the presence of mind to recoil, he would permit himself to imagine what might happen next.

The kiss itself was so fragile and brief it hardly mattered. She would learn only the smell of his cologne, the feeling of his mouth. The most important detail of a kiss was usually the cataloguing of a single fact: is the kiss returned? But *this* kiss, of course, was far too fleeting to be informative. Better he did not return it, in fact, as no man would allow a woman access to the more worthy corners of his mind if he kissed her too readily to start with.

"Sorry," she said, removing her hands from his chest. Balance was a delicate matter; the sending of her desire forward while also tearing herself physically away. Those who did not believe this to be a dance had not undergone the choreography long or devotedly enough. "I'm afraid it cost more energy than I cared to expend," she murmured, "preventing myself from doing that."

Magic was an energy they all knew better than to waste; on some level, she knew he would relate.

"Miss Kamali." These, the first words after kissing her, would forever taste like her, and she doubted he'd escape an opportunity to say her name again. "Perhaps you misunderstand."

"Oh, I'm sure I do," she said, "but I suppose I quite enjoy an opportunity for misunderstanding."

She smiled up at him, and he slowly detached himself from her.

"Your efforts," he said, "would be better spent convincing your initiation class of your value. I have no direct impact on the decision as to whether or not you'll be chosen for initiation."

"I'm very good at what I do. I'm not concerned with their opinions."

"Perhaps you should be."

"I don't make a habit of doing things I should."

"So it appears."

He flicked another glance at her, and this time, to her immense satisfaction, she saw it.

The opening of a door.

"If I believed you capable of sincerity I would recommend you turn and run," he said. "Unfortunately, I think you have every weapon necessary to win this game."

"So it is a game, then." Finally, something she could use.

"It is a game," he confirmed. "But I'm afraid you miscalculated. I am not a useful piece."

She did not, as a rule, miscalculate. Better that he wonder, though.

"Perhaps I'll simply have you for fun, then," she said, but as she did not make a habit of being the one left behind, she took the first step in retreat. "Are the transportation portals that way?" she asked him, deliberately pointing in the wrong direction. The moment his mind would take to replace the incorrect information with accuracy would be enough to catch the shadow of something, and she was right, observing a flicker of something heavily suppressed.

"That way," Dalton said, "just around the corner."

Whatever lurked in his mind was not a complete thought. It was a rush of things, identifiable only by how carnal they were. Desire, for example. She had kissed him, and he was wanting. But there was something else, too, and it wasn't interwoven with the rest the way it sometimes was.

Lust was a color, but fear was a sensation. Clammy hands or a cold sweat were obvious markers, but more often it was some sort of multisensory incongruity. Like seeing sun and smelling smoke, or feeling silk and tasting bile. Sounds that rose out of unseeing darkness.

Dalton Ellery was definitely afraid of something. Tragically, that something wasn't her.

"Thank you," Parisa said, rather meaning it, and proceeded down the corridor to find there was an additional person waiting in the vestibule.

He, she thought, was interesting. There was something very coiled up about him, something rearing to strike, but the best part about snakes was how little they could be bothered to do so unless someone was blocking their sun.

Besides, call it merciless Westernization, but she liked British accents.

"Tristan, isn't it?" she asked, watching him look up from a rather murky swamp of thoughts. "Are you headed to London?"

"Yes." He was half-listening, half-thinking, though his thoughts were mostly unidentifiable. On the one hand they took very linear paths, like a map of Manhattan, but they also seemed to reach destinations that would require more effort than Parisa had energy to follow at the moment. "And you?"

"London as well," she said, and he blinked with surprise, refocusing on her.

He was recalling her academic origin of École Magique de Paris and her personal origin of Tehran, basic introductory details distributed by Atlas.

Good, so he'd been paying attention.

"But I thought—"

"Can you see through all illusions?" she asked him. "Or is it just the bad ones?"

Tristan hesitated for a moment, and then his mouth twisted. He had an angry mouth, or at least a mouth accustomed to camouflaging anger.

"You're one of those," he said.

"If you're not busy, we should have a drink," she replied.

He was instantly suspicious. "Why?"

"Well, there's no point in me going back to Paris. And besides, I need to entertain myself for what remains of the evening."

"You think I'll entertain you?"

She allowed a deliberate flick of her eyes, following the shape of him.

"I certainly think I'd like to see you try," she said. "And anyway, if we're going to do this, we ought to start making friends."

"Friends?" He practically licked his lips with the word.

"I like to know my friends intimately," she assured him.

"I'm engaged." True, but immaterial.

"How wonderful for you. I'm sure she's a lovely girl."

"She isn't, actually."

"Even better," Parisa said. "Neither am I."

Tristan cut her a sidelong glance. "What kept you so long after the meeting?"

She considered what to tell him, weighing her options. This wasn't the same calculation that Dalton Ellery had been, of course. This was purely recreational. Dalton was more of a professional concern, though it was tinged with a bit of genuine craving.

Dalton was chess; Tristan was sport. Importantly, though, both were games.

"I'll tell you over breakfast," Parisa suggested.

Tristan sighed aloud, addressing his resignation to empty air, and then turned back to her.

"I have to do a few things first," he said. "Break things off with Eden. Quit my job. Punch my best friend in the jaw."

"That all sounds like responsible behavior that can wait until morning," advised Parisa, stepping through the portal's open doors and beckoning him after her. "Be sure to schedule in the part where I tell you my theories about what we're not being told, presumably between the broken engagement and the probably well-deserved assault."

He, obligingly, stepped into the portal after her. "You have theories?"

She pushed the button for London. "Don't you?"

They exchanged a glance, both smiling, as the portal confirmed: *King's Cross Station, London, England, United Kingdom.*

"Why me?" said Tristan.

"Why not?" said Parisa.

It seemed they were like-minded. She was inexperienced with

collaboration, but felt that was an important qualification for teamwork.

"I could certainly use a pint," Tristan said, and the doors closed, delivering them to the remainder of their evening.

LIBBY

IT HAD NOT BEEN A VERY GOOD DAY for Ezra, poor thing. This was a rather inevitable outcome, of course, considering he'd had to spend most of it with Libby's parents at her graduation ceremony before she, admittedly, had skipped off mysteriously without warning and then returned to delay any explanation for her absence by tugging him firmly into bed with her. At least he'd gotten sex that day, which she presumed would be a lovely turn of events, but also, his partner in the act had clung to a secretive and knowingly manipulative agenda that had left her distracted and unable to climax, so that was… potentially less lovely for him.

Subsequent pro: she had graciously made him dinner.

Subsequent con: she had also informed him over said dinner that she would be accepting the offer made to her by Atlas Blakely, Caretaker, despite being unable to properly explain why.

"So you're just… leaving?" Ezra asked, warily bemused. He had been mid-sip when Libby began talking and had since forgotten about the wine glass that remained clutched in his hand. "But Lib—"

"It's only two years," Libby reminded him. "Well, one for sure," she amended, "and then hopefully a second year if I'm selected."

Ezra set down his glass, frowning at it.

"And… what is it, exactly?"

"I can't tell you."

"But—"

"You'll just have to trust me," she said, not for the first time. "It's essentially a fellowship," she added in an attempt to explain, but this, unfortunately, had been exactly the wrong auditory cue.

"Speaking of fellowships, I've been meaning to bring it up," Ezra said, brightening, "but I just heard from Porter in the bursar's office that Varona turned down that NYUMA fellowship. I know you weren't excited about the VC job, so if you're still interested in that position, I'm sure I could put in a good word."

Surely he must have known this was the exact wrong thing to say. Shouldn't he? She wouldn't want Nico's cast-offs, and certainly not now.

Though it did leave her with one other thing to explain.

"Well, the thing about Varona is—" Libby coughed. "Well, Varona is... also invited."

Ezra faltered. "Oh?"

"Oh, come on. You can't be surprised." She fidgeted with her utensils, pushing the pasta around on her plate. "You saw us this morning, didn't you?"

"Yes, but I thought—"

"Look, it's the same as it always is," she said listlessly. "For whatever reason, Nico and I can do the same things, and—"

"So then why do they need both of you?" Ezra prompted. Again, the wrong thing to say. "You hate working with him. Not to mention everyone knows you're better—"

"Actually, Ezra, they don't. Clearly they don't," Libby added with a scoff, "since he got the fellowship I wanted. See how that works?"

"But—"

"I can't let him win this time, babe. Seriously, I can't." She wiped her mouth with her napkin, setting it back on the table with frustration. "I've got to set myself apart from him. Don't you get that?"

"Can't you do that by, I don't know," Ezra posed with tacit disapproval, "doing something different?"

He made that sound so simple.

"Look," Libby said, "chances are, only one of us is going to make the cut when the... fellowship," she remembered, narrowly avoiding giving more details away, "determines the final members for its—" A pause. "Faculty." Another pause, and then, "We have the same specialty, which means we'll draw the most obvious comparison. So either he'll be picked and I won't, in which case I'll be back in a year or less, or I'll be picked and he won't, in which case—"

"In which case you win," Ezra exhaled with a hand around his mouth, "and we can finally stop worrying about whatever Varona is doing?"

"Yes." That much, at least, was fairly obvious. "Not that you have to worry about Varona now."

Ezra stiffened. "Lib, I wasn't—"

"You were, actually," Libby said, picking up her glass. "And I keep telling you, there's nothing there. He's just an asshole."

"Believe me, I'm aware—"

"We'll talk every night," she assured him. "I'll come home every weekend." She could do that, probably. Maybe. "You'll barely notice I'm gone."

Ezra sighed. "Libby—"

"You just have to let me prove myself," she told him. "You keep saying that Varona's not better than me—"

"—because he *isn't*—"

"—but it doesn't matter what you think, Ezra, not really." His mouth tightened, probably resentful that she was so dismissive of his admittedly very thoughtful attempts to reassure her, but on this, she couldn't make allowances. "You hate him too much to see how good he really is, babe. I just want the opportunity to learn more, to prove myself. And proving myself by going up against the best in the world means going up against Nico de Varona, whether you believe that or not."

"So I don't get a say, then." Ezra's expression was slightly grim, but mostly unreadable.

"Of course you get a say," Libby corrected him. "You can say, 'Libby, I love you and I support you,' or you can say something else." She swallowed before adding, "But believe me, Ezra, there are only two answers here. If you don't say one, you're saying the other."

She braced herself, waiting. She didn't expect him to make any unreasonable demands, exactly, but she definitely knew he wasn't going to be thrilled. Closeness was important to Ezra; it had been his idea to move in together, and he expected a certain amount of what a therapist might call 'quality time.' He certainly wasn't going to savor the fact that Nico would be there in his absence.

To Libby's immense relief, though, Ezra merely sighed, reaching across the table for her hand.

"You dream big, hotshot," he said.

"That," she murmured, "isn't really an answer."

"Fine. Libby, I love you and I support you." She was briefly permitted a pause for relief; and then he added, "But be careful, okay?"

"Be careful with what," Libby scoffed, "Varona?"

Nico was laughably harmless. Good, certainly, even great if he put his mind to it, but he was hardly capable of schemes. He could get under her skin, maybe—but even then, there was no danger of anything aside from losing her temper.

"Just be careful." Ezra leaned across the table, brushing his lips against her forehead. "I would never forgive myself if I let something happen to you," he murmured, and she groaned. Just the usual white knight shit, then.

"I can take care of myself, Ezra."

"I know." He touched her cheek, smiling faintly. "But hey, what else am I here for?"

"Your body," she assured him. "Plus you make a mean bolognese."

He had her out of her chair in a flash, pulling her into him as she laughed in unconvincing protest.

"I'm going to miss you, Libby Rhodes," he said, "and that's the truth."

So it was final, then. She was really doing this.

Libby wrapped her arms around Ezra's neck, clinging to him for a moment. Maybe she wasn't a damsel in distress, but it still felt nice to anchor herself to something before casting herself into the unknown.

III: BATTLE

CALLUM

IT HAD NOT BEEN A PARTICULARLY COMPLEX MATTER deciding to join the Society at Atlas Blakely's invitation. If he didn't care for the experience, Callum reasoned, he would leave. It was how he generally lived his life: he came and went as he wished. People these decisions affected, if they were angry about his mutability, did not typically stay mad. Preternaturally or otherwise, Callum had a way of ensuring that people came around to see his position on the matter, one way or another. Once he'd made his point, they could always be compelled to act reasonably from there.

Callum had always been aware that word used for his specialty by the Hellenistic University of Magical Arts was not the right word. The manipulist subcategory of illusionist was more often applied to cases of physical specialties: people who could warp things, make them into something else. Water could be convinced to be wine, in the right hands, or at least made to look and taste like it. One of the particularities about the study and reality of magic was that it only mattered, in the end, how things looked or tasted; what they were meant to be, or what were at the start, could be easily dismissed in favor of achieving the necessary result.

But what the Society appeared to know—what *Atlas Blakely* seemed to know, which others typically didn't—was that Callum's work was more accurately defined as a vigorous type of empath. It was unsurprising, really, that he was magically misdiagnosed; empathy was a far more common magical manifestation in women, and thus, when it appeared, it was usually cultivated in a highly delicate, maternal sort of way. There were a number of female medeians who were able to tap into the emotions of others; more often than not, they became marvelous humanitarians, lauded for the contributions to therapy and healing. It was a very feminine thing, to be both magical and saintly. Philanthropy could be worn like jewelry or cosmetics, glittering from the effervescence of their pores.

When the same skill set could be found in men, it was usually too diluted to be classified as magical; more often it was considered an isolated personality trait. In the case of persuasion, a trait with the potential to achieve medeian-level ability—labeled, perhaps, 'charisma' by the non-magical—it would often be put aside in favor of the usual method of going about things: attendance at some famous mortal university, like Oxford or Harvard for example, and then a prosperous mortal career from there. Occasionally these men went on to become CEOs, lawyers, or politicians. Sometimes they became tyrants, megalomaniacs, or dictators—in which case it was probably best their talents went unrealized. Magic, like most other forms of physical exertion, required proper training to wield properly or for any extended period of time; had any of those men ever realized their natural qualities were something they could refine, the world would have been far worse off than it was already.

Naturally there is an exception to every rule, which in this case was Callum. He was saved from any sort of global misbehavior (or rather, the world was saved) by his lack of ambition, which, paired with his love of finer things, meant that he never aspired to world domination, nor to anything even close. Always dangerous, the pairing of hunger with any skill of manipulation; it is an essential law of human behavior that when given the tools to do so, those born at the bottom will always try to claw their way to the top. Those born at the top, i.e., Callum, were usually less inclined to upend things as they were. When the setting was already gilded and ornate, what would be the point of changing them?

Thus, nothing had driven Callum to accept Atlas Blake's offer, but nothing had repelled him, either. He might go through with initiation, he might not; the Society might impress him enough to stay, or it might not. It went without saying, at least, that the building housing the Alexandrian Society was not especially impressive on its own. Callum came from money, which meant he had already seen wealth in a number of its natural forms: royal, aristocratic, capitalist, corrupt… The list went on into perpetuity. *This* form, the Alexandrian variety, was technically academic, though academic wealth was almost always one of the aforementioned forms, if not some combination of all of them.

There was a reason knowledge was reserved for the elite. A self-perpetuating cycle, really, though Callum could not be compelled to criticize it much. After all, he had done nothing but benefit from the inherent classism of higher education. As with most things from which Callum had profited, he questioned very little.

The same could not be said for the others, who had all returned (unsurprisingly) to accept the invitation. The American, Libby Rhodes, was most memorable by how often and irritatingly she spoke, and naturally she had been the first to ask a stupid question.

"We *are* in Alexandria, aren't we?" she asked, her brow furrowing beneath a rather unalluring fringe. If it were up to Callum, he'd have given her a different haircut entirely; something tied up or pulled back, preferably so she'd leave the tips of her hair alone. "I can't say anything looks particularly Alexandrian."

It certainly did not. The interior of wherever they were—distinct from wherever had housed yesterday's meeting, though presumably some equally untraceable location—looked very much like the inside of a London mansion, surrounded by what was surely an English garden as well. Despite the Novas' residency in Cape Town, Callum's family had been invited more than once to pay a visit to the British Royal Family (the Novas had once been close with the Greek royals, hence Callum's very comfortable study at the Hellenistic University in Athens) and he considered the Society's decor to be very similar. Portraits of aristocracy lined the walls alongside a variety of Victorian busts, and while the architecture itself was certainly Greco-Roman influenced, it bore obvious markers of the Romantics, leaning more eighteenth century Neo than genuinely Classical.

Overall, the idea they might have been anywhere other than England was extremely unlikely.

"Well, I suppose there's no harm in saying we are actually in London," confirmed Dalton Ellery, the stiff-looking aide to Atlas Blakely whose energy was immediately guessable; fear, or possibly intimidation. Callum presumed Dalton to harbor a bit of intellectual inferiority, which was the only thing to possibly explain the man's ongoing devotion to academics. If the perks of Society membership were wealth and prestige, why stay here and fail to take advantage?

But, seeing as Callum didn't care, he didn't wonder about it for long.

Instead, he watched Tristan and Parisa, the only two interesting people, who exchanged a rather secretive glance between themselves while Libby, the fringed girl whose anxieties were so prickly and unceasing they nearly set Callum's teeth on edge, frowned with confusion.

"But if this is actually the Library of Alexandria, then how—"

"The Society has changed its physical location several times throughout history," Dalton explained. "It was originally in Alexandria, of course, but was moved soon after to Rome, and then to Prague until the Napoleonic wars, and ultimately arrived here around the Age of Exploration, alongside the rest of imperialism's benefits."

"That," muttered Nico, the Cuban young man who, thankfully, was not quite tall enough to be a threat to Callum's vainer impulses, "is the most British thing I've ever heard."

"Yes, it's very much akin to the British Museum," confirmed Dalton dismissively, "in that every relic from every culture is rather forcibly housed under one monarchical roof. In any case," he continued, as if that had not been a highly brow-raising statement in itself, "there have been countless attempts to house it elsewhere, as one might expect. The Americans had a very strong argument for moving it to New York until 1941, and of course we all know what happened then. Anyway, as I was saying, you'll all be housed here," he said, turning the corner from the gallery to a corridor lined with doors. "Your names are indicated on the placards beside the doors, and your things have been deposited there for you. Once our tour is complete, you will all meet with Atlas and then proceed to dinner. The gong is every evening at half past seven," he added. "Your attendance each evening is expected."

Callum noticed that Tristan and Parisa had exchanged yet another conspiratorial glance. Did they know each other before today, as the two American-trained students did? He paused for a moment to determine it, and then deduced no, they had not met any earlier than the others, though they had certainly met intimately since then.

He felt a flare-up of frustration. He never liked not being among the first to make friends.

"What exactly does a normal day look like?" Libby asked, continuing her tirade of questions. "Will there be classes, or…?"

"In a sense," said Dalton. "Though I expect Atlas will advise you further."

"Do you not know?" asked Reina, the very bored-looking Japanese girl with the nose ring, whose voice was much deeper than Callum expected it to be. She hadn't spoken before then, nor given much indication of listening, though she'd been staring intently at the contents of every room they passed.

"Well, each class of candidates is slightly different," Dalton said. "There are different specialties, making each round of initiates a different composition of skills. Thus, the research you're assigned varies from year to year."

"I don't suppose you're going to tell us what all our specialties are?" prompted Parisa. She, Callum noted, was radiating a certain persuasion herself, though it seemed to be directed at Dalton. Typical; faux-intellectualism would always be appealing to any girl who'd spent too much time in France. It was about as Parisian as bobs, sartorial minimalism, and cheese.

"That," Dalton said, "is up to you. Though I doubt it will be long before you discover them."

"Living in the same house, taking all our meals together? I can only assume we'll be sick to death with knowledge about ourselves in no time," remarked Tristan at a drawl, which prompted Parisa to a smothered laugh that Callum considered supremely false.

"I'm sure you will," replied Dalton, unfazed. "Now, if you'll come this way, please."

Dalton led them through a maze of stately Neoclassicism before arriving in a particularly sun-soaked room of grandeur, the walls of which were lined with books. Reina, who had been glooming disinterestedly through their procession around the house, seemed to have finally woken up a bit, eyes widening.

"This is the painted room," Dalton said. "It is where you will meet Atlas each morning, following breakfast in the morning room. The easiest path to the reading room and archives is through those doors," he added, gesturing with a sidelong glance to his left.

"This isn't the library?" asked Reina, frowning upwards as she eyed the highest shelves. Nearby, a fern seemed to shiver with anticipation.

"No," said Dalton. "The library is for letter writing. And, should you wish it, cream tea."

Nico, who was standing beside Libby, silently made a face of revulsion.

"Yes," Dalton agreed, plucking at a stray thread on his cuff. "Quite."

"Aren't there other people who live here?" asked Libby, peering through narrowed eyes down the corridor. "I thought this was a society."

"Only the archives are housed here. Typically, Alexandrians will come and go by appointment," Dalton explained. "Occasionally there will be smaller groups taking meetings in the reading room, in which case you will be asked not to disturb them, and vice versa."

"Is it really such a simple matter of coming and going?" (Libby again.)

"Certainly not," said Dalton, "though that, too, will be a matter of your discretion."

"But how——"

"What Dalton means," came Atlas Blakely's buttery baritone, "is that there are a number of security measures in place."

At his appearance, Callum and Tristan both turned to face the entrance, the six of them falling reflexively into a line.

"However," Atlas continued, "part of your job as the new class of initiates is to develop a protocol that suits you as a collective. And before you ask what that means," he assured Libby with a smile, "I'm happy to explain. As with all the most crucial secrets, there are quite a number of people who know of the Society's existence. Several organizations have targeted it over the years for robbery, infiltration, or, in some cases, destruction. Thus, we rely not only on the charms in place, but also on the Society's resident class of initiates to maintain their own security detail."

"Wait," said Libby, who was still caught on the prospect of global secrets being widely known. "So that means——"

"It means the first thing to discuss will be your proficiency at magical defense," Atlas confirmed, as a series of chairs materialized behind each of them. "Sit, please," he beckoned, and warily, all six of them took their requested seats; Reina perhaps most warily of all. "I won't be long," Atlas added as a measure of assurance. "Your responsibility this afternoon will be determining your plan as a group. I am mostly here to provide guidance before I leave you to it."

"Has anyone ever stolen anything successfully?" asked Tristan, who seemed to be the most cynical of the group, or at least the first to voice his cynicism.

"Or actually broken in to any degree of success?" Nico added.

"Yes," said Atlas. "In which case, I hope your magical offense is equally as refined as your defense, as you will be asked to retrieve anything that is removed without permission."

"Asked," echoed Reina at a murmur, and Atlas turned to her with a smile.

"Asked," he confirmed, "politely. And from there, dealt with as appropriate."

That was about as well-mannered a threat as Callum might have expected. This was all exceedingly British, from the dome of the so-called 'painted room' to the idea that they would be summoned to dinner by a gong.

Libby, of course, raised her hand tentatively in the air. "How often, exactly, are we expected to defend the Society's…" A pause. "Collection?"

"Well, that depends on the strength of your system." Briefly, a red glow manifested in the corner of the room, and then disappeared. "That, for example," said Atlas, "was a thwarted attempt to enter the Society's perimeter. Though, it's also possible someone simply forgot their keys."

He was smiling, so this was apparently a joke. Callum had the sense Atlas Blakely wanted very badly for them to like him; or, at the very least, he was the sort of person who always had an expectation of being liked.

"As to the subject of the… 'collection,' as you called it, Miss Rhodes," Atlas said with a nod in Libby's direction, "meaning the contents of the Library, that is a more complex matter. You will all gain access to the Society's records in stages; as you earn the Society's trust, you will be permitted further steps. Each door unlocked will lead to another door, which, once unlocked, will lead to another. Metaphorically, of course."

Nico this time: "And these doors…?"

"We'll start with physicalities. Space," said Atlas. "The fundamental laws of physics and how to bypass them."

At that, Libby and Nico exchanged a glance; it was the first time, Callum noted, that Libby did not have one of her spectacularly awkward behaviors on display.

"Once you've proven you can be trusted with the most readily available of our findings, you will move on to the next subject. The five initiates will move even further, of course, over the course of their second year. From there, things become much more specialized; Dalton, for example," said Atlas, with a reference over his shoulder to where Dalton had all but blended into the wallpaper, "works in such a narrow field of expertise that only he is permitted to access those materials at present."

Parisa, Callum could see, found this to be a very interesting trinket of information indeed.

"Not even you?" asked Reina, surprising them once again with her voice.

"Not even me," Atlas confirmed. "We do not, as a society, believe it is necessary for one man to know everything. We don't consider it particularly possible, either, and certainly not very safe."

"Why not?" (Libby again.)

"Because the problem with knowledge, Miss Rhodes, is its inexhaustible craving. The more of it you have, the less you feel you know," said Atlas. "Thus, men often go mad in search of it."

"And how do the women take it?" prompted Parisa.

Atlas gave her a curt half-smile.

"Most know better than to seek it," he said, which sounded, to Callum, like a warning.

"When you say a system," Libby began. Callum flinched, irked again as Atlas turned his attention back to her. She was like a mosquito; the effect of her anxiety wasn't exactly painful, but it did seem to be unrelenting. Callum couldn't sit comfortably in one spot.

"There are six of you," Atlas said, gesturing to the group of them. "You each maintain one-sixth responsibility for the Society's security. How you divide it is up to you. Now, before I leave you to it," he said, seeming to startle Libby with the prospect she might have to go unsupervised, "I will say that while you do not presently have access to everything in the Society's purview, you are very much responsible for the entirety of its protection. Please bear this in mind as you devise your plan."

"Seems a bit counterintuitive, doesn't it?" Tristan remarked. He was, as Callum had predicted, a natural contrarian. "We're responsible for things we can't even see."

"Yes," Atlas agreed, and nodded briskly. "Any questions?"

Libby opened her mouth but, to Callum's immense relief, Nico's hand shot out, pausing her.

"Excellent," said Atlas, turning to Dalton. "Well, we shall all reconvene at dinner. Welcome to the Alexandrian Society," he added, and inclined his head a final time before sauntering through the door, sealing it behind them.

REINA

THERE WAS A MOMENT of guarded curiosity as the remaining six appraised each other in silence.

"You're very quiet," observed Tristan, turning to Callum, the blond South African who sat on his left. "No thoughts on any of this?"

"No pressing ones," said Callum. He had a certain look to him; something very old Hollywood, belonging to the perpetual plague of Westernization that Reina had come to loathe rather than admire, but his voice was soothing, his mannerisms almost comforting. "And you sound quite suspicious."

"My nature, I'm afraid," said Tristan, rather unapologetically.

Parisa, Reina noted, was looking at her intently. It prompted her to a bit of a shudder, bristling at the slight sense of invasion, which in turn upset one of the nearby ferns.

"That's odd," said Libby, for whom the plant had been within sight. She frowned at it before turning back to Reina. "You're... a naturalist, then, I take it?"

Reina strongly disliked being questioned on the subject. "Yes."

"Most medeian-level naturalists have more of a handle on their skill set," observed Parisa, immediately revealing herself to be unpleasant. Not that that surprised Reina at all; most women who looked like Parisa had a lifetime of permission to behave however they liked. Normally she didn't fault them for it, preferring only to stay out of their way, but this sort of shoved-together experience would obviously render avoidance impossible.

She was starting to wish she'd stayed home.

"Oh, I didn't mean to imply—" Libby's cheeks flushed. "I just, I suppose I expected, um—"

"I didn't study naturalism," Reina supplied bluntly. "I specialized in ancient magics. Classics."

"Oh," said Libby, with faint confusion, and Parisa's eyes narrowed.

"What, like a historian?"

"Like one," Reina echoed. Precisely one.

Parisa didn't seem to care for her tone. "So you didn't cultivate your own craft at all?"

"What is everyone's specialty?" Nico interrupted, jumping in as Reina's discomfort heightened. Probably best, as a silent request from her would have had Parisa locked in a chokehold by the very fern she unwisely suspected Reina of being unable to control.

Nico's change in conversation seemed to be more in the interest of sparking conversation with Parisa than it had been defending Reina. "Yours, for example," he suggested to Parisa, prompting her expression to stiffen.

"What's yours?"

"Rhodes and I are both physicists. Well, physics of force, molecular structures, that sort of thing," Nico said. "I'm better, of course—"

"Shut up," muttered Libby.

"—and we have our respective preferred materials, but we can both manipulate physicalities. Motion, waves, elements," he summarized, glancing expectantly at Parisa. "And you?"

"What about me?" Parisa retorted flippantly.

Nico faltered. "Well, I just thought—"

"I don't see why it's necessary that we share the details of our specialties," Tristan cut in sourly. "We're competing against each other, aren't we?"

"But we still have to work together," Libby argued, looking moderately aghast. "Do you really intend to keep your magic a secret for the next year?"

"Why not?" said Parisa, shrugging. "Anyone clever enough to figure it out probably deserves to, and as far as the intricacies—"

"But it's not like we can perform as a group while knowing nothing about each other," Nico attempted, looking as if his intent was to put the others at ease. Reina had a feeling he considered himself likeable enough to manage it, and it was possible he wasn't wrong.

"Even if one of us is going to be eliminated eventually," Nico said, "I don't see how it helps to cripple all of us as a group."

"You only say that because you already told us your specialty," Callum murmured, half-smirking, which made Reina like him less.

"Well, I've got nothing to be ashamed of," Nico said, flaring a little with irritation, which made her like him more. "So unless the rest of you have some sort of insecurity about whatever it is you can do—"

"Insecurity?" Tristan scoffed. "So you're just assuming you're the best in the room, then?"

"I didn't say that," Nico insisted. "I just—"

"He *does* think he's the best in the room," said Parisa, "but then again, who doesn't? Except maybe you," she determined, giving Reina an unfriendly glance.

She, Reina thought, was safely at the bottom of the list of people she intended to be friends with.

"I just think there's some way we can compromise, at least," said Nico. "Shouldn't we have some idea who can do what?"

"I agree," said Reina, mostly because she could see that Parisa and Tristan were resistant. It made no difference to her; everyone already knew her specialty, so she, like Nico and the thankfully now-silent Libby, had no reason not to bolster his argument and pressure the others into confessing. "Otherwise the physical specialties are going to take on the majority of the work, and if I have to waste all my energy on security—"

"Not everything has to be brute force," said Tristan, irritably. "Just because you have physical specialties doesn't mean you'll be doing all the magic."

"Well, you certainly aren't giving me a reason t-"

"Stop," said Nico, and because it was startling, conversation halted. "Who's doing that?"

Reina detested the interruption, but better Nico than Tristan. "Doing what?"

"Rhodes should have spoken by now," Nico said, sliding Libby a glance. She blinked, surprised, and then Nico turned his attention back to the others, peering suspiciously at Tristan, Parisa, and Callum. "Someone convinced her not to. Who was it?"

Tristan glanced at Parisa.

"Wow, thanks," she said drily. "That's not obvious."

"Well, you can hardly blame me for—"

"It's not me," Parisa snapped, irritated now, and Reina fought a smile. Not only was the Tristan-Parisa alliance cracking early, but now it was obvious what Parisa's specialty was: she could either read minds or emotions.

"One of you can influence behavior," Nico accused, adding blisteringly, "Don't."

There was only one option left.

One by one, they gradually turned their attention to Callum, who sighed.

"Relax," he said, crossing one leg listlessly over the other. "She was anxious. I turned it down."

Libby blinked, suddenly furious. "How *dare* you—"

"Rhodes," Nico said. "The air's too dry for this kind of volatility."

"Shut up, Varona—"

"So you're an empath," said Reina, glancing at Callum, "and that means…" A glance at Parisa. "You can read minds," she guessed, determining it unlikely that a society claiming to be the most advanced of its kind would invite two pairs of identical specialties.

"Not anymore," Parisa said with a glare at Tristan. "They've all got shields up now."

"No one can hold that for long," Tristan said, looking suspiciously at Callum. "Especially if we're going to have to guard our emotions, too."

"This is ridiculous," Libby said, having successfully forced out Callum's influence by then. "Listen, I'm the last person to ever say Varona's doing anything reasonable—"

"Who?" said Callum, who was probably being difficult on purpose.

"I… Nico, then, whatever—the point is," Libby exhaled impatiently, "we'll never get anything done if we're all trying to protect ourselves from each other. I came here to *learn*, for fuck's sake!" she snapped, which Reina was exceedingly relieved to hear. Libby may have been annoying, but at least she wasn't afraid to insist on something genuinely important. Her priorities, unlike everyone else's, were in the right place.

"I absolutely refuse," Libby huffed, "to exhaust my magic just to keep you lot out of my head!"

"Fine," said Callum lazily. "I promise not to put any of you at ease, then."

"Hey," Nico snapped. "She's not wrong. I'd like to have some autonomy to my sentience too, thanks."

Tristan and Parisa seemed to agree, though they weren't ready to say so.

"Surely we shouldn't have to explain to an *empath* why none of us want our emotions toyed with," Libby insisted.

Callum waved an indolent hand. "Just because I happen to know what your feelings are doesn't mean I waste time trying to understand them, but fine. I'll behave if she will," he added with a sly glance at Parisa, who glared back.

"I don't influence anyone," she said, irritated. "Not magically, anyway. Because I'm not an asshole."

Sure you're not, thought Reina loudly, prompting Parisa to yet another scowl.

In the absence of any further discussion, the three remaining members had turned to Tristan, whom Reina realized belatedly was the last to reveal his specialty.

"I—" He stiffened, unhappily cornered. "I'm a type of illusionist."

"Yeah, so am I," replied Callum, a doubtful drawl. "A bit of a blanket term, isn't it?"

"Wait a minute," Parisa said, suddenly recalling something. "Your name is Callum *Nova*, isn't it? Of the illusionist Novas?"

The others in the room sat up slightly, expressing interest that even Reina couldn't prevent. The Nova Corporation was a global media conglomerate who secretly or not-so-secretly specialized in illusions; they were dominant in both the mortal and medeian industries, most adept within the industry of cosmetics and beauty. They were fascinating not only for their products, but for their cutthroat business practices. They had put several smaller companies out of business by repeatedly undermining medeian statutes about how much magic could be used in mortal products.

Not that that was the reason Reina was interested at that particular moment. Rather, she had realized that Parisa was probably piecing together the fact that she'd overlooked the person in the room with the most money, and that brought Reina so much satisfaction the weeping fig in the corner joyfully sprouted fruit.

"Yes, I'm a Nova," Callum said, not taking his eyes from Tristan, who had still not confessed to anything. "Though, as you've clearly pieced together, illusions aren't particularly my life's work."

"Fine," growled Tristan. "I can see through illusions."

Immediately, Libby's hand rose somewhere to her cheek, and Tristan sighed.

"Yes, I can see it," he said. "It's just a zit. Relax."

Then Tristan's attention traveled slowly back to Callum, who stiffened in apprehension. Delightful, Reina thought. The only thing better would be if

Tristan informed them that wasn't Parisa's real nose.

"I won't tell them if you won't," Tristan said to Callum.

For a moment, the air in the room was so tense that even the plants grew wary.

Then, abruptly, Callum laughed.

"Let's keep it between us, then," he agreed, reaching out to clap a hand around Tristan's shoulder. "Better to let them wonder."

So there was an us and them now. That was considerably less delightful.

MotherMotherMother, the ivy in the corner whispered with a shudder of consternation, joined by the hissing sound from the nearby fig plant.

Mother is angry, whimpered the philodendron. *She is angry, OhnoOhnoOhno—*

"—'s no point fighting about this," Libby was saying, as Reina quietly engaged a deep inhale, hoping not to spur any nearby greenery to mutiny. "Regardless of what we think about each other, we still have to formulate some sort of security plan, so—"

But before Libby Rhodes could come to any sort of bossy conclusion, there was a low, loud, percussive gong, and the door to the painted room flew open, the house itself seeming to beckon them down the hall.

"Guess we'll have to formulate later," said Callum, rising to his feet and striding forward before waiting to hear what the end of Libby's sentence would have been.

Behind him, Tristan and Parisa exchanged a glance and followed; Nico rose to his feet, beckoning Libby with a grimace. She, however, hesitated in frustration, then turned her attention to Reina instead.

"So, listen," Libby began, shifting uncomfortably from foot to foot. "I know I must have sounded rude before, what with that thing I said about you being a naturalist, but I was only—"

"We don't have to be friends," Reina said bluntly, cutting her off. Obviously Libby was about to extend some sort of olive branch, but Reina had enough *actual* branches to contend with without dragging any metaphorical ones into the picture. She certainly had no interest in making friends; all she wanted from this experience was to gain as much access to the Society's archives as she could.

Though she didn't want to close any doors, either.

"We just have to be better than *them*," Reina pointed out gruffly, gesturing with her chin to the other three, and that, at least, Libby seemed to grasp.

"Understood," she said, and then, gratifyingly, she followed Nico out the door without waiting, leaving Reina to trail behind alone while the painted room's plants mourned her loss.

NICO

Much as Nico resented every syllable of what was about to come out of his mouth, he doubted there was any alternative.

"Listen," he said to Libby, dropping his voice. "I need this to work."

Naturally she was defensive before anything else. "Varona," she began, "might I remind you that you're not the only one here who has something to prove—"

"Rhodes, spare me the lecture. I need access," he told her. "*Specific* access, though I don't know what specifically yet. I just need to make sure I can get into as many of the Society's archives as possible."

"Why?"

She had such a tireless capacity for suspicion when it came to him. Sure, he could tell her that most research existing about the offspring of creatures was either ancient and lost or illegal and not particularly in-depth, but he didn't really want to get into it. Those were Gideon's secrets, not his.

"I just do," he said, and before Libby could open her mouth again, he hastily interrupted. "I'm just trying to tell you that I'm willing to do whatever it takes to move on."

"Nico, if you're trying to intimidate me—"

"I'm not—" He broke off, frustrated. "Rhodes. For fuck's sake, I'm trying to work *with* you."

"Since when?"

For such a smart girl, she could be really stupid.

"Since I noticed the older three are already picking teams," he hissed, gesturing ahead to where Tristan and Parisa had caught up with Callum.

Gradually, understanding began to dawn on Libby's face.

"You want to be some sort of alliance, you mean?"

"You heard what Atlas said. We're doing physical magics first," Nico reminded her. "You and I are going to be better at that than everyone else."

"Except maybe Reina," Libby said, glancing apprehensively over her shoulder. "I can't quite get a read on her, though."

"Whether she is or she isn't, it doesn't matter. Rhodes, we're already at a disadvantage," he pointed out. "There's two of us and one each of them. If anyone's going to get eliminated, one of us is the natural choice."

She chewed her lip. "So what are you suggesting?"

"That we work together." Unheard of for them, considering their mutual enmity, but he hoped she wouldn't take too firm a hand with that particularly dead horse. "We can do more that way, anyway." Astounding that it had taken graduating from NYUMA for them to believe their professors, who had insisted as much for years. "We just can't give the others a reason to think either of us is expendable, that's all."

"If anyone's going to try and make me look expendable, it's you," she pointed out, and Nico sighed.

"Don't be petulant. I'm trying to be mature." Or something. "At the very least, I'm being pragmatic."

She considered it. "But what if an alliance with you isn't in my best interest? I mean, if you *do* prove to be useless—"

"I am not and have never been *useless*," Nico sniffed, "but fine. We'll be a team so long as it's in both our best interests, how's that?"

"And what will we do when it isn't?"

"We'll cross that bridge when we get to it."

Libby hummed in thought again, half-sighing.

"I suppose they *are* a bunch of snobs," she muttered, and added, "And I do sort of already hate Callum."

"Try not to," Nico advised. "Empaths can do a lot with strong emotions."

"Don't mansplain empaths to me." A predictable response, but he could see her starting to concede. "It just seems so ridiculous that we can't all work together," Libby muttered, half to herself. "I mean, what is the *point* of having so much talent in the room if nobody's willing to see where that takes us?"

Nico shrugged. "Maybe they'll get over it."

"Ah yes, because that so frequently happens," Libby grumbled, toying in agitation with her bangs.

She was definitely on the edge of agreement. Nico waited, prompting her to get on with her internal calculations, and she rolled her eyes.

"Fine," she conceded grumpily—which Nico reminded himself was *not* annoying, because it was what he'd wanted and, furthermore, it proved him right. "We're allies until we're not, then. Which I assume will be any moment."

"Love the enthusiasm, Rhodes," said Nico, and she grunted something derogatory in response, the two of them finally arriving in the dining room.

Alliances aside, Nico was feeling quite confident, though he could see Libby was having the opposite reaction. Yes, she had been targeted outright by Callum (a predictable breed of asshole if Nico had ever seen one) and she was much too fragile to contend with Reina's lofty disinterest in her, but that was only because it was in Libby's personal moral code to fret pointlessly about things she couldn't control.

Once she had the opportunity to prove herself, she wouldn't be nearly so mouseish; that much Nico knew from experience. Elizabeth Rhodes was a lot of things, most of them unhelpful, but restrained when it came to her abilities was not even remotely one of them. For once, the chip on Libby's shoulder would probably serve him well.

The sooner she had a chance to be tested, the better, Nico thought grimly, observing over dinner that Callum, Tristan, and Parisa were obviously deluding themselves into thinking that being secretive and more experienced made them into some sort of exclusive club. He almost regretted finding Parisa so attractive, though it was hardly the first time he'd taken a liking to a girl whose primary quality was her inability to be impressed.

Thankfully, dinner was brief. Tomorrow, Dalton informed them at the end of their meal, would be their first full day. Tonight, they would merely be taken to their rooms to get some rest.

Dalton led them back to the long corridor past the gallery, where each of their names were carved into small placards beside the doors.

"It's like boarding school all over again," murmured Callum to Parisa, though of course none of the others could relate. Nico could, given that he'd been sent to New England from Havana the moment his medeian status had been cemented, but he, at least, was conscious enough of his wealth not to point to it. NYUMA had been populated with plenty of students like Libby or Gideon who had gone through mortal schooling most of their lives; coming from magical money, as both Nico and Max had done, wasn't something to boast about unless one wanted to be immediately mistrusted and disliked. For someone who could apparently feel the emotions of others, Callum seemed dreadfully out of touch.

"Speak for yourself," muttered Parisa back to Callum, proving Nico correct, though Callum merely smirked at her.

"You're all adults," Dalton said, catching wind of their muted conversation, "so there are no rules. Just don't do anything stupid."

"No rules?" Tristan echoed, glancing at Libby as if he expected her to faint at the news, which was certainly an accurate assessment of her character. She had always had a bit of a look to her as if she might immediately report any wrongdoing; that she was currently dressed like a page from the spring catalogue for school prefects (square-neck cardigan, pleated skirt, ballet flats) certainly didn't help.

"You can't bring anyone else into the house," said Dalton, as an apparent amendment. "But as it would be near impossible to accomplish anyway, I don't bother including it as a caveat."

"Do you live here as well?" asked Parisa.

"On the grounds," Dalton confirmed evasively.

"If there's any sort of problem—" Libby chirped.

"This is not a school," Dalton clarified again, "and as such, there is no headmaster to alert in the event that any of you find yourselves dissatisfied. If there is indeed a problem, it belongs to the six of you collectively. Anything else?"

Nothing.

"Very well, goodnight," said Dalton, as the six of them wandered off to find their rooms.

Much like the house itself, the bedrooms were incredibly English, each room occupied by identical four-poster beds, reasonably sized desks and wardrobes, and a single vacant bookshelf. Nico's room, which was the first door on the left, was beside Callum's and across from Reina's. Libby looked uneasy as she made her way to the end of the hall with Tristan, which Nico supposed was unsurprising. She had a great fear of being disliked, and he doubted Tristan had ever truly liked anyone. Thus far, Nico's decision to ally himself with Libby wasn't a promising sign for his popularity in the house, but if the situation ever called for changing teams, he was confident he could manage it. Besides, better to be the most tolerable option of the three physical specialties than to be the hanger-on to the other three.

Nico wasted little time getting to bed. For one thing, Gideon had promised to visit, and for another, his power was reliant almost entirely on his physical state. In general, magic was a physical exertion; there was a certain degree of sweat involved, and recovery between bouts of use was a necessity. Nico likened it to the mortal Olympics: someone with natural aptitude could manage the fundamentals of their own specialty quite easily, *perhaps* without even breaking a sweat, but to win a gold medal required extensive training. As for other specialties outside one's own, more of the same. You could certainly *attempt* to succeed in every Olympic sport, but you could just as easily kill yourself trying. Only someone very foolish or very talented would attempt as much as Nico de Varona had attempted.

Luckily, he was both troublingly talented and exceedingly unwise.

"This was extremely difficult," remarked Gideon, manifesting in Nico's head somewhere in the midst of whatever he'd been dreaming before, which he could not now remember. He seemed to be inside some sort of interminable jail cell now, reclining on a narrow cot with Gideon on the other side of the bars.

"Wherever you've gone," Gideon said, "it's a fortress."

Nico glanced around, frowning. "Is it?"

"I can't actually get through," Gideon said, gesturing to the bars. "And I had to leave Max outside."

"Outside where?"

"Oh, one of the realms." They had tried mapping them in college, but it was difficult. Realms of thought were hard enough to grasp, and the realms of the subconscious were extensive and labyrinthine, ever-changing. "He'll be fine. I'm sure he's sleeping."

Nico rose to his feet, approaching the bars. "I didn't realize it'd be so difficult." On second thought, though, he probably should have.

"There are a lot of defensive wards up," Gideon said. "More than I would expect."

"Even mental ones?"

"Especially mental ones." Gideon plucked something in the air like a guitar string. "See that? Someone over there is a telepath."

Parisa, probably, if what Tristan implied was correct, though Nico doubted that particular ward was her doing. It must have been a thread within a larger shield against telepathy, which made sense. Not every variety of theft required a corporeal form of entry.

He glanced up, looking for a camera (or the iteration of one), and spotted it in the corner.

"Well," Nico said, pointing to it. "Try not to say anything too incriminating."

Gideon looked over his shoulder, shrugging. "I haven't got much to say, to tell you the truth." A pause, and then, "Avez-vous des problèmes? Tout va bien?"

"Si, estoy bien, no te preocupes." Anyone watching could probably translate, but that wasn't really the point. "I suppose we shouldn't do this too often, then."

Gideon inclined his head in apparent agreement. "You're not properly sleeping when I'm here," he pointed out. "And judging by this place's security, you're going to need all your energy."

"Yes," Nico sighed, "probably."

"Is Libby there?"

"Yes, somewhere." He grimaced. "Though you're not supposed to know that."

"Well, it was more of a lucky guess, really." Gideon tilted his head. "You're being nice to her, aren't you?"

"I'm always nice. And don't tell me what to do."

Gideon's smile broadened.

"Tu me manques," he said. "Max hasn't noticed you're gone, of course."

"Of course not." A pause. "Y yo también."

"Strange without you around."

"I know." Not really. It didn't feel real yet, but it would soon. "Is it quiet, at least?"

"Yes, and I don't like quiet," Gideon said. "Makes me suspect my mother's going to surface from the garbage disposal."

"She won't, we had a talk."

"Did you?"

"Well, she surprised me in the bath," said Nico. "Still, I'd say she's fairly well persuaded." Or something close enough, he thought grimly.

"Nicolás," Gideon sighed, "déjate."

"I'm only trying to h-"

He broke off as the bars warped, Gideon's face disappearing. He opened his eyes to jarring darkness, someone shaking him awake.

"There's someone here," said a voice he didn't recognize for a moment, and Nico groggily struggled to sit upright.

"What? It's just my friend, he's not—"

"Not in your head." It was Reina's voice, he realized, adjusting to make out the general shape of her face in the dark. "There's someone in the house."

"How do you—"

"There are plants in every room. They woke me." She was using a tone that sounded like *stop talking*. "Someone is trying to get inside, if they aren't here already."

"What do you want me to do?"

"I don't know," she said, brows creased. "Something."

Nico reached over, pressing a hand to the floor to feel the wood pulse beneath his palm.

"Vibrations," he said. "There's definitely someone here."

"I know that. I told you."

Well, better if he could take care of it alone, or close to alone. Reina had probably done him a favor waking him first.

Ah, but he'd said he wouldn't do things alone.

"Wake Rhodes," Nico said on second thought, rising to his feet. "She's in the last—"

"The last room on the right, I know." Reina was gone quickly, without asking questions. Nico crept out into the house, listening for a moment. Libby was better at listening; she was more attuned to waves of things, usually sound and speed, so he gave up and started feeling instead. He could sense the disruption from somewhere downstairs.

The middle door opened, revealing Parisa in the frame.

"You're thinking very loudly," she informed him with palpable distaste, as Libby emerged from her room.

"Shouldn't we wake—"

"What's going on?" demanded Callum, bursting from his door.

"Someone's in the house," said Nico.

"Who?" said Libby and Callum in unison.

"Someone," replied Nico and Reina.

"Many someones," Parisa corrected. She was holding a hand to the wall. "There are at least three compromised access points."

"She's right," said Reina.

"I know I'm right," Parisa growled.

"Has anyone woken Tristan?" asked Libby, looking predictably fretful.

"You do it," said Parisa, disinterestedly.

"No," Nico said. "Rhodes is coming with me."

"What?" said Libby, Parisa, and Callum.

"You heard me," said Nico, gesturing for Libby to follow. "Reina, wake Tristan and tell him to follow. Rhodes, stay close."

She gave him a glare of *don't boss me around*, but he had already started moving.

A good thing he had, too. It was almost immediate from the time they emerged onto the gallery landing.

"Get down," Nico hissed, tugging Libby to the floor as something shot overhead, aimed from the entry hall up to the vaulted landing of the second floor. It was much larger than a bullet, so probably not deadly. Something for temporary immobilization, most likely, which most magical weapons tended to be. But they were expensive, and not particularly useful when fired up at an unknown target, which gave Nico pause.

"Probably a test," said Callum, in something of a low drawl. "Some tactic to scare us into working together."

Possible, Nico thought, though he didn't particularly want to agree with Callum aloud.

"Cover me," he said to Libby.

"Fine," she said, grimacing. "Keep your head down."

Every year, NYUMA held a tournament for the physical specialties; something akin to a game of capture the flag, but with fewer rules and more allowances. He and Libby had never been on the same team, almost always facing off in the final round, but all the games were essentially the same: someone attacked while someone else covered.

Nico rose to his feet while Libby conjured a thin bubble of protection around him, manipulating the molecular structure of the air in their immediate vicinity. The world was mostly entropy and chaos; magic, then, was order, because it was control. Nico and Libby could change the materials around them; they could take the universe's compulsion to fill a vacuum and bend it, warp it, alter it. The fact that they were natural energy sources, twin storage units for massive electrical charge, meant they could not only harness the energy required for an explosion, but they could clear a path of least resistance for it, too.

Still, even batteries had their limits. Single combat was an excellent way to waste a lot of time and energy, so Nico opted to cast a wider net. He altered the direction of friction in the room, sending the entry room's occupants into the furthest wall; helpfully, a thin tendril of plants crept out to twine around them, holding fast.

"Thanks Reina," said Nico, exhaling as he returned the balance of force in the room.

Libby's shield bubble dissipated.

"Is that all?" she asked.

"No," said Parisa. "There's someone in the east wing—"

"And the library," said Reina, before amending irritably, "the painted room."

"Which one?" demanded Callum.

"Are you planning to be useful at all?" Reina countered, glaring.

"If I felt there was any need to be concerned, I probably would be," replied Callum. "As it is, why waste the effort?"

"What's going on?" asked Tristan, who had apparently managed the decency to join them.

"Blakely's testing us," said Callum.

"You don't know that," Libby said. Beneath the gallery corridor, the sound of further entry was imminent, and she had her brows knitted in concentration. "It might be real."

"What do you want me to do with these?" Reina asked, pointing to the men wriggling within the vines of their captivity.

"Well," Parisa said, impatient, "seeing as we don't want them in the house—"

"Varona, do you hear that?"

Before Nico could retort that yes, Rhodes, if she could hear it, *he* could obviously hear it just as well, there was a strange, disorienting ringing from inside his ears; it filled his mind with a vacant whiteness, blinding him behind closed eyes.

He vaguely felt a sharp sting of some kind, like the entry wound of a needle. Something stung his shoulder and he wanted to swat it away, only the screech of white that somehow filled his ears and eyes was debilitating;

paralyzing. He felt a pressure inside his head that threatened to fill the space, like a rapidly expanding tumor.

Then the ringing faded, just enough that he could open his eyes, and he saw that Libby was speaking, or trying to. *Varona*, her mouth was saying, *Varona, it's a way!*

Way? No, not a way.

He blinked, his vision clearing.

A *wave*.

That helped. He tried to raise his right hand and faltered from pain, switching to the left to take hold of the particle of sound and aim it, like a whip, until it cracked. Libby, now freed the effort of dragging him from the sound wave's immobilizing effect, extinguished it with a spark.

"—can't be a test," she finished, and Nico realized the pain in his shoulder was much more than a sting. The wound was slick with blood, and as far as he could tell, that didn't typically happen with magical weapons.

"That," Libby was saying with horror, "is not a fake injury!"

"It's a gunshot wound," observed Parisa. "Whoever they are, they must not be magical."

Made sense, even if the first shot had been some type of magic; certain forms could be easily provided to a buyer with enough money, and medeians were rare enough that sending in a group of them would probably be a waste. Guns were cheaper and perfectly effective; case in point. Nico growled with annoyance, clotting his blood with a wave of his hand.

"But this can't be the Society's doing," Libby protested. "Surely we're supposed to do something!"

"There's at least one medeian here," Nico gritted through his teeth, struggling to rise. He wasn't going to bother with easing the pain, as that would only require more energy than he could spare at the moment. It wasn't a lethal wound by any means, and he would heal it later. "We should split up, I think. I can take care of the rest if Rhodes looks for the medeian."

"The rest?" echoed Callum, doubtful. "That's a mess you've got on your shoulder. It's not a pistol, it's an automatic rifle. You could be dealing with military special ops."

"Thank you ever *so*," replied Nico crassly, as another round was fired from below. He knew perfectly well what he was dealing with, which was precisely the point. "They wouldn't bother arming a bunch of medeians with AKs," he shouted over the sound of weaponry, "just like they wouldn't send in mortals without magical oversight." If it was a military task force of some sort, they were probably being commanded by a medeian. "And if he's good at waves, Rhodes will hear him coming."

"Then we should split up," said Parisa, who was at least very coolheaded.

"Yes, good idea. You stay with me," Nico suggested to her, "Rhodes can take Tristan, and Reina can go with—"

"I'll stay," said Reina.

"What?" said Callum and Libby.

Reina seemed undeterred. "Nico's the one taking on more people. I have combat experience."

Nico glanced at her. "You do?"

"Well, I trained in hand to hand combat," she amended, which sounded an awful lot as if she had merely read a lot of books on the subject. "Besides, you lot seem to think I'm useless at my specialty, don't you?"

"We don't really have a lot of time to argue," Libby pointed out, cutting in before anyone else could speak. "Parisa, take Callum," she said; anything, Nico guessed, to get out of going with Callum herself, "and Varona's right, Tristan can come with me."

"Fine," said Parisa flatly. "I can find the medeian in the house."

"Good, and we'll check the access points—"

That was about as much Nico had the patience to discuss when it came to logistics. By then his arm had gone a little numb, probably because his mind was leaping ahead to the prospect of fending off intruders.

He had been very, very good at the physicist tournament. Voted MVP four years running, in fact, and as good as Libby may or may not have been (fine—she *was*, but still), she had never once beaten him. Nico had a taste for adrenaline, and besides, he had to see someone about a bullet wound. In his not-so-humble opinion, he was rather richly owed.

"Come on," Nico called to Reina, leaping atop the gallery's bannister and beckoning her after him into the hail of gunfire below, shielding himself with a hand outstretched. "Meet you down there."

"Varona," Libby sighed, "you do realize there are *stairs*—"

He wasn't listening. Shots were fired, surprise surprise, but he was ready for them now. He slipped one as easily as he might have ducked a punch, catching the uniform that suggested he'd been right; this was some sort of military task force. Fun! Exciting. All of them against him; how terribly unfortunate they hadn't thought to bring a party twice as large. He curled the floor in slightly, funneling them all into an invisible drain. Better that way, to see how many. He counted six and smiled to himself, returning the floors to how they'd been. The gunmen stumbled, then shot towards him.

It was Reina, to Nico's surprise, who took aim first, sending a bolt of something very crude but very fast into the chest of an oncoming gunman. It knocked the wind out of the gunman, sending the butt of his rifle flying into the face of his comrade. By the sound of his swearing, Nico guessed American, maybe CIA. That, he thought with a shiver of anticipation, would be very exciting indeed. He had never been important enough to merit assassination before.

More shots were fired, which certainly wouldn't do; one bullet wound was plenty. After waiting a moment to take the impact through a temporary shield of his making, Nico took hold of the nearest gunman and aimed him in a circle, prompting the others to launch themselves behind the aristocratic furniture for cover. A little tug of gravity out from under them sent them floating in slow motion, the rifles drifting from their hands. Nico summoned their weapons and disassembled them with a single, explosive blow, sending the components flying like shrapnel as the ordinary forces in the room returned.

There, he thought. Now let's really have a fight.

Reina seemed to be managing well enough with hand-to-hand combat; Nico caught a glimpse of her from the corner of his eye. She moved like a bull, attack after attack, and the force of her blows remained unfinished but heavy, unmistakable. He was a bit more finessed, more agile. The first gunman, now armed with a small utility knife, came for him with a blind overhand right hook, which Nico happily ducked, sending the gunman stumbling with a loud slur of profanity.

That, Nico thought, was certainly British English. CIA *and* MI6, perhaps? How flattering.

Reina handled two of the gunmen, landing a hard but accessible shot to immobilize one thigh while Nico narrowed the remaining four men to three, twisting the gunman's knife around for a blow to the kidney. He brought three to two with some tricky shots to the head, dazzling with a few careless jabs before shooting upwards with an uppercut, snapping the gunman's neck back.

All it took was a little precision to guide his non-dominant, uninjured hand.

It made sense, really, that whoever was trying to break into the Society would not have sent an entire company of medeians. Surely they knew what sort of security measures they were trying to breach, and a pack of special operatives could conceivably do just as much damage without sacrificing a drop of valuable magical blood. Yes, they would have to be accompanied by a medeian to break the security wards, but nobody Nico was facing now was dangerous unless he allowed them to be. Perhaps unsurprisingly, he wasn't particularly in the mood to be killed.

The two remaining gunmen weren't stupid. They attacked side by side, making Nico the point of an isosceles triangle; a basic tenet of two-on-one combat, and therefore easy enough to predict. As was Nico's decision to force them into an Orion's belt, sprinting towards one while firing a blast of force at the other. For Nico, magic was merely an augmentation of his natural aptitude; he was sure-footed, well-balanced, compact and quick without any help from his powers, which would need to be preserved as much as possible. He could waste it, ending the fight sooner and requiring more time to recover, but he knew better than to do something short-sighted. These men may not have been magical, but *someone* here was, and they would surely prove it soon enough. Nico intended to be ready when they did.

He used only enough to give his blows the equivalency of electrocution, sending one gunman (now fully disarmed with the help of a summoning charm and the burying of the gunman's own knife into the muscle of his quadricep) stumbling backwards, temporarily immobilized, while the other shot forward, missing Nico by an inch.

Nico, regaining control of the gunman's knife, slipped just in time to avoid a shot aimed for his wounded shoulder—which, he supposed, was a bit of a giveaway as a pressure point, seeing as it was currently covered in blood. Luckily, his reflexive counter led his opponent directly to the spot of difficulty he'd hoped for, and his next slip, calculated to intercept the gunman barreling forward from behind him, caused the second gunman to make contact with the first.

Then he felt a little rumble underfoot; a warning, and a reminder that these were not the only intruders left in the house. Caught between the final two, Nico loosened the pull of gravity again to levitate himself parallel to the ground, slitting one's carotid with the knife in his hand while aiming the arch of his foot into the sternum of another. The final gunman took the effect of Nico's kick like a blow to his heart, halting mid-gasp and collapsing just as Reina drove a blade into the side of her assailant's head.

Nico was about to turn and whoop—to congratulate her with a hand on her shoulder for having done slightly more than read a book—when he felt the unsettling sound enter his head again; this time, the dial had been turned so high he rose off the ground, floating in full-bodied paralysis.

Was that all this medeian could do? Waves? He supposed there was a reason only six of them had been chosen for the Society; not every medeian had both power *and* skill. This one seemed to have only one talent. In the medeian's defense, though, it was a highly useful talent, and Nico was rendered instantaneously weak, having bled copious amounts during all the moments he wasn't concentrating on clotting the wound to his shoulder. If he hadn't already made such an expenditure of effort, this would have been no trouble at all to resist. He could overpower most medeians on strength alone, but not while he was crucially injured.

Still, it would have to be done. It would hurt, but it would have to be done.

Nico summoned what remained in the reserves of his abilities, half-exhausting himself in the process, and was surprised by a little spark; a jolt, somewhere in the unfeeling palm of his hand. It was a rush of something, like an electrical current, and Nico felt it leave him in a burst; an expulsion with the force of a gasp and the volume of a scream.

It had to have been Reina, but he couldn't think about what had caused it just then. He had seconds before the medeian conjured another sound wave, so he shoved a cluster of magic—power, energy, force, whatever anyone wanted to call it—directly into the body of the waiting medeian.

The sound of his shot meeting its target was a woman's cry of pain, and Nico cleared the fog and dust from the air, waiting until he and Reina could both clearly see her.

"Well," Nico said to Reina, glancing at the medeian who was struggling to her feet. "Do you want to go first, or should I?"

He wasn't particularly surprised when Reina smiled grimly, taking a step forward.

"I'm sure there's room for both of us," she said, placing a hand on his shoulder as Nico gladly summoned what sparked from his veins.

TRISTAN

SOMEWHERE, TRISTAN CAUGHT THE SOUND of a deafening explosion, followed by the unmistakable whoop of Nico de Varona's laughter.

He was *enjoying* this, Tristan thought with disgust. When they'd last left Nico behind, gunshot wound and all, his steps had been so careless and at ease he looked like he was dancing, slipping between gunshots; as if gravity itself worked differently for him, which it probably did. Tristan hadn't known anyone with the broad specialty of 'physicist' before, finding that most physical medeians had the narrowest fields of skill. With immense power typically came the ability to influence only certain things: Levitation. Incandescence. Force. Speed. Tristan hadn't known it was possible for someone to be capable of all of that, and, by the looks of it, possibly even more. Physical magics were draining enough that Nico should have been exhausted by now, but he wasn't.

He was *laughing*. He was enjoying this, and meanwhile, Tristan was going to be sick.

In Tristan's mind, he had accepted the easier job; he was only going to 'secure the perimeter,' or whatever this sort of activity could be called. If anyone was going to shoot at anything, he reasoned privately, it was going to be all those guns aimed at Nico, whom Tristan hadn't particularly liked to begin with. He knew the type—loud, showy, full of meritless bravado, like most of his father's gang of witches. They all had violent streaks they barely concealed with a slavish devotion to rugby, and Tristan had assumed Nico was one of those. Young, brash, and prone to fights he couldn't win.

Apparently Tristan was wrong. Nico could not only win, he could also do it with a gunshot wound to the shoulder of his dominant hand.

Even more alarmingly, he wasn't the only one who could.

It was with immense reluctance that Tristan had initially agreed to split off with Libby, who had been little more than an irritation that Tristan suspected of being too insecure to last a day. Only chivalry (or something akin to it) had kept him from wandering off instead with Callum and Parisa, who had taken a left turn based on something the latter could read in the house's mind. Tristan had thought, Well, someone's going to have to keep an eye on the poor little annoying girl, or how else would she survive having no one to answer her thousand questions?

But then, of course, he'd been blindsided by a pack of what appeared to be spies with guns, and he was now having to rely on said annoying girl *much* more heavily than he cared to admit.

"Get down," Libby snapped as another gun fired, this time from somewhere behind them. It was, at least, a refreshing change of pace from her usual apprehensive mumbling. If there was one thing to be relieved about given all this, it was that Libby Rhodes was far more capable than she looked.

Tristan was beginning to regret not befriending any of the three physical specialties. Nico would have been ideal, given that he seemed to be a powerhouse of energy. The magic radiating from him was more refined than any Tristan had ever seen, and he'd seen quite a lot in his capacity as an investment analyst. He'd met with medeians claiming to power entire plants with the equivalent of nuclear energy who didn't have the raw talent Nico had, and who certainly didn't have his control. It occurred to Tristan, unhappily, that Libby and Nico may have come off as the least threatening for being the youngest and least experienced, but he suddenly doubted they were as juvenile as they seemed. He wished now that he hadn't drawn a line between him and the others, because he doubted it would be easy to un-draw.

It was all an unpleasant reminder that Tristan's father, a witch capable of moderate levels of physical magic, had always considered Tristan a failure. From the start, Tristan had been slow to show any signs of magic, barely able to qualify for medeian status when he reached his teenage years. An unsurprising outcome, considering they had spent so many years before that concerned he wasn't even a witch.

Was that why he'd chosen to do this? Atlas Blakely had told Tristan he was rare and special and therefore he'd thought yes, fine, time to drop everything I spent years tirelessly cultivating in order to prove to my estranged father that I, too, can do something wildly unsafe?

"Do you know any combat spells?" Libby panted, giving Tristan a look that suggested he was the most useless person she'd ever met. At the moment, he suspected he might have been.

"I'm… not good with physicalities," he managed to say, ducking another shot. These men seemed to be different from the group Nico had taken on in the drawing room, but they were definitely also outfitted with automatic weapons. Tristan didn't know prodigious amounts about the intersect of magic and tech in warfare, seeing as James Wessex had chosen to handle any matters of weapons technology himself, but he suspected these were mortals using magically enhanced scopes.

"Yes, fine," Libby replied, clearly impatient, "but are you—"

She broke off before something he suspected to be the word *useful.*

Which, as Adrian Caine had always made an effort to point out, Tristan had never been.

"Just come on," she said in frustration, pulling him after her. "Stay behind me."

This, Tristan thought, was a mildly infuriating turn of events. For one thing, he didn't have a lot of experience being shot at. This was supposed to be an academic fellowship, for fuck's sake; he hadn't expected his time in the Alexandrian archives to involve ducking behind the closest piece of gaudy furniture he could find.

He could have stayed at Wessex Corp and never been shot at in his entire life. He could have simply told Atlas Blakely to shove it and gone on holiday with his fiancée; he could be having vigorous, herculean sex right now, waking up to discuss the future of the company with his billionaire father-in-law over an expertly blended Bloody Mary. Did it matter that Eden was a tiresome adulteress or that James was a capitalist tyrant if it meant never having to break a sweat aside from a drunken family game of badminton?

At the moment, it was unclear.

Libby, at least, was starting to take some initiative with her defense, having discarded any further hesitation in favor of survival. Whoever had broken in, they were covered head to toe in black and moving acrobatically around the room, like a small pack of ninjas. That felt like a childish thing to say, but there it was: there were three or four ninja-things coming after them, and Tristan couldn't think of the first thing to do. There was so much magic in the room it was difficult to see anything but hazy, translucent leaks.

Libby turned and aimed at something; an expulsion of power that was directed at nothing.

"You missed," he said, a muttered I-told-you-so moment that he would have decorously avoided if not for how potentially life-threatening all this was, and she glared at him.

"I didn't miss!"

"You absolutely did," he said through his teeth, pointing. "You missed by about five feet."

"But he's down, he's—"

Hell on earth, was she blind? He should have stayed with Nico. "What are you talking about? You might have broken a lamp, fine, but it's only Edwardian—"

"I didn't—" Libby broke off, blinking. "You're saying there's nothing there?"

"Of course there's nothing there," he growled in frustration, "it's—"

Bloody Christ; was he stupid?

"It's an illusion," Tristan realized aloud, scowling at his own failure to see the obvious, and then, without any further wasted time, he took hold of Libby's shoulders and aimed her, pointing.

"Right there, see it? Straight ahead."

She fired again, this time setting off a round of bullets by stopping their progression mid-air and instigating mass combustion. The gunman was blown backwards, the air littered with shrapnel, and the force of the explosion set off a momentary fog of smoke. Libby was frightfully incendiary, which Tristan suspected was something to conserve as much as it was a timely relief. It was probably going to cost her the same amount of energy as whatever Nico had been doing downstairs, so best not to fire incautiously while they didn't know how many others they would still face.

"What does the room look like to you?" he asked in her ear, trying to concentrate as the smoke cleared. All he could make out were flares, torrents of magic.

"I don't know… dozens of them, at least," she said, grimacing. He could see she was battling frustration; for someone with her obvious control problems, the presence of illusions must have been particularly nightmarish. "The room's crawling with them."

"There's only three left," Tristan told her, "but don't waste energy. Let me see if I can find the medeian who's casting the illusions."

Libby gritted her teeth. "Hurry up!"

Fair enough. He lifted his head to glance around, trying to determine who, if anyone, was doing the casting. He couldn't see any indication of magic being produced, though he did spot a bullet—a real one; Libby must have not been able to tell it from the illusioned ones—just in time to throw up a fairly primitive shield, which dissolved on impact as Libby jumped, alarmed.

"The medeian's not here," Tristan said, which was possibly the most troubling conclusion he could have reached. "Let's get rid of these three and move."

"Aim me," she said without hesitation. "I can take out three."

Tristan didn't doubt it.

He took hold of her left arm, guiding her just as one of the gunmen fired another round of bullets. As with before, Libby's explosion ricocheted backwards into the assailant, though Tristan didn't wait to see if he'd achieved his intended results. The others were moving, and quickly, so he pulled her into his chest, aiming first for the one coming towards them and then, with a little added difficulty, at the one who was slipping from the room.

"They're headed that way," he said, pulling Libby up and racing after the escaping gunman. "Must be where the medeian is. Can you—"

A thin bubble of atmospheric change warped around them, sealing itself with a little slurp of vacuumed pressure.

"Thanks," he said.

"No problem," she panted, as Tristan caught traces of magic and followed its trail to land them in one of the sitting rooms.

The illusionist was easy to find, even before they had fully entered from the corridor; the cloaking enchantment was obviously expensive, covering most of the room and reaching into the nearby access points. Tristan held Libby back, watching the medeian first to see if he was working with someone else.

It looked like he was, though it wasn't clear if whoever the illusionist was working with was a remote partner or someone else in the house; he was typing rapidly into a laptop that didn't seem to be magical at all. Probably programming security cameras to be able to see, if Tristan had to guess, which meant they had seconds to spare. If not for having to control the illusions at the same time, the illusionist would have known they were there already.

"Go," Tristan said to Libby, "while he's not looking."

She hesitated, which was the one thing he'd hoped she wouldn't do.

"Do I shoot to kill, or—?"

In that exact moment, the medeian's eyes snapped up from the laptop screen, meeting Tristan's.

"NOW," Tristan said, more desperately than he had hoped to sound, and Libby, thank bloody fuck, threw up a hand in time to stop whatever was coming towards them. The medeian's eyes widened, obviously startled at the prospect of being overpowered, while Libby advanced towards him, shoving the force of the medeian's own expulsion backwards.

The medeian wasn't going down without a fight; he tried again, and this time Libby's response was like a bolt of lightning, snapping the medeian's control with a lash of something around his wrists. Tristan heard a cry of pain, and then a mutter of something under his breath; some basic obscenity, Tristan suspected, though his Mandarin was rusty.

"Who sent you?" Libby demanded, but the medeian had scrambled to his feet. Tristan, concerned the medeian might conjure more illusions as a defense, leapt forward, taking hold of Libby's arm again and raising it.

"Which one?" Libby gasped. "He split."

"That one, there, by the window—"

"He's multiplying!"

"Just hold steady, I have him—"

This time, as Tristan locked Libby's palm on the trajectory of the medeian's escape, he caught a glimpse of something; evidence of magic that hadn't been clear from afar. It was a little glittering chain, delicate like jewelry, that abruptly snapped.

In that precise moment the medeian turned his head, eyes widening in anguish. It had been a linking charm, but it was gone now.

"He had a partner but he doesn't anymore," Tristan translated in Libby's ear.

She tensed. "Does that mean—"

"It means kill him before he gets away!"

He felt the impact leave her body from where his fingers had curled around her wrists. He could feel the entire force of it pumping through her veins and marveled, silently, at being so close to what felt like live ammunition. She was a human bomb; she could split the room, the air itself, into tiny, indistinguishable (except to Tristan) atoms. If Adrian Caine had ever met

Libby Rhodes, he wouldn't have hesitated to buy her somehow; he'd have offered her the biggest cut, given her the highest privilege of his little witchy cult. He was like that, Tristan's father; male, female, race, class, it didn't matter. Optics were nothing. Usefulness was paramount. Destruction was Adrian Caine's god.

Tristan turned his head away from the explosion, though the heat of the blast was enough to sting his cheek. Libby faltered, struggling for a moment from the effort, and he locked an arm around her waist, half-dragging, half-carrying her from the room.

He kept moving until he saw Parisa, who emerged from one of the lower floors onto the landing of the stairwell, white-faced. Callum was at her side.

"There you are," said Parisa dully, sounding like she'd seen a ghost.

"What happened?" Tristan asked them, setting Libby back on her feet. She looked a little woozy, but nodded to him for release, disentangling herself from his grip.

"I'm fine," she said, though she remained braced for another attack, shoulders still tense.

"Just ran into another medeian downstairs," Callum said. "Some spy organization from Beijing. A combat specialist."

Tristan blinked with recognition. "Did the medeian have a partner?"

"Yes, an ill-"

"An illusionist," Tristan confirmed, exchanging a knowing glance with Libby. "We got him. How did you know they were spies?"

"Aside from the obvious? She told me," said Callum. "It was just her and the partner who were magical, everyone else was mortal."

A distraction, probably, while only one of the medeians broke in.

Libby was testing her joints, still glancing around in paranoia. "She told you there was no one else? She could have easily been lying."

"She wasn't," Callum said.

"How do you know?" Libby pressed, suspicious. "She could've just—"

"Because I asked nicely," Callum said.

Parisa would have known—or could have, assuming the medeian hadn't been using any mental defensive shields—but she, Tristan noticed, hadn't said a word on the subject.

"You okay?" Tristan asked her, and she shuddered to cognizance, glancing up at him with a look of temporary displacement.

"Yeah. Fine." She cleared her throat. "As far as I can tell, the house is empty now."

"Was it just one group?"

Parisa shook her head. "Whoever Nico and Reina took out, they were a group, then the partners we took out, and someone else who was working alone."

"Not alone," came a voice, as the four of them looked up, instantly assuming various positions of defense. "Not to worry," chuckled Atlas, who had Dalton trailing at his heels. "It's only me."

"Is it actually?" Libby whispered to Tristan, who was mildly impressed. Paranoia clearly suited her, or perfectionism, or whatever this was. She no longer trusted her own two eyes, and long-term, that was probably for the best.

"Yes," he said. "It is."

She nodded gravely, but didn't say anything.

"The agent taken out by Miss Kamali was sent by your former employer, Mr. Caine," Atlas said, glancing at Tristan. "We always expect to see someone from Wessex Corp, mind you, so that was unsurprising."

Tristan frowned. "You… *expect* to see them?"

At precisely that moment, Nico bounded euphorically up the stairs, Reina following like the slip of a shadow behind him.

"Hey," Nico said, gorily disfigured. His thin white t-shirt was caked in blood from his shoulder and his nose was broken, though he appeared not to have noticed. He thrummed with adrenaline, acknowledging Atlas with an overeager nod. "What's going on?"

"Well, Mr. de Varona, I was just informing the others about the operatives you faced this evening," Atlas replied, opting not to comment discourteously on Nico's appearance. "You and Miss Mori took out a military task force."

"MI6?" Nico guessed.

"Yes, and CIA," confirmed Atlas. "Led by a medeian who specialized in—"

"Waves, yeah," Nico supplied, still buzzing as he glanced at Libby. "How'd you come out, Rhodes?"

Beside Tristan, Libby stiffened.

"Don't look so thrilled, Varona, it's monstrous," she hissed, though Atlas answered for her.

"With Mr. Caine's help, Miss Rhodes dispatched one of the world's most wanted illusionists," said Atlas, giving Tristan an additional nod of deference. "Her partner, a hand-to-hand combat specialist, was dispatched by Mr. Nova. They are both favored operatives of the Guǐhún, an intelligence operation from Beijing. Conveniently, they were both wanted globally for war crimes," he informed Libby kindly, "which we will be pleased to inform the authorities they will not have to concern themselves with anymore."

"Did we miss anyone?" asked Libby, who clearly couldn't be deterred from her apprehension, but before Atlas could open his mouth, Reina had spoken.

"Yes. Two got away."

The other five heads swiveled to hers, and she shrugged.

"They couldn't get what they came for," she said placidly. "Wards were too complex."

"Yes," Atlas confirmed. "Miss Mori is correct. There were, in fact, two medeians from the Forum who attempted unsuccessfully to penetrate the defensive wards of the library's archives."

"The Forum?" asked Callum.

"An academic society not unlike this one," Atlas confirmed. "It is their belief that knowledge should not be carefully stored, but freely distributed. I confess they greatly misunderstand our work, and frequently target our archives."

"Why do you know all this?" asked Tristan, who was growing rather frustrated by the Caretaker's upsettingly careless tone. "It sounds as if we were all sitting ducks for something you already knew was going to happen."

"Because it was a test," Callum cut in.

Atlas gave him an impatient smile. "Not a test," he said. "Not strictly speaking."

"Try speaking less strictly, then," Parisa advised tightly. "After all, we did nearly get killed."

"You did not nearly get killed," Atlas corrected her. "Your lives were in danger, yes, but you were selected for the Society because you already possessed the tools necessary to survive. The chance that any of you might have died was—"

"Possible." Libby's lips were thin. "Statistically, that is," she added, inclining her head towards Atlas in something Tristan disgustingly guessed to be deference, "it *was* possible."

"Many things are possible," Atlas agreed. "But then, I never claimed your safety was a guarantee. In fact, I was quite clear that you would be required to have some knowledge of combat and security."

Nobody spoke; they were waiting, Tristan expected, to be less annoyed about the fact that while they had never specifically signed anything saying they preferred *not* to be shot at in the middle of the night, some principles of preference remained.

"It is the Society's practice to 'leak' the date of the new members' arrival," Atlas continued in their silence. "Some attempts at entry are expected, but it was never for us to know who or what those attacks would be."

"The majority of the attempts were deflected by preexisting enchantments," Dalton added, surprising them with his presence. "The installation allows us to see the ways our enemies may have evolved."

"Installation," Nico echoed. "What is that, like a game?"

He seemed delighted about having been invited to participate.

"Merely common practice," said Atlas. "We like to see how well our potential initiates work together."

"So, in short, a test," said Callum, sounding none too pleased about it.

"A tradition," Atlas corrected, with another steady smile. "And you all did quite well, truth be told, though I hope having seen each other in action allows you to put together a more thorough defense system. Collaboration is very important for the sort of work we do here." He turned to Dalton, arching a brow. "Don't you agree, Mr. Ellery?"

"As I said, every class of initiates consists of a unique composite of specialties," Dalton supplied neutrally, addressing them as a group. "You were selected for a team as much as you were chosen as individual members. It is the Society's hope that, moving forward, you will act accordingly."

"Yes, quite," Atlas concluded, returning his attention to the group of them. "There will of course be some relevant details to see to as far as any structural or magical damage, but seeing as the house has now been emptied and the wards have resumed their usual work, I would invite you to get some rest and revisit the house's security in the morning. Good night," he offered crisply, nodding to them as a group, and then turned on his heel, followed by Dalton.

Parisa, Tristan noted, watched Dalton go with intense and possibly excessive interest, frowning slightly in his wake. Tristan waited for the others to move—first Reina, who headed to bed without a word, and then Callum, who rolled his eyes, followed by Nico and Libby, who immediately started arguing in hushed tones—before he approached Parisa, sidling up to her as she turned away in troubled thought.

"What's wrong?" he asked.

Her gaze flicked up to Callum, who was a few strides ahead of them.

"Nothing," she said. "Nothing."

"Doesn't look like nothing."

"Doesn't it?"

Only in that Callum looked perfectly unchanged.

"What happened?" Tristan asked again.

"Nothing," Parisa repeated. "It was just…" She trailed off, and then cleared her throat. "It was nothing."

"Ah yes, nothing," Tristan said drily. "Right."

They reached their rooms, lingering at the start of the corridor as the others filed off to bed. Nico barked something disapproving at Libby— something about "Fowler will fucking live for fuck's sake"—and then only Tristan and Parisa remained in the hall.

He paused beside her door, hesitating as she opened it.

"I was thinking," he said, clearing his throat. "If you wanted to—"

"I don't at the moment," she said. "Last night was fun, but I don't really think we should make it a regular thing, do you?"

He bristled. "That's not what I meant."

"Sure it was," said Parisa. "You've just had a near-death experience and now you want to stick your prick in something until you feel better." Tristan, who was much too English for this conversation, rather resented her choice of words, though she cut him off before he could express his demurral aloud. "It's evolutionary," she assured him. "When you come close to death, the body's natural impulse is procreation."

"I wasn't that close to death," Tristan muttered.

"No? Well, lucky you." Parisa's expression hardened, her eyes darting to Callum's bedroom door.

Not that Tristan had doubted it before, but 'nothing' had most definitely been 'something.'

"I thought you liked him," Tristan commented, and Parisa bristled.

"Who says I don't?"

"I'm just saying—"

"I don't know him."

Tristan contemplated the value of asking a third time.

"Something clearly happened," he allowed instead. "You don't have to tell me what it was, I just—"

"Nothing. It's nothing." She gave him a defensive glance. "How was little miss sunshine?"

"Libby? Fine. Good," Tristan corrected himself, as it didn't seem fair not to give her credit. She may not have been able to get out easily without him, but he wouldn't have gotten out *at all* without her. "She's good."

"Needy little thing, isn't she?"

"Is she?"

Parisa scoffed. "You should see the inside of her head."

Tristan was already quite certain that was a place he had no interest in being. "I doubt we'll be friends," he said uncomfortably, "but at least she's useful."

There it was again. Useful.

The one thing he was not.

"Self-deprecation is such a waste," said Parisa, sounding bored by the prospect of his interior thoughts. "Either you believe you're worthy or you don't, end of story. And if you don't," she added, opening the door to her room, "I certainly don't want to chance ruining the high opinion of you I may have mistakenly gotten from last night."

Tristan rolled his eyes. "So I'm *too* good, then? Is that the problem?"

"The problem is I don't want you getting attached," Parisa said. "You can't just replace one high-maintenance woman with another, and more importantly, I don't have time for your daddy problems."

"By all means, let me down gently," drawled Tristan.

"Oh, I'm not letting you down at all. I'm sure we'll have our fun, but certainly not two nights in a row," Parisa said, shrugging. "That's sending entirely the wrong message."

"Which is?"

"That I wouldn't eliminate you if given the chance," she said, and slipped inside her bedroom, shutting the door.

Great, Tristan thought. It was such a confounding reality that Parisa was beautiful even when she was being mean; *especially* then, in fact. She was also much more beautiful than Eden, which said a lot about beauty, and about cruelty, too.

He had such a talent for finding women who put themselves first. It was like he was some sort of sniffer-dog for emotional fatality, always able to dig it up from the one person in the room who would have no trouble making him feel small. He wished he were less attracted to it, that brazen sense of self, but unfortunately ambition left such a sweet taste in his mouth, and so had Parisa. Maybe she was right; maybe it *was* daddy problems.

Maybe after a lifetime of being useless, Tristan simply wanted to be used.

IV: SPACE

LIBBY

"So," Ezra said. "How's it going?"

"Oh, you know," Libby said. "Fine."

"...*fine*?" Ezra gave a little groan; half-charmed, half-doubtful, accompanied by an eye roll she could hear through the phone. "Come on, Libs, I just went on for ten minutes about my supervisor's affinity for onion bagels. I think you can probably come up with something to tell me about your new job."

Well, magnificent. She thought she'd escaped any necessity for confession, given her dutiful half-listening to said story about supervisor and bagels along with the likelihood that she could slip casually into phone sex, but evidently not. It was just what she needed, really, to have to tell someone who would want to know everything the absolutely nothing she was allowed to explain.

"It's a fellowship," Libby began, chewing the inside of her cheek. "We do… you know. Fellowship things. Research."

There. That was one way to put it. A boring one, ideally, inviting no further questions.

"What are you researching?"

Alas.

"Oh, um…"

"There has always been an intersect between magic and science," Atlas had said upon introduction to their first topic of study, leading them inside what he referred to as the reading room. It was a split level, high-ceilinged open space with a series of tables in the center, most of which were occupied with nothing aside from one or two chairs and a small reading lamp. Illumination was minimal in the bottom half of the room, so as to not disturb the literature itself, while the top level glowed faintly with track lighting, looked down from a balcony lined with shelves.

At the moment they entered, a middle-aged man had glanced down from above, observing their entry and nodding to Atlas.

Atlas, in return, gave the visitor a courteous wave. "Bom dia, Senhor Oliveira," Atlas offered in greeting, startling Libby slightly with the reference to someone she was fairly certain was currently the chairman of the medeian offices of Brazil.

"In any case," Atlas continued, tonally unchanged, "much of what exists in the Society's archives draws no separation between magic and science; that distinction is more often made in later centuries, particularly pre-Enlightenment and post-Protestant Reformation. The scientific reflections of antiquity, such as the many works of Democritus we have in the archives—"

(Here Reina suddenly came alive from her usual half-comatose look of wanting to be elsewhere. Unsurprising that she would be interested; Democritus wrote dozens of texts on ancient atomism, nearly all of which would have been classified throughout Reina's classics education as 'missing.')

"—indicate that most studies on nature, and of the nature of life itself, do not suggest any preclusion of magic. Indeed, even some medieval studies of heaven and the cosmos suggest both scientific and magical study; take, for example, *Paradiso* by Dante, which manages an artistically interpreted— but not inaccurate—understanding of the Earth and its atmosphere. The mystique of Dante's heaven may be attributed to both scientific and magical forces."

Most of their 'lessons,' if one could call them that, were Socratic discussions that took place in one of the outrageously stuffy drawing rooms, various places redeemed only by the presence of their countless first edition texts. Any additional books—anything referenced during the day's discussion, for example—were easily summoned from the archives; in fact, they were *so* easily available that a handwritten copy of Heisenberg's notes once appeared beside Libby on the table even before she had spoken her curiosity aloud.

("Interestingly," Atlas said, "Heisenberg's uncertainty principle is based, in large part, on a major misconception. Perhaps you might have heard that on the evening he first began his calculations, Werner Heisenberg had been watching a man a little ways before him who seemed to appear beneath a lamp, then disappear into the night, and appear from another pool of light, so on and so forth. Naturally, Heisenberg's estimation was that the man was not actually disappearing and reappearing, but simply becoming visible and invisible due to light sources; thus, if Heisenberg could reconstruct the man's trajectory by its interaction with other things, the same could be done for electrons, which is a tenet of physics that has been proven time and time again. Unfortunately," Atlas chuckled, "the man that poor Werner was watching was actually a medeian called Ambroos Visser, who could very much disappear and reappear at will, and who happened to be having a marvelous time doing so that very evening. Post-death, Ambroos came to lead the poltergeist society at that very park in Copenhagen, and today he is deeply revered for his contribution to our understanding of atomic spectra.")

"Lib?" Ezra asked, startling Libby back to their phone call. "Still there?"

"Yes, sorry," she said, blinking. "What was the question?"

He gave a low laugh, the sound of it muffled into the receiver. He must have been in bed, turning onto his side to prop his phone against his ear. "What are you working on at the moment?"

"Oh, um… ecological conservation. In a sense." That was sort of true, if one considered the process of terraforming hostile environments to be an ecological study. The previous afternoon, Libby and Nico had spent nearly all their energy trying to alter the molecular makeup of the painted room, hoping to tweak the nature of its atmosphere to their preferred specifications. They had been told to stop, though, in a rather snippy tone, when Reina said the fig plant in the corner was suffocating.

"We're just trying to understand basic principles of science and magic so we can apply them to… bigger projects."

Like, for example, wormholes. So far, Nico and Libby had managed to successfully create one wormhole, which had taken two weeks of research and an entire day of casting to accomplish. Ultimately, Nico had been forced to test it himself, because no one else was willing to take the chance they might accidentally wind up on Jupiter. (An impossibility, technically, as it would have taken at least ten thousand Nicos and Libbys to power anything even close to that magnitude of power and precision, but still, Tristan in particular had looked as if he'd rather eat his own foot than test it out.)

In the end, it took Nico from the first floor corridor of the west wing to the kitchen. In typical Nico fashion, he now used it on a regular basis.

"Well, it's understandable if it doesn't feel interesting yet," said Ezra. "Most of academia can feel fairly pointless while you're in the early research phase. And probably for quite a while after that, I imagine."

"That's... true," Libby permitted hesitantly, not wanting to admit that the creation of a wormhole was actually not a pointless thing at all, even if it meant Nico was constantly and inconveniently disappearing and reappearing with snacks.

As far as Libby knew, they were the first ones who had ever managed to do it, even on a micro level. If there were sufficient power sources in the future—if, by chance, some medeian was born somewhere with nuclear energy in their fingertips—then they could easily do the same thing in space, in time... in spacetime! In fact, if any government agencies knew they had done it, they could easily get enough medeians together to bolster a magical space program. She had wanted to call NASA the moment they managed it, only then she remembered it would ultimately be controlled by a politician (any politician, somewhere, or at least a whole flock of them, some which would inevitably be less competent than others), and as Atlas often said, most forms of knowledge were better reserved until they were certain such revelations wouldn't be abused. Even if Libby *could* manage to successfully terraform Mars, there was no guarantee it wouldn't bring about a second global Age of Imperialism, which would be disastrous and destructive. Better they kept it in the archives.

"—'s Varona?"

"What?" Libby asked, having been daydreaming about planetary exploration again. "Sorry, I was just—"

"I just wondered how things were going with Varona," Ezra said, sounding slightly more tense now than when he'd laughed her inattention off before. She supposed Ezra would never not sound tense about Nico, and understandably so; she had a practice of bristling at the sound of his name, too. "Is he being... you know. Himself?"

"Oh, well—"

At that precise moment, Libby heard a burst of nonsensical Nico-sounds from the gallery, which meant he was probably sparring with Reina again. That had begun almost immediately after the installation ('installation' being Atlas' word for all of them nearly dying on their very first night as part of the Society) and now, Nico and Reina had a habit of doing what appeared to be daily martial arts workouts together.

It was strange, obviously. It had all the hallmarks of Nico's pre-established habits and customs while manifesting in a new and disturbing way. Not that

Nico had ever been particularly devoted to wearing shirts, for example, but coming across him without one, dripping sweat and colliding with Libby in the hallway only to slime the front of her blouse with his perspiration, was now all too frequent an occurrence.

Admittedly, the ease of Nico's comradeship with Reina, or whatever it could be called, had bothered Libby at first. Terrible as it was to acknowledge, Nico was currently the closest thing Libby had to a friend. Reina had made it clear she had no interest in being amicable with Libby, and the others certainly hated her (in the case of Callum, that feeling was deeply mutual), so the potential loss of Nico was a blow; something Libby had never thought she'd say about Nico de Varona, or the lack of him.

She was particularly resentful of the fact that Reina and Nico had bonded over their joint foray into violence, both because it meant Libby might lose Nico's alliance—thereby chancing her own elimination once the others felt free to confess their collective dislike—*and* because it was annoying that Nico had spent four years hating Libby only to befriend a girl who almost never spoke except to scowl.

"Don't pout, Rhodes," advised Nico. By then they had all taken to exploring the grounds within the Society's wards; the house was surrounded by a lovely manicured lawn, a grove of trees, and some roses, beside which had been the first site of Nico and Reina's communal venture into recreational pugilism.

It was sometime in the early weeks when Nico had first pulled Libby aside, her shading her eyes from the high summer sun and him chirpily toweling the sheen of sweat from his chest. "I still need you," he assured her, ever his effervescent, pompous self.

"Oh, good," Libby said drily, "thank heavens I'm still of some use to you."

"Actually, I've been meaning to tell you something." Nico wasn't listening, having grown entirely too used to her sarcasm by then, but he surprised her with a conspiratorial hand on her elbow, tugging her around the collection of rose bushes that she supposed counted as a garden to the English. "I've noticed something about Reina."

"Varona," Libby sighed, "if this is going to be gross—"

"What? No, nothing like that. If anything I'd want to sleep with—well, never mind," he muttered, "that's not relevant. The point is, trust me, you *want* me to get Reina on our side," he assured her, dropping his voice in a manner she supposed he found provocative. "We need her, and I'm not even sure she understands that. Or why."

"Do *you*?" prompted Libby doubtfully. It wasn't as if Nico had ever been notorious for his talents of perception. For example, he had somehow managed to miss that Libby's best friend at NYUMA, Mira, had been sickeningly in love with him for the entirety of their schooling.

(Before *and* after he slept with her. Fuckboys, honestly.)

"I sorted it out by accident," Nico admitted, again dismissing Libby's loyal efforts to undermine his masculinity on Mira's behalf, "so your skepticism isn't entirely the worst, but yes, I do. Reina is—" He broke off, frowning. "She's like a battery."

Libby blinked. "What?"

"Well, I've been thinking about it, and what is a naturalist except for a type of energy source, right? I don't know how she's doing it or what she's tapping into, but think about it, Rhodes." Nico seemed to be imploring her; irritatingly, as if the gears in her head were not already turning precisely as his had turned. "I noticed it when we took on the waves medeian at the installation. When I was touching her, it was like I had an extra power source."

(The epiphany and its corresponding conversation had occurred pre-wormhole. Truthfully, they wouldn't have managed it at all if not for Nico figuring this out about Reina, but Libby certainly hadn't confessed that to his face. Nor did she plan to.)

"We'll have to test it," Libby said, glancing over her shoulder. It was a bit exciting, discovering that their alliance was an alliance indeed; he had clearly waited until they were alone to share his suspicions. "Do you think she'd be on our side?"

"Rhodes, she's already on our side," Nico scoffed, which at first Libby attributed to his indefatigable arrogance, but then, thankfully, he went on to support the allegation with actual evidence. "We don't talk much," he clarified, gesturing to his recent bout of physical activity, "but there's no question she definitely loathes Parisa. And she doesn't make a secret of not trusting Tristan or Callum."

"Nor should she," Libby murmured to herself.

This appeared to have sparked some secondary, tangential epiphany in Nico de Varona's manic web of thoughts. "You were with Tristan that night,"

Nico observed aloud, holding up a water bottle and pouring some of it over his head (splashing Libby, which she did not appreciate) before consuming what remained. "How was he?"

Ah yes, Tristan. A complete enigma, as far as she was concerned.

"He can do something strange," Libby admitted, brushing a droplet of water from her brow before it made her bangs all wonky. She was growing them out, which meant they were inconceivably annoying. "You know how he said he can see through illusions? I didn't realize that means he doesn't necessarily see them while they're being used."

"What, at all?"

"No. Not at all. He had to ask me what I thought the room looked like."

"Huh, weird." Nico paused thoughtfully, chewing on the lip of his water bottle. "Useful, you think?"

"Very. Well," Libby amended after a moment's thought, "it's a useful skill, at least. Though I'm not sure whether it qualifies as enough to keep him from being eliminated. Much as I hate to admit it," she sighed, "an empath and a telepath could be much more helpful allies when we move out of the physical sciences."

"Better a telepath than an empath, don't you think? If we had to choose," Nico said.

"You only say that because you like Parisa," Libby muttered under her breath, and Nico gave her an unforgivably broad smile.

"Can you blame me, Rhodes?"

"Varona, honestly." No, of course she couldn't blame him; Parisa was, hands down, the most beautiful girl Libby had ever seen in her life. Luckily, Libby was not a useless boy and did not focus on extraneous details like Parisa's looks. "Your dick aside, she's really not a team player. I'd hardly call her an asset when it comes to working as a group."

"True," Nico said, who must have taken a blow to the head to actually consider taking something she said seriously. "She's been weird to Callum, hasn't she?"

Libby gave Nico a glance intended to indicate that they were *all* weird to Callum, and rightfully.

"True," Nico repeated.

"What's the deal with this, anyway?" Libby asked him, gesturing warily to his relationship with Reina. "Are you two, like—?"

"It's exercise, Rhodes," Nico said, flexing his stomach for emphasis. "I told you, we don't talk much."

"Okay," she sighed, "but do you… I mean. Are you two, you know——?"

"What do you care?" He gave her one of those smug, dazzling grins that she loathed to the core of her being. "Don't tell me you're jealous."

Christ Almighty. "Oh, shove it, Varona," she said, turning to leave. There was really only so much Nico she could take in one sitting.

He, however, had caught her arm before she left, tugging her back. "You're not telling Fowler about any of this, right?" Nico asked her. "If I can't tell Gideon, you certainly can't tell Fowler."

"Ah yes, because your roommate and my boyfriend are exactly the same scenario," Libby said with a roll of her eyes.

"I'm just saying——"

"*Relax*, Varona, I'm not telling him anything."

"Not even about the installation, right?"

"Hell no. Are you kidding?" She'd wanted to tell him at first, but a single moment's consideration had reminded her that Ezra would lose his mind if he knew she'd been in harm's way. He was one of those old-fashioned types; a white knight, even though she hardly needed rescuing. "Absolutely not."

"Where's Tristan's head at?" Nico asked, having already discarded the thought of Ezra and moved onto whatever thing he'd have to conquer next. "Do you think we can get him on our side?"

"Do we *want* him on our side?" Libby asked doubtfully.

"Why, you don't like him?"

"It's not that." Truthfully, she'd been prepared to dislike Tristan much more than she did. "He's smart, I'll give him that," she conceded, thinking of the way he'd helped with their calculations much more than either Callum or Parisa. Tristan's background as an investor in magical technology made him intensely knowledgeable, even if his practical inexperience with physicalities precluded him from contributing much magically. "He's just also very, um——"

"Grumpy," said Nico.

"Well, I wouldn't——"

"He's grumpy," Nico repeated.

"Varona, I'm trying t-"

"He's *grumpy*," Nico said loudly.

"Maybe he's shy," countered Libby, unconvincingly.

And then, because that had fooled no one, she sighed, "I don't think there's anything *wrong* with him, I just… Well, for one thing, he almost certainly doesn't like me," she said, and then stopped, dismayed with herself for sounding so much like a child.

"I don't like you either, Rhodes, so I hardly think that's relevant," said Nico, proving himself reliable, if nothing else. "And besides, it seems fairly obvious that Tristan doesn't like anyone, so you can't take it personally."

"I don't." Not really. "I'm just saying I'm not ready to be in an *alliance* with him. Or with Reina, for that matter," she added quickly. "She might be useful and all that, but it's only been a few weeks."

"I didn't say we should devote ourselves to her body and soul," Nico said. "I just think she's, you know." He smiled broadly, vengeful in his delight. "Moderately epic."

High praise from someone who considered Libby to be only somewhere in the bottom twenty worst people he'd ever met (or so he told her once during a heated argument third year at NYUMA). Not that Libby was jealous of Reina; it was clear, at least, that Nico intended to see his alliance through with Libby, and that was really all she needed from him at the end of the day.

Would it have been nice to have an ally who was also a friend? Yes, sure, maybe. She had thought for half a second that maybe Tristan would have warmed to her after their brush with danger, but he had been deliberately keeping his distance from her since then. She supposed that might have been in her head; she was the youngest, after all, and Tristan was somewhere around the same age as Callum, so maybe that was why they seemed to be increasingly together. Maybe the fact that Callum clearly didn't like her (or her emotions, anyway, which in her defense, *she* didn't care for, either) was making Tristan less inclined to like her, too.

In that case, Tristan was not only an idiot, but also hardly someone whose instincts she could trust. It hadn't required much to convince Libby that Callum was bad news, and even Parisa seemed to agree. If Tristan couldn't see it, then…

"He's not worth your energy, Lib."

"I know," Libby said, before remembering that Ezra was talking about Nico, not Tristan, and that oh, yeah, she was still on the phone talking to Ezra. "I mean—sorry," she amended with a blink, "Varona's fine, I was just—
"

"Is there someone else?"

"Hm?" Drat, more things she couldn't talk about, like who was in the program with her. "No, I was just—"

There was a quiet knock at the door.

"Hang on, Ezra—Yes?" Libby called, covering the receiver with one hand.

"It's Tristan," came the voice from the other side. Perfunctorily, and with a sense of wishing the interaction was already over with, as one might expect from all of Tristan's interactions.

"Oh, um—" That was a surprise. "One second. Ezra?" she said, returning to her phone call. "Can I call you back?"

There was a pause.

"I'm about to head out, Lib, it's getting late here. Tomorrow?"

"Tomorrow," she promised, mildly relieved. "I love you."

"Love you." Ezra hung up and she rose to her feet, padding to the door and pulling it open.

For someone who didn't care much for illusions, Tristan Caine certainly was one. It was a Saturday, meaning they all had the day off from their usual work—assuming nobody breached their recently updated security measures, that is—but Tristan was fully dressed (smartly, with a tucked-in shirt and a J. Crew sleeve-roll and everything, like he was heading to a brief but critical lunch meeting), holding a newspaper tucked under his arm. Libby was willing to bet that Tristan had gone down for both breakfast and lunch already that day, which they had the option of taking in their rooms on the weekends. It was as if the appearance of normalcy was a crucial piece of Tristan Caine's identity.

"Yes?" she asked, a little breathless from her jaunt to the door.

He was as inscrutable as always, peering down at her in his hawkish way. "Do you still have the Lucretius?"

"Oh, yes, of course—hang on. Come in."

She left the door open for him, turning to sort out where she'd left the book. "Working on a Saturday?" she asked him, peering around for it in her pile of things. She hadn't planned to touch the manuscript any time soon; she was rather intent on spending the day in her yoga pants, recovering in advance of whatever massive energy output she'd need to produce on Monday.

"I just want to have another look at it," he said.

"Truthfully, I don't know if it'll be much help," she said, finally spotting it in the pile beside the nightstand. She wasn't the neatest person alive, nor was she the best at rising early. All in all, she felt woefully inadequate next to Tristan, who was so pulled together he nearly sparkled. "I can't say it has much in it that hasn't been addressed by later works."

"There's something about time," Tristan said, "isn't there?"

"Sort of. Nothing concrete, but—"

"I'd like to see for myself," he told her curtly, and she blinked.

"Sorry, I wasn't trying t-"

"Don't apologize," he said impatiently. "I just have a theory I'd like to test."

"Oh." She held the book out for him, and he took it. Before he could leave, though, she cleared her throat. "Any chance you'd like to tell me what theory you're testing?"

"Why?"

"I… curiosity, I guess." Incredible how he made it feel like a capital crime just to ask him a simple question. "I *do* actually care about the research we do, you know."

He bristled slightly. "I never suggested you didn't."

"I know, I'm s-" She broke off before apologizing again. "Never mind. You can hang onto it, by the way," she said, gesturing to the book. "I don't think there's anything useful. Theoretically, I suppose the idea that time and movement aren't separate functions is an interesting baseline, but that's hardly unique to—"

"You and Nico manipulate force, correct?"

She was startled, first by the interruption and secondly, by having her abilities addressed.

"What?"

"Force. Yes?"

"Yes, force." He seemed to be playing with something in his head, so she added, "We use it to alter the physical makeup of things."

"Why couldn't you make a wormhole through time?"

"I—" That wasn't what she expected his follow-up to be. "Well, I… theoretically I suppose we could, but that would require understanding the nature of time to begin with."

"What would you need to know in order to understand?"

He didn't seem to be mocking her; she hazarded an attempt to explain without getting defensive at being asked a moderately obvious question.

"Well, time's not a physical thing," Libby said slowly. "Var- Nico and I can manipulate things we can see and feel, but time is... something different."

"You can't see or feel it?"

"I—" Again, she stopped, a little taken aback. "Wait a minute. Are you telling me that you *can*?"

He regarded her for a moment, mildly troubled.

"I didn't say that," he amended. "I just want to be prepared for whatever we do on Monday."

It didn't seem worth it to point out that Tristan had done almost nothing the past few weeks as it was. Aside from posing theoretical arguments to guide their experiments, he hadn't contributed all that much.

But she supposed it wasn't his fault he hadn't. At least he worked hard, didn't he? He was reading and annotating all the texts, working on his own over the weekend. And maybe if he could see differently than she could when it came to illusions, he could see other things differently, too.

The idea that maybe Tristan, like Reina, had some additional talent that Libby could make use of and report back to Nico filled her with a little thrill. Why should Nico de Varona be the only one to sort out what a person was good for?

"There's a theory that quanta *is* space," Libby said, exciting herself with the prospect that she might have stumbled onto something. "That space itself isn't emptiness, but a fabric of tiny individual particles. So, I assume that time could be made up of similar particles? The gravitational potential is—"

"Look, I appreciate the book," Tristan said, "but I don't really have anything to chat about."

"Oh." The word slipped out of her defeatedly. "Right, sorry."

Tristan's jaw tightened, annoyed, and she grimaced.

"Not sorry," she amended, forcing a smile. "I only meant—"

"You don't have to be sorry for existing, you know," Tristan cut in irritably, and then he turned to leave, prompting Libby to wish she'd stayed on the phone with Ezra instead of answering the door.

Ezra was so good about being supportive. That was why she liked him, really. He was her number one fan, her tireless champion. He believed in her so much and so powerfully that it always made her feel there was someone in her corner, and at times like these, she longed for something to make her feel centered. Secure.

"Rhodes," Tristan said, startling her into noticing he'd paused in the threshold before exiting the room. "Thank you for the book."

She blinked, and then nodded.

"Hope it helps," she said.

He shrugged and closed the door behind him, leaving her to fall back on her bed with a sigh.

CALLUM

PARISA DIDN'T TRUST HIM NOW. It radiated from her, suspicion, her misgivings warping irreparably in the air between them. Considering their respective talents, she must have known he was aware of how she felt; of the corrosion atrophying their potential from one side. That she hadn't bothered to conceal it could only mean she had no intention to repair it, and if she did not care to repair it, then it appeared she had chosen to draw a line.

Which was too bad, not only for the obvious reasons, but also because it meant Callum had been mistaken. He had taken Parisa for the sort of girl who admired when a man took control of a situation instead of leaving her to do the work herself.

Evidently not.

In terms of allying himself with the others, Libby was out for obvious reasons, and so was Nico. Reina was an island, so that was useless, but Callum would have to befriend someone. Not to keep from being eliminated, of course; he could persuade them if it really came down to it, or if he even decided to stay.

It was more an issue of entertainment, and since Callum wasn't entertained by books or research, he would have to find stimulation in a person.

Luckily, one potential source still remained.

"You look distressed," Callum commented to Tristan, leaning over to speak with him in pseudo-privacy. "Something bothering you?"

Tristan's gaze slid to his, and then back to Libby and Nico. "Aren't you seeing this?"

"I'm seeing it."

"And you're *not* distressed?"

Callum smiled thinly.

"I suppose I don't see much use for having a black hole in my living room," he said.

It wasn't as if Callum was unaware that what Libby and Nico (and, he supposed, Reina) were doing was relatively monumental. He could understand, theoretically speaking, why magically modeling a previously unexplained phenomenon was a matter of significance, and for purposes of the Society, he could acknowledge it as the sort of thing belonging somewhere in the archives. There was no question of academic value.

It all just seemed terrifically impractical, and Callum was a practical sort of man.

"Most people are stupid enough that this sort of information is useless," Callum offered Tristan in explanation. "Why bother understanding the universe when everything it's made of exceeds basic human comprehension?"

"But they just proved a major element of quantum theory," Tristan said, frowning. He, Callum noted, couldn't take his eyes from what they'd done. "Those two twenty-something medeians just created something that all of human history has tried to understand and couldn't."

He sounded unreasonably awed, in Callum's view. Unsurprising; it was all dreamland all the time in this house. Clearly somebody needed a reality check.

"Those two twenty-something medeians put into practice a theory that has been all of human history in the making," Callum corrected Tristan, trying to shine a little much-needed pragmatism on the situation. "Though, again, I don't know what possible use could come out of dropping something into a black hole and watching it bounce back out again."

Tristan finally managed to tear his attention from Nico and Libby's molecular sleight of hand, glancing sharply at Callum. "You're serious, aren't you?"

"Lethally, I'm afraid," said Callum. "I think it's a clever parlor trick."

"Parlor trick," Tristan echoed, disbelieving. "And what is it *you* can do, then?"

Tristan was being facetious, of course, merely proving a point and not genuinely asking, which was a pity, as the answer would have been decently silencing. For starters, Callum could make the twin cosmologists do anything he wanted. That meant, among other things, that he could take ownership of that black hole quite easily himself. If he were in a particularly enterprising mood, he could go a step further and persuade every person in the room to leap inside it.

Across from them, Parisa stiffened.

"I dislike physical magics," Callum said eventually, turning his attention back to Tristan. "Gives me a sort of unidentifiable itch. Like a scratch in my throat."

It took a moment, but Tristan did catch the undertones of a joke. Good, so he wasn't totally inept, then.

"At least tell me," Tristan sighed, "that you can recognize the significance of what's happening here."

"Recognize it? Yes, certainly. An enormous magical event," Callum confirmed, "which will soon be swallowed up by some other enormous magical event." That was how all of science worked, anyway. They were all pieces of some other eventual thing. The atom was part of the atomic bomb. Cataclysm, carnage, world wars, subprime mortgage lending, bank bailouts. In Callum's mind, human history was interesting because of humans, not science. Because humans were idiots who turned the elements of life into a weapon. The only interesting thing Libby and Nico had accomplished so far was to successfully terraform a miniature model of the moon, because it meant the moon could eventually be conquered. Someone would try to build Rome anew, or start a new Vatican. It would be madness, and therefore interesting.

More interesting, anyway, than studying the altered carbon levels or whatever it was they'd managed to do.

"On the bright side, there haven't been a thousand questions," Callum commented at dinner that evening, gesturing across the table to Libby with his chin after Tristan had taken the vacant chair beside him. The table was currently occupied with the sound of low chatter between Nico and Libby, who were comparing notes; Parisa had already excused herself for the evening, and Reina was absently spooning food into her mouth while she pored over the duplicate of some ancient journal.

"I will regret leaving Rhodes' element," Callum added at a murmur, "if only because that will no longer be true."

Tristan gave a reluctant sort of smirk, as if principles of moral superiority had compelled him not to laugh, but only just. "You really don't like her, do you?"

"Some people are flawed and interesting," Callum said with a shrug. "Others are just flawed."

"Remind me not to ask you what you think of me," Tristan said.

"Actually," Callum said, "I rather think you should."

Tristan said nothing.

"I know you're very suspicious of me," Callum said, before amending, "Of everyone."

"I find people to be largely disappointing," Tristan commented.

"Interestingly, so do I."

"Is that considered interesting?"

"Well, seeing that my specialty requires me to grasp most details of human nature, yes, I think so," Callum said. "Knowing what I know, I should really find other people fascinating, or at least valuable."

"And do you?"

"Some. Most, I find, are just replicas of others."

"Do you prefer good people," Tristan asked tangentially, "or bad?"

"I like to have a bit of both. Discord," Callum replied. "You're a prime example."

"Am I?"

"You want to be loyal to Parisa, which is interesting," Callum observed, as Tristan gave a little involuntary twitch of acknowledgement. "For a woman you slept with once, you seem to feel you owe her something. Same with Rhodes."

Tristan blanched. "I hardly think they're the same category."

"Oh, they're not," Callum agreed. "You feel you owe Rhodes your life. Parisa you simply *want* to owe your life to."

"Do I?"

"Yes. And you want very badly to mistrust me on her behalf." Callum gave Tristan another wary smile. "Unfortunately, you also find me appealing."

"In what way?"

"Nearly all of them," Callum said, adding with a glance between them, "You're not alone in that."

Tristan was silent another moment.

"You seem to have done something to Parisa," he noted, and Callum sighed.

"Yes, I do seem to, don't I? Pity. I like her."

"What did you do? Insult her?"

"Not that I know of," Callum said, though the real answer was no, he had not insulted her. He had *scared* her, which was the only sensation Parisa Kamali could not abide. "But I think perhaps she'll come around." She was the sort of person who would always do what was best for herself, even if it took her some time to puzzle it out.

"You don't concern yourself much with being liked, do you?" Tristan asked, half-amused.

"No, I don't." Doubtful Tristan would be capable of understanding that, but the sensation of being liked was extraordinarily dull. It was the closest thing to vanilla that Callum could think of, though nothing was truly comparable. Being feared was a bit like anise, like absinthe. A strange and arousing flavor. Being admired was golden, maple-sweet. Being despised was a woodsy, sulfuric aroma, smoke in his nostrils; something to choke on, when done properly. Being envied was tart, a citrusy tang, like green apple.

Being desired was Callum's favorite. That was smoky, too, in a sense, but more sultry, cloaked and perfumed in precisely what it was. It smelled like tangled bedsheets. It tasted like the flicker of a candle flame. It felt like a sigh, a quiet one; concessionary and pleading. He could always feel it on his skin, sharp as a blade. Piercing, like the groan of a lover in his ear.

"Being liked is fairly ordinary, I'm afraid," Callum said. "Intensely commonplace."

"How unimpressive," Tristan said drily.

"Oh, it can be helpful at times. But I certainly don't aim for it."

"How exactly do you plan to avoid being eliminated, then?"

"Well," said Callum patiently, "for one thing, you won't let it happen."

Tristan raised a hand to release a scoff into his palm, curling his fingers around it. "And how won't I?"

"Rhodes listens to you. Varona listens to her. And Reina listens to him."

Tristan arched a brow. "So your presumption about me is…?"

"That you will not want to eliminate me." Callum smiled again. "It's really quite simple, don't you think?"

"I noticed you didn't include Parisa in your calculations. Or me, for that matter," Tristan said in his usual drawl, "though I'm willing to overlook that for the sake of argument."

"Well," Callum said, "a telepath is useful, of course, if your goal is to interfere with someone's thoughts. But do you know how infrequently people actually think?" he prompted, raising his glass to his lips while Tristan, inescapably in agreement, offered the echo of a soundless laugh. "With very rare exceptions, emotions are far stronger. And, unlike thought, emotion can be easily manipulated. Thoughts, on the other hand, must be implanted or incepted or stolen, which means a telepath will always burn more energy than an empath when magic is being used."

"So you think you are the more useful option, then?"

"I think I'm the better option," Callum clarified. "But more importantly, I think that, at the end of the day, you understand me more than you care to admit."

The statement rang with relative clarity. Callum had almost no doubt that whatever reasoning the others had to dislike him, Tristan would find his rationale more persuasive. Tristan's cynicism, or his disillusionment, or whatever it was that left him so bitterly disenchanted with the world, was useful that way.

"My offer is this," Callum said. "I am on your side."

"And?"

"And nothing," Callum said. "Surely you see this is a game of alliances? I am your ally."

"So then I should be yours?"

At that precise moment, Libby looked up. She had already adopted a habit of skirting Callum's attention (probably wise) and so managed to lock eyes with Tristan by accident before quickly looking away, returning to her conversation with Nico.

Tristan tensed; aware, probably, that he had just been caught in discussion with Callum, whom none of the others were in a rush to befriend.

"Parisa is not an ally," Callum cautioned Tristan, who cleared his throat. "Neither is Rhodes. As for the others, Varona and Reina are pragmatists; they will side with whoever will take them the furthest."

"Shouldn't you do the same, and wait," Tristan advised, "to see if I have any value before trying to recruit me?"

"You have value," Callum said. "I hardly need assign it to you."

Across the table, Nico exclaimed something unintelligible about gravitational waves and heat. Or perhaps time and temperature. Or perhaps it didn't matter at all, not even remotely, because unless Nico wanted to be some sort of medeian physicist chained to a laboratory for the rest of his life, nothing would come of it. The purpose of the Society was to get in, get access, and then get out. Remaining here, as Dalton Ellery had done, was pointless. The best of them would seek to parlay the influence of the Society, not bind themselves to the annals it contained.

Callum was the sort of person readily built to go far, Society or no Society. Tristan was the same, though in a different way. Callum could smell it on him: the ambition, the hunger, the drive. It was on the others, too, but not nearly so strong, and certainly not so close to longing. Nico had a hidden agenda (it was tightly sealed, tasting of metal) and perhaps the others had their reasons, but only Tristan truly *wanted* it, with his whole being. It was salty, savory, like salivation itself.

The only person who was as starved and desperate as Tristan was Reina, and there was certainly no point trying to win her. Not yet. She'd take whichever side she needed to when the time arose.

Libby was so unthreatening as to be a non-factor. Thus, Callum did *not* factor her into his personal calculations. If he ever needed another black hole, he'd simply seek her out in whatever mundane government job she accepted after being eliminated from this group. True, there was an as-yet unidentified link between Libby and Tristan—perhaps as a result of their experience during the installation—but that would be a simple enough matter to resolve. Tristan quietly resented her, or resented her abilities, and that was an uncomplicated emotion to play with. Callum could twist it easily around his finger, turning it steadily to hate.

As for Parisa, she was a difficulty. Callum had understated her abilities to Tristan for obvious reasons, and that was only with regard to her technical specialty. She was a better medeian than Callum, who had never been a particularly devoted student, and she was immensely calculating. Fatally, even. She was the one enemy Callum didn't want, but she had already drawn the line, so he'd have to knock her pieces off the board quickly.

Callum didn't want to waste time toying with Parisa's pawns; he wanted her king.

"I have to admit, I am a little sick of the physicist show," Tristan murmured to himself, staring with an intensity he didn't know was envy while Libby and Nico, for unknowable and unimportant reasons, tried reversing a boiling cup of water.

Ah, inevitable acquiescence. How bountifully sweet.

"Let's have a nightcap," Callum suggested, rising to his feet. "Do you take your scotch neat?"

"I'd take it in a barrel at this point," said Tristan.

"Excellent. Have a good night," Callum said to the others, rising to his feet and making his way from the dining room to the painted room.

Reina didn't look up as he went, nor did Nico. Libby did, which was why Callum had said it to begin with. She would see Tristan following in Callum's wake and feel more isolated than she already did, and without even a blink of effort.

Poor little magic girl. So much power, so few friends.

"Good night," Libby said quietly, not looking at Tristan.

People were such delicate little playthings.

NICO

THE APPEARANCE OF EILIF in the drain of his bathroom sink was not ideal. A diverse sampling of "fuck" fell out of Nico's mouth in at least three languages, and Eilif, who had surfaced from somewhere in the plumbing, slurped out from the drain to perch herself on the lip of his sink, rolling her eyes. She said something impatient in rapid Icelandic, or possibly Norwegian, and Nico, who was exceptionally naked, gave her a glare intended to remind her that being quadrilingual was, while probably a worthy endeavor, not something he was in the mood for becoming today.

"It's just me," she said in English. "Calm down."

"First of all, no," said Nico, finding that a necessary and accurate starting point. "Secondly, how did you get in here?" he demanded, pivoting around for any Society-related consequences as a result of the mermaid who'd just broken into his bathroom. The usual red light in the corner, signaling a broach of the wards, troublingly did not appear. "This shouldn't even be *possible*—"

"Well, it took some time to find you, but eventually I sorted out where you were. Called in a few favors, that sort of thing. I need you to lift the wards concealing my son immediately. You look well, Nicolás," remarked Eilif, all in one liquid train of thought. "Nearly delicious enough to taste."

"You," Nico grunted, "need to stop that. And what do you mean 'a few favors'?"

"Oh, I know where you are," she drawled, beginning to toy with her hair. She was slightly blue, as always, and exceptionally vascular, so that Nico could see the indigo rivers splicing like kintsugi over her bare breasts. "It wasn't very difficult. Naughty," she chided as a preening afterthought.

"You still shouldn't have been able to get in," Nico said gruffly.

"Nicolás, how is it my fault if your creature wards were left unattended?"

Fair. It had crossed his mind briefly at the time they'd set them up, but he couldn't very well tell everyone else why he needed to guard against one mermaid in particular.

Well—he *could* have, but he doubted anyone would take it seriously. Besides, Eilif wasn't dangerous to him. Just… fishy, and mostly unhinged.

"Now, about my son," Eilif began.

"No," said Nico flatly, because despite Eilif presenting little danger to *him*, Gideon was a separate concern. "Do you know what it cost me to put up that ward in the first place? Leave Gideon alone."

"Well." Her pale lips pursed. "I see *you* have no understanding of progeny."

"Neither do you!" Nico snapped. "You use him, Eilif, and he hates it. If Gideon wants you out, you're staying out."

In answer, Eilif's eyes dropped to his hips.

And then lower.

And she stared.

And stared.

"Stop cursing my dick," said Nico impatiently. "I'm not going to change my mind."

Eilif threw her arms up with a sigh. "You know, I'm getting very tired of you," she informed him shrilly. "Shouldn't you die soon? Gideon's had at least seventy mortal years by now."

"He's twenty-two," Nico said.

"What? Impossible," Eilif scoffed.

"I threw him a birthday party," Nico said. "Which, by the way, you missed."

She waved a hand, uninterested as usual in the traditional customs of motherhood. "Then he's been a child for centuries, at least!"

"He's not a child, he's an adult. He's at approximately a quarter of a mortal lifespan."

"That doesn't sound right—"

"Well, it is!" Nico said indignantly, and Eilif gave a loud, cerulean groan.

"Give me my son," she barked, unconstrained. "He needs me!"

"No, he doesn't."

"How will he eat?"

"He eats *fine*."

Her eyes narrowed, unconvinced.

"You know, we were fine before you," she accused him, bemoaning it with a sullen howl.

"That's not even close to true," Nico said. "You left your infant son in the woods of Nova Scotia and then proceeded to show up every few years just to make him chase you through the dream realms. I wouldn't call that being 'fine,' unless we're only counting you."

"Who else would we be counting?" Eilif demanded, and then paused. "Ah yes. Gideon."

"Yes, Gideon." How eminently exhausting. "Your son, remember?"

"GIVE ME MY SON," Eilif said hotly, trembling now with fury. "I don't like it. I don't like *you*. Give him to me. Sweet Nicolás," she murmured, with her melodic hell-purr of sirenic persuasion. "My darling, don't you dream of riches?"

"Stop," he said.

"But—"

"No."

"But I want—"

"You can't."

"BUT HE'S MINE," Eilif wailed, shuddering with temper before resolving to a juvenile sulk. "Fine, have him. I'll be back," she promised in her most simpering tone, and then she threw herself into the sink, swallowed up by the drain again.

"Varona, what the hell is going on in there?" came Libby's voice from the corridor.

"Hell," Nico confirmed. "But don't worry, it's been wrangled." Or it would be soon.

"Whatever," Libby muttered, the sound of her footsteps heading back to her room.

A quick text to Gideon—*meet me in the usual spot?* followed by a hasty *everything's fine!*—ensured an early night.

"What did you do?" Gideon said the moment Nico sat up, resuming his place inside the jail cell of the Society's subconscious wards. "Something interesting, I hope."

"Bored, Sandman?" Nico asked him, stepping close to the bars.

Gideon shrugged.

"I guess," he said. "There's only so many books you can fall asleep reading."

"Well, don't watch too much television," Nico said. "You always end up in the dangerous realms when you've been exposed to excessive violence and I'm sorry, but you're just not very good with firearms."

Gideon gave a theatrical sigh. "Stop scolding me, Nicky," he said, "you're not my mother."

It was a joke, but Nico winced at the reminder. Gideon, catching it, abruptly froze.

"Oh no," Gideon said, paling at once, and Nico sighed.

"It's fine, Gideon, I have it handled, I prom-"

"What did she say?"

"Nothing, I told you, it's f-"

"Nicolás," Gideon said fiercely. "What did she say?"

So much for it's fine, Nico thought. Not that he'd ever been very good at lying to Gideon.

"Nothing much, really," he said. "She seems to… want you for something."

"Yes, I know she does," Gideon said, scrubbing tiredly at his cheek with one hand. "She always does eventually. I thought she had actually left me alone this time, but—"

He broke off, and again, Nico winced.

"You," Gideon realized aloud, glaring at Nico. "You set up a ward against her without telling me, didn't you?"

"What? That's crazy," said Nico.

"Nico, you had no *right*—"

"That's ridiculous, of course I did—"

"—you can't just interfere without telling me—"

"—I was *going* to tell you; in fact, I'm sure I already did! It's not my fault if you didn't read the minutes closely—"

"—for the last time, my mother is *my* problem, not yours—"

That, of course, was met with a growl of frustration. "Haven't you figured out by now that I *want* your problems?" Nico demanded, half-shouting it, and thankfully, Gideon's mouth snapped shut. "Your pain is my problem, you idiot prince. You little motherfuck." Nico rubbed his temple wearily as Gideon's lips twisted up, half-laughing. "Don't laugh. Don't… don't look at me, stop it. *Stop* it—"

"What are these pet names, Nicky?"

"Shut up. I'm angry."

"Why are *you* angry?"

"Because you seem to think for some stupid reason that you should be handling everything on your own—"

"—when really *you* should be handling it on *your* own, is that it?"

Touché. The bastard.

"Gideon, for fuck's sake, I'm rich and extremely handsome," Nico growled. "Do you think I have my own problems? No, I do not, so let me have yours. Put me to use, I beg you."

Gideon rolled his eyes. "You are," he said, and exhaled, "*unbearable.*"

"Yes. And you are safely hidden from your mother right now, so hush. But she is definitely looking for you," Nico conceded, which had been the primary warning he'd intended to pass along. "The ward will hold for a while yet, but it's only a matter of time before she breaks it. Or pays someone else to break it." Eilif was unfortunately much worse than the usual finfolk; largely in that she had friends in low places, most of them possessing uncompromised access that many people and governmental organizations wished they didn't.

"I could stay here," Gideon said thoughtfully. "In the realms?"

It would work, but not forever. "You still have a body."

"Yes."

"A *mortal* body—"

"Well, it looks like a mortal body, anyway."

"It's aging, isn't it?"

"It appears to be, possibly, but—"

"We'll figure it out someday," Nico assured him. "Your lifespan and all that. Your natural diet," he enumerated idly, "where to put the litter box, how to give you proper exercise. You know, the usual care and keeping of hybrid creatures—"

"Though I suppose none of it will matter if my mother kills me first," Gideon remarked.

Nico sighed, stepping back from the bars for a quick count of three, and then stepped back.

"Do not," he said with a long-suffering scowl, "say things like that."

But Gideon, who customarily looked amused by everything Nico did, only smiled.

"Don't worry about me, really," he said, for probably the millionth useless time. "I don't think she'll actually kill me. Or if she does, it'll be an accident. She's just very careless."

"She nearly drowned you twice!"

"I might be misremembering that."

"I don't think there's a way to misremember!"

"In her defense, she didn't know I couldn't breathe underwater. The first time, anyway."

"That," Nico said, aghast, "is *not* a defense!"

Gideon, though, was laughing.

"You know, Max is perfectly unbothered by all of this," he said. "You should consider doing what he does."

"What, dragging my ass across the carpet?"

"No, and he's stopped doing that," Gideon said. "Thankfully."

"Gideon, I just want you to be okay," Nico told him pleadingly. "Por favor. Je t'en supplie."

"I am, Nico. Worrying about me is just your excuse to avoid your own life—which, by the way, I know nothing about," Gideon pointedly reminded him. "Are you planning to tell me anything, or am I just always going to be your princess in the tower?"

"You'd make a terrible princess, first of all," Nico muttered. "You haven't the figure for a corset *at all*, and as for the rest, believe me, I would if I could—"

"But you can't," Gideon preemptively supplied, and grimaced. He glanced away before looking back, adding, "You know, I do worry about you, too. Your vanity aside, I do think you have plenty of problems without fixating on mine."

"Like what?" Nico scoffed, emphatically gesturing to his full head of hair.

"I… never mind." Gideon shrugged. "I'm just saying, this is a two-way street."

"Well, I know that, don't I? I would never devote myself so magnanimously to someone who failed to notice how interesting I am."

"And you are very devoted."

"As devoted as I am interesting," Nico confirmed, "so you see how we've reached a détente."

Gideon gave him a look like he'd swat him on the nose with a newspaper. So, the usual.

"Estás bien?" Gideon asked.

Yes, strangely, Nico was doing quite well indeed. He and Libby were very nearly getting on, arguing only about academic things ("It's one thing to stop time and another to try to move it around" was his take on the subject of her latest theory, but of course she'd had Arguments) and he and Reina were doing fine, and in general Nico ate well and didn't want to murder the people around him. (He could do without Callum and Tristan, but he'd suffered more distressing opposition before.)

Sure, he missed normal things, like the freedom to go places that weren't this house and also, sex—but he had a feeling it was best that he didn't sleep with anyone here. He'd probably let Parisa do whatever she wanted to him, and that was just not a good look for anyone.

"Je vais bien," Nico said conclusively.

"Good," said Gideon. "Then I'll let you get back to sleep."

"What, already?" Nico said, frowning. "But—"

Gideon snapped his fingers and Nico sat up in bed, gasping. He was back in his body, back in the Society's manor house. Back in the place he'd never technically left.

Beside him, his phone buzzed.

Go to sleep.

Nico rolled his eyes. Dumbass.

See u in my dreams, he joked.

His phone buzzed in his hand.

Always, Nicolás, always.

REINA

As far as Reina was concerned, she had already received extravagant returns on her investment in joining the Society. By the close of summer, only a quarter through their allotted year, she'd already wound up with riches. True, she had left very little behind, so perhaps the upfront sacrifice had been minimal, but the point remained that she was enjoying herself, in her way. The access she had to the Society's archives—to the reading room itself—was everything she had longed for. It was precisely what she had dreamed the Library of Alexandria would contain, and that was only at the surface level; the most elementary access to ancient scientific and magical thought. Having managed a mere three months' worth of research on the physics of force and space, Reina had already seen the grimoire by Circe *and* the lost oeuvre of both Democritus and Anaximander.

Which meant that her continuing motivation was, at an extreme minimum, only to not *lose* access. These were the ancient works in animism, naturalism, cosmology, but what would come from the medieval medeians, who could have only contributed in secret? What about the Enlightened? Would she see the works of both Isaac Newton and Morgan le Fay? Impossible to tell until she got there, which meant, quite inescapably, that she must.

Reina spent more of her free time in the reading room than the others of her initiate class, testing the limits of which texts she could access regardless of the subject at hand, which was why she was slightly more aware of who else came through the Society's doors on an occasional basis. There was one Society member in particular Reina recognized: Aiya Sato, a woman who sat on the board of directors for a massive tech conglomerate based out of Tokyo. Aiya was the youngest self-made female billionaire in the mortal economy and a celebrated medeian as well. Her face was a frequent feature, each of her feet securely settled in both worlds.

"Oh, you must be Miss Mori," said Aiya. The two of them were both waiting for the results of a summoning from elsewhere in the archives, and Aiya, a consummate networker, had struck up conversation in their native dialect. "Tell me, how was the installation?"

Reina gave few details, never having been one for conversation. Aiya, however, was very chatty.

"I suppose it must be very different with Atlas Blakely at the helm," she was saying, at which point Reina stopped her.

"Were you initiated long ago?" It seemed impossible. Aiya looked very young, hardly over thirty.

"No, not very. Only one class before this, in fact."

"You were in Dalton Ellery's initiation class?"

"You know Dalton?"

"He still researches here."

Aiya blinked, surprised.

"I would have thought Dalton would be the first to move on," she said, looking a bit unsettled. "I can't imagine what he'd still be doing here."

"Is it not customary for some members to stay on?"

"Oh, it is, but not Dalton," Aiya said, puzzled. "You know what his specialty is, don't you?"

Reina struggled to think of anything he'd said or done that seemed particularly noteworthy.

"No, I don't think so."

"Dalton's an animator," Aiya offered emphatically, as if that should mean something.

"He can bring things to life?"

"Things?" Aiya said, and chuckled to herself. "Yes."

Reina frowned. "Is he—"

"Oh no, not a necromancer," Aiya corrected quickly. "That is, he *can* do it, but he prefers the inanimate and metaphysical, or at least he did when I knew him. You know he's from somewhere in the woods of Denmark? Or perhaps the Netherlands. I can never remember when it comes to the Nordic countries, and he dropped the 'Von' I think—but the point is, there are legends in his village about a boy who can spirit entire forests to life, even the wind itself. He's modern mythology." She smiled faintly. "I can't imagine why he'd have agreed to stay behind, though I suppose he's quite young still. And he was always Atlas' favorite."

"I thought Atlas had been the Caretaker for some time," Reina said, recalling that Aiya's comments about Atlas had been the thing to spark her interest in the first place.

Aiya shook her head. "No, it was someone else for quite a while. An American, for nearly half a century. His portrait is here—" She waved a hand disinterestedly. "Somewhere."

"But you know Atlas?"

"He was essentially what Dalton is now, I believe. To tell you the truth, we didn't see our Caretaker much; Atlas did most of the work. Do you see him frequently?"

"Atlas?"

"Yes."

"Yes, almost daily."

"Hm. Odd." Aiya smiled. "Though I suppose he was always very enthusiastic."

"Is it common for researchers to take over the position of Caretaker?" Reina asked. Researcher appealed to her; Caretaker, with all its corresponding logistics and politics, did not. "Will Dalton be next?"

"Well, to be honest Dalton is precisely the sort of person who would want to be a Caretaker rather than a researcher, but no," Aiya said. "Atlas was a special case. Caretakers are usually selected by the Society's board of trustees from well outside its internal functions."

"Any reason for that?"

"Something about not drawing from a poisoned well, I'm sure. Not in Atlas' case, of course," she added as an afterthought. "He would have been a natural choice for it; he's so well-liked. Dalton, though… a mystery." A frown. "I would have thought him more likely to pursue something else."

Their books arrived side by side. Reina's was a duplicate of Leucippus' *The Great Cosmology*. Aiya's was untitled.

"Do you come back to the archives often?" Reina asked.

"No, not very," said Aiya. "Still, it is a valuable resource. There is much more than you can imagine contained within these walls."

She tucked the book into her bag, turning to Reina with a smile.

"Please do enjoy your time here," she said. "It's all worth it, truly. I had my doubts at first, but in the end, you really must believe me. I would do it over, easily."

"Was it difficult?" Reina asked. "The elimination process."

Briefly Aiya's smile faltered. "Initiation itself, you mean?"

"No, I mean... is it difficult," Reina attempted to phrase, "choosing which of your initiation class to eliminate?"

"Oh, yes. Unimaginably." The smile resumed. "But as I said, it is worth it. Have a wonderful day," Aiya said, offering Reina a polite, deferential bow and turning quickly away, the sound of her stiletto heels echoing through the reading room.

Reina had the sense that she had just had a very strange interaction, though she couldn't quite explain why. The sensation stuck with her for most of the following days, flitting in and out of her thoughts without deriving any solid conclusions.

Between working, sparring with Nico (Reina had felt he was the stronger hand-to-hand combatant and also, she needed the exercise), and reading for pleasure, there wasn't much time to concern herself with the irrelevant or the unimportant. She was quite content, really, though she had the vague sense that the others around her weren't.

MotherMotherMother, one of the ferns whined one day, fawning droopily over a shelf. *Mother there is troubletroubletrouble in the air, Mother pleaseplease do you see it?*

At first Reina assumed it was the unholy alliance burgeoning between Callum and Tristan. They had always been very likely to be found in each other's presence, seeing as a line had (intentionally or not) been drawn between the physical specialists and the others, but lately it was becoming less likely to see one without the other. They were frequently in furtive conversation; usually Callum leaning in while Tristan spoke. Reina had thought it was a good thing, or at least a perfectly fine thing, as it meant that Parisa would not have Tristan glued to her side. Gradually, though, it became more evident that Parisa was being punished for something; whether her punishment was coming from Tristan's hands or Callum's was relatively unclear.

The trouble with Tristan, and the reason Reina sometimes preferred Callum, was his meanness, his bite. It was sharp, brittle, and made unavoidably more malicious due to his...

Intelligence was an underwhelming word. Tristan was more than simply witty or clever or knowledgeable; he was *quick*, and always the first to see when something was wrong. At first Reina thought he was nitpicking, being contrary just for the sake of contradicting something, but it had become increasingly obvious that unless Tristan knew exactly what to correct, he didn't bother speaking. He had, for better or worse, a breathtaking apathy to almost everything, which only collided with derision when something was problematically out of place. Reina could not decide whether that intuitive cruelty was worse with Callum, who couldn't be bothered with any of their work, or with Parisa, who seemed to find herself above it.

Parisa's outward demeanor didn't change; not because she was suffering and trying to hide it, much to Reina's disappointment, but because she was distracted. She didn't seem to feel the loss of Tristan at all, and it wasn't until the drooping fern bemoaned the state of oxygen in the room that Reina identified the cause.

"There is a natural transition from space to time," said Dalton, who was standing beside Atlas, as he often was. "Most modern physicists, in fact, do not believe there is any distinction at all. Some do not even believe that time exists; at least, not in our fictionalized conception of it, where it can be traveled in some sort of linear way."

The reminder of Dalton Ellery's existence in the world brought Reina back to her conversation with Aiya, prompting her to think again of Aiya's confusion over Dalton's decision to return. In Reina's opinion, Dalton seemed a natural academic—the epitome of 'those who can't do, teach'—and yet Aiya had looked as though the prospect of such a thing was incomprehensible. The idea that Dalton might be withholding a powerful magical ability that had required more than two years' time to master was intriguing; even compelling.

And Reina, finally spotting the way Parisa's eyes fell on Dalton, was clearly not the only one compelled.

She supposed it explained a lot of things; why Parisa was often unaccounted for, for one thing, and why the loss of Tristan, Parisa's initial paramour of choice (or so it seemed) was not particularly bothersome to her. Immediately, Reina's conflict about whether Callum and Tristan were ganging up on Parisa vanished, leaving her with a sense of disappointment in its place.

Of course Parisa was plotting something. She wasn't a woman the same way Reina was a woman, or the way Libby was. She was a woman in the weaponized sense, the kind who would step on others to keep herself at the top, and from the looks of it, she was having no trouble getting what she wanted.

Even to Reina, the glance between Dalton and Parisa was intensely loaded. Whether something had happened between them already or not was unclear, but there was no doubt some version of it would be happening again soon.

"What are you doing?" Reina asked bluntly, cutting off Parisa's path through the house during one of their afternoons away from research. "What exactly is the point?"

Parisa's eyes slid to hers, irritated. "What?"

"Read my mind," Reina suggested facetiously. Parisa's glance in return was equally annoyed.

"Why should there be a point? He's attractive. I'm bored." As Reina suspected, Parisa had clearly read her thoughts already.

"You can't honestly think I'm that stupid," Reina said. "Nor do I think *you're* that stupid."

"Thank you, I think," Parisa said, bristling in her lofty way, "but is there any reason you oppose this, or are you just rejoicing in being obtuse?"

"I don't give a damn what you choose to do," Reina said. "But I don't like it when things don't make sense. I don't trust it, and I don't trust you."

Parisa sighed loudly. "Shouldn't you be off playing with one of the other children?"

It never stopped being outrageous how the older three looked down on Libby and Nico, though it was far more ridiculous when people speculated separating them; venturing, as Callum often muttered, that one was more bearable than the other. In Reina's mind, they were binary stars, trapped in each other's gravitational field and easily diminished without the other's opposing force. She wasn't at all surprised when she discovered one was right-handed (Nico) and the other left (Libby).

"Deny it all you like, but those two have already proven their value," Reina said. "What have you contributed so far?"

"What have *you?*" Parisa snapped. "You're an academic. You can be an academic with or without the Society."

Whereas Parisa was the oldest type of working woman in the book.

"Oh, very nice," Parisa said, hearing Reina's not-so-carefully concealed distaste. "You think that's what this is? I'm some sort of gold-digging succubus and now you're going to drag me before the magistrates?"

"'Succubus' is more flattering than the word I had in mind," said Reina. Parisa rolled her eyes.

"Look, I can see—even if you can't—that you think you ought to feel sorry for me. It's nice of you. And totally unnecessary." Parisa's mouth tightened. "Callum is not punishing me. He's trying to beat me, but he won't. And you might wonder who you should choose between us, but I can tell you right now: if you knew what I know, you'd choose me over him every time."

"Then why not tell us what you know?" Reina demanded, only half-believing her. "If you hate him so much."

"I don't hate him. I feel nothing toward him. And if you knew what was good for you, so would you," Parisa warned, as the potted Calathea in the corner shivered prophetically. "Now, are we done here?"

Yes. No. In a way, Reina had gotten exactly what she'd come for. Parisa was pursuing Dalton; confirmed. Parisa had something against Callum; confirmed. The 'why' of it all remained a bit distressing.

Unfortunately, Parisa could see as much.

"You know why you don't understand me?" Parisa answered Reina's thoughts, stepping closer to lower her voice. "Because you think you've figured me out. You think you've met me before, other versions of women like me, but you have no idea what I am. You think my looks are what make me? My ambitions? You can't begin to know the sum of my parts, and you can stare all you like, but you won't see a damn thing until I show you."

It would be too easy to argue. It would be precisely what she wanted.

Not that silence was any different; Parisa looked unduly satisfied.

"Don't envy me, Reina," she advised softly, turning to say it in Reina's ear. "Fear me."

Then she made her way down the corridor, disappearing from sight.

PARISA

SHE COULD ALWAYS TELL where he was in the house. For one thing, there were huge amounts of magic around him; knots of it, tangled, and they seemed to arise in bursts, like flames. For another, his thoughts were less guarded when he was working, owing to the fact that he typically worked alone. He was very often alone, unless he was walking the grounds with Atlas or instructing the six of them in some way, or if he were working with Society members who came in for special projects.

At night he slept very little; she could hear his thoughts buzzing, localizing around something she couldn't identify from far away, until she recognized the sound of something unmistakable.

Parisa.

Why sex? Because it was so easily emotionless, uncomplicated, primal. A straightforward return on baser urges. Because thoughts, however malformed or misshapen they might become in the heat of the act, could not be so readily protected during something so chemical, and they certainly did not disappear. Good sex was never mindless; it merely meant concentration was elsewhere, not gone. Parisa knew her craft well enough to know that, and thus, she knew she'd succeeded the first time she kissed him, slipping something in the latch of his thoughts so she'd always be invited in.

She'd kept her distance afterwards, but the summer had been long enough for him to wonder. He was thinking increasingly about her, and she'd already visualized him enough in private to know which places she wanted to touch first; where she planned to put her lips, her hands, her teeth. She had given him the thrill of her presence; leaning over when he gestured to something, filling his atmosphere with her perfume.

He knew the contents of her file, just like he knew the others. He knew her skill set, her history. Which meant that he knew the touch of her hand, brushing his when she passed him on the stairs or in the hall, was only the surface of an unimaginable depth. Once, she poured herself a glass and sat in his presence across the room, unmoving. Saying nothing. Bringing some champagne to her lips, letting it settle across the bed of her tongue. She had felt the vibration of his thoughts, the tension between them, which kept him from concentration. He read the same sentence eighteen times.

Tonight, he was alone in the reading room. To his credit, he didn't look very startled to see her, though he had the presence of mind not to reveal his relief.

"You shouldn't," he cautioned, leaning wearily back in his chair. He didn't specify whether he meant that she shouldn't be there or that she shouldn't come closer, but she was, so she did. He didn't argue, nor did he seem to give any indication he intended to. His mind was, at present, a sealed vault.

In her experience, that was hardly something he could maintain for long.

"You seem tired," Parisa said. She wandered closer, running her fingers over the wood of the table. She brushed the corners of his books, placing the tactility of her skin at the forefront of his mind. He closed his eyes when she slid her hand from his arm to his shoulder, letting it hover in place for a moment. They had touched countless times by then; innocently, but often enough that memory would do half the work for her. "Something wrong?"

"You shouldn't be here." She could see the skin of his forearms pebbling at the brevity of their contact. Not everything was a matter of telepathy.

"I thought there weren't rules?"

"I wouldn't call this a rule."

It was unfortunate that restraint looked so good on him. He was tense in all the right places, poised for a fight. "What would you call it?"

"Inadvisable." His eyes were still closed, so she slid the tips of her fingers up to his neck, floating them over the hollow of his throat. "Possibly wrong."

"Wrong?" Her fingertips danced below his collar, tracing his clavicle. "Don't tempt me."

He caught her hand in a sudden motion, circling her wrist with his fingers.

"Are you being careful, Parisa?"

She had the sense he wasn't talking about the here and now.

"Should I be?" she asked.

"You have enemies. You mustn't."

"Why not? I always have enemies. It's unavoidable."

"No. Not here. Not—" He broke off. "Find someone somewhere, Parisa. Don't waste your time on me; find someone in your initiation class, someone reliable. That or make yourself indispensable somehow."

"Why," she said with a laugh, "because you don't want me to leave?"

"Because I don't want you to—"

He broke off, eyes snapping open.

"What do you want from me?" he asked her quietly, and before she could open her mouth, he said, "I'll give it to you if it means you'll work harder at playing this game."

There it was again; the acrid sense of fear.

"Is it answers?" he pressed her. "Information? What is it? Why me?"

She slid out of his grip, stroking his hair from his temples.

"What makes you so sure I want something? Dalton." She had wanted to say his name, to test it out experimentally, so she did. She could see on his face how viscerally he suffered for it.

"You do. I know you do." He inhaled sharply. "Tell me what it is."

"What if I tell you I don't know?" she murmured, maneuvering from behind his chair to position herself against the table, leaning back on her palms. His hands seemed to levitate in a trance, moving of their own accord to find her hips. "Maybe you intrigue me. Maybe I like a puzzle."

"Play a game with someone else, then. Nico. Callum."

The mention of Callum's name gave her an involuntary bristle, and Dalton looked up, brows furrowed.

"What is it?"

"Nothing." The room was lit from above, but down here there was only the single desk lamp to cast illumination over Dalton's features. "I have no interest in Callum."

Dalton lips brushed the fabric of her dress; above her sternum, below the hollow of her throat. His eyes closed, then opened.

"I saw what he did, you know. I watched." Dalton gestured evasively around. "There are surveillance enchantments, wards everywhere, and I was watching the two of you at the time. I saw it."

"So you saw him kill her, then." The reminder nearly gave Parisa a shiver; or would have, if she were less responsible with her own control.

"No, Parisa."

Dalton reached up, touching her cheek; a single brush of his thumb, right over the bone.

"I saw her kill herself," he said softly, and though it was the worst time, surely the wrong one, Parisa instinctively pulled him closer. Impulsively, she wanted him in her grasp.

She had nursed his affinity for her, making him crave her like an addict. One drop and he would go too far. He gave in easily, readily; perilously, like madness. His hands clutched her hips and he set her roughly at the edge of the table, inciting a burst of heat.

"People can do unnatural things. Dark things, sometimes." He sounded hungry, ravenous, desperate. His lips brushed her neck and she sighed; something she'd done countless times before and would do countless times again. Still, it was different even when it was the same, and with him it was unprofessionally persuasive.

This was the magic of sex, the animation. Something coming alive inside her at his touch.

"Can't you strike a deal with the devil if it means getting what you want?" he whispered.

Her eyes fluttered shut and she thought of Callum.

Aren't you tired? All this work, all this running, none of it you can ever escape; I can feel it in you, around you. You feel nothing anymore, do you? Only erosion, fatigue, depletion. Your exhaustion is all you are.

Parisa shuddered and pulled Dalton closer, so that his pulse aligned with hers. Both were arrhythmic and unsteady.

What are you fighting for? Do you even know anymore? You can't leave this behind you. They will chase you, hunt you, follow you to the ends of the earth. You already know this, you know everything. How they will kill you a thousand different ways, bit by bit. Piece by piece. How they will destroy you, little by little, by robbing your life from you.

Her hands traveled over Dalton's spine, nails biting into the blades of his shoulders.

Your death will have to be at their hands, on their terms, not yours. They will have to kill you to keep themselves alive.

She felt him come closer to breaking, teetering on the edge.

You have a choice, you know. You have only one true choice in this life: live or die. It is your decision. It is the only thing no one else can take from you.

Dalton's lips, when they met hers, were spiced with something; brandy and abandon. She slid her fingers through his hair, reveling in his shiver that tugged her closer, like a reflex from a fall. She reached behind her, shoving the books aside; Dalton slid his hands under her dress, wrapping his hands around her thighs.

That gun you're pointing at us… Do you even know who we are? Do you know why you're here?

"Promise me," Dalton said. "Promise me you'll do something."

Turn the gun around.

"Dalton, I—"

Pull the trigger.

Parisa gasped, blood and madness coursing through her when he shoved the dress up her legs, drawing her closer. In her mind, she watched the assassin's death again, over and over. *Turn the gun around.* The smell of fire, a woman's blood spraying at her feet. *Pull the trigger.* Callum hadn't even lifted a finger. He'd barely drawn breath. *Turn the gun around.* He had looked that woman in the eye and convinced her to die. *Pull the trigger.* Her death had cost him nothing; not even a second thought.

Was that the kind of devil Dalton meant?

"I am not good," Dalton told her, rasping it into her mouth. "No one here is good. Knowledge is carnage. You can't have it without sacrifice."

She kissed him hard; he fumbled with her dress and dropped to his knees, tugging her hips towards him. She felt the hard edge of a book stabbing into the base of her spine, then the indelible sweetness of Dalton's mouth; his kiss, his tongue and his lips. Her back arched off the wood, accommodating her quiet sigh. Somewhere in Dalton's mind things were coming loose; a door was opening. She slid inside and sealed it shut behind her, tugging at the roots of his hair.

What was in here? Nothing much. Even now, even in his head, he was careful. She could only find fragments, remnants of things. Fear, still. Traces of guilt. He needed to come untied, come undone. She could pull a few strings and glimpse his insides, find the source of it, if she could set him on a path bound for destruction. She tugged him to his feet, hastily flaying open the zipper of his trousers. There wasn't a man alive who couldn't sink into her with the blankness, the blindness of ecstasy. Satisfaction was obstructive that way. She yanked at his hips, clawed into his spine, bit into the muscle of his shoulder. If they were caught like this, so be it. They'd be caught.

He had imagined this before; she could watch the evidence of it like a flipbook in his mind. He had already had her a hundred different times, a thousand ways, and that she could see them now was promising. There was a weakness in his defenses, and it was her. Poor thing, poor little academic, trying to study his books and keep her distance when really, he was fucking her on her hands and knees in the abscesses of his tired mind. Even this—taking her here, on the table covered with his notes—he had seen before: prophecy. It was like he had spirited this very vision to life.

They both gasped. He wanted the two of them close, her securely fastened in his arms, and so did she. From here she could taste the burning edges of his thoughts. He wasn't just afraid of something; he was afraid of everything. He hated this house, the memories in it. The memories themselves were knives, glinting in the light. They pricked her fingers, warning her away. *Turn the gun around. Pull the trigger.* There were demons in here; devils. *Can't you strike a deal with the devil if it means getting what you want?* There was boyhood in here too, juvenile and furious and small. Once, he had brought a dead sapling back to life, only to watch it wither away and die regardless.

The taste of him on her tongue, real and imagined, was burnt sugar, wild adoration, tender rage. Poor thing, poor desperate thing. Parisa recalled the thoughts in Reina's head, which the naturalist couldn't quite control; *Dalton is something, he's something important, he knows something we don't.*

I know that, you stupid girl, thought Parisa, and I never miss my mark.

"Dalton," she whispered, and this would have to be the first of many times, because as much as she would have liked to lose herself in him, that was the one thing she couldn't do right now. He wanted to tell her something; something he felt was desperately important, something he couldn't say aloud, and if she didn't take it now, he might lock it further inside him. He might seal it away. She said his name again, twisting it around her tongue, fitting it to the shape of her indelicate longings: "Dalton."

"Promise me," he said again, and he was ragged this time, wretched and weak, and she was struggling to maintain her thoughts. What did he want her to know? It was something powerful, almost explosive, but it warped and waned. He wanted her to know, but couldn't tell her. He wanted something, something he couldn't confess aloud; something that could devastate them both.

What was it? He was close now, closer, and she had her legs snaked around his waist, her arms locked around his neck. What did Callum have to do with it? *Turn the gun around. Pull the trigger.* The knot inside her tightened, swelling up and pulsing in her veins. Her heart was quick, too quick, her muscles straining. Dalton, Dalton, Dalton. He was as good as she wanted him to be; traumatically so. This was a torment she would seek again and again. The trauma of him was exquisite, the vice of his intimacy combative and honeyed. Oh, he was full of lies and secrets, only some of which he wanted to keep. What had he done, what did he know, what did he want?

She only saw it in the moment she let go, soundlessly crying out between his lips. So it was *her* intimacy he wanted, then; only when she was vulnerable, taking pleasure at his hands, could he forget what she was long enough to let her see. She came and his mind went with her, eruptive in relief.

It was a fragment of an idea; the fractured sliver of a larger truth. So small and so sharp she almost missed it, like a thorn on a root underfoot. She stumbled on it: he wanted her not to die. *Parisa.* The small voice she'd heard, it was part of that same thought, the same fear. *Parisa, don't go. Parisa, please, be safe.*

It slid into her mind like a splinter, a sliver. It was such a tiny thought, so innocuous, buried indiscreetly in a shallow grave of apprehension. He had countless worries, jagged little aches of thought, but this one was so easy to find she could trip over it, and she had.

She reached up, clawing a hand around his jaw.

"Who's going to kill me?"

She had asked quickly enough that there would be no time to prevent his answer. Already he was exposed for her—enraptured, undone. Remorse would set in later, maybe resentment, maybe regret. For now, though, he would never be more hers.

The words had left her lips for him to swallow; aptly, he gulped them down his throat.

"Everyone," he choked aloud, and then she understood it.

They will have to kill you to keep themselves alive.

V: TIME

TRISTAN

THERE WERE TIMES WHEN Tristan's natural inclination towards cynicism served some larger, more enduring toxicity; a vast, chronic paranoia. Any rare glimpses of optimism were swiftly dealt with, a virus his mind and body leapt to attack, and thus were ultimately beaten into submission. Feelings of hope? Cancerous. There was a constant sensation for Tristan that if things seemed to be going well, half of him was sure he was in the process of being mightily tricked.

Which was why the possibility he could do more with his magic than he had ever been aware of before joining the Society was so stupendously upsetting. Were there logical reasons this might be true? Yes, of course. All skills became more refined when they were properly trained, particularly magical ones, and since Tristan had been either unidentifiable or misclassified for the majority of his education, it followed that he might not have experienced the true spectrum of his abilities until now.

Did that stop him from wondering if he were slowly going mad instead? No, absolutely not, because the possibility remained that he and the others were being quietly but effectively poisoned. (It would be a complex con, but a good one. If this was how he died, so be it. Whoever planned it would obviously deserve their intended result.)

It was difficult to explain, which was why he hadn't. To anyone. He sensed he was letting off certain undercurrents of agitation, though, which was a suspicion Callum served to reinforce, always glancing over at Tristan reassuringly when he was feeling most unhinged. It was the conflict of the thing; the *tension*. The difficulty of seeing one thing and knowing another. Strangely, it had been something Libby said that did it; she had commented on Tristan's ability as if it were notable that he couldn't see her version of reality, and from there it had been a tumble of deduction.

It all hinged on a basic, undeniable fact: that what Tristan could see and what others could see were different. Other people, according to both Callum and Parisa, saw things based on their experiences, on what they were taught, on what they were told was true and what wasn't. Einstein himself (surprisingly not a medeian; almost certainly a witch, though) had said there was no reality at all except in the *relations* between systems. What everyone else was seeing—illusions, perceptions, interpretations—were not an objective form of reality at all, which meant that, conversely, what Tristan could see... *was*.

He could see, in some sense, reality itself: a true, unbiased state of it.

But the closer he looked, the fuzzier it got.

It was late one night when he couldn't sleep, sitting cross-legged in the center of his mattress to test his eyesight again. Of course, it wasn't his *actual* eyes he was using; it was some other form of looking, which he supposed was his magic, though he hadn't progressed to knowing what to call it yet. Mostly, if he concentrated, he could see little particles of things. Like dust, almost, where if he focused in on one thing, he could watch its trajectory, follow its path. Sometimes he could identify something from it; a mood, which took the form of a color, like an aurora, which was still somehow none of those things, because of course he hadn't honed the sense required to name it. He wasn't hearing or smelling reality, and he certainly wasn't tasting it. It was more like he was dismantling it layer by layer, observing it as a model instead.

It had the same logical progression most other things possessed. Take the fire that had been burning in the hearth, for instance. The weather was getting colder now, moving briskly into autumn, and so Tristan had fallen asleep to the light dancing, shadows falling, the smell of flames warming the air as flakes of ash floated down to the base of the wood. He knew it was fire because it looked like fire, smelled like fire. He knew from experience, from his personal history, that if he touched it, he would burn. He knew it was fire because he had been told it was fire; that much had been proven countless times.

But what if it wasn't?

That was the question Tristan was struggling with. Not about the fire specifically, but about everything else. A very existential crisis, really, that he no longer knew the difference between what was true, objectively, and what he merely *believed* to be true because it had been told to him that way. Was that what happened to everyone? The world had been flat once; it was believed to be flat, so in the collective consciousness it was, or had been, even if it wasn't.

Or was it?

It was giving Tristan such a monumental headache that he didn't even stop to question why someone would be knocking on his door at this hour. He simply waved a hand and summoned it open.

"What?" he said, Tristan-ly.

"Turn down the cataclysm, would you? It's the middle of the night," said Parisa, Parisa-ly. She, he noted, was fully dressed, if a bit... rumpled. He frowned at her, and she shut the door behind her, leaning against it.

"I obviously didn't wake you," Tristan commented in observation, wondering if she would take the bait and explain.

Unsurprisingly, she did not. "No, you didn't wake me. But as a general rule, you could stand to calm down," she said, and then stepped further into the room.

Moonlight fell on her from the window in a panel; just narrow enough that he could see the little furrow of concern in her brow. Each of Parisa's expressions were so artful they could hang in the Louvre, and not for the first time, Tristan wondered what on earth her parents must have looked like to achieve such outrageous genetic symmetry.

"Actually, my parents aren't particularly attractive," said Parisa blandly. "And my face isn't technically symmetrical." She paused, and then, "My breasts certainly aren't."

"I know." He hadn't specifically noticed, but it felt like the right thing to remind her; that he had been in a position to know, at least. Several positions. "And is that supposed to be self-deprecation? Or humility?"

"Neither. Beauty is nothing." She waved it away and stole towards him, settling herself on the edge of his bed. "Everyone's perception is flawed. They have standards drilled into them by cultural propaganda. Nothing anyone sees is real; only how they perceive it."

How very topical, Tristan thought grimly. Which might have been intentional on her part, though at the moment he didn't care to dwell on which of his thoughts she was or wasn't using.

"What is it?" he asked her. "Clearly something's bothering you."

"I've just discovered something. I think." She toyed with her fingers, tapping them mindlessly in her lap. "I'm not sure yet whether it will be in your best interest to tell you."

"In *my* best interest?"

"Well, you're right, it wouldn't be in yours. You wouldn't take it well at all." She glanced at him, eyes narrowing. "No, I can't tell you," she determined after a moment. "But regrettably, I do want you to trust me."

"Perhaps you're unfamiliar with the concept of trust," Tristan pointed out, assuming that she almost certainly was, "but it is very rarely based on nothing. Correct me if I'm wrong, but you're suggesting that you'd like me to blindly trust your judgment despite having multiple things you're unwilling to tell me?"

"I know the inside of your head, Tristan," Parisa reminded him, the same way he'd commented on his intimacy with her, albeit more confidently. She had actually taken stock of his details, whereas he, with her, had been mostly preoccupied. "You wouldn't take it well."

"Ah, wonderful," Tristan muttered. "You even condescend beautifully."

When she shifted towards him on the bed he caught a hint of her perfume, only it wasn't hers entirely. Parisa had a signature scent, a spectrum of florals. At the moment, there were traces of cologne, musks of something masculine and smoky, which, to Eden's credit, Tristan's former fiancée had always been very careful to prevent. Eden Wessex might not have known that Tristan could see through her illusions, but she was a very dutiful adulterer. He had considered it—still considered it, in fact—to be one of her primary strengths.

"This Society," Parisa said, jolting him back to the point. "It's not what I thought. They're telling us at least one lie."

The restless feeling of resistance bristled again, rearing up in protest. Again, the usual torment: Tristan wanted to believe the Society was giving him something he could not have gotten otherwise. He was suspicious of what that something was. Now, Parisa was tipping the scales once again, feeding his inexhaustible doubt.

"I don't think there's anything to be done about it," Parisa remarked curtly. "Not yet. But I think it's worth knowing who we work for."

Tristan frowned. "Atlas, you mean?"

"Or is it?" she posed, pursing her lips. "There are some answers I need to dig up, I think, but in the meantime, you need to be careful."

He hated to continuously express his bewilderment, but there was nothing for it.

"Me?"

"Callum is influencing you," said Parisa. "I don't know if he's doing it magically or otherwise, but he wants something from you. He's willing to blind you to accomplish it."

"I'm not a damsel, Parisa. I don't need rescuing."

That, much to the dismay of his vanity, only served to amuse her. "Actually, I think you're precisely a damsel, Tristan." She reached out, touching his cheek. "I know you don't trust Callum," she said, murmuring it. "I think that's precisely what he's using against you. He's presenting you with his reality, thinking his candor will appeal to you, but you're not listening, are you, Tristan? You're not listening to what he really is, even when he says it to your face."

Tristan stiffened. "If I don't trust him, then what does it matter?"

"Because even if you don't trust him, you *believe* him. He is influencing your perception by confirming everything you already believe to be true. He's planting things in you, and I worry."

Her thumb stroked his jaw, floating over his lips. "I worry," she said again, quieter.

Tristan's immediate reflex was to mistrust Parisa's softness.

"What did he do?" he asked her. "What could have possibly upset you so much?"

"It didn't upset me. It unsettled me." She pulled away. "And if you really must know, he convinced the illusionist to kill herself."

Tristan frowned. "So?"

"So, don't you see? His weapon is *us*. Our beliefs, our weaknesses, he can turn them against us." From the faint light through the window, Tristan could see the tightening of her mouth. "He finds the monsters we keep locked away and sets them loose, so why would I ever want him to see mine?"

"Fine," Tristan permitted evasively, "but couldn't you do the same? You can read minds. Should we regard you with the same suspicion?"

Parisa rose agitatedly to her feet.

"There is a difference between what we are capable of and how we choose to use it," she snapped.

"Maybe so, but if you want me to trust you, you'll have to give me a reason," Tristan pointed out. "Otherwise, how are you any different from

Callum?"

She gave him a glare so sharp he could feel it, cutting himself on its edge.

"Callum," she said, "doesn't need you, Tristan. He wants you. You should ask yourself why that is."

Then she slipped out of his room and did not speak to him again for four days.

Not that it bothered him too immensely. The silence of temperamental women was a very common feature in his life, and anyway, he did not know what to make of her... warning? Threat? Unclear what she wanted, though he was privately pleased she hadn't gotten it. He hated giving people what they wanted, especially if it was unintentionally done.

He was also extremely distracted. They were covering the many theories about time, beginning with attempts at time travel by witches in the Middle Ages; a conversation which also included, for some reason, the prominent European attempts at extending the mortal lifetime. In Tristan's mind, the concept of time should have been covered in the physical magics, not historical or alchemical failures. Perhaps it was just an excuse to give them more access to another magical period in history.

He was beginning to steal away privately more and more, pursuing his own research in the ancient texts they'd been reading about the construction of the universe before doubling back to the mysteries he felt unsolved. Why hadn't their wormhole successfully traveled through time? Did it really require *more* magic to influence time, or had they simply not gone about it correctly? He tried to draw it once, scribbling it in his notes while Dalton droned on about Magellan and the Fountain of Youth, but nothing came of it.

Nothing, that is, until Libby sought him out.

It wasn't clear at first that she'd been intentionally looking for him. He had assumed she merely stumbled on him in the painted room after dinner and would therefore hastily leave. It became apparent, however, that the stumbling was really just another side effect of her natural presence, and so he glanced up expectantly.

"I had a thought," she said.

He waited.

"Well, Varona and I both had a thought. I mean, I *thought* of it," Libby clarified hurriedly, "but I needed him to test it, and, well, I don't know if you're willing to hear it, but I noticed your drawing the other day and—not that I was prying, I just… oh god, sorry," she said, mangling what might have been a blissful end to that sentence. "I didn't mean t- Well, the thing is—"

"Spit it out, Rhodes," said Tristan. He had just been on the verge of something, maybe. (Probably not, his brain reminded him. Wishful thinking.) "I haven't got all day."

"Right, well, alright." Her cheeks burned furiously, but she came closer. "Can you… try something with me?"

He gave her a look intended to express that he would consider it, if—*and only if*—it meant she would get to it and leave him alone.

"Right," she said, clearing her throat. "Watch this."

She plucked a small rubber ball from her pocket and tossed it, letting it bounce three times before freezing it in place.

"Now watch while I reverse it," she said.

It bounced three times backwards and landed snugly in her hand.

"Okay," Tristan said. "And?"

"I have a theory," Libby said, "that it looked different to you than it did to me. To me, I did the exact same thing forwards and backwards. I could have gone ten seconds back in time and noticed nothing different from before I threw the ball. But you," she said, trailing off, and waited.

Tristan thought about it.

"Do it again," he said, and her face immediately relaxed. Relief, he suspected, that he might have actually noticed something, or was at least giving her the opportunity to *make* him notice.

She tossed the ball again, letting it bounce three times, and froze it.

Then she summoned it back, same as before, and caught it in her hand.

"See something?" she said.

Yes. Not something he could explain, but there was some element out of place. A rapid motion around the ball, barely visible.

"What did you expect me to see?" he asked her.

"Heat," she said, breath quickening. Clearly she was excited; childishly so. "The thing is," bubbled from her lips, "according to everything I've read, it's possible time is measurably no different from gravity. Things moving up and down? Gravity. Things moving backward and forward? Force, of course, depending on the dimension—but also, in some respect, *time*. If the clocks had been stopped, if nothing had changed, there would be no physical evidence that I hadn't reversed time itself when I reversed the ball's motion. The only real way you could know that we *haven't* traveled in time—aside from trusting your understanding that we haven't," she provided as a caveat, gesturing around the room to her experiment, "is that heat was produced by the ball hitting the ground, and heat can't be lost. Thermal energy bouncing the ball has to go somewhere, so as long as that hasn't vanished, then we haven't moved back in time."

"Okay," Tristan said slowly, "and?"

"And—"

She stopped.

"And... nothing," she concluded, deflating a little. "I just thought—" She broke off again, faltering. "Well, if you can see heat, you could also see time, don't you think?" she said, nudging her fringe aside. "If what you're seeing is even more specific—electrons or something, or quanta itself—then the next step is to manipulate it. I've been thinking about it for ages," she informed him, again becoming Studious Libby, who temporarily lost her anxious ticks. "With the illusions, with that medeian that I—"

She broke off on the word *killed*, clearing her throat.

"You told me what you saw," she clarified, "and I used that information to change my surroundings. So, if you told me what you saw when it came to time—"

"You could use it. Change it." Tristan chewed the thought for a moment. "Manipulate it?"

"I guess it depends on what you were seeing," Libby said carefully, "but I think, if I'm right about what you can do, that if you could identify the physical structure of time, then yes. We could maneuver it somehow." She was breathless with exhilaration; the thrill of a problem nearly solved.

"Though, if you're busy," she amended with a floundering blink, "we could always try it another t-"

"Rhodes, shut up," said Tristan. "Come here."

She was clearly so pleased that she didn't bother opposing his tone, instead bounding over to sit beside him. He stopped her and rose to his feet, gesturing her into his chair.

"You sit," he said. "I'll stand behind you."

She slid into his seat and nodded as he concentrated once again.

Whatever this particular magic was, when he focused it hard enough, things became grainy. When he did the equivalent of squinting, it was like the zooming of a microscopic lens. Things were blurrier at the edges, but he could see things, smaller and smaller. Layers upon layers, motion growing more rapid the closer he got.

"When you manipulate gravity," he said. "What does it feel like?"

Libby closed her eyes, holding out a hand.

With the flat of her palm, she pushed down. The pressure nearly dragged Tristan to his knees.

"Like a wave," she explained belatedly. "Like things are floating in an invisible current."

Tristan conjured his understanding of linear time, turning it over in his mind. Where might the misconceptions have been? That it was linear, he supposed. That it moved forward and backward. That it was ordered. That it was irrelevant to concepts like heat.

There it was; when he dismissed his expectations, he found it. It was the only thing moving at an identifiably constant pace, though it varied from different levels throughout the room. Faster higher up, slower lower down. Not the same constancy of the clock on the wall, which was close to the ceiling's apex, but near Libby, it was regular. As regular as a pulse. He could see it, or feel it—or however he was experiencing it—at what he presumed to be sixty beats per minute right where Libby's hair brushed the tops of her shoulders, flipping girlishly out. It was getting long; it had grown at least an inch since they'd arrived.

Tristan reached forward, resting a hand on Libby's arm, and started tapping the pattern of the motion.

"Is there something that feels like that in this room?" he asked her.

She closed her eyes again, frowning. Then she reached for his hand, pulling it just below her clavicle, resting it on her breastbone and jarring him slightly out of his rhythm, his fingers brushing bare skin.

"Sorry," she said. "Need it somewhere I can feel it."

Right. It would ricochet through her chest that way.

Tristan located the precise beat he was looking for and tapped the pattern again, waiting. For another ten, twenty beats, he tapped it out like a metronome, and by the time he reached forty beats or so, Libby's eyes shot open.

"I found it," she said, and then, with a motion of her hand, the pattern Tristan had been watching went still.

To his disbelief, *everything* went still.

The clock on the wall had stopped. Tristan himself, the motion of his breath, had been suspended, and he suspected the blood in his veins had been, too. Nothing moved, though he could look around somehow, or feel around, experiencing himself newly within the space he'd taken up. His hand was still resting on Libby's chest, his thumb below the collar of her shirt, no longer tapping. She had the strangest look on her face; nearly a smile, but somehow louder. It burned with resilience, with triumph, and then he processed it: she had done this with intention, with skill.

With his help, Libby Rhodes had *stopped time*.

She blinked and everything fell back into place, careening into motion. It had been nothing more than a lag, a momentary resistance that had been nearly unidentifiable, but even so, Tristan could see the sweat on her brow. It had not cost her nothing.

She rose to her feet too quickly, spinning to face him in her fervor, and nearly collapsed. He caught her with one arm around her ribs and she struggled upright, grasping his shoulders for leverage.

"I could do more if I had Nico," she said, staring at nothing. At his chest, but also at nothing; staring down the barrel of her thoughts, rapidly calculating something. How to do it again, or do more, or do better. "I couldn't hold it alone, but if I had him, or maybe Reina... and you showed me how to move it first, then maybe we could—Well, maybe if I'd just... drat, I should have—"

"Rhodes," Tristan sighed. "Listen—"

"Well, I don't know what we could do, to be honest," she confessed worriedly. "If this is how time moves, then everything is a bit different, isn't it? If time is a force that can be measured like any other—"

"Rhodes, listen—"

"—at very least we could *model* it, couldn't we? I mean, if you can see it, then—"

"Rhodes, for fuck's sake!"

She looked up, startled, to find Tristan staring (exasperatedly, he assumed) down at her.

"Thank you," he said, and then exhaled, irritated. "Jesus, fuck. I just wanted to say thank you."

That abysmal fringe of hers was getting outrageously long; it had fallen into her eyes. She brushed it away with one hand, lowering her chin slightly.

"You're welcome," she said, her voice soft.

The silence that followed, a rarity indeed, was filled with things Tristan generally hated. Floaty, swollen things, like gratitude, because now he understood that he hadn't imagined any of it; she had proven that for him. She had proven that whether what he had was blindness or madness, it could still be put to use somehow. True, he might be little more than a lens through which to view things, but he was a scope, a necessity. Without him she could not see it. Without him, she could not *do* it.

What a relief it was, being a cog in something that actually turned for once.

"What's this?" came a voice behind them, and Tristan immediately released her, taking a jarring step back. "Odd," remarked Callum, sauntering into the room as Libby felt for the chair behind her, rapidly flustered. "Doing homework, children?"

Tristan said nothing.

"I should go," Libby mumbled in reply, and dropped her chin, hurrying to the door.

Callum watched her leave, half-laughing to himself.

"Can you imagine? Being like that. Born with all that power and still not good enough, still desperate to flee the room. Sad, if you think about it." Callum pulled out one of the free chairs, sinking into it. "Someone really ought to take that power away from her and put it to good use."

Explaining what she had just done was unlikely to change Callum's mind. If anything, it only served to prove his point. "At least she's relentless," said Tristan.

"Her? She's entirely relenting, Caine." Callum was still smiling; his opinion of Libby, however low it happened to be, wasn't nearly enough to stifle his mood. "Have any interest?"

"In her? Not remotely." Tristan slid into the chair where Libby had been. "But I can certainly see why she was chosen for this."

"I rather can't believe that's still a thing you question," remarked Callum. "What does the 'why' really matter? Aside from your personal taste for intrigue, that is."

Tristan slid a glance at him. "Don't you wonder?"

"No." Callum shrugged. "The Society has its reasons for choosing us.

What matters is my choices. Why play their game," he added, smile glinting again, "when I can play my own?"

Callum doesn't need you. He wants *you,* Parisa's voice reminded Tristan. *You should ask yourself why that is.*

"There's that doubt again," Callum said, ostensibly delighted by whatever he could read from Tristan. "It's so refreshing, really. Everyone else has this irritating frequency, full of jolts and jerks, but then there's you. A steady, pleasant base."

"And that's a good thing?"

"It's like meditation." Callum closed his eyes, sinking lower in the chair. He inhaled deeply, and then, slowly, opened them. "Your vibes," he drawled facetiously, "are absolutely resplendent."

Tristan rolled his eyes. "Want a drink?" he said. "Could use one."

Callum rose to his feet with a nod. "What are we celebrating?"

"Our fragile mortality," Tristan said. "The inevitability that we will descend into chaos and dust."

"Grim," Callum offered appreciatively, closing a hand around Tristan's shoulder. "Try not to tell Rhodes that or she'll start decaying all over the place."

Because he could not resist, Tristan asked, "What if she's tougher than you think she is?"

Callum shrugged, dismissive.

"I'm just curious," Tristan clarified, "whether that would please you or send you into a spiral of existential despair."

"Me? I never despair," said Callum. "I am only ever patently unsurprised."

Not for the first time, Tristan considered how the ability to estimate people to the precise degree of what they were must be a dangerous quality to have. The gift of understanding a person's reality, both their lightness and darkness, without the flaws of perception to blur their edges or lend meaning to their existence was... unsettling.

A blessing, or a curse.

"And if I disappoint you?" Tristan prompted.

"You disappoint me all the time, Caine. It's why I'm so very fond of you," Callum mused, beckoning Tristan toward the library and its finer bottles of vintage scotch.

NICO

IT STOOD TO REASON, given Eilif's appearance in his bathroom sink, that the wards had a hole of some kind. Not that magic was so easily simplified to concrete matters of holes or solidity or otherwise, but for all intents and purposes, the wards intended to keep people out of the Society must have been faulty on the basis of precisely that: they were intended for *people*.

The library's archives, at least, had seen fit to provide Nico with something of a primer on creatures and their respective magics, for which he had required Reina's knowledge of runes and antiquated linguistics to fully grasp. There had been no recent treatises on the subject, owing first to hunting and then to the (not-dissimilar) prospect of academic study that was hardly distinct from captivity. The practice of "conservation" where it came to magical species had become so mistrusted among the creatures themselves that, according to Gideon, most had either disappeared or chosen to align themselves—as his mother had—with fairly dubious magical sources.

"My father is either dead or hiding," Gideon had explained to Nico once, "not that it matters which, as I don't expect to ever hear from him. I'm quite sure I have siblings all over the world, belonging to any variety of species. Doubtless he acknowledges none."

Gideon had said it in a factual manner at the time, wholly unemotional about the prospect, and Nico hadn't bothered to question him any further. Gideon already had plenty of psychological trauma without adding a father fixation to the mix, so if anything, the absence of Gideon's father was probably a blessing.

Nico's single concern was, as always, keeping Gideon's mother out. Once the Society's perimeter was secured, he could return his attention to the study of Gideon's remaining fractures without fearing he'd become responsible for a massive security breach.

Despite trusting Reina to accurately translate runes for him as he'd requested, Nico had hoped not to have to explain the reasons for his little foray into rare extracurricular study. True to form, Reina required little explanation.

"As far as I can tell, magic is magic," she said, hardly looking up from where she scanned the page in the reading room. She sat with her legs curled under herself on the chair, her entire frame defensively enveloping the book as if she feared someone might suddenly snatch it from her hand. "Most creatures' genetics are no different from a human's than an ape's. Just a matter of evolutionary distinctions, that's all."

"Mutations?"

She glanced up, eyes slightly narrowed. "Genetic, you mean?"

Nico bristled at the implication that he might have meant aberrations. "Of course," he said, perhaps more passionately than necessary.

"No need to be brutish," she remarked, expressionless. Then she returned her attention to the page. "The difference in magical ability appears to lie in the customary form of usage," she said, eyes roving over the page with only the slightest break in motion; a sidelong glance to what Nico guessed was a back-talking plant somewhere in the corridor. "That's true," she conceded grumpily, presumably to the plant, though she slid her attention upward to fix Nico with a studious look of contemplation.

"It's smaller," she said.

He frowned. "What is?"

"The—" She paused, cursing quietly under her breath, or so he assumed. "Output," she eventually produced from somewhere in her multilingual lexicon. "Usage, power, whatever the word is. Creatures produce less, or rather, waste less."

"Waste?"

"Ask Tristan," she said.

"Ask Tristan what?"

Nico spun at the sound of Libby's voice to find her lingering in the doorway, hesitantly half-in, half-out.

"Nothing," said Nico, at the same moment Reina said, "How much magic humans produce."

"Humans," Libby echoed, flitting inside with a flare of interest. "As opposed to what?"

"*Nothing*," Nico repeated, more emphatically this time as Reina returned her attention to the book, muttering an unblinking, "Creatures."

Libby turned to look at Nico, expectant. "Creatures, Varona, really?"

Her brow was arched beneath her mass of fringe, which he positively loathed. It was one thing for her to be nosy, and another thing entirely for her to regard him with so much palpable doubt.

Just what did she expect him of bollocking up this time?

"I wanted to be certain of something," he supplied evasively, with the tone of blistering impatience he knew she would find repellant. There was always a chance she'd leave if he pestered her enough.

"Okay, and what does Tristan have to do with it?"

Evidently her curiosity had been all too successfully piqued.

"I haven't the slightest idea," Nico retorted, though much to his dismay, that was enough to make Reina finally remember to explain herself.

"Tristan can see magic being used," she said from behind her curtain of black hair.

"How do you know that?" asked Libby, which to Nico's ear sounded unnecessarily accusing, as if she resentfully suspected Reina and Tristan of having some sort of weekly brunch wherein they discussed their private lives and secret wishes.

"Observation," Reina replied, which Nico could have told Libby was the obvious answer. Reina spoke little and saw much, though what Nico liked most about her was that she considered most of what she viewed to be substantially unimportant, and therefore not worth discussion.

Unlike Libby, who felt precisely the opposite.

"Tristan," Reina continued, "can see magic in use. As I was explaining," she said, cutting a demonstrative glance to Nico to indicate a return to her previous subject, "creatures have a more refined use of their own magic. They channel it better, more efficiently. It's—" Another pause for the lexicon. "Thinner. Narrow. Spun like thread, not like—" Another pause. "Fumes."

"I suppose Tristan has used the word 'leak' to describe magic before," Libby murmured thoughtfully to herself. "Though we could probably ask him to explain it more fully."

The idea of asking Tristan Caine for anything that was not a scowl or muttered clip of sarcasm was enough to sever what remained of Nico's limited patience.

"No," he snapped, and would certainly have summoned the book from Reina's grasp and stormed out if not for the way she shielded it with her entire body. "This isn't about you, Rhodes."

She bristled. "What's it about, then?"

"Nothing. Certainly nothing I need you for."

Libby's eyes narrowed, and Reina curled more determinedly around the book, tacitly assuring them both that she had no interest in what would follow and would certainly be of no help.

Nico, who had fought often enough with Libby Rhodes to know when a larger explosion was impending, abandoned the matter of the book and spun to take the stairs, irritated. He had done well enough for himself without a library's help before. He would simply see to the matter of the wards without further discussion.

Or not. Behind him, Libby's unshakable footsteps were dogged and crisp.

"Varona, if you're planning to do something stupid—"

"First of all," Nico said, spinning curtly to address her as she stumbled into his back, "if I were to elect to do something stupid, I would not require your opinion on the matter. Secondly—"

"You can't just run around playing with things unnecessarily just because you're bored," Libby retorted, sounding matronly and exhausted. As if she were his mother or his keeper, which she resolutely was not. "What if you're needed for something?"

"For what?"

"I don't know. Something." She glared at him, exasperated. "Perhaps it stands to reason, Varona, that you shouldn't do stupid things simply because they're stupid. Or does that somehow not compute?"

"If I'm bored, *you're* certainly bored," Nico offered in retaliatory accusation. "Just because you won't admit it doesn't make it any less true. And following me around to see what I do wrong gives you a bit of a thrill, doesn't it?"

"I," Libby replied hotly, "am not following you around. I'm putting myself to good use. I'm using the research we're learning and applying it where I can, which is precisely what you should be doing."

"Oh, truly? How magnificent for you. How scholarly you are," Nico gushed in plaintive mockery, reaching out to pet her head. "That's a good girl, Rhodes—"

She swatted his hand away, the air around them crackling with the sparks of her intemperance. "Just tell me what you're up to, Varona. We could go about it faster if you just asked me for—"

"For what? For help?"

She fell silent.

"Would you have asked *me* for help, Rhodes?" Nico countered, aware how thinly skeptical his voice sounded. "We aren't different people now just because we've come to a single agreement. Or have you forgotten we're still competing?"

He regretted it the moment he said it, as it wasn't what he meant. He hardly needed to make an enemy of Libby, and certainly did not aspire to waste time on any rivalries beyond what was necessary for initiation. He did, however, need her to stay out of his private business, and in this case, he very much did *not* want to hear the inevitable lecture on how he'd inadvertently allowed a misbehaving mermaid into the house. He doubted it would be brief, and he knew it would be followed extensively with questions, none of which he planned to answer.

"So that's your idea of an alliance, then." Libby's voice was flat with anger.

No, not anger. Something more bitter, less malicious than that.

Brittle sadness.

"Let's not pretend this is something it isn't," Nico said, because the damage had already been done, and it wasn't as if she'd ever been known to forgive him. "We're not friends, Rhodes. We never have been, we never will be—*and*," he added, giving in to a burst of frustration that mixed unrelentingly with guilt, "since I can't simply *ask* you to leave me alone—"

She spun away, the last glimpse of her expression one of hollow disappointment. Nico watched her dismount the stairs, taking a sharp turn to disappear from sight as a little echo of Gideon suddenly tutted softly in his head: *Are you being nice to Rhodes?*

No, of course not. Because there wasn't a person in the world who could make him feel less adequate simply by existing, and besides. He had wards to fix.

Nico slid irascibly up the remainder of the stairs, taking a turn at the gallery in the opposite direction of the painted room and bedrooms. He would need privacy to work uninterrupted, which meant the ground floor was not an option, and upstairs contained plenty of unnecessary stages for empty grandeur where no one ever went. He closed himself into one of the gilded drawing rooms (it had long ago stopped being a place for aristocratic dances or whatever purpose the British required rooms to draw) and set himself to the task of mindful pacing, once again engaging the twitchy need for motion he habitually found expelling from his limbs.

Ultimately the wards were gridlike, ordered, and therefore easily surveyed for something out of place, which at first glance was nothing. The six of them had designed the structure of the security system in a spherical globe, within which a tightly woven fabric of magical defenses cloaked the Society and its archives. Physical entry would be easily repelled by the shell of altered forces surrounding the house, while intangible magical entry was readily sensed by the internal system of woven, fluid sentience.

How, then, had Eilif managed to slip them in order to wind up in his sink? Probably best to check the pipes.

Nico closed his eyes with a grimace and examined the house's plumbing, feeling at the edges for the warps of magic he recognized as his own, or possibly Libby's. In terms of magical fingerprints, their signatures were almost identical; a consequence of similar training, perhaps. Nico felt another bristle of guilt or irritation or allergies and shrugged it away, trying to focus more, or possibly less. Intuitively it didn't matter which specific element of magic belonged to him. Libby's or his own, it would respond just as obediently, mastered by the skill regardless of the hand that cast it.

Sure enough, upon closer inspection there were numerous bubbles and blemishes, little bastardizations of security from what Nico could feel around the pipes and then, upon further scrutiny, between the layers of insulation in the walls. Not enough to prevent a *person* from emerging corporeally through the cracks—compression was a difficult task, requiring enough energy to set off the house's internal sensory wards before any conceivable success of entry—but for Eilif, or for some other creature attempting entry? Possibly, if what Reina said about refinement of power was true. It wasn't as if air ducts or other methods of entry had never been neglected before, and in this case, Nico could feel the way the house's infrastructure strained beneath their wards, corroded by magic and hard water and whatever else eroded metal over time. He wasn't much of a mechanic, but perhaps that was precisely the problem. The medeians elected for the Society were academicians, not tradesmen, and they certainly weren't chosen for their efficiency at knowing when an old house required maintenance. Sentient though it may have been at times, it was still a physical structure, and Nico's element was physicality. Perhaps this was always meant to be his (or Libby's) responsibility to maintain.

Magic was no different from rot, corrosion, temperature change, overuse. Contractions and expansions and chipping and peeling and movements of time and space. Funny how laughably simple everything was in the end, even when it belonged to the immeasurable, or the invaluable. Nico would simply have to repair the areas where the wards were weakened, reinforcing them with custom bandages where they may have waned and warped.

Whether his remedies would hold would be a matter of adhesion, which was… slightly difficult, but hardly impossible. Nico would simply bend back into shape what he could and then cover up what he could not.

Distantly Nico was aware he was considering something Gideon would deem "irresponsible"—or possibly it was Libby calling it that, and Gideon was standing somewhere over her shoulder in Nico's head, grimacing in agreement. Max would not care either way, which Nico foggily pieced together was something he positively adored about Reina. He could go and grab her now, he thought, considering that the extra burst of energy he seemed to consensually borrow from her might be wise to have at present, but at the disastrous implication he might have been behaving unwisely ("Something stupid," Libby irked snottily in his head) he promptly nudged the idea away, flicking it aside with a twitch of dismissal.

So what if he overexerted himself, just this once? His power was renewable, easily replenished. He would be sore for a night or three and then the discomfort would pass, and no one would have to know the mistake he'd made initially by overlooking it. If Libby lorded it over him that he was more tired than usual, so be it. It wasn't as if he was much use in the realm of time, anyway. He had no interest in fountains, youthful or otherwise.

The bristle of recalling his current uselessness was enough to secure Nico's decision. He disliked the anxiety of listlessness, which was as constant to him as Libby's unrelenting undercurrent of fear. Fear of what? Failure, probably. She was the sort of perfectionist who was so desperately frightened of being any degree of inadequate that, on occasion, the effort of trying at all was enough to paralyze her with doubt. Nico, meanwhile, never considered failure an option, and whether that was ultimately to his detriment, at least it did not restrain him.

If Libby made the mistake of thinking herself too small, then Nico would gladly consider himself too vast by contrast. If anything, the opportunity to swell beyond the ceiling of his existing powers ignited him. Why not reach further, for things beyond the limits of his current grasp? Even when the options were to reach the sun or collide flaming with the sea, safety was a uselessness Nico de Varona couldn't abide.

So he started with the easiest tasks: unraveling clusters that had formed around the little gapings of the house. Magic was then thinner at the points of disentanglement, so he reinforced them with his own, sealing them until power flowed smoothly instead of being sucked up into little vacuums of inefficiency. It was a mix of push and pull, easing the entropy of decay into orderly avenues of traffic. The house itself resisted, straining a little, and sweat dripped in thin rivulets down the notches of Nico's spine. His neck ached a little from a muscular knot he'd hardly noticed before, but which throbbed now with discomfort and strain. Evidence, he surmised belatedly, of his weeks of physical misuse while working with space. It wouldn't be the first time he would be instructed (or berated) to stretch.

He ignored the pins and needles in the nerves that pricked up the length of his neck, shoving aside the pinch that reverberated upwards, thudding, to his head. A headache; marvelous. Possibly he was dehydrated, too. But stopping now would mean having to start up again later, and Nico loathed a task unfinished. Call it hyper-focus, but his fixations were what they were.

Finding no further bird-nests or clumps, Nico set himself to the task of metallurgy, purifying the toxicities that were the result of erosion over time. Briefly he became aware of something nagging at his memory, an old half-attended lecture; *magic cannot be produced from nothing much as the case with energy there is no difference Mr de Varona would you be so kind as to lend us your attention please*, and then there was an echo of laughter as Nico must have replied irreverently and yes, fine, this unit of study belonged to the principles of time, didn't it? The inconvenience of knowing his mind had tucked away things for future use, which were in fact too late, because the truth of the matter—that Nico was a mere human currently trying to power the regeneration of a physical structure vastly more sizable than himself—was hardly helpful now that he'd started. He felt the rumble of the ground beneath him; something else slipping out from his control. He may have miscalculated the velocity at which this house would drain him, greedily suckling at what he had intended to carefully measure out. He'd cut himself open too widely, bleeding magic without being able to keep pace or cauterize the wound.

Hm. What to do, at this point? *Keep going* was the only answer Nico had ever known. Failure, stopping, ceasing to be or to do was never an option. He gritted his teeth, shivering with a chill or a shudder of power that left him like an expulsive, painful sneeze. Ouch, fuck, bless you, the sort of burst that could ultimately break a rib or burst a blood vessel, which most people were not aware a sneeze could do. Funny how that worked; the innocent fragility of being human. There were so many ways to break and so few of them heroic or noble.

At least Libby could use his eulogy as a posthumous lecture, or so he assumed. "Nicolás Ferrer de Varona was an idiot," she would say, "an idiot who never believed he had limits despite being heartily assured so by me, and did you know it was possible to die from overexertion? *He* knew, of course, because I told him so plenty of times, but, surprise surprise, he never listened—"

"Varona." He heard Libby's voice from somewhere in the pit of his stomach, the chatter of his teeth limiting him to nothing more than a grunt in reply. "Jesus Christ."

She sounded as disapproving as she always did, so there was no telling whether she was real or imagined. The pounding in Nico's head was deafening now, the ache from his shoulders to his neck enough to blind him with the pressure between his eyes, behind his sinuses. He could feel the fabric of his shirt being peeled from his chest and stomach, probably soaked through with sweat, but there was no stopping, not now, and why waste it? He had fixed the cystic areas of magical build-up and rot, and so turned his attention to the vacancies and gaps.

He could feel himself being dragged toward heat, waves of it unevenly covering him through flickers of what must have been flame. The so-called 'great room'—the room for which there was a drawing room to begin with— had a hearth, so presumably Libby, if she were actually there and not merely in his imagination, was doing her damndest to keep him from a chill. She must have had plans to sweat out the fever of his effort, which was a lovely thought, all things considered, but possibly insufficient. Worst case, it would be no different from the bandages Nico was currently affixing to the house's decay; makeshift decoration to slow an eventual demise.

But of course he was only being dramatic. He was not going to die.

"You insufferable manchild. You idiot prince." Her fondest derivative for him, or at least her most frequent. So much so it felt like something he may have accidentally colonized and put to use. "You are not going to do something so utterly unforgivable as to waste your talent and die, I won't have it," Libby informed him, jerking his shoulders upright.

He would have mumbled I know that Rhodes shut up had he not been busy focusing on the task of not dying, and more specifically, on aiming what was currently oozing out of him, which was probably something he needed to survive.

"You deplorable little Philistine," Libby said. "What on earth were you thinking? No, don't answer that," she grumbled, shoving him none-too-gently so that his back rested against something hard, like the leg of a Victorian chair. "Just tell me what you're doing so I can help you—even though I ought to defenestrate you from that window instead," she muttered in an afterthought, ostensibly to herself.

Nico grunted something in response, because what remained to be done would be exceedingly draining and, at the moment, impossible to explain in words. Nearly everything that could be sealed or reinforced had been sealed and reinforced, and all that remained were the areas of decomposition, spoiled and thin and requiring less a bandage than an amputation, reconstruction from the inside out. Reversing damage, asking chaos to be structure, was enough to sap him completely, wringing out what little remained. He could feel it in the convulsions of his intestines, the way magic was now being taken from his kidneys, his heart, his lungs.

"You can't just give yourself away like this," Libby scolded, ever the admonishing schoolmarm, but then she had taken his hand gruffly and laced it with hers. "Just show me."

Most likely the moment she touched him she could already feel the direction his power had taken. They'd had a knack for it from the beginning, a way of becoming the other's beginning and end. They typically declined to do so, of course, because it was invasive. Because him using her or her using him was like temporarily trading limbs, swapping joints. For the rest of the day he would feel like he was lifting Libby's hand instead of his own or bending Libby's knee to take a step, and he knew she felt the same way. He would look up to catch her eye and she would grimace like he had taken something from her, and yes, whatever she'd taken from him was equal in value as what she'd had before, and it wasn't as if either of them had done it on purpose—but still, she was missing something that he now possessed, and vice versa.

They struggled to properly disentwine, or worse. They each became strange, molded copies of the other.

It was only when they had started using their magic to replicate the effects of space that the sense of borrowed power and stolen limbs had stopped feeling like a gruesome, halfhearted sex act and more like true synchronicity. There was a harmony to it when they were reaching together, like the gratified spreading of a broader pair of wings. Difficult to explain what the difference was, except for the sensation of having finally uncovered a proper use, an ideal purpose. They were still inhumanly powerful, yes, but they had been without aim, without direction, so that alone the use of their abilities felt retroactively clumsier, less refined. Combined it was purified and focused, untarnished and distilled.

Nico took a breath without strain for the first time in several minutes and registered with private relief that the joining of Libby's power with his own had done more than simply alleviate his task. It left him in a cleaner, more precise stream, less the leak that Tristan might have called it (and that Nico would not have called it before if not for realizing how *un*-leak-like it now seemed to be) and more sleek, contoured and smooth.

Within minutes the pipes had been fixed. Seconds later the wards pulsed without disruption. Nico spent what power remained on a thorough sweep of their spherical perimeter, which left him in an unsteady rush. No faults this time, no little skips of error. No flaws to snag on the wave of his surveillance.

Libby released him and shifted, dragging slightly as she moved.

"Why?" she said after a moment.

Nico opened his eyes with difficulty, the bleary image of her manifesting at his side. The red of the walls with its gold accents seemed to blur beside her hair, the silhouette of her closed eyes. She wasn't fully exhausted, not like he was, but there had definitely been a toll. She had shouldered some of his burden for him.

"I'm sorry." He managed to croak it out, rasped and insufficient though it was.

"You'd better be." Libby slid a hand to the floor, pressing her palm flat against it. "Still a little tremor," she noted.

"Is that—" Fuck, his mouth was unbearably dry. "Is that what brought you here? A tremor?"

"Yes."

Of course it was. She'd make a big fuss of it, naturally, of the disruption he'd caused and how little control he possessed over his abilities, when really, *she* was the only one who could feel it. Per usual it would be his fault, and inevitably she would lord it over—

"You are unfairly talented. Upsettingly good," Libby sighed with a tactile hum of envy, and then her eyes fluttered open. "Doing that much magic..." She twisted around to look at him, fixing him with a scrutinizing glance. "I would never have attempted it alone."

"I shouldn't have attempted it alone." No point denying that now.

"Yes, but you almost managed it. You might have done fine without me."

"'Almost' and 'might have' wouldn't count for much if I'd been wrong."

"True, but still." She shrugged. "It wasn't as if you didn't know perfectly well I'd come."

Nico opened his mouth to argue that of course he'd known no such thing, but on second thought, he wondered if she wasn't a little bit right about that. There was a safety net, whether he acknowledged it to her or not, when she was around. He couldn't get away with much without her noticing, and surely he'd known that on some level, consciously or otherwise.

"Thank you," he said, or possibly mumbled.

She looked pleased, or smug.

"Why were you repairing the house on your own?" she said, briskly shoving their repulsive moment of benevolence aside. "Reina could have helped you," she added as an afterthought.

Nico found it miraculously tactful that she had not suggested herself, so as a reward, he offered, "If I were going to ask someone for help, Rhodes, it would have been you."

"Empty words, Varona," was her reply, equally accommodating. "You never ask anyone for help."

"Still, it's true."

She rolled her eyes, leaning over to press a thumb to the pulse at his wrist. "Slow," she observed.

"I'm tired."

"Anything else?"

"Headache."

"Drink water."

"Yes," he growled, "I fucking *know* that, Rhodes—"

"Any aches? Swelling?"

"Yes, yes, and yes; yes to all of it—"

"You should probably sleep," she commented blandly.

"For *fuck's sake*, I just said I—"

"Why?" she interrupted, and though Nico was exhausted, though he did not want the argument that was sure to follow and though he would have very much preferred to crawl into his bed and sleep for at least the next twelve hours, he still said the one thing he knew she would not accept.

"I can't tell you."

His voice sounded dull, even to him.

Predictably, Libby said nothing. He could feel the swell of her tension beside him, anxiety curling defensively around her like Reina's arms had wrapped around the book. Something of her own to protect, to keep safe, to keep hidden.

Much as he hated to admit it, Nico resented himself most when he made her feel small.

"Just... please don't make me tell you," he amended raggedly, hoping the last-ditch effort at sincerity might persuade her not to suffer more.

She was quiet for a moment.

"You said it was an alliance," she said.

"It is." And it was. "It's an alliance, Rhodes, I promise. I meant what I said."

"So if you need help...?"

"You," Nico assured her quickly. "I'll come to you."

"And if *I* need anything?"

She was primly juvenile, tit-for-tat. For once, though, he didn't begrudge her that.

"Me," he confirmed, relieved to be able to offer something. "I've got you, Rhodes. From here on, I swear."

"You'd better." She sounded satisfied with that, or at the very least relieved. "You owe me big time after this little jaunt of idiocy."

"I knew you'd eventually get self-righteous about it." He added a little groan, just to maintain some semblance of decorum. No need to frighten either of them with too brisk a departure from their usual animosity.

"Still," she sighed. "You'd tell me if you were in any real danger?"

"We're not anymore."

"That's not an answer, Varona."

"Fine, yes." Another groan. "I'd tell you if we were, but for what's worth, we're not."

"But we were?"

"Not danger, exactly. But there were some… oversights."

"And now?"

"Check the wards yourself if you don't believe me."

"I already did." She paused again anyway. "The pipes, really?"

"What, you don't grasp the fundamentals of home ownership, Rhodes?"

"God, I hate you."

Ah, normalcy.

"Likewise," Nico agreed, struggling to his feet. Libby, true to form, did not attempt to help him, instead merely watching with amusement as he dragged himself upright from the foot of the chair.

Instantly, Nico suffered the swift retribution of a muscle contraction in his thigh, a stab of pain that reverberated through his leg while he struggled unsuccessfully to remain aloft, stifling a whimper.

"Charlie horse?" Libby guessed tonelessly.

"Shut up," Nico gritted through his teeth, eyes supremely watering.

"Don't be such a baby."

She waved a hand and the ground slid out from beneath him, sending him sprawling forward with an unsteady lurch. The heels of his hands hit the sheets of his bed, the room tilting to deposit him fully within the walls of his bedroom until he collapsed there in a fit of throbbing limbs, not bothering to protest.

"Thanks," Nico managed to slur into his mass of pillows, tumbling headfirst into bed without any effort to fully undress. His shirt, he realized with faint but fading awareness, remained resolutely elsewhere, probably still soaked with sweat, and worse, he still hadn't drunk any—

Nico blinked as a glass of water surfaced pointedly atop his nightstand.

"Fucking Rhodes," he muttered to himself.

"I heard that," came Libby's reply outside his door.

But by then Nico was already well on his way to sleep, dreamlessly out like a light.

PARISA

So it was not a game, then. That, or it was a highly sadistic one.

It was only in retrospect that Parisa realized Atlas and Dalton had never specified that one of the six would be sent home; only that one of the six would be *eliminated* in a decision made by the others. Five would choose one to go, but the conditions of their departure had never been made clear. She had thought, initially, that it was a rather arbitrary—albeit civilized—method of ensuring that only the best and most dedicated moved on.

Now, though, everything made a twisted sort of sense. Why would the world's most exclusive society of academics ever permit one of its potential members to *leave*? It would be a security risk at best; even if the eliminated medeian parted amicably from the others—already a significant *if*—people were reliable only for being careless with information.

Only the dead kept secrets. The moment she realized it—tripping over it in Dalton's mind—everything else fell into place.

"One of us has to die," Parisa had said aloud, testing it out to see how it would feel against the backdrop of reality. That Dalton was still inside her at the time was a secondary concern, until he went rigid.

"What?"

"That's why you don't want me to lose. You don't want me to be the one who dies." She pulled away to look at him. "A bit drastic, don't you think?"

He looked neither relieved nor undone by her knowing. At best, he was resigned to it, and though he tried to pull away, she locked him in place, still processing.

"You killed someone, then." She registered it with a blink. "Is that what you keep locked away? Your guilt?"

"You used me," he observed tangentially, confirming his suspicions for himself.

Which was quite obviously sufficient for a yes.

"But what possible reason could there be for killing an initiate?" Parisa pressed him, uninterested for the moment in the task of soothing his ego. As if a woman could not enjoy sex and read minds at the same time! They had not even disentangled and already, Dalton was looking for ways to make her the villain of his femme fatale narrative, which was hardly something she had time or patience for. "Ridding the world of a medeian, and for what?"

Dalton drew back, fumbling with his trousers. "You're not supposed to know about this," he muttered. "I should have been more careful."

Liar. He'd clearly wanted her to know it. "Perhaps we shouldn't dwell on things we're not supposed to know," Parisa remarked, and Dalton slid a glance at her, the taste of her so idly sweet on his tongue that even she could see him curl his thoughts around it. "Are you going to tell me why," she pressed him, "or should I just run off and tell the others how this is all an elaborate fight to the death?"

"That's not what it is," Dalton said mechanically. That was the company line, it seemed. She wondered if he were capable of delivering any other explanation, contractually or otherwise.

"Magic comes only at a price, Parisa. You know that. Some subjects require sacrifice. Blood. Pain. The only way to create such magic is to destroy it."

His thoughts were cloudier than that; less finite. "That's not why," Parisa observed.

"Of course it is." Now he was impatient, jittery. Possibly he simply disliked being contradicted, though she suspected there was more to it than that. "The subjects contained in the library are not for everyone. They are rare, requiring immense power and unimaginable restraint. There's a reason only six are chosen—"

"Five," Parisa corrected him. "Five are chosen. One is slaughtered."

His mouth tightened. "Don't call it a slaughter. It isn't a slaughter. It's—"

"A willing sacrifice? I highly doubt that." She gave a sharp laugh. "Tell me which of us would have agreed to this if we knew one would have to die for it, hm? And besides, I can see there's more to it." She peered at him carefully, waiting to see if he would reveal anything, but he had sealed himself into a vault again. He had already given away too much, or simply wanted her to believe he had. Whether that had been his intention or not remained unclear.

"You wanted me to know, Dalton," she reminded him, deciding to accuse him openly and see where that went. "I don't think you're careless enough to let me get close to you otherwise. But if you want me to act on your warning, then you'll have to explain to me why it exists. Otherwise," she scoffed, "what reason would I have to stay?"

"You can't leave, Parisa. You've seen too much."

That, and he did not seem to think she would do it even if she could. There was no panic, no frenzied concern as he said it; entirely fact.

It was unfortunate his certainty was so merited. After all, what life could she possibly go back to after this?

She straightened her skirt, adjusting her undergarments, and rose to her feet.

"Dalton," she said, and took hold of his collar. "You know I did more than use you, don't you?"

His tongue slid over his lips. "More than?"

"I enjoyed you," she assured him, and tugged him closer. "But I'm afraid I'll have quite a few more questions when I've thought this all through."

His hands found her waist blindly. They would itch for her now, she was sure. He would wake in the middle of the night to find the shape of her formed between his vacant palms.

"Perhaps I'll give you nothing," he said.

"Perhaps you will," she agreed.

It would be a matter of weeks before they found themselves in a compromising situation once again.

By that point they had moved into time theories, and Parisa, who specialized in cognizance, was able to do far more than she had with the predominantly physical magics. Most theories of time and its motion were quietly psychological; that a person's experience of time could be shaped by thought or memory. Pieces of the past seemed closer, while the future seemed at once nonexistent, distant, and rapidly approaching. Tristan was clearly intent on proving the significance of quantum time theory (or something), but Parisa was focused on the obvious: that the *actual* function of time was not a matter of its construction, but the way it was experienced by others.

It was the first time the library had begun revealing things exclusively to her, giving her its usual pseudo-sentient tug in one direction or another, and she had begun to venture into the historical texts she'd thought so little of at first. Not Freud, of course; Western mortal psychology as a self-conscious mode of study was, unsurprisingly, several centuries too late. Rather, Parisa immersed herself in the scrolls from the Islamic golden age, nipping at a half-formed hunch and uncovering that the Arabic astronomer Ibn al-Haytham had observed about optical illusions the same thing Parisa had observed about the human experience in general—namely, that time was an illusion of itself. Nearly every theory of time was rooted in a fallacy, and manipulation of it as a concept was largely accomplished through the mechanism of thought or emotion. Callum was much too lazy to focus on the latter, but Parisa dove into the early psychological medeian arts—Islamic and Buddhist, mostly— with a fervor that surprised all of the others.

All of them, that is, but Dalton.

"I told you," he said, finding her alone in the reading room one night.

She allowed him to think he'd surprised her. "Hm?" she said, playing at startled.

He slid a chair over to sit beside her at the table. "Is this al-Biruni's manuscript?"

"Yes."

"Are you studying reaction time?" It was Biruni who had first begun experimenting with mental chronometry, which in this case was the lag between stimulus and response; how long it took for the eyes to see something and the brain to react.

"How do you know what I'm studying?" Parisa asked, though she didn't need to.

Because they both knew he could not take his eyes off her, of course.

"I can see you're working a theory," he said. "I thought perhaps you might want to discuss it."

She permitted a half-smile. "Should we whisper about differential psychology? How salacious."

"There is an intimacy to intensive study that even I find unsettling," he said, shifting towards her. "The expression of an unformed thought."

"Who says my thoughts remain unformed?"

"You share nothing with any of the others," he noted. "And I advised you to find an ally."

She brushed his knee with hers. "And haven't I found one?"

"Not me." He looked wryly amused, though he didn't pull away. "I told you, it can't be me."

"What makes you think I need an ally? Or that I would allow myself to be killed?"

Dalton glanced around, though it was unlikely they'd be overheard. Parisa could feel no other active cognition in the house, except perhaps for Nico. He had a somewhat frequent visitor, a telepathic one of sorts, though he was never fully conscious when it happened.

"Still," Dalton said. An appeal; *believe me, listen to me.*

Crave me, fuck me, love me.

"What is it about me? You don't trust me, clearly," Parisa observed. "I don't even think you'd want to trust me if you could."

He gave her a curt, telling smile. "I do not want to, no."

"Have I seduced you, then?"

"I think conventionally you have."

"And unconventionally?"

Her hair had slipped over one shoulder, catching his eye.

"You torment me a bit," he said.

"Because you think I might not want you?"

"Because I think you might," he said, "and that would be disastrous. Calamitous."

"Having me, you mean?" It would fit the archetype of her. Seduce and destroy. The world was filled with poets who thought a woman's love had unmade them.

"No." His lips twitched ironically. "Because you would have me."

"How bold of you." Unlikely, too. She had yet to identify his nature. Was he humble or boasting? Had he been recklessly led astray, or was she the one being led somewhere with intention? The idea he might be toying with her precisely the way she toyed with him was brutally intoxicating, and she twisted to face him. "What would happen if I wanted you?"

"You would have me."

"And?"

"And nothing. That's it."

"Do I not have you now?"

"If you did, wouldn't you find it dull?"

"So you're playing a game, then."

"I would never insult you with a game." He glanced down. "What is your theory?"

"Who did you kill?" she asked.

There was a brief stalemate between them; tension unsettled.

"The others," Dalton observed, "have suggested we focus on the mechanics of time. Loops."

Parisa shrugged. "I have no need to rebuild the universe like blocks."

"Why not? Isn't that power?"

"Why, simply because no one else has done it? I don't need a new world."

"Because you want this one?"

"Because," Parisa said impatiently, "the power it would take to create one would only destroy countless things in its path. Magic has costs. Didn't you say it yourself?"

"So you agree, then."

"With what?"

"The Society's rules. Its elimination process."

"Its murder game, you mean," corrected Parisa, "which is itself insulting."

"And yet you remain, don't you?"

Unwillingly, she felt her eyes travel askance to her notes.

"I told you." This time, Dalton's smile broadened. "I told you. Even knowing the truth, you would not say no."

"Who did you kill?" Parisa asked him. "And how did you do it?"

He tugged the page from below her arm, glancing over it.

She sighed, remembering what he said about the intimacy of academia. He liked her most when she was vulnerable, didn't he? When he had a piece of her that she had not wished to give up. Pleasure unadulterated, or knowledge unshared.

"Memory," she said, and Dalton glanced up. "The experience of time through memory."

He arched a brow.

"Time travel," Parisa explained, "is simple, provided you are traveling through one person's perception of time. Perhaps," she demurred, agitated in anticipation of inevitable misunderstanding, "that might be considered less interesting to my unsubtle associates—"

"They study what they specialize in, as do you. Go on," Dalton said.

"It's not very complex," she told him; surprised but not displeased by his dismissal. "Intelligent people respond more quickly to stimuli, therefore intelligent people experience time faster, and may be perceived to have more of it. Intelligence is, in some senses, also an illness—genius is frequently a side effect of mania. Perhaps some would have such an excess of time that they are experiencing it differently. Also, if time could be consumed differently, it could also be preserved. And if a person had an excess of time—"

"They could travel throughout their own experience of time differently," Dalton concluded.

"Yes," Parisa said, "in essence."

He curled a hand around his mouth in thought, contemplating it.

"How would you measure intelligence? Or would it be magic, in this case?"

"Who did you kill?" asked Parisa.

"He was not well liked," said Dalton, surprising her again. She had not expected an answer. "Not that it's an excuse," Dalton added.

"Was he dangerous?"

Dalton's brow furrowed. "What?"

"Was he dangerous," Parisa repeated. "To either you or the Society?"

"He—" Dalton blinked, retreating slightly. "The Society did not determine whether he lived or died."

"Didn't they? In a sense," Parisa said. "They selected six candidates knowing that one would be eliminated. Don't you think they have an idea which one they find expendable?"

Dalton blinked again.

And again.

His thoughts went cloudy and reformed; a different shape this time.

"How did you kill him?" Parisa asked.

"Knife," said Dalton.

"Ambush?"

"Yes. A bit."

"How Roman of you."

"We were heavily intoxicated." He scrubbed wearily at his jaw. "It is not easy, taking a life. Even when we knew it was required."

Compulsory anything was not a concept Parisa enjoyed. "What if you had not done it?"

"What?"

"What if you had chosen not to kill someone," Parisa repeated, clarifying as Dalton's thoughts unraveled a second time. "Would the Society have stepped in?"

"He knew," Dalton said, which was not an answer. "He knew it would be him."

"So?"

"So he would have killed one of us instead, if he could have." A pause. "Probably me."

Ah, so that explained his fear, or at least part of it.

Parisa reached out, brushing Dalton's hair from his forehead.

"Have me in your bed tonight," she said. "I find I'm besieged by curiosity."

His sheets were crisply white, cleanly tucked. She took great pleasure in unmaking them.

There were other times.

Once, she found him in the gardens. It was early, cold, and damp.

"The English," she said, "over-romanticize their own dreary winters."

"Anglophilia," said Dalton, turning towards her. His cheeks were bright, spot lit by twin buds of cold, and she reached for him, taking his face between her hands to warm them.

"Careful," he warned. "I may take this for tenderness."

"You think I'm not tender? Seduction is not all lethality," said Parisa impatiently. "Most people want only to be cared for. If I had no softness, I'd get nowhere at all."

"And where do you want to go this morning?"

"Nowhere you cannot take me," she said.

"Flattery is part of seduction," he said, "isn't it?"

"Inescapably, yes."

"Ah. I regret being such a straightforward case."

"No one is ever straightforward."

He half-smiled. "So we're not simple, we're just... all the same?"

"A flaw of humanity," said Parisa, shrugging. "The compulsion to be unique, which is at war with the desire to belong to a single identifiable sameness."

They were out of sight already, up too early for anyone else to stir, but he pulled her into the nearby grove of birch trees anyway, concealing them.

"You make me so common," he said.

"Do I?"

"Think how interesting I could be to someone else," he suggested. "A homicidal academic."

"You're not uninteresting," she said. "Why did he want to kill you?"

"Who?" The pretense was so very tiresome, but apparently necessary.

"How many people have wanted to kill you, Dalton?"

"Probably very many."

"How deliciously uncommon," she offered evasively.

He drew her into his arms, hips flush against hers.

"Tell me something," he said. "Would you have wanted me more if I had denied you longer?"

"No," Parisa said. "I'd have found you a considerable idiot if you had."

She toyed with loop of his trousers, turning over stones in her thoughts.

"Tell me about the Forum," she said, pleased to see the evidence of momentary startlement. "I find I've been wondering about this Society's enemies. Specifically, whether they may be right." She hadn't forgotten that the Forum's agents alone had been able to escape after slipping the Society's wards during the installation.

Despite his initial flicker of surprise, Dalton seemed relatively unfazed. "Why should I know anything about the Forum?"

"Fine," she sighed, disappointed but unsurprised, "then tell me why he wanted to kill you."

"He had to kill someone," Dalton said with an air of repetition, "before they killed him."

"Were you too weak or too strong?"

"What?"

"Either he chose you as a target because you were too weak," she clarified, "or because you were too strong."

"What do you think?"

She glanced up to find Dalton watching her closely.

"You must have chosen me for a reason yourself," he remarked, shrugging. "Was it because I was weak, or strong?"

"Are you making yourself a parable?"

"Maybe."

"Why," Parisa countered, "did you think it would be dangerous for me to have you? Who would it be dangerous for?"

"Me," said Dalton. "Among others."

"And yet you lack quite a bit of self-preservation, don't you?"

"Most likely."

"Is that why he wanted to kill you?"

She'd meant it as a joke, pushing him to see what might come to light even if she aimed blindly, but he seemed to regard her with new severity.

"I want to try something," he said. "Meet me tonight."

"Where?"

"My room. I want to see how good you are."

"We've already tried that," she said drily, "and I believe we both rose admirably to the occasion."

"Not that," he said, though he was obviously not opposed. "I only meant I'm going to spend the day burying something. A thought."

"An answer?"

"Yes."

A little thrill coursed through her.

"I thought you wouldn't play games with me?"

"This isn't a game. It's a test."

"What do I get if I pass?"

"An answer."

"*The* answer?"

"Yes, fine." A pause. "It will drain you."

"Good," she said invitingly.

"I already know what you can do without trying. I want to see what happens when you try."

She shivered with anticipation. She had missed the sensation of operating in her element.

"Alright," she said, flexing her fingers. "Then I'll try."

By the time she reached his private chambers, slipping in quietly when the others had gone to bed, Dalton was already sleeping. There was an hourglass beside the bed, with the implication clear enough: there was a time limit to this test. She flipped it, closing her eyes, and lay on her back beside Dalton, finding the rhythm of his pulse. It would be a matter of sinking into her own consciousness to locate the edges of his, then the effort of seeking out the most difficult doors to open.

When she opened her eyes, it was to a tangle of thorns.

"How very cliché," she sighed, spotting the labyrinth that led to the castle. "I have an hour to reach the princess in the tower, is that it?"

An hour of his experience, that is, and all indications suggested he was particularly brilliant. She turned to the side, glimpsing a handful of non-native fungi sprouting along the path of thorns.

"Subtle," she said drily, and plucked one, letting it turn to sand in her palm.

Mental chronometry. She was playing with his concept of time, collecting it for her use. She conjured, for purposes of allusion, a fashionable set of thin-plated armor, tucking the grains of excess time away.

The process of traversing the thorns was merely designed to waste her energy. Working her own magic inside his head was exponentially more effort than doing it in the physical universe; power worked like a traffic jam that way. One car slowing down meant a wave of amplified delay, and likewise, the use of magic outside Dalton's mind compounded to a phantom degree of effort inside it. If she used the extra time she collected, she would exhaust herself. If she did not, she would run out. It was a clumsy set of rules, but clever enough, particularly for someone who was not primarily telepathic.

Not that any of this was primitive in the least; the kingdom Dalton had built in his head could not have been erected in a day, not when a lesser medeian would not have managed it in a lifetime. The labyrinth was unstable, constantly shifting, but grandiose and complex. Whatever the secret was that Dalton Ellery had locked away, it did not want to be found, and he must have had extraordinary capabilities to be so capable of keeping it from her.

She expected, given the sophistication of his mental defenses, something to force her out; flame was easy for the mind to conjure, and small brush fires leapt up through cracks, incandescent tongues to light her path. When she was attacked by spectral guards, she wasn't surprised. They had been hastily cloned from one conception, and all fought mechanically—the same pattern of blows, over and over. Again, impressive for the work of an amateur, but this was only a test. Dalton had already made it clear he didn't want her to die, so perhaps that was why his mind could not truly bring itself to threaten her. It was only designed to give her something to prove.

She took the tower steps two at a time, sprinkling sand as she went. The armor she'd made had begun to rust. She, corporeally, was fading. Time was running out.

The castle itself was well formed, uncreatively imagined. Based, most likely, on somewhere Dalton had once been, though there were details she hadn't expected: each individual torch was lit upon the wall with a flame that responded uniquely to changes in the air, and the colors in the tapestries must have been selected, not recalled. She took the central staircase, following the path set for her, but could see that the rooms flanking it were furnished and filled; they were crafted, not copied.

The corridors narrowed, leading her upwards from landing to landing until she stepped onto a winding, circular staircase. At the top of the stairs were three tower rooms; these, unlike the others, were shut. She had time to open all three, but only long enough for a glimpse. If she wanted to fully search their contents, she would have to choose one.

Inside the first door was herself. *That* Parisa—Dalton's Parisa—turned in Dalton's arms to look at where the real Parisa stood in the corridor, expectant. Ah, so he had given her the opportunity to see what he truly felt about her, then. Uninteresting.

She opened the second door, finding a memory. A stranger, and Dalton with a knife in his hand. So that was what had happened. Tempting.

The third door contained only a locked chest. To break it might require more time than she currently had, though she paused when she realized the setting. It was a Roman plaza; a forum. *The* Forum.

She hesitated, stepping inside, but then stopped. This could wait. That, or it was an answer she could find on her own.

So she turned, darting back into the hallway to thrust open the second door.

Almost immediately, she was hurled into Dalton's consciousness, living it from his memory, though it had not begun where she thought.

"—you sure?"

It was a whisper from a young man to a young Dalton, who was nearly unrecognizable. His hair was the same, his appearance as meticulous as always, but there was something about his face that was distinct. A decade younger, true, but filled with something.

No. *Absent* something.

"Once we do this, we can't go back." It was a tawny-skinned young man who spoke with an unfamiliar accent. "Can you live with it?"

Dalton was only half-listening. He was charming something idly; the air surrounding his open book flickered and twisted, a small storm forming above the page.

"I wouldn't have to," Dalton said. Eerily, he turned to Parisa. "People think it's the meaning of life that matters," he said, and she blinked. She wasn't sure how he was manipulating his memory to speak with her, but there was no doubt that he was. "It's not the *meaning*. Everyone wants a purpose, but there is no purpose. There is only alive and not alive. Do you like this?" he asked, abruptly shifting in tone. "I made it for you."

He turned back to the other young man before Parisa could answer.

"I could bring you back," he suggested.

Even Parisa could see that this younger Dalton did not sound genuine.

"I thought you said you couldn't do that?" the young man asked.

"I said I don't. But of course I *can*." Dalton twisted again for another sidelong glance, giving Parisa an unnerving smile. "I'm an animator," he told her, which the other young man did not appear to hear. "Death does not register for me with any sort of permanence. Except my own, which I suppose explains what I did next."

He turned back to the young man. "There is nothing to say we can't bring you back," he said. "Maybe it's an additional test? Maybe there's always an animator, and therefore no one actually dies."

There was a flash of something; a knife. It glinted in Parisa's own hand.

Then she felt a lurch; the unmistakable entry of the blade into flesh.

Then, without warning, she was sitting alone.

"I shouldn't be doing this, but you have to listen to me." It was Atlas Blakely, pacing, and Parisa glanced down, recognizing Dalton's clasped fingers as her own. "It's you they want to kill, Dalton. The others have agreed on you."

"How do you know?" came out of Parisa's mouth, which was Dalton's.

"They're afraid of you. You unnerve them."

"Rather small of them," said Dalton irreverently, before conceding, "Fine. Let them try."

"No." Atlas spun. "You must change their minds. You *must* survive."

"Why?"

"The Society needs you, whether they see it or not. What can they do with him? There have been others like him before. Men like him become wealthy, become rich, that's all. They contribute to the global oligarchy and that's it, that's the end. You are necessary in other ways."

There was a rip, a small tear, and then Dalton was sitting before her again like a sunspot Parisa tried fruitlessly to blink away, returning to her armored form within his mental tower's small room. They were alone this time, and Dalton—this young version of him—was leaning forward, inches from her.

"They got used to me," he said. "And I didn't like killing. I'm an animator," he added, as if that explained everything. She supposed it did, in part.

"You bring life," she remarked.

"I bring life," he agreed.

She could see the evidence that he had been tampered with, the jerks of his motions so unlike the fastidious Dalton she knew. It was unclear how honest he was being with her; his memories had clearly been altered, either by the corruption of his past experience or by the clever hand of his present self.

"Are you using me?" she asked him, wondering if she might have permitted herself to be lured somewhere unwise.

His younger self smiled brilliantly.

"I wish you'd seen the other room," he told her. "We'd have both enjoyed it immensely. This one is dull."

"You lied to him," she observed. "You told him you would bring him back?"

"He never actually agreed to do it," said Dalton. "I think he knew I wouldn't."

"Kill him, or bring him back?"

"Neither, I suspect."

"So he told the others to kill you?"

"Yes."

"And you persuaded them otherwise?"

"Yes."

"Was it difficult?"

"No. They were just happy it wasn't them."

"And why didn't you bring him back?"

"Too much work," said Dalton, shrugging. "And anyway, I was wrong."

"About what?"

"About everything." Another shrug. "Someone always dies. They have to."

This version of him wasn't at all what she imagined.

"What's the Forum?" she asked him.

"Boring," said Dalton. "Society rejects."

"You don't find that interesting?"

"Everyone has enemies."

She couldn't help feeling a mismatch; some glitch of something, details that didn't follow.

"Why are you still here?" she asked him.

He stole forward, prowling towards her sleekly, and in that moment, she registered what he was. He flickered slightly, moving in bursts.

"Are you an animation?" she asked, forgetting her previous question.

Dalton's mouth twisted wryly. His lips parted.

Then Parisa felt a hand on her collar, dragging her backwards.

"Get out," said a deep voice. "Now."

She jolted upright, or tried to, but found that the return to her own consciousness had left her lying paralyzed on her side. The real Dalton was holding her head, and gradually, as she resumed occupation in her body, she realized she had been seizing. She was choking, half-retching on what she registered belatedly was her tongue.

She had overexerted herself; the hourglass beside her had long since run out, and by the look on Dalton's face, it had taken a significant amount of effort to wake her.

She scrambled away from him, blinking. "What was that?"

He frowned. "What was what?"

"That voice at the end, was that—?"

She stopped, blinking.

There was something about Dalton's face now; not that it was older, which it was. He must have been in his early twenties in his memory, but this was more than that. The expression he wore was different now, more steeped in concern. She had not tried to read his younger self's thoughts at the time, thinking she was speaking directly with them—they were, after all, both inside *his* head—but retroactively, she could see she'd been wrong.

Whatever he had been then, his current self did not contain any trace of it. It was a loose thread fraying; something that had come undone, and then been severed.

"You're not whole," she realized aloud, "are you?"

He stared at her. "What?"

"That thing, the animation, it was—"

"You never started the test," he cut in slowly, and then it was her turn to stare at him.

"What?"

"Where were you?" he pressed her, concerned now. "I could feel you, but—"

She felt a shudder of uncertainty.

"What was it?" she asked. "Your test."

"A bank vault," he said. "With a combination lock. A puzzle, in essence."

So what had she broken into inside his head, then? Strange. More than strange. The situation he described sounded straightforward, even elementary. In short, something she would expect from someone who was not a telepath, unlike the thing she'd found.

"What did your bank vault contain?" she asked warily.

"A bit of parchment, nothing important... It was only supposed to take a few minutes to find. Where were you?" Dalton said again, more urgently, but this time, Parisa didn't answer.

Wherever she had been, she was growing increasingly certain that Atlas Blakely had been the one to pull her out.

REINA

THEY WERE GIVEN LEAVE around the December holidays to return home if they wished, which Reina firmly did not.

"Shouldn't someone stay behind to tend the wards?" she asked Dalton privately.

"Atlas and I will be here," he said. "It's only a weekend."

"I don't celebrate Christmas," she said, displeased with the inconvenience.

"Most medeians don't," he agreed, "but the Society hosts its annual events during the mortal holidays."

Reina frowned. "We're not invited to the Society events?"

"You're potential initiates, not members."

"But we're the ones who live here."

"Yes, and one of you," Dalton said neutrally, "will not remain by the end of the year, so no. You're not invited."

The idea of going home (a meaningless concept by now) was unfathomable. Detestable, even. She was currently in the middle of a fascinating manuscript she had seen Parisa with; a medeian work on the mystical study of dreams by Ibn Sirin, which led Reina to a curiosity about the concept of realms within the subconscious. Nico had expressed some interest in it as well, which she considered a point of distinct significance. As with the runes he had asked her to translate, there was no telling what he wanted a book on dreams for; he had no interest in historical psychology, or in anything he couldn't turn into a miracle of physics (Nico was very sulky when he was not permitted to be incomprehensibly astounding), but regardless, it was nice to have someone to discuss it with. The others were usually very private about their research, guarding their theories as secrets.

Nico was always the most open with her, going so far as to invite her to New York for their winter recess. "You'll loathe Max," he said happily while they were sparring, referring to someone Reina gathered to be one of his flat mates. "You'll want to kill him and then five minutes after you've left you'll realize you actually love him. Gideon is the opposite," he added. "He'll be the best person you've ever met, and then you'll notice he's nicked your favorite sweater."

Reina faked a hard right, which Nico read like a book. He slid backwards, one hand on his cheek, the other falling with inconceivable arrogance to match the quirk of his smile, and gave her a little beckon of *uh huh, try again*.

The idea of staying in a place occupied by boys in their early twenties gave Reina an unpleasant itch. "No thanks," she said.

Nico was not the type to be insulted by these things, and predictably, he wasn't. "Suit yourself," he said with a shrug, ducking a wide hook as Reina caught Libby glancing over at them, a little half-frown on her lips. She was looking forward to seeing her boyfriend, or so she said, though Reina wasn't convinced. Libby's boyfriend (none of them could remember his name, or perhaps Libby had never actually told them what it was) seemed to exclusively call at unwelcome times, leading Libby to make a face of irritation when she glanced at her screen. She denied her annoyance, of course, most vehemently to Nico, but as far as Reina could tell, Libby's Pavlovian response to any mention of her boyfriend was to quickly stifle a grimace.

In anticipation of their brief leave, the others mostly shared Reina's reluctance. Tristan appeared to dread the prospect of leaving, probably because he had burned such a wide variety of bridges in order to come in the first place; Parisa was irritated about being temporarily deposed, prissy as always; Callum, true to form, didn't seem to care much either way. Only Nico seemed to have any genuine interest in going home; then again, Nico was so adaptable in general that Reina suspected he could make anything comfortable enough to stand it for a time.

The past few months had been relatively peaceful ones. They had all fallen into a rhythm of sorts, and the disruption of their fragile peace felt especially inconvenient, even troubling. True, they hadn't *bonded*, per se, but they had at least warmed enough to exist in each other's physical space without persisting tension. Timing, Reina thought, was a sensitive thing, and the house plants made no secret of mourning her impending absence.

In the end, Reina decided to stay in London. She had never ventured beyond the grounds of the Society's manor house, so now she was ostensibly a tourist in her own city. On her first day, she toured the Globe Theatre, then wandered the Tower. On the second day, she took a brisk morning walk through the Kyoto Garden (the trees shivered cheerfully, thrumming with frosted whispers as they recounted their origins), followed by a visit to the British Museum.

She had been looking at the Utamaro painting of the Japanese courtesan when someone cleared his throat behind her, causing her to bristle with impatience.

"Purchased," said a South Asian gentleman with thinning hair, addressing her in English.

"What?" asked Reina.

"Purchased," the gentleman repeated. "Not stolen."

His accent didn't sound entirely English; it had a mix of origins.

"Apologies," he amended, "I believe the technical term is 'acquired.' The British do hate to be accused of theft."

"As do most people, I assume," Reina said, hoping that would be that. Unfortunately, it wasn't.

"There is some service to it, at least," the gentleman continued. "Here the treasures of the world are on display, not hidden away."

Reina nodded vacantly, turning to leave, but the gentleman turned after her, falling into step at her side.

"Every five years, six of the world's most talented medeians disappear," he remarked, and Reina's mouth tightened. "A few of them emerge two years later in positions of power and privilege. I don't suppose you have any theories?"

"What do you want?" Reina asked impatiently. If that was considered rude, so be it. She didn't feel any particular need to be polite.

"We expected you to be in Tokyo," said the man. A continuation of his earlier thought, as if she had not interjected at all. "We'd have been here sooner, in fact, but you're not easy to track down. With a family like yours—"

"I am not in contact with my family," Reina said. "Nor do I wish to be bothered."

"Miss Mori, if you would indulge me for just a moment—"

"You clearly know who I am," said Reina. "So shouldn't you know, then, that I have turned down every offer I receive? Whatever you imagine I accepted, I did not. And whatever it is you plan to offer me, I decline it as well."

"Surely you must feel some obligation," said the man. "A scholar like yourself, you must think it valuable to have access to the Alexandrian records."

Reina stiffened; Atlas had always said the Society was known among certain groups, but still, she hated to think the place she prized so mightily could be referenced with such open disregard.

"What good are the archives," the man pressed, catching the look on her face, "when only a small percentage of the world's magical population can ever learn from them? At least the artifacts contained in *this* museum are offered to the whole of the mortal world."

"Knowledge requires caretakers," said Reina flatly. "And if that's all—"

"There are better ways to care for knowledge than to hide it away."

Another version of her might have agreed with him. As it was, though, she spared him half a glance.

"Who are you?"

"It's not who I am, but what I stand for," said the man.

"Which is?"

"Freedom of information. Equality. Diversity. New ideas."

"And what do you think you will gain from me?"

"The Society is inherently classist," said the man. "Only the highest trained medeians will ever reach its rank, and its archives only serve to secure an elitist system which has no oversight. All the world's treasures under one roof," he prompted, "with only a single organization to control its distribution?"

"I," Reina said, "have no knowledge of anything you speak."

"True, you are not a member yet," the man agreed, dropping his voice. "You still have time to make other choices. You are not bound to the Society's rules, nor to its secrets."

"Even assuming any of this were true," Reina muttered, "what would you want from me?"

"It is not what we want from you, Miss Mori, but what we can offer you." The man slid a card from his inside pocket, handing it to her. "Someday, should you find you are trapped by the choice you've made, you may contact us. We will see to it that your voice is heard."

The card read *Nothazai*, either the man's name or his pseudonym, and on the back, *THE FORUM*. A reference, of course, to a subversion of everything the Society was. The Roman Forum was a marketplace of ideas, the most celebrated meeting place in the world. It was the center of commerce, politics, and civility. In short, where the Society cloistered itself behind closed doors, the Forum was open to all.

But there was a reason the Library of Alexandria had been forced to hide in the first place.

"Are you truly the Forum?" Reina asked neutrally. "Or are you simply the mob?"

When she glanced up, he—Nothazai—had not looked away. "It is no secret what you can do, Reina Mori," he said, before amending, "At least, it is no secret what you *could* do. We are citizens not of a hidden world, but of a global economy; an entire human race. It is a troubled world we live in, ever on the brink of progress and regression, and very few are given the opportunity to make true changes. Power like the Society's does not elevate this world; it only changes hands, continuing to isolate its advantages."

It was an old argument. Why have empires and not democracies? The Society's version of an answer was obvious: because some things were unfit to rule themselves.

"You think I can contribute nothing from where I stand, I take it?" Reina prompted.

"I think it is obvious you are a blend of broad dissatisfactions, Miss Mori," said Nothazai. "You resent privilege in all its forms, including your own, yet you show no desire to unmake the present system. I think someday you will awaken to your own conviction, and when you do, something will compel you forward. Whoever's cause that will be, I hope you will consider ours."

"Do you mean to accuse me of some sort of tyranny by proxy?" Reina asked. "Or is that an unintended consequence of your recruitment tactics?"

The man shrugged. "Is it not a proven fact of history that power is not meant to exist in the hands of the very few?"

"For every tyrant, there is a 'free' society which destroys itself," said Reina, who knew enough ancient history to grasp the faults of hubris. "Power is not meant for those who misuse it."

"Is not the worst tyranny that which perceives itself to be noble?"

"Greed is greed," said Reina flatly. "Even if I accepted your perception of the Society's flaws, why should I believe your intentions any different?"

Nothazai smiled. "I only suspect, Miss Mori, that you will soon change

your position on the matter, and when you do, know that you will not be left to
your own devices. Should you require an ally, you have one," he offered, and
bowed low.

The symmetry of the moment reminded her of something.

"Are you some sort of Caretaker?" she asked him, thinking of Atlas
Blakely's card. Inexplicably, she remembered what Atlas had said about
the others who might have taken her place; a traveler, as he had specifically
mentioned, whatever that meant.

Were the members of the Forum merely Society castoffs?

"No, I am nothing important. The Forum cares for itself," said Nothazai,
and turned away before pausing, doubling back half a step. "By the way," he
added in an undertone, "perhaps you know already? The Tokyo billionaire
Sato has just won parliament's special election, displacing the incumbent
candidate."

The mention of Aiya was startling, though Reina tried not to let it show.
"Why should Aiya Sato matter to me?"

"Oh, she doesn't, I'm sure. But it's very interesting—she was the one
who uncovered the incumbent councilor's corruption. Almost as if she had
information the government itself did not. The incumbent denies it, of
course, but who to believe? There is no other evidence aside from Sato's own
dossier, so perhaps we'll never know."

Briefly, Reina recalled what Aiya had summoned during their brief
interaction in the reading room: an unmarked book. Reina quickly blinked
it away, obscuring it. Even if this man were not a telepath, there were other
ways to prod inside her head.

"Assassinations," Nothazai said. "Development of new technology that
enters mortal copyrights, but never public domain. New weaponry sold
only to the elite. Space programs developed in secret for warmongering
nations. Biological warfare that goes unreported; illness that wipes out the
unmentionables, left to the fringes of poverty."

"You blame this on the Society?" Broad claims, and as far as Reina
considered feasible, unknowable ones.

"I blame the Society," Nothazai clarified, "because if it is not its job to
cause such atrocities, then why not undertake the effort to prevent them?
Inevitably, it must stand to gain."

Somewhere in the administrative offices, a small fern dying of thirst let out a thin, wailing scream.

"Someone always gains," said Reina. "Just as someone always loses."

Nothazai gave her a brisk look of disappointment.

"Yes, I imagine so. Good day, then," he said, and slipped back into the museum's flow of traffic, leaving Reina to look down at his card.

An odd thing, timing. She'd had a feeling, hadn't she? That something would disrupt the peace she'd found within the Society the moment she stepped outside its walls. It was a narrow window to reach her without the Society's wards; only a matter of hours remained before her return, which was much too specific to guess.

Could this, like the installment, have been another test?

The idea that anything would keep Reina from initiation into the Society was enough to reflexively curl her fingers, crumpling the card within them to a stiff, unwelcome ball.

The others could do with power what they wished. She tossed the card into the bin and strode out into the cold, ignoring the seedlings that sprouted up between cracks in the sidewalk. The argument itself, that she should turn on the Society in order to save the world, was ludicrous. Look at her talents, for instance. Wouldn't the Forum be the first to have her sacrifice her autonomy, all to sustain a planet that had irresponsibly overpopulated itself? There was such a thing as asking too much, and she had known the demands of others all her life.

Depending who viewed it, Persephone had either been stolen or she had run from Demeter. Either way, she had made herself queen. The Forum, whatever they were, had misjudged Reina poorly for being free of principle, when in fact her principles were clear: she would not bleed out for nothing.

If this world felt it could take from Reina, so be it. She would gladly take from it.

VI: THOUGHT

LIBBY

LIBBY SLAMMED THE APARTMENT DOOR SHUT, turning to find Ezra waiting expectantly in the living room behind her.

The unfortunate thing about Manhattan apartments was the incredible lack of having any other space to be. That, and thin walls. Not being overheard by *someone* was probably never going to be an option so long as she lived in this city. She'd ruled out privacy the moment she signed the NYUMA student contract, which was a fact that moving in with her first year R.A. three years later had not improved. Funny that.

"I take it you were listening," Libby said gruffly, and Ezra slid one hand in his front pocket, buying time before his response.

"Yes." He cleared his throat. "Listen, Lib—"

She knew what was coming next. For one thing, it wasn't as if she'd come home to the promise of sex and chocolates or whatever. The fight had begun the moment she walked in the door, and two days later, it still hadn't been resolved. The fact that he needed her to beat the same dead horse was starting to feel inhumane to both of them (and the horse).

"I already told you," she sighed, cutting him off, "I'm not going to tell you anything, Ezra. I can't."

"Yes, you've made that abundantly clear," he replied, too sharply, and then he grimaced, recognizing the combative undertones in his own voice. "Look, I don't want to fight about it again—"

"Then don't."

She paced away from the door, suddenly desperate for motion. He followed, ceaselessly orbiting her until she thought she might choke.

"I'm just worried about you, Libby."

"Don't be." A softer tone would help, probably.

Not that she had one to spare.

"What am I supposed to do? You come back after six months without warning and you can't even tell me where you've been. Now you have people knocking on the door upsetting you, and you're trying to... to what? *Hide* them from me?"

"Yes. Because this has nothing to do with you," said Libby, still brusque with impatience. "I've always known you didn't trust me, Ezra, not fully, but this is getting out of hand—"

"This isn't about trust, Libby. It's about your safety." *This* again. "If you're in over your head somehow, or if you've gotten caught up in something—"

She tightened a fist. "So you think I'm stupid. Is that it?"

"Libby, don't. You're my girlfriend; you're important to me. You, for better or worse, are my responsibility, and—"

"Ezra, listen to me carefully, because this is the last time I'll say it."

She took three steps to close the distance between them, slamming the book shut on the last argument she planned to have today.

"I am *not*," Libby said flatly, "yours."

She didn't wait to see if he would argue. The look on his face suggested that whatever came next, she wasn't going to enjoy it. She thought about packing a bag, summoning her things. She thought about screaming or crying or making demands; making a mess, in general.

But in the end, it was all so exhausting she simply turned and pulled open the door, planning nothing beyond the certainty of walking through it.

Immediately: a coat would have been a good idea. She shivered in the dark, glancing up the block toward Nico's apartment. A thought, definitely, but if there was ever anyone to be unsympathetic—or even sympathetic, but in an *enormously* unhelpful way—it would be Nico, who had loathed Ezra on sight.

Not to mention that if she went to Nico, she'd have to discuss the visitor she'd just received.

"Elizabeth Rhodes?" the woman had asked in her Bronx accent. If not for the expensive scarf tied around her natural hair, she might have looked like one of those campaigners who stopped people on the street to talk about the environment or veganism, or possibly the hazards of imperiling their immortal souls. "If I could just have a moment of your time—"

Libby shivered and turned left, heading for the train station.

She wondered why they had not been warned that other organizations might come recruiting. Atlas had mentioned the Forum's existence, fine, but he'd left out that for two days of their initiation period, they would be vulnerable to interception.

Was it a trial of some sort, as the installment had been? Was her loyalty being tested?

"Miss Rhodes, surely you've thought about the natural elitism of the Society's mere existence," the woman, Williams, had said. "No one else in your family is magically trained, are they? But I wonder," Williams mused softly. "Could the Society have saved your sister if they had ever shared what they had known?"

It was a question that Libby had asked herself hundreds of times before. In fact, for a time it had left her sleepless, particularly when she was first approached by NYUMA. The thoughts, torturous and destructive, were always the same: If she had only known more, or if she had just been trained sooner, or if someone had told her earlier...

But she already knew the answer. For years, she'd researched at length. "There is no cure for degenerative diseases," she replied, with the confidence of someone possessing dismal, intimate knowledge of the fact.

Williams had arched a brow. "Isn't there?"

It was a trap of some sort. Whether it was a test or not, it was certainly a trap. Someone was toying with her personal history, manipulating her with it, and Libby didn't care for it. If there was one thing she'd learned from working alongside Callum, it was that feeling too much or too fully only meant she wasn't thinking with her head.

It wasn't the Society's fault, Libby had argued in response, that capitalism prevented medeian healthcare from being available to mortals. If medeian methods were priced according to empathy, then yes, fine, perhaps one could blame the research for existing privately—but it would have gone through both the mortal and medeian corporations first; it would have come at so inflated a cost that even if a cure existed, it would have bankrupted her family to try and use.

"So your sister deserved to die, then?" asked Williams blankly.

Which was when Libby had slammed the door.

She had not spoken about Katherine to anyone in years. She thought of her sister from time to time, but only distantly, as something she kept at arm's length. As a measure of sanity, she had ruled out wondering whether something could have been done; in fact, she had already driven herself half mad considering it. The idea that a stranger might have suddenly brought everything to the surface felt a bit manipulative, and certainly unwelcome.

Was this the Society's doing? They would know about Katherine Rhodes, whom Libby had called Kitty as a child, and whom her parents had rightfully adored. Katherine, who had died at sixteen to Libby's thirteen, wasted away in a hospital bed at the whims of a magicless body that slowly killed her. The administrators at NYUMA, when asked, had told Libby her abilities had likely not come to fruition until after the stress of losing her sister had faded away. Katherine, they said, had been ill for years, requiring most of the attention from her parents, and thus Libby would not have focused on her abilities even if she had noticed she had them. It would take work to catch up, they said.

"Could I have saved my sister?" she asked, because survivor's guilt was sharpest in retrospect.

"No," they told her. "Nothing exists to reverse the effects of her illness, or even to slow it."

It had taken Libby two years of manic research to prove them right, and then two more to finally lay thoughts of her sister to rest. She might not have managed it at all if not for Nico; "Oh, buck up, Rhodes, we've all got problems. Doesn't mean you get to waste the time she never got," was his take on the situation—confessed to him at the height of finals delirium, and clearly a massive mistake—at which point Libby had slapped him, and eventually Ezra had intervened. Nico was placed on probation and Libby told herself she would beat him in every class if it killed her.

She kissed Ezra for the first time that same night.

The Society would have known all that, minus the inconsequential details of her personal life. They would have known about Katherine, so maybe this *was* a test, but it wasn't as if the circumstances of her origin story weren't easily discoverable information for anyone who wanted them. A late-blooming medeian with a dead sister? Not terribly complicated to put the pieces together, particularly for an organization with comparable resources. Either the Society knew precisely what to taunt her with in order to test her loyalty, or the Forum had wanted to give her a compelling reason to doubt the Society.

Either way, there was only one place Libby currently wanted to be.

She passed through the doors to Grand Central and took the stairs, finding the medeian transports to take her back to London. It was technically too early to return—they'd all been told not to do so until tomorrow—but she had helped build their security, hadn't she? Twice over. Nothing in the wards sufficiently defended against her entry; for all intents and purposes, it had been more of a polite request than a mandate in any official capacity.

She passed the entry rooms, heading for the reading room, but stopped at the sound of voices; a low wave of sound, meaning hushed tones. She frowned, listening closer for the particularities, and turned swiftly, making her way to the painted room.

Ah, so she had not been the only one to come running back, then.

Parisa and Tristan were on the floor of the painted room, drinking a bottle of something with their backs to the light of the crackling fire. Parisa, unfairly beautiful as always, had her head resting on Tristan's lap, dark hair spilling over his thighs; the slit of her fashionable slip dress had been drawn up so high the full length of her slender leg was fully visible, nearly to her hip, and likewise, Tristan's shirt had fallen open, left half-undone to reveal the curve of his chest below the shadow of his clavicle.

A languid smile was curled over his lips, though it was partially distorted by the bottle he drew up to them. He swallowed with a laugh and Parisa reached blindly upwards, the tips of her fingers brushing his mouth.

It wasn't as if Libby hadn't already known that Parisa and Tristan were sleeping together. Well—she hadn't *known*, exactly, but she wasn't surprised to find evidence of it now. It wasn't as if they had many options within the house, and if Nico had already made it plenty clear that Parisa was his first choice, was it any surprise she'd be Tristan's, as well?

Libby thought for a moment of Tristan's hand on her pulse and swallowed, shoving it aside.

It wasn't as if she cared what they did. After all, she had a boyfriend.

A boyfriend she had recently fought with.

One she would rather not see.

But…

But.

A boyfriend nonetheless.

"Well, don't you look distressed," remarked Parisa drily. She drew herself upright, taking the bottle from Tristan's hand. "Perhaps you ought to join us."

Libby blinked, caught off guard. She hadn't realized they'd seen her.

"I," she began, and faltered. "This is… this is obviously private, so—"

"Have a drink, Rhodes." Tristan's voice was a low rumble, his eyes darkly amused. "You clearly need one."

"We won't bite," added Parisa. "Unless you're into that sort of thing, of course."

Libby glanced over her shoulder, still compelled to leave for the reading room.

"I was just going to—"

"Whatever it is, it'll still be there in the morning, Rhodes. Sit." Tristan beckoned her with his chin, gesturing to the spot next to him.

Libby hesitated, unsure whether this was her precise choice of company, but the idea of not being alone was… tempting. And Tristan was right, whether he knew it or not. Driving herself mad all over again could be easily ventured anew tomorrow.

She stepped forward and Parisa smiled approvingly, reaching up to hand her the bottle. Libby collapsed on Tristan's other side, taking a sip.

"Oof," she said, wincing as it burned. "What is this?"

"Brandy," said Parisa. "With a few more fermented spices."

"Meaning…?"

"Meaning absinthe," said Tristan. "It's absinthe."

"Oh." Libby swallowed, already a little bowled over by the effect of her single sip.

"Let me guess," Parisa sighed, reaching over Tristan to take the bottle from Libby. "You don't drink much?"

"Not particularly," Libby said.

Parisa drew the bottle back to her lips, which were stained a dark red. The dress was a navy blue, almost black, and Libby instantly wished she had the requisite sophistication to pull it off.

"You can pull it off whenever you'd like," remarked Parisa, chuckling into the bottle.

Libby felt her cheeks flush. "I just meant I could never wear anything so…" She coughed. "I just don't do trends very well."

Parisa leaned forward, handing the bottle back to Libby. The strap of her dress slipped blithely from her shoulder, draping against her arm and floating over what Libby now realized necessitated the absence of a bra.

"I meant it literally," Parisa said as Libby brought the bottle to her lips, and while Libby choked on her swallow, Tristan laughed.

"You must have gotten a visit from the Forum as well," he said to Libby, who had only just recovered from an eruption of absinthe-tainted coughs. "What deeply personal revelation did they make about you, then?"

"You tell me," Libby said, taking another swig. The last thing she wanted to be for this conversation was sober; she already felt juvenile and inept as it was.

"Well, it's all very dull for us, unfortunately. My father's a crime boss, same old, same old," said Tristan, adding to Libby's look of confusion, "Nasty piece of work. Adequate witch, though."

"Is he?"

"You've never heard of Adrian Caine?" asked Tristan. Libby shook her head, and Tristan's smirk cracked slightly. "I'm joking. I didn't expect you to run in London's seedy underbelly."

"Is he like the Godfather?" asked Libby.

"A bit," said Tristan. "Only less paternal." He took the bottle from her hand, not bothering to wait for her to release it before he took a long swig. "He'd love you," he added after swallowing, shaking himself like a dog from the burn.

Libby glanced sideways at him, waiting to see if that was supposed to be an insult. Tristan met her glance, arching a brow in expectancy.

It didn't seem to be.

"And I, of course, am a whore," remarked Parisa, as Libby choked on her swallow once again. "I'm sure there's a better word for it, but at present I can't be bothered to think of any."

"An escort, perhaps?" asked Tristan.

"No, nothing so professional. More like an exceptionally talented philanderess," Parisa said. "It started shortly after I finished school in Paris. No," she amended, recounting it in her head, "I believe technically it began while I was *in* school, though it was only a hobby then. You know, like how the Olympics only celebrates the achievements of amateurs."

Libby left the follow-up questions to Tristan. "It started with a professor, I presume?"

"Yes, naturally. The academics are the most brutally deprived, or so they remain convinced. Really they're all equally obscene, only they live in such a slender fragment of reality they'd never come out of their offices to see who else was fucking."

"Fucking you, you mean, or fucking in general?"

"In general," Parisa confirmed, "though also me."

Tristan chuckled. "And from there?"

"A French senator."

"Quite a leap, isn't it?"

"Not really. Politicians are the least discerning and the first to expire. But it's always important to have one and get it out of one's system."

"Was it enjoyable, at least?"

"Not in the slightest. My briefest affair, and the one of which I am least fond."

"Ah. And after the senator…?"

"An heir. Then his father. Then his sister. But I never liked the family holidays much."

"Understandable. Did you have a favorite among them?"

"Of course," said Parisa. "I just adored their little dog."

Libby glanced between the two of them, slightly dumbfounded. She was uncertain how they could speak so openly and so… *flippantly* about Parisa's sexual exploits.

"Oh, it comforts him, really, not that he'll ever admit it. Knowing the truth of my sordid nature only confirms Tristan's deepest suspicions about humanity," Parisa replied to Libby's inner thoughts, catching her sidelong glance. "I'm confident Tristan could be stabbed mid-climax and still find the strength to groan out 'I was right' before succumbing to the cavernous embrace of death."

"You're not wrong, though from here on I'll be checking for knives," said Tristan ambivalently, which should have been confirmation of his involvement with Parisa, but instead it only bewildered Libby further.

Were they something or weren't they?

"We aren't," said Parisa, "and anyway, he likes you, Rhodes. Don't you, Tristan?" she asked, turning to him.

Tristan held Parisa's eye for a moment as Libby's intestines twisted with silent discomfort, the rest of her unsure how to react. It was a joke, of course. True, Parisa could read minds, but it wasn't that. It was obviously just teasing.

Wasn't it?

"I like Rhodes well enough, I suppose," was Tristan's underwhelming response, as Libby briskly determined that now would be a marvelous time for an immediate change in subject.

"So the Forum tried to… blackmail you?" Libby asked them, clearing her throat. "Extort you or something?"

"Something like that," Parisa confirmed with a roll of her eyes. "I'd have considered it, too, only it was so very unpleasant the way they went about it. So brusque and outright." She shuddered, disapproving. "I've had torrid affairs with less indecency."

"You actually *considered* it?" Libby spluttered through her swallow, somewhat unable to differentiate between the burn in her stomach and the one in her chest at the thought. "Seriously?" Her voice, much to her dismay, had gone shrill with disbelief. "But what if it's—"

"A trap? I doubt it," said Parisa. "That doesn't seem the Society's style."

"But the installation—"

"Was them placing us out as sitting ducks," Tristan supplied, "but not technically a trap."

Libby supposed he was right, though she frowned to recall Parisa's original point.

"Still. You considered taking the Forum's offer?"

"Oh, of course," Parisa confirmed, taking the bottle from Libby's hand and pausing its path in front of Tristan. They exchanged a glance; Tristan's brow arched. Then he tilted his head back, permitting Parisa to pour a little absinthe down his throat, and licked the excess moisture from his lips, choking up a laugh as she spilled it down his chin. "Oops," she said, smoothing it away with the pad of her thumb, and then drew the bottle to her lips. "Anyway," she said, taking a swallow and handing it back to Libby, "it's not as if I have any reason to be loyal to the Society yet. I'm not initiated, am I?"

"Well, no," Libby conceded, frowning as she accepted the bottle. "But still, isn't it a bit—"

"Disloyal?" Parisa guessed. "Perhaps, though I'm hardly known for my fidelity." She gave Tristan a sidelong glance. "What about you?"

"Me? I'm a one-woman man, Miss Kamali," said Tristan, half-smiling. "Most of the time."

"Most of the time," Parisa echoed with approval. "But surely not all?"

Libby took a long pull from the bottle, suddenly feeling she needed much more of whatever poison it contained.

"Why, um," Libby began, and Parisa turned to her. "Can I ask you—?"

"Why sex?" Parisa prompted, as Libby's cheeks burned again, heartily chagrined. "Because I enjoy it, Elizabeth. And because most people are idiots who'll pay for it, and existence in society costs money."

"Yes, but isn't it…" She trailed off. "Well—"

"You want to know if I find it demeaning to have sex with people for money," guessed Parisa flatly, "is that it?"

Immediately, Libby wished she'd said nothing. "I just… you're obviously very talented, and—"

"And I use my talents well," Parisa agreed, as Libby drew the bottle back to her lips clumsily, if only for something to do with her hands. "And it is attitudes like yours which make certain I will never be denied. After all, if we could all have boundless, fulfilling sex whenever we liked, why would we ever bother with monogamy? Stigma like yours keeps you subjugated, you know," Parisa remarked, tipping Libby's bottle upwards to ensure a longer sip.

Libby felt the liquid spill around the sides of her mouth and closed her watering eyes, suffering the still-unfamiliar sting. The taste of anise marinated the thickness of her tongue, foreign and bittersweet.

"Don't you ever detest the necessity of emotional attachment?" Parisa murmured, the tips of her fingers brushing Libby's throat before toying, idly, with the tips of her hair. "Men in particular are draining, they bleed us dry. They demand we carry their burdens, fix their ills. A man is constantly in search of a good woman, but what do they offer us in return?"

Flickers of Libby's irritation with Ezra filtered through her mind. "On another day, I'd have a better answer to that," she muttered, and felt the reward of Tristan's most disdainful laugh against her elbow. She shifted, leaning into his chest, and let the vibration carry through her bones. "But still, you're a telepath, Parisa. Those are rare, and you're exceptionally good, I know you are. I just…" Libby shrugged. "I don't see what you gain from it."

"You do things, don't you, to make things easier for yourself?" asked Parisa. "You don't use your magic to walk up the stairs, but you defy gravity all the same, don't you?"

"So?" asked Libby. Tristan leaned over for the bottle, his fingers brushing hers. "I don't see what that has to do with anything."

"Well, because to you, sex is purely physical, when in fact the mind opens along with everything else," said Parisa. "To try to overpower someone's mind, to make it subject to my own, is a waste of time. When he's inside me I hardly have to lift a finger to know precisely what he is, what he wants. He'll tell me so himself without my asking. And why impress my demands unnecessarily, wasting energy and effort? I can make people loyal to me simply by offering them something they want above all else, which costs me nothing to give."

That made a bit of sense to Libby. Tristan's arm slid around her back as he adjusted his posture, brushing the inch of skin between the top of her jeans and the hem of her sweater.

"So you use them," Libby said, clearing her throat. "Your... paramours?"

"I *enjoy* them," Parisa said, "and they enjoy me."

"Is it only men?"

Parisa paused to moisten her lips, half-smiling.

"Most women are less in love with the partners they choose than they are simply desperate for their approval, starving for their devotion," she said. "They want, most often, to be touched as no one else can touch them, and most of them inaccurately assume this requires romance." She reached forward, taking the bottle from Libby's hand. "But the moment we realize we can feel fulfilled without carrying the burdens of belonging to another—that we can experience rapture without being someone's other half, and therefore beholden to their weaknesses, to their faults and failures and their many insufferable fractures—then we're free, aren't we?"

It took Libby a moment to realize that Parisa had set the bottle aside, forgotten. Instead Libby had been feeling Tristan's arm against the small of her back, smelling the roses from Parisa's long hair, draping like a curtain within reach. She could see the little gloss of alcohol on Parisa's lips, and the strap of her silk dress she still hadn't fixed, slipping further down her shoulder. Libby could hear the undertone of suggestion in Parisa's voice, as spiced as the absinthe, as warm as the noisily crackling fire.

"You underestimate your power, Libby Rhodes," said Parisa.

Libby held her breath as Parisa came closer, half-straddling Tristan's lap to take hold of Libby's face, smoothing her hair back from her cheeks. Libby, paralyzed, sat perfectly still as Parisa's lips brushed hers, warm and soft. Delicate and inviting. She shivered a little despite the heat, and meanwhile Tristan's hand stole up her spine, traveling carefully over the notches. She kissed Parisa back tentatively, lightly.

"You're mocking me," Libby whispered to Parisa's mouth, withering a little in agony.

Parisa pulled back halfway, pausing to glance at Tristan.

"Kiss her," she suggested. "She needs to be convinced."

"And you're leaving me to do the convincing?" prompted Tristan drily, as Libby's heart pounded in her chest. "I rather thought that was your expertise."

Parisa glanced at Libby, laughing melodically.

"Oh, but she doesn't trust me," murmured Parisa, reaching out to toy with Libby's hair again. "She's curious about me, fine, but if I do it she'll only get up and run."

She let her hand fall, sliding her palm around the slats of Libby's ribs.

"I'm not mocking you," Parisa offered Libby softly. "I'd be happy to have a taste of you, Miss Rhodes," she mused, and Libby shivered again. "But it's not simply that. You're useful, Libby. You're powerful. You," Parisa concluded with another fleeting kiss, "are someone worth knowing well, and fully, and—" She broke off, the tips of her fingers stroking up the inside of Libby's thigh. "Perhaps deeply."

Libby was startled by the sound from her lips, mouseish and yearning.

Parisa lifted a brow knowingly, turning to Tristan.

"Kiss her," Parisa said again. "And do it well."

"And if she doesn't want me?" Tristan asked, glancing at Libby.

The moment their eyes met, Libby tried to conjure Ezra. She tried to think of something, anything, to remind her that she had left him at home, left him behind, but she could see only glimpses of her own frustration, her fury, her irritation. She tried, fruitlessly, to see him, and saw only Tristan instead.

Helplessly, Libby felt the pounding of her heart the way she had once felt Tristan's touch, ricocheting through her chest like tribal drums. She had stopped time with him, once. This was the problem: that within these walls she wasn't Ezra's, wasn't one of his trinkets or possessions or pets, but entirely herself. She had stopped time! She had recreated a mystery of the universe! Here she had done as she pleased and she had done it well, fully, deeply.

She was powerful on her own. She did not need his oversight. She did not want it.

"You'll have to tell me what you want, Rhodes," Tristan said, and if his voice was gravelly with something, it might have been the absinthe. Or it might have been the fact that he was looking at her like he had already undressed her, already kissed her, already peeled her underwear from her hips with his teeth. Like he was already glancing up at her from the foot of her bed, his broad shoulders securely locked between her thighs.

"Shall I tell him, or will you?" Parisa asked with a quiet laugh, giving Libby a knowing glance. She stroked Tristan's cheek with the knuckle of one finger, teasing along the bone until she brushed his mouth, beside his lips.

Libby couldn't decide what was more troubling; the thoughts she was having about Tristan, or the fact that Parisa could see them and still didn't believe Libby was capable of taking what she wanted.

What *did* she want?

Libby glanced at Tristan and felt it again; that little sway, the pulse of time stopping. It had been so unlike her, so much more about feeling and instinct than anything she'd ever done before. Whether a result of her sister's loss or her own psyche, Libby thought constantly, relentlessly, perpetually wavering between states of worry or apprehension or, in most cases, fear. Fear of ineptitude, fear of failure. Fear she'd do it wrong, do it badly; be the disappointing daughter who lived instead of the brilliant one who died. She was afraid, always, except when she was proving herself to Nico, or letting Tristan lead her blindly, forcing her to trust in something she couldn't see.

She took hold of Tristan's face with one hand and pulled him close, dragging his lips to hers, and he let out a sound in her mouth that was both surprise and relief.

She kissed him.

He kissed her back.

It was enough of a thrill to have Tristan's tongue in her mouth, his arm wound tightly around her ribs, but then Libby reached out further, finding the silk of Parisa's slip dress. Parisa's hand slid over Libby's hip and when Tristan pulled away, catching his breath, Parisa kissed Libby's neck, the tip of her tongue tracing a line across Libby's throat. Libby slid a hand gracelessly up Parisa's thigh and Tristan groaned in Libby's mouth; evidence Parisa's other hand must have found an equally suitable location.

Was this actually happening? It appeared it was. Remnants of the absinthe burned in Libby's chest, sending her thoughts scattering. Tristan pulled her astride his lap and Parisa tugged at her sweater, casting it aside to join the near-empty bottle.

For a moment, half a lucid thought flashed through Libby's mind before reverting to base sensations: hands, tongues, lips, teeth. Somehow Tristan's chest was bare, and she dug her nails into the fibers of his muscle, his skin sparking where she touched it.

Things progressed hastily, drastically, euphorically. She tasted from them both like sips from the bottle, and they each had her like the last laugh. If she would regret this, that was for tomorrow to decide.

"Don't let me wake up alone," she whispered in Tristan's ear, and it was quiet and fragile, crystalline, like glass breaking, the splinter of a hairline fracture that crept up from an unsteady base. Her vulnerability was misplaced among the multitude of sins, but she didn't care. She wanted Parisa's hair wrapped around her knuckles, she wanted Tristan to put her in positions she'd undeniably shiver to recount, but she wanted this, too. To be connected to someone undeniably, even temporarily, at least until the first garish rays of light came through.

Fleetingly, at the back of her mind, Libby knew things would always be different between them now, irreversibly so, and a saner piece of her wondered if that had been Parisa's intention from the start. She'd practically spelled it out already, that sex was a means of asserting control—of creating strings, chains of obligation, where there had been none before—but whether Libby was being used or maneuvered or devoured, she didn't care, she didn't care, she didn't care. It was enough to taste, to feel, to touch, instead of think. Enough to be that free of feeling.

Enough, for once, to *feel*, and nothing else.

CALLUM

SOMETHING HAD HAPPENED to Tristan.

It was immediately apparent upon Callum's return to the Society's London house. He had arrived in the late afternoon after spending their compulsory two days in Mykonos (he had no intention of going back to Cape Town, where the chance he would be expected to work was unfortunately much too high to risk) and begun scouring the house, starting with Tristan's two most likely places in the morning: the library for tea, or the reading room for research. Callum had counted on the appearance of a particular version of Tristan upon sharing some significant news; namely, that someone, and in this case everyone, had left out a very important caveat about the Society's initiation process.

Instead, though, he found Tristan in the door frame of the painted room, staring blankly at the floor.

"I presume you've had a visit from the Forum," Callum began, and paused. Tristan looked more haggard than usual, as if he'd been up all night, and there were fumes of remorse and nausea coming off him in waves. "Christ," said Callum upon closer inspection, taken aback. "What on earth did you get up to while we were all away?"

"Nothing. Just a bit knackered," was the mumbled response, only half-coherent. Tristan's voice was rasping and low, and the look of thorough misery on his face was enough to give Callum a second-hand migraine.

"Sauced, too, by the looks of it." Normally Tristan was better about holding his alcohol; it was one of the primary reasons Callum liked him. There was much to be said about a man who habitually remained upright.

"Absolutely fucking bladdered," confirmed Tristan, pivoting slowly to face Callum and holding his hand to his head. "I'd do something about it, only the prospect of managing anything at all sounds positively exhausting."

Understandable. Most people struggled with a hangover, and medeians even more so. Alcohol was a poison, after all, and magic was easily corrupted.

"Here," Callum said, beckoning Tristan towards him and pressing his thumb to the furrow between his brows. "Better?"

It didn't take much to alleviate a headache. Even less to make the headache *feel* as if it had been alleviated.

"Much." Tristan gave Callum a fleeting look of gratitude. "Did you enjoy the opulent shores of Greece, Your Highness?"

"You were invited, as you may recall."

"Yes, and I should have gone, clearly."

"Well," Callum said, "next time. In any case, there's something very interesting I thought you ought to know."

"If it's about the Forum, I received a visit as well. From a rather unpleasant sort of bloke, if I do say so myself."

"Actually, no," said Callum. "Or not entirely, anyway." He gestured outside. "Fancy a walk? Fresh air might do you some good."

The gardens, which accommodated roses of all varieties, were always a tolerable temperature, despite the presence of snow. Inside the house, a clatter indicated Nico had returned along with Reina, and, presumably, Libby.

"I suppose now we'll have to hear endlessly about Rhodes' beloved inamorato," sighed Callum.

To his surprise, Tristan became rapidly uncomfortable, going blank. "I suppose," he mumbled, and Callum frowned. It wasn't the discomfort that eluded him, but the obvious deflection; Tristan was magically keeping him out, preventing himself from being interpreted. The others did it often, sending up intangible shields whenever Callum approached, but never Tristan, who would have considered it a waste of effort.

Odd.

"Anyway," Callum said, "this Society has an interesting little mechanism. The 'elimination,' as they call it? Is perhaps too true a term."

It had not been very difficult to find the truth at the core of the Forum recruiter's intentions. It seemed that although the contents of the Society's collection remained a secret, its true nature was not.

"One candidate," Callum said, leaning closer, "must die."

Immediately he anticipated Tristan's posture to stiffen, or his dark gaze to narrow, as it usually did. Perhaps Tristan would even confirm that he'd had suspicions, which he nearly always had. He was a man so beloved of his own misanthropy that he would surely express less horror at knowing the truth than he would a lack of surprise at uncovering it.

"That's madness," said Tristan, without any particular feeling.

Callum's jaw tightened, irritated.

So Tristan already knew, then.

"You didn't tell me," Callum observed aloud, and Tristan glanced up, grimacing.

"I only just found out, and I'd forgotten for a moment."

"You'd *forgotten*?"

"Well, I—" Tristan fumbled, his wall of neutrality momentarily slipping. "I told you, it was… a strange night. I haven't quite finished processing."

If this version of Tristan was anything, 'unfinished' was certainly the right word.

"Care to postulate aloud?" prompted Callum. "After all, you've ostensibly become aware that one of us will have to be murdered." He bristled with irritation at not being the one to reveal that trivial little tidbit of information. "Who told you? No, don't answer," he grumbled as an afterthought. "It was Parisa, wasn't it? You were with Parisa last night."

Tristan looked moderately relieved. "I… yes, I was, but—"

"How did she know?"

"She didn't say."

"You didn't ask?" Unfathomable. Under any circumstances Tristan would have made demands.

"I—" Tristan stopped, wavering again. "I was distracted."

Callum stiffened. Of course Parisa had taken the opportunity to secure her alliance with Tristan the one way she knew how. Callum had been Tristan's primary confidant for months; surely she would have suffered that loss by now and tried something to repair it.

"You know," Callum remarked, "there is no fate so final as betrayal. Trust, once dead, cannot be resurrected."

Tristan glanced up sharply. "What?"

"With the Society," Callum clarified smoothly. "They're lying to us, or at least misleading us. How shall we respond?"

"I imagine there has to be a reason—"

"You," Callum echoed, and then scoffed. "*You* imagine there to be a *reason,* really?"

"Well, is it any wonder?" Tristan said defensively. "And anyway, maybe it's another trick. A test."

"What, making us think we have to kill someone? Clearly you don't understand the damage of such an exercise," Callum said gruffly. "There is nothing so destructive as thought, and especially not one that can never be rescinded. The moment a group of people decide they can be rid of someone permanently, what do you suppose happens next?"

"You're saying you wouldn't do it?"

"Of course not. But succumbing to the demands of a Society whose precursor for entry is human sacrifice? You can't tell me you've simply accepted it without question." Callum was sure of that much. "Even Parisa wouldn't consider it unless there was something significant in it for her. As for the others, Reina wouldn't care, and perhaps Varona could be persuaded, but certainly Rhodes would—"

Callum stopped, considering it. "Well, by that measure, I don't see the elimination falling to anyone other than Rhodes."

"What?" Tristan's head snapped up.

"Who else would it be?" Callum prompted, impatient. "The only person with fewer friends than Rhodes is Parisa, but she's useful, at least."

"You don't find Rhodes useful?"

"She's half of a set," said Callum. "Varona has precisely Rhodes' talents, only in a less obnoxious package."

"Varona is not Rhodes," Tristan said, the edges of his shield flickering a little. "They are not interchangeable."

"Oh, stop. You only can't imagine killing Rhodes because it would be like drowning a kitten," said Callum. "She'd fuss the whole time."

"I—" Tristan turned away, sickened. "I cannot believe you're actually discussing this."

"You're the one who seemed entirely unfazed by the idea we'd be asked to commit a murder," Callum pointed out. "I'm simply trying to sort out how you expect it to take place."

"Varona will never agree to kill Rhodes," Tristan said. "Nor will Parisa."

"They'll have to choose someone, won't they?"

"Maybe they'll choose me," Tristan said, blinking rapidly. "Perhaps they should."

"Oh, for fuck's sake, Tristan." A little fuse of Callum's temper sparked. "Must you be so very small all the time?"

Tristan cut him a glare. "So I should be more like you, then?"

This was obviously going nowhere.

"Have a nap," Callum said, pivoting away in annoyance. "You're a terrible bore when you're unrested."

He had hoped they'd have some sort of strategy session, determining which of the others they could most stand to lose, but it seemed Tristan was currently handling everything with exceptional ineptitude. Callum stalked through the corridors, returning to his room when he nearly collided with Libby.

"Rhodes," he said gruffly, and she glanced up, face draining of color, before hurrying past him without a word.

If there was one thing Callum loathed about himself, it was the prison of his deduction. So, Libby and Tristan were suffering the same intolerable human illness of shame and alcoholism. Wonderful. Clearly something had happened between them, and Tristan had not told him.

Again, Tristan had not told him.

Callum reached the corridor of private rooms and pushed open the door to Parisa's bedroom, shutting it behind him.

"No," said Parisa lazily. "And don't bother with Reina, either. Well—no, on second thought, that I would very much like to see," she mused, lifting her head to prop it up with one hand. "I suspect she'd bite your dick if you even tried it. Shall we have a wager and find out?"

Parisa, unlike the others, reeked of nothing. None of Parisa had come loose. She did not even seem particularly dehydrated. She seemed...

Smug.

"What did you do?" asked Callum bluntly.

"What I do best," said Parisa.

"What did Rhodes have to do with it?"

"You know, I rather like Rhodes," Parisa hummed thoughtfully. "She's very... sweet."

Her smile curled up thinly, taunting, and Callum understood he was being toyed with.

He relaxed a little, relieved. Finally, someone who could play.

"They're idiots," he said, prowling over to recline beside her on the bed.

"All of them."

"Everyone's an idiot," Parisa replied, tracing mindless patterns on her duvet. "You should know that as well as anyone."

"What did you do?"

"Changed them," she said with a shrug. "Can't reverse that sort of thing."

That was the peril of thought. Thoughts were so rarely dismissed once they'd been picked up and toyed with, and a mind successfully altered could rarely, if ever, revert.

Worse were feelings. Feelings were never forgotten, even if their sources were.

"No, you can't," Callum slowly agreed. "But why would that matter to you?"

"Why wouldn't it?" She shrugged. "It's a game. You know it's a game."

"No matter the stakes?"

She blinked with surprise, and then her expression fell away.

"Did you kill them this time?" she asked tightly.

"Kill who?"

"Whoever it was. From the Forum."

"No, not particularly."

She stared at him. "Not *particularly*?"

"Well, if he dies later on, that's really not my doing. They're his feelings," said Callum, shrugging. "How he chooses to process them is not my responsibility."

"My god, you're an absolute psychopath," said Parisa, sitting fully upright. "You don't feel any empathy at all, do you?"

"An empath with no empathy," echoed Callum. "Surely you hear how foolish you sound?"

"You can't just—"

"And what did *you* do, hm?" prompted Callum. "You can hear their thoughts, Parisa. You can change them, as you've just willingly confessed. By default you are no less interfering, and was your cause any more noble than mine?"

"I don't *destroy* people—"

"Don't you?" Callum asked her. "From what I just saw, Tristan and Rhodes look severely devolved. They are not who they were before."

"Devolved," Parisa said, "is hardly the word I'd use. And it's certainly not the same as destroyed."

Callum shifted an inch closer to her on the bed, and she leaned away, repulsed.

"You hate me because we're the same," he told her softly. "Haven't you come to that conclusion yet?"

She bristled, distractingly lovely in her fear. "We are not the same."

"How are we different?"

"You feel nothing."

"Whereas you feel sympathy but act regardless. Is that it?"

Parisa opened her mouth, then closed it.

"We are not the same," she said, "and what's more, you overestimate yourself."

"Do I?"

"You think you're more powerful than I am, don't you?"

"You have to work much harder to accomplish the same result. If I am not more powerful, I certainly have a more extensive vault from which to draw."

"The others know better."

"Do they? Perhaps not."

He could feel pieces fitting together for her, melting smoothly into place. An effortless joining. Her process of thought was so elegant, so pleasing. It was so satisfying to watch her make decisions, unlike other people. Normal people were so messy and unkempt. Parisa poured out her thoughts like honey, and though Callum couldn't read them the way she could, he could intuit other things far more clearly.

For example she thought, rather foolishly, that she could win.

"Shall we prove it?" Parisa prompted him. "Maybe you're right. After all, *you* clearly think we're the same, so for all intents in purposes, so must they. Thoughts, feelings, this is all the same to them." Again they were conspiratorial in their agreement. Even safely out of Callum's reach, surely Parisa could feel the way they were bound by similar circumstances. "They ought to have a chance to know the truth of what each of us can do."

"A battle of wits?" Callum replied.

"Of course not," she said. "Why do battle when we could simply... play a game?"

He slept well that night, untroubled. In the morning, they persuaded their referee.

"We do have a specified lesson for the day," said Dalton in his stuffy academic's voice. "And I hardly think this is necessary."

"The present research subject is thought," said Parisa. "Is there no value in observing a practicum on the subject?"

Dalton glanced uneasily between them. "I don't know if it's appropriate."

"Oh, go on," said Nico, who was intensely bored by the subject matter as usual. "We've got to eliminate someone eventually, don't we? Seems worth knowing what the other magics can do."

"Yes, Dalton, we will be eliminating someone quite soon," Callum agreed smoothly. "Why not allow us to determine who has the greater capability now?"

Dalton, out of anyone, would know the difference between Callum and Parisa's talents. After all, he was busy keeping her out of his head and holding Callum at bay as well, preventing either from being able to manipulate his moods—which meant Dalton was frequently overworked when they were in the same room, allowing things to slip between the cracks.

That Dalton had been sleeping with Parisa for months was, if still a secret among the others, not a very well kept one, and certainly not to Callum. More than once Callum had witnessed Dalton experiencing Parisa within every parapet of his being without touching her, with only the silhouette of former senses; muscle memory for lovers. At arbitrary times throughout the day, Callum could taste and feel and smell her anew, like the ghosts of someone else's aching.

He wondered if that was something to use against Parisa. Would she care for one amorist to find out what she'd done with two of the others…? Likely not, Callum thought with disappointment. She seemed the sort of person one only loved at one's own risk, and he doubted she had ever made (or kept) a promise.

"Well," Dalton said uncomfortably, "I suppose it needn't take long."

"One hour," said Parisa. "But no interference."

That, Callum thought, was quite an interesting request.

Perhaps even a stupid one.

"What's the purpose of a referee if there can be no interference?" prompted Tristan gruffly. He, Callum thought, would be a challenge for later. Already he had glanced furtively at Libby twice; he would need to be reminded how to choose his allies well.

"Just someone to stop us when the hour is up," Parisa said, glancing pointedly at Dalton. "No more, no less."

"No astral planes, either," said Callum. "Dull for the audience."

"Fine," said Parisa. "Corporeality only."

They shook on it, taking their places on opposite sides of the room.

"Rhodes," Callum said. "Turn your anxiety down."

Across the room, Parisa's mouth quirked.

"Don't worry about him, Rhodes," she said. "He'll be fine."

Warily, the vibration of Libby's unceasing agitation faded somewhat.

They waited in silence until the clock met the hour.

"Start," said Dalton.

"Why are you here?" asked Parisa promptly, and Callum chuckled.

"You want to do this as a debate? Or an interrogation?"

"Varona," called Parisa to Nico, not taking her eyes from Callum's. "What do you not do at the beginning of a fight?"

"Most things," replied Nico ambivalently.

"And why not?"

"Don't know the traps," he supplied, shrugging. "Have to learn the other person's rhythm first before you deal the heavy blows."

"There," said Parisa. "See? Even Varona knows."

Callum scoffed. "Is that what we're doing? Sparring? I thought the purpose was to differentiate ourselves from the physical specialties, not conform to them."

Parisa's smile twisted upward.

"Answer the question," she said.

"Very well. I joined because I had no other pressing plans," said Callum, "and now, I believe, it's my turn to ask you a question. Correct?"

"If you'd like," said Parisa obligingly.

"Marvelous. When did it occur to you that you were beautiful?"

There was a twitch between her brows, suspicious.

"It's not a trap for your modesty," Callum assured her. "Not much of one, anyway, when surely we can all confirm it for a fact."

"My modesty is not at issue," Parisa replied. "I simply fail to see the relevance."

"It's an opening swing. Or, if you prefer, a control."

"Is this some sort of polygraph?"

"You asked me why I was here in order to gauge some sort of truth from me, didn't you? Given your own parameters, surely I can do the same."

"Fine." Parisa's mouth tightened. "You're asking when I knew I was beautiful? I've always known."

"Well, surely that's true in some sense," Callum said, "but you're not just ordinarily beautiful, are you? You're the kind of beauty that drives men to warfare. To madness."

"If you say I am."

"So, when did you first understand it? Your power over others. Men, primarily," he said, taking a step towards her. "Or was it a woman first? No," he determined, catching the motion of her bristling in response. "Of course it was a man."

"Of course it was a man." She echoed it with a smile. "It always is."

"You have a loneliness to you, you know," Callum said, "but it's a bit... manufactured, isn't it? You're not an only child; that would be a different sort of loneliness. Like Rhodes," he said, gesturing over his shoulder, "she's lonely and alone, but not you. You're lonely because you choose to be."

"Perhaps I simply loathe other people," said Parisa.

"What's your sister's name?" asked Callum, as Parisa blinked. "You were close, of course, until you weren't. Your brother has some sort of strong name, I suspect; masculine, difficult to fracture. He's the heir, isn't he? The oldest, and then your sister, and then you. He favored you, your brother, and your sister turned you away... and she didn't believe you, did she? When you told her what you saw inside his mind."

He could see Parisa faltering, forced to relive the shadows from her youth.

"Let's see," Callum said, and snapped his fingers, populating the walls with images and tones from Parisa's past. "Money, that's easy enough." It would be false, a painting, unlike something she could do from his head, which would be a photograph. It was an inexact science, being an empath, but the important thing was to identify the proper sensations. For example, the golden light of her childhood and privilege. "Obviously you were well educated. Private tutors?"

Her jaw tightened. "Yes."

"That stopped after a time. You adored your tutor, of course. You love to learn. But your brother, he didn't like you paying so much attention to someone who wasn't him. So sad! Poor little Parisa, princess of her family, locked inside her vault of riches like a sweet, caged bird. And how did you get out?" He considered it, splashing an image of her former self onto the wall. "Ah, of course. A man."

The hazy illustration of young Parisa was swept away, carried off on the wind.

"Walk with me," said Callum, and immediately Parisa's knees buckled, lacking the strength to fight him. The others, he was sure, would follow, equally entranced. "More room this way. What was I saying? Ah, yes, someone saved you—no, you saved yourself," he amended, "but you made him believe it was his doing. Was it… your brother's friend? Yes, his closest friend; I can feel the betrayal. He expected something from you for his efforts… eternal devotion? No," Callum laughed, "of course not. He wanted something much more… accessible."

He paused, glancing at her, and the image of her following them along the walls as they walked was pulled into a darkened room, the light around it suddenly extinguished.

"How old were you?" he asked.

He watched Parisa swallow, her mouth gone dry.

"Eighteen," she said.

"Liar," he replied.

Her lips thinned.

"Fifteen," she said.

"Thank you for your honesty," Callum replied. He turned to the stairs, directing her up them. "So, you must have been what, eleven when you knew?"

"Twelve."

"Right, right, of course. And your brother was seventeen, eighteen…?"

"Nineteen."

"Naturally. And your sister, fourteen?"

"Yes."

"So troubling. So very, very troubling." Callum reached out to brush her cheek and she shrank away, repulsed. He laughed. "So it's me you hate, then?"

"I don't hate you."

"You don't *want* to hate me," Callum replied, "because you suspect me of committing terrible crimes with such silly things as hatred."

He stepped into the ballroom, holding out a hand. "Shall we?"

She glared at him. "You want to dance?"

"I want to see if you can keep up," Callum assured her.

She rolled her eyes, but took his hand.

"I assume you think you're winning," she remarked, beginning an uncannily perfect waltz once he set his hands upon her waist, though he would have expected no less. Somewhere, music was playing. He assumed that had been her work.

"You tell me," he said. "You're the one who can supposedly read my thoughts."

"You spend most of your existence in the singular belief that you're winning," she said. "To be honest, Callum, there's nothing so very interesting to read."

"Oh?"

"There's not much going on in there," Parisa assured him, her neck beautifully elongated as she carried out the waltz's steps. "No particular ambition. No sense of inadequacy."

"Should I feel inadequate?"

"Most people do."

"Perhaps I'm not most people. Isn't that the point?"

"Isn't it just," Parisa murmured, glancing up at him.

"You're so very guarded with me," Callum told her disapprovingly. "It's rather starting to hurt my feelings."

"I wasn't aware you had any feelings available to hurt."

He spun her under his arm, conjuring a little flash of color to marinate the walls.

"Was this it?" he asked, gesturing to the crimson. "I'm not quite sure I have the precise hue."

"For what?"

But he could feel her stiffen in his arms.

"Your wedding dress," he replied, smiling politely, and for a moment, she froze. "How is your husband, by the way? Alive, I assume. I imagine that's why you changed your name, went to school in Paris? You don't strike me as the career-oriented type, so I assume you were fleeing something. And what better place to hide than within the walls of a magically warded university?"

He felt the low undercurrent of her rage and felt keenly, acutely blissful.

"Oh, it's not the worst thing," he told her. "Plenty of teenagers have run from their tyrannical husbands before. Did your brother try to stop it? No, of course not," he sighed to himself, "he never forgave you for turning from him, and this was your punishment."

Parisa stepped back, dazed, and Callum held out a hand to her.

"You've been running a long time," he murmured to her, brushing a loose curl from her cheek. "Poor thing." He pulled her into an embrace, feeling the low swell of her misery greet him like a wave inside his chest. "You've been running for your life since the moment you were born."

He felt her sag against him, drained slightly, and he angled her shoulders beneath his arms, guiding her out of the ballroom.

"It wasn't your fault, you know," he told her, adjusting his arm to fit her waist as he led her up the stairs, up past the bedrooms and to the terrace on the top floor. She was gradually deflating, sentiment beginning to bleed out of her as if he'd sliced a vein. "People think beauty is such a prized thing, but not you. Not yours. Your beauty is a curse."

"Callum." Her lips were numb, his name slurred. He brushed his thumb over her bottom lip, half-smiling.

"Do you hate them?" he whispered to her, lightly kissing her cheek. "No, I don't think you do. I think, quietly, you suspect you deserve this, don't you? You drive people to madness; you've watched it happen. You see them set eyes on you and you know it, don't you? The way it looks, the way it feels. Perhaps you consider yourself a monster for it. It would explain your fear of me," he told her softly, taking her face in his hands. "Secretly, you believe yourself to be far worse than I have ever been, because your hunger is incurable. Your wants are insatiable. You never tire of making people weak for you, do you? The perversity of your desire scares you, but it's easier to think I might be worse."

They reached the terrace, Callum nudging the doors open for their entry. Parisa's feet met the wet marble, nearly slipping as the London rain fell. It splashed over the Greco-Roman farce that was the Society's decor, droplets sliding like tears from the marble cupids, the white-washed nymphs.

Callum tucked one of her hands in the crook of his arm, leading her around the rooftop's perimeter.

"You must wonder sometimes if it would be easier not to exist," he commented.

Parisa didn't answer, staring instead at her feet. Her shoes, fashionable as always, were suede and ruined, soaked through from the rain within minutes. Her hair fell lank over her shoulders in the wet, though of course her beauty was undiminished. He had never seen a woman's eyes shine so dully and still remain so bright. The haunted look in them heightened her beauty, in his mind. She had never been so lovely, so broken. She made devastation look like riches, like jewels.

"Did they hurt you?" he asked.

She dragged her gaze up, sickened. "Who?"

"Everyone."

Her eyes shut briefly, and she swayed. Her lips parted to mumble one word.

"Yes."

Callum stroked the drops from her cheeks, her lips. He pressed a kiss to the furrow between her brows; comforting, tender. Sweet.

"They don't have to hurt you anymore," he said, and stepped away, leaving her to stand alone.

She was burning on low now; a simmer that threatened to flicker, a glimmer poised to go out. Funny thing about rain, really, how it always made things seem so dismal. London did that naturally, of its own accord. The foggy grey was so spectacularly akin to loneliness, which Parisa was inescapably awash in. She was so saturated in it that she was the only thing that shone.

Callum watched Parisa turn her head, gazing out over the gardens, taking in the view of the city from where they stood. She was still staring, half-unblinking, when she reached out for the railing, closing her hand around it and settling into the breeze with a shiver. She was so empty now he doubted much would ignite her. Perhaps a spark, but then nothing.

Isolation was a powerful weapon. Forced isolation more so.

He did her the honor of watching, at least, as she climbed onto the railing. To her credit, she took little time to decide; she wasn't one for second-guessing. He was proud of her, nearly, for being so strong that way, for taking things into her own hands. He kept his gaze on hers, reassuring. He would not be revulsed by her choice.

When she fell, Libby gasped.

Unfortunate, Callum thought internally. He'd forgotten the others were there, being focused instead on Parisa's emotions, which were engulfing. She was so lovely, her sadness so pure. Her anguish was the most wonderful thing he'd ever tasted.

"No," sputtered Libby, half-hysterical. "No, you can't—what—"

"Why didn't you stop them?" Nico demanded, rounding on Dalton, who shook his head, numb.

"It hasn't been an hour," he said, visibly dumbfounded.

"Are you mad?" Tristan spat, seeming to fumble for words. His eyes, Callum observed, were widest, though it was difficult to tell which emotions were uniquely his. Callum could feel a variety of things from Tristan: sadness, disbelief, and then, at the tail end, distrust.

Ah, he thought with a grimace, and looked up, catching Parisa's eye as she smiled at him.

"Time to wake up," she said, and snapped her fingers.

In an instant, they were all back in the painted room, standing still, clothes dry.

As if they had never moved.

"I said no astral planes," Callum said, irritated, though he had to give her credit. He hadn't noticed anything; not one detail of the house had been amiss, and the rain had been a nice touch.

"So I should be dead, then?" she scoffed. "And anyway, we weren't on an astral plane. We were in someone else's head."

"Whose?"

"Nico's," Parisa said, as Nico blinked, startled. "Sorry," she added insincerely, turning to him.

Retroactively, Callum realized why she had begun with such a simple question, electing to misdirect him while she addressed Nico within the first minute. Clever girl, he thought grimly.

"You were rather an easy target, Varona. Guileless," Parisa offered to Nico in explanation. "Fewest impermeable walls."

"Thank you?" Nico said, though he was staring at her, still unconvinced that she was real.

"That's an hour," said Dalton, exhaling with relief as he glanced at his watch. "Though I'm not sure how to declare a winner."

"Callum, of course," said Parisa. "He did the most magic, didn't he? I could hardly even fight back," she said, turning to him.

"Did I?" he echoed, and watched her mouth twitch.

"Yes," she said. "I may have put us somewhere you couldn't actually harm me, but you beat me nonetheless. You broke me, didn't you? So you've won."

But he could feel the triumph radiating from her; it was sickening and putrid, rancid and rotting. She was overripe with it, devolving to decay. She was deadness taking root in fertile soil, resurrecting in the abundance of his loss.

He had genuinely broken her, that much was undeniable. Her death, even in noncorporeal form, had been real. But still, there was no question she'd let him find the pieces to break, knowing he would do it. Nothing she had revealed to him was a lie, but in taking advantage of her weakness, he'd revealed far more of himself. She, after all, understood thought: specifically, that something, once planted, could never be forgotten.

Now Callum's mistake was obvious: he had thought to prove himself strong, but nobody wanted strength. Not like his. Strength was for machines and monsters; the others could not relate to faultlessness or perfection. Humans wanted humanity, and that meant he would have to show evidence of weakness. He could see Tristan failing to meet his eye and knew it, that Parisa had beaten him, but this was only a single round. For his next trick, he would have to let the smokescreen of what he'd been today disappear.

"Callum, then," said Dalton, turning to the others. "Would anyone like to review what we saw?"

"No," said Reina flatly; speaking, for once, for all the others. She turned to Parisa with something like sympathy, which Callum observed with a grimace.

He would have to make them believe he could be weak. Perhaps only one person would be willing to believe it of him, but Parisa had already proven that to be considerable enough.

There was no stopping what one person could believe.

TRISTAN

IT HAD STARTED with a question.

"What do you think we should do?" Tristan had asked, summoning the bottle of absinthe and raising it to his lips.

He should have known Parisa would have an answer. For every question, but specifically that one. She would not have come to him empty-handed.

"I say," she replied, cleverly undoing one of the buttons of his shirt, "we should make our own rules."

That night was a blur to consider in retrospect, which was something Tristan wished he could have said at the time. Unfortunately he had been perfectly clear-eyed and conscious when he slid his tongue between Libby's lips, knowing both who she was and what he *ought* to have been—which was, ideally, able to prevent himself from stumbling into depravity and, quite probably, doom. Regrettably, he wasn't.

Parisa may have been the reason this all started—cleverly, and with what Tristan assumed to be centuries of atavistic female guile—but he had made no attempts to stop, and there was no recovering from what he now understood he craved.

And truly, it was a *craving*, nothing so intentional as wanting. Some chemical reaction was responsible, or demonic possession, or some tragic malformation that other people wrote books about surviving. The absinthe had certainly encouraged him, spreading like warmth through his limbs, but whatever it was Tristan suffered, he was faintly aware he'd been suffering it already. The symptoms preempted the condition, or perhaps the condition had existed (blindly, deafly, and dumbly) all along.

That Libby Rhodes was primarily a physicist was never to be discounted. Even now, her touch rumbled through his bones like the tremors of the earth itself.

Not that she seemed to be fixating much on what had passed between them.

"Electrons," Libby said without preamble, startling Tristan. He had recently begun trying to fiddle with the dials of his magic while listening to music, or otherwise disabling or distracting one of his senses. At the moment, he had been filling his ear canals with ambient noise while thinking about the taste of her mouth.

"Sorry, what?" he said, relieved that only Parisa could read his mind. (Fortunately, she was not in the room.)

"How small can you see?" asked Libby.

That wasn't much clearer. "What?"

"Well, you seem to be able to focus on the components of things," she said, still not addressing any of the more obvious things, like how they had slept together somewhat recently.

He had woken up in bed with her—with *her*, not Parisa—and had expected to find something more similar to the usual Libby Rhodes. Apprehension, regret, guilt, any of the above. Instead he'd awoken to Libby reading a manuscript, glancing at him as he sat up with difficulty.

"We don't need to talk about it," had been the first words out of her mouth. "In fact I'd prefer if we didn't."

Tristan had managed somewhat miraculously to straighten, squinting at her. His mouth was inconceivably dry, his head pounding, and he was being treated to merciless flashes of things he'd recently done and felt and tasted.

"Fine," he managed, though she paused, clearly hitting some sort of internal snag.

"What were you doing back here with Parisa last night, anyway?"

Dehydration wasn't going to make this conversation any easier. "She asked me to come. Said she had something to discuss." He could hear the coldness in his voice and paused, unsure whether it was worth getting into what Parisa had revealed about the Society under these uniquely troubling circumstances.

"Oh." Libby glanced away. "Well, if you don't want to tell me—"

For fuck's sake. He would have to now, wouldn't he?

"Rhodes," he began, and stopped.

There was no way she would take it well.

Though, keeping it from her would be morally quite worse, given how he had spent the previous evening. There was something about waking up naked in someone's sheets that made Tristan quite unwilling to subject her to secret group homicide.

Where to start, even if he could? Parisa had told him that in order for five to be initiated, one had to die. They had never been choosing someone to *be* eliminated; they were responsible for choosing someone *to* eliminate. The whole time they had been led to believe this was civilized and fair, but really it was primitive and shameful and, if Parisa was right, then they were possibly under the thumb of an organization that killed and had been killing for thousands of years.

But Tristan expected some form of panic, and so determined perhaps a half-lie would be best.

"Are you familiar with the trolley problem?" he asked Libby instead. "Where you find yourself at a lever in control of a runaway trolley—"

"And you either kill five to save one, or kill one to save five. Yes, I know it."

What a miraculous coincidence it was, that he would be having this conversation with her in her bed during the study of thought. Of course, where it came to magic, thought was less about philosophy than it was about the compulsions of it, and how it could be read or toyed with or interpreted.

In this case, ethics would have to do.

"Would you?" he asked, and when Libby frowned, he clarified, "Kill one to save five."

"Parisa summoned you here for a thought experiment?"

"What?"

Libby waited, and he blinked.

"Oh. No, she was—Well, it was about the Forum. Apparently—" More hesitation. He had never been so hesitant in his entire life, and wished desperately that he were clothed for this. Or that he had not known it to begin with.

Parisa was right. Thoughts, once planted, could not be forgotten. He could not unthink the way it felt to run his fingers over the bone of Libby's clavicle, his thumb hovering above her throat like he could slice it or adorn it, or both.

"Apparently," he attempted again, "Parisa's visit from the Forum rather made her... think."

"About the Society, you mean?"

"Yes. Sort of."

"What does that have to do with the trolley problem?"

"Well, someone gets eliminated, don't they? In this case you kill one to save yourself. Not literally, of course," Tristan rushed to add. "But… conceptually."

"I never cared much for thought exercises," said Libby warily. "And besides, the experiment does hinge a bit on who the people are, in some cases."

"Suppose the one person was me, then. Would that change things?"

He attempted a lightness to the suggestion, though of course the reality of knowing what he knew rendered things immensely more disconcerting than Libby could possibly guess. Then again, she wasn't exactly Parisa. He doubted Libby would inform him she'd be rid of him while they were still in bed together, and he was right.

"You don't really think I'd eliminate you, do you?" she asked, frowning, and went on to say something entirely not what he'd expected: "Your potential is fully unrealized. If anyone needs the Society, Tristan, it's you. I think even Atlas can see that."

That, Tristan thought, was both extremely helpful while being thoroughly not helpful at all.

Never had he known someone so positively bewildering. How could someone catastrophize the mundane at every possible turn only to readily assert her stance on such serious moral transgressions? She made him feel mad, insane, unstable. True, she was somewhat uninformed about the details (his fault), but there were markers of sensible logic here: she would not eliminate him because his power retained the most potential. Not because of who he was, or even what he was, but what he could be. That hadn't been anywhere near the top of his concerns, nor even counted among Parisa's, as far as he had known. She merely wanted Tristan because she trusted him on some level, he suspected. Perhaps it was a circular sort of thing, the way his usefulness to her was what proved him useful.

Meanwhile, there was no predicting where Libby Rhodes might find solid intellectual ground. Tristan, naturally, was so unsettled as to topple at every possible juncture. Did he want this so badly he would kill for it? Sometimes the answer was unquestionably yes. What was being human except to crave things unreasonably? Parisa could build worlds inside a person's mind. Tristan knew now—though he hadn't then—that Callum, for better or worse, could destroy a person's soul without lifting a finger. He had thought Libby and Nico were powerful—that Reina was *leaking* raw magic, overflowing with it to the point of near-irresponsibility—but knew nothing of himself, or where he fit among them. Admittedly, Tristan was not the most useful now, but the return on his investment might be greatest of all.

Did he even understand what existed at his fingertips? Did any of them?

Morality, what little Tristan had of it, tugged him between schools of thought, forward and backwards. "I do what's necessary," had been Adrian Caine's take on most of his sins, and while it was (academically speaking) a legitimate philosophical standpoint, it was rather repugnant when left unconstrained by things like 'mercy' or 'compassion' or even 'guilt.' Worse, if there was one thing Tristan had always aimed to be, it was well to the left of whatever his father was.

Of course he could not *kill* someone; certainly not over access to a few books. (Rare ones. In the hands of the most powerful medeians he'd ever known. As part of a custom that had existed for centuries, so therefore wasn't it...?)

(Never mind.)

In any case, if he did this—or even accepted it as a thing he *could* do—would he ever be able to forgive himself? Could he live with whatever remained of his conscience? Funny how quickly humans could adapt to things. He had once believed he could marry Eden Wessex and serve her father dutifully, never questioning whether he wanted more; or, as the case may have been, whether he *craved* it. He was starting to think his solidarity with the person he'd once been had been a much more stable time, and perhaps much healthier. It had been like regular exercise, productive diet habits, broken by a blissful, gorging binge. Now he had everything he could want; power, autonomy. Sex. Christ, the sex. And all it took was killing one person, but who would it even be? It wasn't as if they could all agree on someone.

Unless.

"What if it were Callum?" he asked.

(Purely for the sake of argument.)

Libby frowned. "What, you mean kill Callum to save... me? The rest of us?"

"Yes." It made Tristan anxious even to think of suggesting it, though luckily Callum wasn't in the house. Callum's presence, like Reina's, was readily identifiable by excess traces of magic. With all Callum's illusions, though, it was difficult to discern what was actively in use and what wasn't.

"Say it was Callum on one side of the tracks, and the rest of us on the other."

"Oh." Libby blinked, and her eyes widened. "Well, I—"

Tristan waited, bracing himself. He wasn't entirely sure what he wanted her answer to be. It was, to her, a hypothetical question, so it wasn't as if this was enough to really determine her stance.

Still, he was rather taken aback when she said, "I'm not doing that."

"What?" had been his gut response, delivered so sharply it rattled his entire aching brain from the depths of his many upsetting thoughts. "What do you mean you're not doing that?"

"I'm not killing someone," she said, shrugging. "I won't do it."

"Well, suppose you won't have a choice," he said.

"In the thought experiment, you mean?"

He hesitated, and then said, "Yes, in the thought experiment."

"Everyone always has a choice." She chewed the inside of her cheek, tapping the manuscript in her lap to the wave of something he probably couldn't hear. "Would you?"

"Would I what?"

"Kill Callum."

"I—" He blinked. "Well, I—"

"Or me." She glanced at him sideways. "Would you kill me?"

"No." No, not her. What a waste it would be for anyone to rid the world of her power, her capability. What an absolute crime against humanity. That was an easy conclusion, even if sex were not part of the equation. "No, of course not, but—"

"What did Parisa say?"

It occurred to him that Parisa had said something precisely the same, only drastically different: *I'm not doing that.*

"I think," he said slowly, "Parisa would plot some sort of mutiny. Take over the train." He managed a grim laugh that hurt his throat, stinging. "Kill three and save three, somehow, just so she didn't have to do precisely as she was instructed."

"Well, there's that for choices," said Libby, shrugging, as if anything he'd said were a plausible option. Tristan blinked, attempting to formulate thought, but was interrupted by the motion of Libby carefully marking her place in the manuscript, turning to face him.

"I should probably talk to—" A pause. "I need to, um. My boyfriend is," she began, and then faded into silence. "I should probably tell him."

"You aren't going to…" Fuck. "What are you going to tell him?"

She chewed her lip. "I haven't decided."

"You're not going to—" Stay.

"I don't know. I don't think so." A pause. "No."

"So…"

The fact that Tristan could neither fully speak nor fully keep from speaking was a rather upsetting one. He longed for the presence of mind to say nothing, to wander out of here like someone who did this sort of thing all the time, but at the moment he suffered only pinpricks of dehydration and total, unfettered stupidity.

"So you're just going to tell him, then? Straight out?"

"I don't know. I need to think about it," she said.

Clearly she meant alone, which was fair. This thought exercise, unlike the previous one, was not designed for peer review. The impulse to ask *think about what?* temporarily flooded Tristan's consciousness, but muscle memory kept him from lingering overlong. Bad enough that he'd done what he'd done; he did not want to suddenly become the sort of person who lingered. He had limbs accustomed to impassive distance, and to his relief, he put it between him and Libby Rhodes with ease.

Weeks later, he had still heard nothing from her. Their first few interactions had been slightly awkward, with occasional averted glances and one truly precarious collision that involved his palm inadvertently skating her hip as they passed each other between tables in the reading room, but there had been no further discussion. There had been no deliberate contact of any kind, nor anything outside of hello or good evening or please pass the bread.

Until, of course, "Electrons."

"What do you mean electrons?" Tristan asked, feeling groggy and stupid. Ironic that the research spent on thought would leave him so utterly bereft of any, even after nearly two months. Their current topic of precognition (and its study of history's most famous precognitors, like Cassandra and Nostradamus) had done absolutely fuck-all to prepare him for this sort of interaction, which could only be described as nightmarishly unexpected.

"If you could break things down as small as an electron, you could alter them chemically," Libby said. "Conceivably, that is."

"Oh." He cleared his throat. "Well, it seems a bit more of a... later topic, doesn't it?"

"What, chemistry?"

"We're still on psychokinesis."

"Well, that's not unrelated to thought in general," she said. "I actually thought of it when we were discussing the mechanics of the future. By the way, have you thought any further about time?"

She had such a ceaseless way of making him wonder what on earth she was talking about.

"About... time?"

"About whether you can use it." She, unlike him, seemed blissfully unaware that this was the first time they were speaking to each other privately since he had woken up in her bed. "Precognition is proof the future can be accessed through thought, so why not physically as well? Not to mention that time is a dimension none of the rest of us can even imagine the shape of, much less see." She fixed him with a direct, unnerving glance. "Unlike you."

"What, you think I can—?" His misdiagnosed illusionist training was failing him. Magically speaking, he hadn't the faintest idea what sort of language could be used to describe what she was suggesting. "*Traverse* time?"

"I have absolutely no idea, Tristan," she said. "That's why I'm asking you. It just seems as if you probably have some way to use it, don't you?"

"Use what?"

"Your specialty."

"What about it?"

"Well, it's yours, isn't it? So presumably you're the one who should be using it, not me."

Foggily, he produced an argument, plucking it from somewhere. "Plenty of magical specialties are designed to be used together. Most naturalists work with—"

"I'm not saying that." Libby tilted her head, brushing her fringe to one side. She had grown it out; now it was nearly long enough to tuck behind her ear, a fact of which Tristan was troublingly assured. "There's nothing wrong with it not being yours to use. I simply suspect otherwise."

"Why?"

"Why what?"

"Why suspect otherwise?"

"Truthfully, it's really more of a guess than a suspicion. What does Parisa think?"

"I—" He stopped, taken by surprise yet again. "What?"

"Actually, speaking of Parisa." Another abrupt change, just as Tristan thought he'd managed a grasp on the conversation. "Do you suppose she's changed her mind?"

Rather than continue asking the same question, Tristan folded his arms over his chest, waiting.

"About the whole… elimination thing," Libby clarified, intuiting correctly that he hadn't the faintest idea where she was going with any of this. "Seems like she might have changed her mind after the whole Callum thing. You know, the trolley problem?"

"Oh." Right. The small issue of Parisa's death by Callum. "Yes." Tristan fought a sudden chill. "In fairness, I think she always knew that about him."

"Well." Libby cleared her throat. "I suppose there might be some merit to the whole thing."

Tristan arched a brow. "Some merit to… killing Callum?"

"You saw him, Tristan." Libby's mouth was a new, grim form of determination he'd never seen from her before. "He didn't know it wasn't real, did he? He had no idea he was in some sort of… augmented reality in Varona's head," she said with a frown, "so *Callum's* reality is that he could be rid of Parisa at any time, and easily. So maybe that's something to consider in the experiment."

"That some people should die?"

"That some specialties shouldn't exist," she said conclusively.

That, Tristan thought, was certainly a jarring realization to come to.

"It's a moral dilemma for a reason, Rhodes." His mouth was dry again, though for what reason, he wasn't entirely sure. Perhaps because she'd just unintentionally decided which of them she'd murder, which she might one day actually do.

Precognition. Terrible. He spared no envy for Cassandra.

"There isn't a correct answer," Tristan said slowly.

Libby's smile twisted slightly, eyes drawn up to his.

"I suppose not," she observed, mostly to herself, and then, astoundingly, began walking away.

Suddenly, Tristan felt a bit mad with disbelief at the concept that Libby could wander over, suggest to him that he was capable of doing something utterly impossible, and then wander off again without addressing the thoughts that had been plaguing him for weeks. Could he kill someone? Could *she*? Had they signed over their souls the very moment they set foot in this building? Had they become something they would not have been otherwise, now contorted beyond recognition from what they'd been? Were they not yet the deformities they would *ultimately* be? What the fuck was he supposed to do with electrons—how could he possibly *use time?*—and had she broken it off with her boyfriend or not?

Tristan's hand shot out before he could stop himself.

"Rhodes, listen—"

"Ah," came Callum's voice, cutting in just as Libby whirled around, eyes wide. "I thought I felt some lingering distress. Is Tristan pestering you again, Rhodes?"

"No, of course not." She cleared her throat, glancing at Tristan's hand, which he removed from her arm. "Just think about it," she said quietly, "would you?"

Then she gave Callum's shoes a wordless glance and ducked her head, leaving the room.

"So skittish, that one," said Callum, glancing after her and turning back to Tristan. "She doesn't know, does she?"

"No." He still couldn't bring himself to tell her. "And anyway, suppose it isn't true?"

"Suppose it isn't," Callum agreed, falling into the chair beside Tristan's. "How do you imagine they make that announcement, I wonder?"

"It could be a trick," Tristan said. "Or a trap. Like—"

"The installation? And the Forum?"

Tristan sighed. "Suppose they just want to see what we're capable of."

"Suppose it's real," Callum mused alternatively. "I don't suppose you have a lead, do you?"

"A lead?"

"A target would be the less sensitive term," Callum said. "Or a mark."

Tristan bristled a little, and Callum's perpetual smile thinned.

"Do you find me callous now, too, Tristan?"

"A cactus would find you callous," mumbled Tristan, and Callum chuckled.

"And yet here we are," he said, summoning a pair of glasses, "two peas in a pod."

He set one glass in front of Tristan, pouring a bit of brandy he procured from the flask in his jacket pocket.

"You know, I don't remember the first time I realized I could feel things other people couldn't," Callum commented anecdotally, not looking up from the liquid in the glass. "It's just… always been there. I knew, of course, right from the start that my mother didn't love me. She said it, 'I love you,' just as often to me as she did to my sisters," he continued, shifting to pour himself a glass, "but I could feel the way it lacked warmth when she said it to me."

Callum paused. "She hated my father. Still does," he mused in an afterthought, picking up his glass and giving it a testing sniff. "I have a guess that I was conceived under less than admirable circumstances."

He glanced up at Tristan, who raised his own glass numbly to his lips. Like always, there was a blur of magic around Callum, but nothing identifiable. Nothing outside of the ordinary, whatever Callum's ordinary even was.

"Anyway," Callum went on, "I noticed that if I did certain things; said things a certain way, or held her eye contact while I did them, I could make her… soften towards me." The brandy burned in Tristan's mouth, more fumes than flavor. "I suppose I was ten when I realized I had *made* my mother love me. Then I realized I could make her do other things, too. Put the glass down. Put the knife down. Unpack the suitcase. Step away from the balcony." Callum's smile was grim. "Now she's perfectly content. The matriarch of the most successful media conglomerate in the world, happily satisfied by one of the many boyfriends half her age. My father hasn't bothered her in over a decade. But she still loves me differently; falsely. She loves me because I put it there. Because I made myself her anchor to this life, and therefore she loves me only as much as she can love any sort of chain. She loves me like a prisoner of war."

Callum took a sip.

"I feel," he said, blue eyes meeting Tristan's. "I feel immensely. But I must, by necessity, do it differently than other people."

That, Tristan supposed, was an understatement. He wondered again if Callum were using anything to influence him and determined, grudgingly, that he did not know.

Could not know.

"I," Tristan began, and cleared his throat, taking another sip. "I would not wish to have your curse."

"We all have our own curses. Our own blessings." Callum's smile faltered. "We are the gods of our own universes, aren't we? Destructive ones." He raised his glass, toasting Tristan where he sat, and slid lower in his chair. "You're angry with me."

"Angry?"

"There's not a word for what you are," Callum corrected himself, "though I suppose anger is close enough. There is bitterness now, resentment. A bit of tarnish, or rust I suppose, on what we were."

"You killed her." Even now it felt silly, inconceivable to say. Tristan had been numb at the time, only half-believing. Now it felt like a distant dream; something he'd invented when his mind had wandered one day. The call of the void, that sort of thing. Gruesome ugliness that danced into his thoughts and back out, too fleeting and horrid to be true.

"It seemed like the honorable thing at the time," said Callum.

It took drastic measures not to gape at him. "How?"

Callum shrugged. "When you feel someone's pain, Tristan, it is difficult not to want to put them out of it. Do we not do the same for physical pain, for terminal suffering? Under other circumstances it's called mercy." He took another sip from his glass. "Sometimes, when I suffer someone else's anguish, I want what they want: for all of it to end. Parisa's condition is lifelong, eternal. Degenerative."

He set the glass on the table, empty now.

"It will consume her," he said, "one way or another. Do I want her to die? No. But—"

Another shrug.

"Some people suffer bravely. Some clumsily." He glanced up, catching Tristan's look of uncertainty. "Some do so quietly, poetically. Parisa does it stubbornly and pointlessly, going on just to go on. Just to avoid defeat; to feel something more than nothing. It is, above all, vanity," Callum said with a dry laugh. "She is like all beautiful things: they cannot bear the idea of not existing. I wonder whether her pain will grow sharper or more dull after her beauty fades away."

"And what about those of us who don't suffer?" asked Tristan, fingering the lip of his glass. "What worth do we have to you?"

Callum scrutinized him a moment.

"We all have the exact curses we deserve," he said. "What would I have been, had the sins that made me been somehow different? You, I think, have a condition of smallness, invisibility." He sat up, leaning forward. "You are forced to see everything as it is, Tristan," Callum murmured, "because you think you cannot be seen at all."

Callum slid the glass from Tristan's fingers, leaning across the table. He smoothed one hand over the bone of Tristan's cheek, his thumb resting in the imprint of Tristan's chin. There was a moment just before it happened where Tristan thought perhaps he had wanted it: touch. Tenderness.

Callum would have known what he wanted, so perhaps he had.

"I feel," said Callum, "immensely."

Then he rose to his feet, long-legged and lean, leaving only the glass where he had been.

It went without saying that for days after, Tristan was quietly in torment. Callum, at least, was no different in his intimacy. They were friends primarily, same as ever, accustomed to their evening digestifs by the fire. There was a companionship to Callum, an ease. There were moments when it seemed Callum's fingers twitched towards Tristan's shoulder, or skated reassuringly between the traps of Tristan's scapulae. But they were only moments.

Libby, meanwhile, kept coolly away, and Tristan's thoughts of time with her meandered inevitably to the matter of time itself.

As spring began to break unseasonably early, creeping out from beneath the winter chill, Tristan found himself repeatedly outside, approaching the wards that surrounded the Society's estate. Magic at its edges was thick and full, identifiable in strands as voluminous as rope. There were threads of it from other classes, other initiates, which made for a fun, sleepless puzzle. Tristan would toy with the pieces, pulling at their ends like fraying thread, and watch for any disruption in the pulse of constancy.

Time. The easiest way to see it—or whatever of it Tristan could identify—was to stand there, nearly out to the street, and to exist in many stages of it at once. It wasn't a normal activity, per se, but none of this was.

Their supervision seemed to have decreased over time; coincidentally or not, none of them had seen much of Atlas since they had each been confronted by the Forum, which led to an odd sort of tiptoeing among the Society's residents. Each had developed their own odd habits, and this was Tristan's. He stood in silence, twisting dials he only partially knew how to use, and hoped—or, rather, assumed—that something would happen if he only looked long enough.

The trouble was his imagination. Libby had said it: hers was too small. Tristan knew the falseness of geometry, the idea that the world contained other dimensions that they were not yet programmed to understand. But he had learned shapes as a child, so naturally he looked for them now. To stare into the familiar and somehow expect to see something new felt so frustrating as to be thoroughly impossible. Yes, Tristan could see things other people could not, but he didn't believe his own eyes when he saw them. A child told habitually of his worthlessness was now a man bereft of fantasy, lacking the inventiveness to lend him a broader scope. Ironically, it was his own nature that crippled him most.

Only once did Tristan run into someone while he did this. He looked up, startled, to suddenly see a young man facing him, staring at the house as if he couldn't quite see it, or perhaps like he was looking at something entirely else.

"Yes?" asked Tristan, and the man blinked, adjusting his attention. He wasn't particularly old, probably Tristan's same age or a bit younger, and had slightly overlong black hair, plus a general look of rare untidiness. As if he were the sort of person who didn't usually spill coffee on his collar, but he had done so today.

"You can see me?" asked the man, incredulous. Tristan supposed he might have been using a cloaking illusion, but was interrupted before he could ask. "Well, never mind, that's obvious," the man sighed, mostly to himself. He was not British; he was extremely American, in fact, albeit different from whatever sort of American that Libby happened to be.

(Tristan wondered why she had come to mind, but hastily dismissed it.)

"Obviously you can see me or you wouldn't have said anything," the man remarked in something of a continued amiability, "only I've never actually encountered another traveler before."

"Another... traveler?" asked Tristan.

"Usually when I do it everything's a bit frozen," said the man. "I knew there were other kinds, of course. I just always thought I was existing on a plane that other people couldn't see."

"A plane of what?" asked Tristan.

The man gave him a bemused half-frown. "Well, never mind, I... suppose I'm wrong." He cleared his throat. "In any case—"

"What are you looking at?" asked Tristan, who was academically stuck on the point at hand. "Your surroundings, I mean." He hoped to determine whether they stood in the same place physically, or only temporally. Or perhaps neither, or both.

"Oh." The man glanced around. "Well, my apartment. I'm just deciding whether to go inside."

"I don't think I'm on the plane you're on, then. I think I can just see it." Tristan paused, and then, because he wasn't entirely sure he wanted the encounter to end, "What are you deciding?"

"Well, I've just not entirely made my mind up about something I've got to do," said the man. "Actually no, it's worse. I think I've already decided what I'm going to do, and I just hope it's the right thing. But it isn't, or maybe it is. But I suppose it doesn't matter," he sighed, "because I've already started, and looking back won't help."

That, Tristan thought, was certainly relatable.

"I won't keep you," Tristan said. "I'm just... playing around a bit, I think."

Calculations had started, albeit unhelpfully. It seemed they were both on the same plane of something—time was the only plausible explanation— but how had Tristan arrived there? Either it had happened so subtly he didn't know how he was doing it (and therefore he might have done it before, or might do it accidentally again) or he had done something to initiate the mechanism and failed to write it down. He ought to start cataloguing his meals, his socks. Every step he took differently, just in case something he did managed to drag him to another corner of reality.

"Yes, well, play responsibly." The man gave Tristan a lopsided grimace. "I'm Ezra, by the way."

"Tristan," said Tristan, offering Ezra a hand to shake.

"Tristan," echoed Ezra, brows twitching as he accepted Tristan's grip. "But you're not—?"

Tristan waited, but Ezra stopped, clearing his throat.

"Never mind. Best of luck, Tristan," he said, and strode forward, gradually disappearing into the thick fog that covered the house's lawn.

Once Ezra had disappeared, it occurred to Tristan that he had done something. What it was he hadn't the slightest idea, but he had done it, and so he turned on his heel and marched himself into the house, launching up the stairs.

He could tell Libby. She would probably exceed him in enthusiasm, meaning that he would have the freedom to derisively say things like 'calm down it's nothing' even if he did not feel them. Unfortunately she would also ask several questions, trying to unpuzzle things as she always did. She was an architect of details, constantly in the trenches of construction. She would want to see how things moved, what parts were in play, and of course Tristan would have no answers to any of it. She would look up at him, wide-eyed, and say anything else? and he would say no, that's all he knew, sorry he even brought it up at... three.

In the morning.

Tristan sighed, stepping back from Libby's door and shifting to face the frame beside his own instead, knocking once.

Callum arrived at the door shirtless, his hair mussed. Behind him, Tristan could see the rumpled sheets, still warm from where Callum had lain there moments before, breathing deeply in solemn slumber.

It was strange how Tristan did not know how Callum looked to the others. He wished sometimes that he could venture inside someone else's head the way Parisa could, just to see. It was a curiosity now. He knew Callum did something to his hair, to his nose. He could see that enchantments were used there, but could not piece together their effect. Instead, Callum appeared to Tristan as he always did, with hair that wasn't quite blond and the forehead that was noticeably high; the jaw that was so square it looked perpetually tensed. There were things available to fix, if one were in the business of fixing. Callum's eyes were close-set and not as blue as he could make them if he tried. Possibly Callum could even afford the enchantments that made them permanent; even mortal technology could fix a person's eyesight. Medeian charms afforded to the son of an agency of illusionists meant that even Callum might not remember the way his face looked undone.

"I see you," came out of Tristan's mouth before he had decided fully what to say, which was probably best, as it might have been 'I don't want to be alone,' or worse, 'I don't know what I want,' both of which Callum would know by looking. What a terrible thing it was to be so tragically exposed.

Callum shifted away from the door, beckoning him in with a motion. Wordlessly, Tristan stepped inside.

NICO

NICO SLIPPED TO THE INSIDE of a right cross and missed a hard incoming hook, running directly into Reina's fist and swearing loudly in a mix of highbrow Spanish and rural Nova Scotian slurs.

(Once, Gideon had taught him how to say something in Mermish—which was a blend of Danish, Icelandic, and something Nico classified as vaguely Inuit—but had also warned him that, pronounced incorrectly, it would summon a sort of half-ghost, half-siren sea-thing, so it hardly seemed worth it to use. Max was not particularly helpful with profanity, as he was stubbornly prone to overuse of the same one: "balls.")

"You're out of sorts," remarked Reina, wiping sweat from her brow and eyeing Nico as he stumbled back, dazed.

It took a moment, but eventually his eye stopped watering.

"Maybe you're just getting better," mumbled Nico half-heartedly.

"I am, but that was your mistake," Reina observed with her usual regard for his feelings.

"Yes, fine." Nico slumped down to sit on the lawn, sulking a bit. "I suppose let's call it, then."

Reina gave the grass a derogatory look (it may have insulted her; she had mentioned once that certain types of English lawns had a tendency to be excessively entitled) but eventually sat uncomfortably beside him.

"What's wrong?" asked Reina.

"Nothing," said Nico.

"Fine," said Reina.

It was, in nearly every sense, the opposite of the encounter he'd had shortly before this one.

"You're lurking," Parisa had called to Nico from inside the painted room, turning a page in her book without looking up. "Stop lurking."

Nico froze outside the door frame. "I'm not——"

"Telepath," she reminded him, sounding bored. "You're not only lurking, you're pining."

"I'm not pining."

(Okay, so maybe it wasn't totally different from his conversation with Reina.)

"Just come in here and tell me what's bothering you so we can move this along," said Parisa, finally glancing up from what Nico was surprised to see was a vintage copy of the X-Men comics.

"What?" she prompted impatiently, following his line of sight to the comic with a look most closely described as exacting. "Professor X is a telepath."

"Well, I know," said Nico, fumbling.

"You don't think he's based on a medeian?"

"No, I'm just… never mind." He paused, rifling the hair at the back of his head with a grimace. "I'll just—you're busy, I'll—"

"Sit down," said Parisa, shoving out the chair across from her with her foot.

"Fine. Yes, alright." He sat heavily, clumsily.

"You're fine," said Parisa. "Stop fretting."

"I'm not fretting," Nico said, bristling a bit from the wound to his manhood, and she glanced up.

It was really so desperately unfair she was so pretty, Nico thought.

"I know," she said. "That's my origin story, if you've been paying attention."

Immediately, Nico faltered again. "I know," he said, more to his feet than to anything. Was this what it was like to be Libby? He was almost never so oafish, nor so concerned with his own oafishness. He'd met plenty of pretty girls, and certainly a handful of attractive mean ones. He should have been prepared for this.

"I'm not mean," Parisa corrected, "I'm brusque. And before you facetiously blame a language barrier," she added, pausing him once he opened his mouth, "I am also conversationally trilingual, so that's not an excuse."

"A toast to your linguistic superiority, then," grumbled Nico, stung.

Parisa glanced at her page, flipping it.

"Sarcasm," she remarked, "is a dead form of wit."

Reference to mortality of any sort was enough to make Nico flinch, and

Parisa glanced up at the motion of it, sighing.

"Just say it," she suggested, tossing the comic aside. "I can't have you tiptoeing around like this, Nicolás. If you go soft then I'll have to be soft, and I can't begin to tell you how little time I have for pretense—"

"You *died*," Nico said, "in my *head*."

Parisa paused for a moment, possibly to dip a toe inside the head in question. She was barefoot, he realized, observing the petal-pink of her toenails where they rested on the chair beside his. He focused purely on the observation, hoping it would be less telling than anything else she might find running through his thoughts.

"Don't concern yourself with the me in your head," Parisa said eventually. "She doesn't exist, Nico. Only I do."

Good advice, theoretically. In this case, it barely applied.

"I feel responsible somehow," he admitted, "which is—"

"Ridiculous," she supplied.

"—I was going to say possibly unfair," he corrected, "but still. Why—?" He stopped.

"Why did I choose to use your head and not one of the others?" Parisa prompted. "I told you, Nico, because you're the least capable of guile."

"Sounds like an insult."

"Why?"

"Makes me sound... I don't know." He was mumbling, half-shamed. "Naïve."

"What is this, machismo?" Parisa sighed.

Nico shifted in his chair, glancing at her toes again.

"For what it's worth, it's you I'd most want in bed," she remarked, subjecting him to untold decades of trauma simply by holding his gaze while she said it. "It's rare that I'm selfless enough to keep my distance, truthfully, and rarer still that I summon any restraint. Unfortunately I find myself with such a pressing desire not to ruin you."

He slid a hand to where her feet were idly sat atop the chair beside his, stroking a finger along one arch. "Who says you'd ruin me?"

"Oh, Nico, I would love for you to be the one to ruin me," she said flippantly, shifting to rest her feet in his lap, "but much to my own detriment, I wouldn't allow it; and anyway, you do things much too openly, with far too much of yourself. You'd fuck me with your whole heart," she lamented, "and I can't put you in that sort of danger."

"I am capable of casual sex," said Nico, wondering why he felt the need to make it true. He curled his palm around her heel, drawing it up to the bone of her ankle and caressing her calf slowly, molding his hand to the shape of her.

"For you, it can either be good or it can be casual," she said. "And I can't take the chance of having one without both."

She dug her toes into his thigh, sliding down in her chair.

"What do you do in your dreams?" she said, and then, "You speak to someone," she answered herself, drumming her nails along the wood of the table. "I can hear you doing it sometimes."

"Oh." He cleared his throat. "I... it's really not my—"

"Not your secret to tell, I know, only I already know it, so there's very little telling involved. His name is Gideon," Parisa produced matter-of-factly, like a familiar character she had plucked from the pages of a comic book. "He worries you constantly. Gideon, Gideon, Gideon... he is in your thoughts so often I think his name sometimes myself." She sighed a little as Nico continued to work his palms mindlessly into the slender muscle of her calf, strumming the tender fibers of her. "He's a traveler, isn't he, your Gideon? Not a telepath." She closed her eyes, exhaling again when Nico's fingers brushed the inside of her knee. "From what I can tell he operates in dreams, not thought."

"Actually," said Nico, and stopped.

Parisa eyes opened and she shifted her leg again, this time adjusting so the arch of her foot sat perilously atop Max's prized vulgarity of choice.

"Actually?" she prompted.

For once she wasn't smiling coyly. She didn't intend to seduce him into an answer. She meant to crush him if he did not.

Nico liked her more for that, which was troubling.

"Don't be troubled," she assured him. "You may be the only person who likes me for the right reasons."

He rolled his eyes, taking her foot in his hands again. "Do you think there's an intersect between dreams and thought?" To her pause of expectation, he clarified, "I've been trying to do research on it but it's no use, really. I don't know what I'm looking for."

"What is he?" she asked him. "Gideon."

He kneaded the bone above her arch, stroking it with his thumb. "A creature, technically."

"Hybrid human?"

"Well—" Nico bit the inside of his cheek. "No. Half mermaid, half satyr."

"Oh." Parisa's smile twitched, and then broadened. "Human-shaped? Where it counts, that is."

He glanced up at her. "Is that meant to be funny?"

"Yes. A bit." Her tongue slid over her lips, rendering her faintly girlish. "I can't help my appetites."

"He's got a dick, if that answers your question." He switched gruffly to her other foot, tugging punitively at her pinky toe. "Not that I—" More hesitation. "I'm just saying, I've lived with him for a long time. Things happen."

"So you've seen it?"

Nico glanced up, defensive, and she shrugged.

"I've seen plenty," she told him. "I wouldn't judge you."

"It's not like that," he muttered.

"Fine, machismo again." She nudged his knee with her heel. "Don't be cross."

"I'm not, I'm just—"

"So Gideon can travel in dreams, then?"

"Gideon… can," Nico said slowly. "Yes. Sorry, yes."

"Oh." Parisa sat up, abruptly removing both feet from his lap. "You've done it too?"

"I—" He felt his cheeks flush. "It's a private question."

"Is it?"

No.

"Fine, I do it," Nico said with a grimace, "but don't ask me how I—"

"How do you do it?"

He gritted his teeth. "I told you, it's—"

"Describe Gideon's penis," Parisa suggested, and in the pulse of panic that followed, she had clearly plucked something from his head. "Ah," she said, "so you transform, then? Well, that's certainly impressive. More than." She nudged him again, delighted. "Brilliant. Now we can never fuck," she said, seemingly content with that conclusion, "as I make a point never to sleep with people who are more magical than me."

"That can't possibly be true," said Nico, gently devastated.

"I," Parisa replied, "am very magical. The Forum must have been especially eager to get their hands on you," she added as an afterthought, which meant nothing to Nico. He frowned, bewildered, and she tilted her head, apparently recognizing his blankness for what it was. "Did you not get a visit from the Forum while you were in New York?"

Nico thought back to that weekend, trying to recall if anything had been out of place.

"Oi," Gideon had said at one point, "someone's trying to get in." Nico, who had been in his customary form of a falcon, said nothing, but gave a brisk little flap of his wings to suggest they could well and rightly fuck off. "Right then," said Gideon, "that's what I thought."

"Well," sighed Parisa, dragging him back to the point, "never mind, then. You wanted to know about dreams and thought?" she asked, and while Nico had until that point been highly insistent on keeping what he knew of Gideon's condition a secret, he recognized the motion of a rare door opening. Somehow, he had earned a key to Parisa Kamali's sincerity, and he did not plan to waste it.

"You read a book," Nico said, "about dreams. Reina told me."

"Ibn Sirin's book, you mean?" asked Parisa. "Though it's said he abhorred books, so probably a lesser medeian wrote it."

"Yes, that one. I think." He fidgeted. "I wondered if you had any—"

"I do," Parisa confirmed. "One theory, mainly." She paused, and then, "What do dreams look like when you're in one?"

"They have a topography," Nico said. "They're in… realms, for lack of a better word."

"Like an astral plane?"

"I wouldn't know," said Nico, "seeing as the only one I've ever been on was the one you created in my head, and I didn't know I was in it."

"Well, you remember how it looked and felt," she pointed out, and he considered it.

"Indistinct from reality, you mean?"

"Pretty much," she agreed. "Our subconscious fills in the blanks. If anyone, particularly you, had looked closely at any of the details, you would have known we were not in reality. But most people do not look closely unless they are given a reason to look."

"Well, then yes, dream realms feel the same," he said. "Like reality."

"I suspect dreams are their own astral plane," Parisa said. "Only they are absent time."

"*Absent* time?"

"Yes. Are you ever aware of time when you're traveling with Gideon?" she asked, and Nico shook his head. "Is he?"

"Not particularly, no."

"Well, perhaps your theory is close. Dreams may well be the intersect of time and thought," Parisa said thoughtfully. "There are plenty of studies to show that time moves differently in dreams, even to a calculable extent. Possibly no differently than how time moves in space."

That was an interesting theory. "So time could move faster or slower in dreams?"

"Instinctually it follows," she said, shrugging, and added, "Gideon must have quite a lot of control to be able to pull himself in and out at will."

Nico had never considered it that way, but Gideon did have a keen sense for when to return. Nico, always in bird form, just assumed Gideon wore some sort of wristwatch.

"Why do you worry about him so much?" asked Parisa, interrupting Nico's internal pondering. "Aside from the matter of your friendship."

Nico opened his mouth, hesitating, then closed it.

Then, gradually, opened it again for, "He's... very valuable."

He didn't want to get into detail about what Gideon's mother regularly asked him to do. Steal things, usually, and typically on behalf of medeians. She was something of a con woman, as far as Nico could tell. With ocean ecosystems changing and the increasing privatization of magic, the modern mermaid evidently could not be counted on to limit herself to the usual exploits of the sea.

Equally unclear, in Nico's view, was whether Gideon was or wasn't a criminal. Gideon certainly considered himself one, hence Nico's careful secrecy on his behalf, but Nico had never liked the thought of it. When Gideon was a child he had simply done as his mother asked, not understanding the details of what he'd been tasked with or who they'd been contracted for, and once he became aware of the consequences, he had stopped, or tried to. People, Gideon said, were inclined to go mad when something was stolen from inside their thoughts, and he no longer wished to be part of it.

But it hadn't taken Gideon long to realize that hiding from his mother (and her employers) was far more easily said than done.

"Ah, yes," Parisa murmured to herself, "I suppose his abilities would be easily monetized. Plenty of people would pay to take ownership of something in a dream if they knew such power existed." She stared off for a moment, thinking. "So what exactly is it you're looking for in the archives?"

Confessing the truth was something of a difficulty, but it didn't seem worth keeping to himself. If anyone was going to be able to help him—or to have no particular agenda in knowing what he knew—Nico supposed it was Parisa.

"What he is, I suppose," Nico admitted. "What his powers are. What his life span is. Whether anyone has ever existed like him before." A pause. "That sort of thing."

"He craves a species, I take it?"

"In a sense."

"Pity," she said. "Very human of him, to long for a collective."

They sat in silence for a moment. Nico had a feeling Parisa was in her own thoughts rather than his at the moment, which was an interesting observation. She seemed to revolve within a solitary orbit, the energy in the room suddenly collecting around her in tendrils of curiosity rather than expelling outward, as other people's contemplation tended to do.

"You should have something," Parisa said after a moment. "A talisman to carry with you."

Nico blinked, looking up. "What?"

"Something to keep with you. Something you keep secret. So that you know where you are," she explained, "and whether you exist on a plane of reality. Your friend Gideon should carry one, too."

"Why?"

Nico stared in puzzlement as Parisa rose to her feet, stretching languidly.

"Well, you haven't identified it yet, but the reason you can't let go of what you saw inside your head is because you didn't know you were inside it." She turned to look at him, half-smiling. "It's a favor, Nico. You ought to have a talisman. Find one and keep it with you, and then you'll never have to wonder what's real."

She turned to leave, expressing every intention to exit the room without further discussion, but Nico leapt to his feet, catching her arm to pause her.

"You don't think Callum would really hurt you, do you?" he asked, his voice more urgent than he would have preferred it to be. An hour before, even five minutes ago, he would never have attempted such a spectacular display of vulnerability, but now he needed to know. "In real life, I mean. In actuality. Whatever that means."

Her eyes narrowed slightly in calculation.

"Doesn't matter," she said, and turned away, but Nico tugged her back, imploring her.

"How can it not matter? You can see inside his head, Parisa. I can't." He released her, but kept the pull of conspiracy between them. "Please. Just tell me what he really is."

For a moment when she looked at him, Nico thought he saw uncharacteristic evidence of tension in Parisa's face. Vestiges of a secret soon to be known; a truth wanting out. She made the decision in the second her eyes met his, but even with the improbability of the conversation they'd just had, he couldn't have prepared himself for how her answer would shake him.

"It doesn't matter whether Callum plans to hurt me," she said, "because I'll kill him before he does."

Then Parisa had leaned closer and said something that Nico had taken like a blow, still reeling even after hours had passed.

"What is it?" Reina asked again, startling him back to their conversation. She was normally comfortable without speaking, but presumably he had been silent for too long.

Nico tugged at a blade of grass, plucking it free. He wondered if Reina could hear it scream when he did so, and flinched at the reminder that the universe had some voice he couldn't hear. Another detail among many he couldn't un-know. A blissful piece of foregone ignorance, belonging to a person he would never be again.

"Would you kill someone to have all of this?" he muttered to Reina, though he regretted having asked the question as soon as it fell out of his mouth. Would she ask him why, and would he be able to answer if she did?

But he needn't have worried. She didn't even spare a breath.

"Yes," she said, and closed her eyes, warming silently in the grass.

VII: INTENT

REINA

THE REALM OF THOUGHT wasn't totally uninteresting as a topic of study, but even so, Reina was pleased to move on. The breaks in subject matter were particularly intriguing because there was always a sense of some invisible, underlying fabric; that they were being directed by currents they couldn't necessarily see until they'd already absorbed it, swallowed it whole.

Reina had the benefit of being raised amid Eastern philosophies as opposed to Western, which meant she trusted general policies of oneness. Suchness, as it were. She understood, in a way the others did not, the existence of polarities, a mysticism of opposition: that acknowledging the presence of life meant accepting the presence of death. That knowledge necessitated ignorance. That gain meant loss. Ambition suggested contentment, in a sense, because starvation implied the existence of glut.

"Luck is a matter of probability," said Dalton. He wasn't always assigned the role of lecturer, which was probably for good reason. He didn't seem to care for it, as if they had dragged him away from something more important; he had an air of wanting to be elsewhere, or generally belonging to thoughts a great distance from theirs. Still, they had grown familiar enough with him by then that his presence was less that of an administrator and more like a cook they rarely saw, or a housekeeper. Someone providing them with sustenance but not interfering much with their daily lives.

"Luck," Dalton continued, "is both a magic and a science that has been studied in detail, by medeians and mortals alike. It is chance, but with a loaded die: the lean of likelihood toward a favorable event. For obvious reasons, one's proclivity for luck is a valuable commodity. Also a common magic, even for the lowest rungs of witches. Now, the issue of unluck—"

"Unluck?" echoed Libby, bewildered.

(Reina had no such confusion. The existence of luck necessarily implied its opposite.)

"Unluck," Dalton confirmed, "for lack of a better term, is the purposeful disruption of probability. Jinxes, hexes, curses—"

"Battle magic?" asked Nico, who despite his best intentions had a tendency to be mercilessly literal.

"Unluck," Dalton repeated. "Hexes are of course the most direct form; intentional bad luck caused to the victim. The other two—"

"Jinxes are inconveniences, entanglements," said Libby. "And curses are deliberate harm?"

She always seemed to phrase things in the form of a question even when she was certain, ostensibly out of a desire to appear unthreatening. (As if any of them would be threatened by something they were all required to study as first year students at university, if not sooner.)

"Academically, yes," confirmed Dalton. "But for the Society's purposes, we are less concerned with the results of such magic than we are with their construction. Which curses have proven most effective and why, that sort of thing. Mostly," he said, his attention straying, as it often did, to Parisa, "how the disruption of luck can be used to unmake a man, unsettling him from the design—or rather, the lack of design—his path should naturally take."

Parisa's dark eyes held his for a moment. Dalton cleared his throat.

"Nature is chaos, magic is order, but they are not wholly unrelated. Bloodlines," Dalton continued, "are a common carrier for mechanisms of unluck—genetic continuity. Very common that a curse will follow genealogy in some way or be passed on to progeny. That sort of magic is much more complex than it seems; anything with such lasting consequences requires a certain degree of sacrifice and loss to the caster."

Reina's commentary was rare, but sometimes necessary. "Why?"

The plants beside her slithered with glee, coaxing her to speak further. *MotherMother soothe us with your voice it pleases us to hear you!*

She crossed one leg over the other, irritated.

"Why?" echoed Dalton at her interruption, looking once again as if he wished he were left alone with his thoughts. "Because although magic and nature have different forms, they are not inseverable: magic has aspects of nature, nature has aspects of magic, and to take one away from either is a corruption to both their forms. It is the disintegration of naturalism itself. A man with a curse will upset the balance of things, warping the universe around him. Luck magic is a corruption as well; for any corruption to hold, the caster must accept, in some way, a fracture—a piece of themselves forever broken, in payment for the imbalance they have caused."

"I don't want to know why it's necessary," Reina said bluntly. "I want to know why it works."

Dalton fixed her with a narrow glance.

"Sacrifice has magic of its own," he said. "The decision to do something is itself a change, a rupture to the state of the world's natural order. Would things happen in the caster's favor regardless of interference? Yes of course, probability meaning that all outcomes are, conceptually, possible," Dalton said, droning on methodically. "But to set one's sights on one particular outcome is to necessitate a shift in some direction, enduring and irreversible. We study the realm of consciousness because we understand that to decide something, to weigh a cost and accept its consequences, is to forcibly alter the world in some tangible way. That is a magic as true and as real as any other."

"Are you suggesting magic is some sort of spiritualism?" said Reina.

Mother is telling the truth!, Mother speaks truth!, she is made of it!

"Sometimes," Reina went on gruffly, "you treat magic like a god, like an energy, and sometimes like a pulse. It's an unscientific vibration when convenient, but we already know its behaviors can be predicted, and therefore purposefully changed."

Dalton said nothing, waiting for her to make her point, so Reina persisted, "You make magic its own entity, but it has no autonomy of choice. No research shows that magic deliberately chooses how to honor the intentions of the caster—it simply does or doesn't work, depending on the caster's abilities."

"So magic has no sentience of its own, you mean?"

Reina nodded, and beside her, Parisa's expression took on some degree of contemplation.

"Magic is not a god," Dalton agreed, "it is a tool. But it does respond discreetly to the distinctions of its user's intentions, however subtle those may be. It is a matter not unlike general relativity," he said. "Intent cannot change the foundation of science or magic as a whole, but we know from observation that its outcome can change relative to its use."

"So whether an arrow hits its target depends on both the skill of the archer and the definable laws of momentum," said Libby. "Is that what you mean?"

"Yes and no," said Dalton. "It is not so simple an equation. The rules of lethality are not limited by one constraint or two, but by many. When it comes to magic, the question is not merely a matter of the archer," he explained, "but also of the arrow itself. Sometimes the arrow is made of stone, sometimes steel, sometimes paper. If the arrow itself is weak, even an immensity of skill can sometimes fail."

"Does the archer's intent forge the arrow in addition to aiming the bow?" asked Nico, frowning.

"Sometimes," said Dalton. "Other times, the arrow is forged by something else."

"Does the arrow forge itself?"

Libby again. Dalton turned to her slowly, regarding her for a moment in silence. She seemed to mean one thing—*If magic is the arrow and we are the archers, how much control do we have over its flight?* —but appeared to have ultimately asked quite another.

Is magic the tool, or are we?

"That," Dalton said eventually, "is the purpose of this study."

Callum and Tristan had not spoken yet, which wasn't entirely unusual, nor was it unusual that they paused to exchange a glance. At one point it had been Tristan initiating the glances, almost as a measure of security; checking to see if his left leg still existed, or if he were still wearing the shirt he'd put on before breakfast. Now it was Callum who was doing routine maintenance. Observing the functions on a passenger train; protecting his assets.

Reina turned to look at Nico, who had lost interest in the philosophical underpinnings of the conversation. She wondered if he were still thinking about what Parisa had told him, and then proceeded to wonder what his intentions were.

She was fairly confident Nico wouldn't kill her. (Her plants slithered back, hissing in distaste at the prospect of anyone doing otherwise.) Of course, practically speaking, Reina was fairly certain no one would; she was neither at the top nor the bottom of anyone's list, which made her neither potential target nor potential victim. Beneath it all, they were equally ambitious— individually, they were all starved for something—but the polarities of the group were the ones whose incongruity couldn't be rectified. The presence of Parisa implied the existence of Callum, and that was the tension the others were unable to stand. Unused to the necessity of opposition, they would find it necessary to choose.

Reina turned to look at Parisa, considering her own choices. On the one hand, she would happily be rid of Parisa. On the other, Parisa had played her game well; Reina doubted anyone could convince Tristan or Libby to kill her. No, scratch Libby from consideration altogether. She wouldn't actively choose anyone—too skittish. Unless Libby would kill Callum? A possibility. After all, Libby had been the most bothered by Parisa's astral death.

At the reminder of the incident in question, Reina turned to observe Callum again, more closely this time. The plant behind him shivered, and Reina frowned in agreement; it was Callum who had unsettled them all, and even the simplest forms of life could feel it. Callum was the obvious choice, only there was one major obstacle to unanimity: Tristan. Would Tristan agree to kill Callum? No, most likely not, and that explained Callum's need to check on him regularly.

It seemed the incident between Callum and Parisa had split the remainder of them into factions—people who were bothered by death and people who weren't—and Tristan was the meridian.

Maybe they should just be rid of Tristan.

Parisa turned to her with one brow arched. (Reina had been careless; settling perhaps a bit too clumsily on the idea.)

Don't pretend you've ever really had a friend, thought Reina in silent reply. *You'd turn on him in a moment if it suited you.*

Parisa's lips twitched up, half-smiling. She gave a small shrug, neither confirmation nor denial, then returned her attention to Dalton, who was just beginning to discuss curses on forms of consciousness when the door opened behind him, revealing the rare appearance of Atlas in the frame.

"Don't let me interrupt," said Atlas, though of course he *had* interrupted, unquestionably. He was dressed in a full suit as always, though he appeared to have come from somewhere; perhaps a meeting. Having never held the position of Caretaker in an elite secret society, Reina was unsure of his daily activities. She watched him remove the hook of his umbrella from his arm and set it beside the door, leaning it on the frame.

At one point, this had been normal. When they first began their work, Atlas had been present nearly every morning, but, like Dalton, he had taken several steps back once they'd grown comfortable with the Society's work. His appearance now shifted the chemistry in the room, noticeably altering its atmosphere.

Dalton nodded in acknowledgement, opening his mouth to continue his list of suggested reading, but before he could, Libby had tentatively raised a hand in the air.

"Sorry, sir," she said, turning to Atlas, "but since you're here, I wondered if we were going to discuss the details of initiation at any point."

The rest of the room froze.

Dalton, Reina observed, had fallen robotically still, instantly short-circuiting. Nico was mortified, but a very specific kind of mortification: the particular dismay of having forgotten to do something important, like having left the house with the oven on. Tristan's gaze was fixed straight ahead as if he had not heard the question (impossible) and Callum was fighting laughter, as if he hoped to replay the moment endlessly until he'd wrung all the amusement out of it that he possibly could.

Parisa was the least startled. Presumably she had known what Libby was going to ask before she had said anything aloud, given the mind-reading, but surely there was no doubt for anyone in the room that whatever secrets the others were carrying, Parisa held them, too.

Only Libby was patently empty-handed.

"We've all been here nearly a year," Libby pointed out. "And by now we've all received visits from members of other organizations, haven't we?"

No one spoke in confirmation, but that didn't appear to deter her in the slightest.

"So, it just seems as if we should have been told by now what comes next," Libby concluded warily, glancing around. "Is there going to be some sort of exam, or—?"

"Forgive my brevity," said Atlas. "As a group, you are to have selected a member for elimination by the end of the month. As for the details, it's a bit early to discuss them."

"Is it?" asked Libby, frowning. "Because it seems as if—"

"The Society has done things a very particular way for a reason," said Atlas. "This may not seem clear right now, but I cannot permit expediency to outweigh the importance of our methodology. Logistical efficiency is only one among many concerns, I'm afraid."

It was clear that Libby wasn't going to receive any further answers; even more obvious was her discontent with the prospect of continued ignorance.

"Oh." She folded her arms over her chest, turning back to Dalton. "Sorry."

Dalton went on, returning half-heartedly to his lecture, and for the rest of the afternoon, nothing was noticeably out of place.

As far as Reina was concerned, however, something monumental had been achieved that afternoon. She was certain now that only Libby remained in the dark, which meant that if the rest of them were aware of the terms for initiation and they still hadn't left, then they must have all secretly come to the same conclusion Reina had.

They were each willing to kill whoever they had to in order to stay. Five out of six arrows were not only sharp, they were lethal, and now they were readily aimed.

Briefly, Reina felt the tug of a smile across her face: Intention.

MotherMotherMother is aliveeeeee!

TRISTAN

"MAYBE WE SHOULD KILL RHODES," remarked Callum over breakfast.

At which point Tristan stopped chewing, swallowing thickly around his toast.

Callum slid a glance to him, half-shrugging. "It just seems practical," he said. "She and Varona are a pair, aren't they? Why keep both?"

Tristan's response was slow. "Then why not suggest killing Nico?"

"We could, I suppose." Callum reached for his coffee, taking a sip. "I could be convinced."

He replaced the cup on the table, glancing at Tristan's waylaid toast. "Everything alright?"

Tristan grimaced. "We're discussing which among us to *murder*, Callum. I don't think I'm expected to go on eating."

"Aren't you? You're still here," Callum observed. "I imagine that means you're expected to go on doing everything precisely as you normally would."

"Still." Tristan's stomach hurt, or his chest. He felt nauseated and broken. Was this what Dalton meant about a person being fractured? Perhaps they were being disintegrated on purpose, morality removed so as to be stitched back up with less human parts. Maybe in the end his former beliefs would be vestigial, like a foregone tail. Some little nub at the base of his philosophical spine.

It was astounding how easily he had come around to the idea. Shouldn't he have balked, recoiled, run away? Instead, it seemed to have settled in like something he'd always suspected, becoming more undeniably obvious each day; of course someone had to die. Immense magic required a power source, and a sacrifice of this nature would be precisely that: immense.

For him, anyway.

"Maybe it won't work if you feel nothing," Tristan murmured, and

Callum looked up sharply.

"What?"

"I just meant—"

What *had* he meant? This was Callum, after all. "Never mind."

"You had faith in me once." Callum's fingers tightened around his cup. "Not anymore, I take it?"

"Well, it's just—"

"This is what I do to survive," Callum said, his voice harsh now with something; betrayal, maybe. Tristan flinched, remembering what Callum had said: *Trust, once dead, cannot be resurrected.* "I thought you understood that about me by now."

"I did. I do," Tristan corrected himself. "But you just sound so…"

"What, callous? Cold, indifferent, ambivalent?" A pause. "Or do you mean cruel?"

Silence.

Callum turned his head to glance expectantly at Tristan, who didn't look up. "You still don't get it, do you?"

Tristan said nothing.

"We are this way because of what we *have*, not what we lack," Callum said, suddenly bristling with impatience. "Who would Parisa be if she had not seen her brother's thoughts? If Reina had not been leached upon from birth?"

"Callum," Tristan managed to say, "I was only trying to—"

"To what? To vilify me? In the end we will make the same choice, Tristan. In fact, we have made it already." Callum's mouth was thinly lined; tight with malice, or pain. "Eventually, you and I will both decide to kill someone. Are you less guilty simply because you've been the one to unravel more?"

Foggily, Tristan thought to say yes. He thought to argue: *This is guilt, it is human, your decisiveness is robotic, like a machine. In the end I could not carry on as I was, I could not become a false version of myself, I have a beating heart inside my chest and where is yours?*

He didn't.

"You are here," Callum said, "because you crave something from this as much as I do. Power, understanding, it doesn't matter which. Maybe it's knowledge you want, maybe not. Maybe you're here because you plan to walk out of this Society and take over James Wessex's company the moment you do. Maybe you'll bankrupt him, send his daughter into ruin. Maybe this is vengeance for you, reprisal, whether you plan to admit that to yourself or not."

Tristan swallowed heavily.

"Maybe you can see others, Tristan, but I can see the parts of you that you won't allow yourself to see. That's my fucking curse, Tristan!"

Callum slammed a fist against the table, rising to his feet.

"There isn't a person alive who can see themselves as I see them," Callum snarled, and it did not sound like a warning. Not a threat. "You want to believe that your hesitation makes you good, makes you better? It doesn't. Every single one of us is missing something. We are all too powerful, too extraordinary, and don't you see it's because we're riddled with vacancies? We are empty and trying to fill, lighting ourselves on fire just to prove that we are *normal*—that we are ordinary. That we, like anything, can burn."

He pivoted as one hand fell to his side, exasperated.

"We are medeians because we will never have enough," Callum said hoarsely. "We aren't normal; we are gods born with pain built in. We are incendiary beings and we are *flawed*, except the weaknesses we pretend to have are not our true weaknesses at all. We are not soft, we do not suffer impairment or frailty—we imitate it. We tell ourselves we have it. But our only real weakness is that we know we are bigger, stronger, as close to omnipotence as we can be, and we are hungry, we are aching for it. Other people can see their limits, Tristan, but we have none. We want to find our impossible edges, to close our fingers around constraints that don't exist, and *that*," Callum exhaled. "That is what will drive us to madness."

Tristan glanced down at his forgotten toast, suddenly feeling drained.

Callum's voice didn't soften. "You don't want to go mad? Too bad, you are already. If you leave here the madness will only follow you. You have already gone too far, and so have I."

"I won't kill Rhodes," said Tristan. "I can't do it."

Callum paused a moment, stiffening, and then he resumed his seat, waving a hand over his coffee to replenish its warmth.

"Yes," he said without expression. "Parisa made sure of that."

For the rest of the day, Tristan felt dazed, as if he'd suffered a wound that hadn't clotted. The constant questioning of himself, of others, was viciously acute. It was one thing to be understood by someone else, to be exposed by them, and another (however inevitable it was) to be misused by them. Both

Parisa and Callum had seen pieces of Tristan that he either didn't or couldn't understand; both fundamentally distrusted the other. What, then, had they seen in him that they could each use to their advantage? He was caving in on himself beneath the weight of his doubt, uncertain.

Nothing was concrete anymore. Time did not exist and neither did infinity. There were other dimensions, other planes, other people who could use them. Maybe Tristan was in love with Callum or Parisa or both or neither, maybe he actually hated them, maybe it meant something that he trusted them both so fucking little and they didn't mind, having known it all along. Maybe the only parts Tristan couldn't see were himself and his place in their game between each other.

What Tristan wanted was to believe in something; to stop staring at the pieces and finally grasp the whole. He wanted to revel in his magic, not wrestle with it. He wanted something, somewhere, that he could understand.

He was pacing while he postured. Movement didn't help the blur of things half-seen, but sitting still was not an option. He closed his eyes and reached out for something solid, feeling strands in the air. Their wards were gridlike, difficult to disturb, like bars. He paused and tried something different: to be part of them, participant instead of observer.

He felt himself like a flicker of existence, both in place and not. It was meditation, in a sense. A focus on connectedness, and the more embedded in his own thoughts he became, the less he was able to place himself in any physical reality. In the absence of sight, sense and memory could tell him where he was: hard wooden floors, the smell of kindling burning in the furnace, the air of the Society mansion, occupied by magical contortions he himself had made—but in the interest of unlearning his preconceptions, he discarded them. He was nowhere, everywhere, everything and nothing. He abandoned the necessity of taking a form or a shape.

Bewilderingly, it was Parisa's voice that spoke to him.

"You ought to have a talisman," she said. "Find one and keep it with you, and you'll never have to wonder what's real."

Tristan's eyes snapped open, alarmed, but upon recalling himself in reality, he confirmed that he hadn't moved from where he'd remembered himself last. He still sat on the floor of the painted room, surrounded by no one and nothing.

Where had he gone in that instant, or had he actually moved at all? Had

Parisa been inside his head somehow, or had it been a memory? Was it her magic or his own?

So much for not wondering what was real.

In the end, Tristan shook himself, rising to his feet. After a pause to think, he took a small scrap of paper, scribbling something on it and tucking it into his pocket.

Callum looked up when he entered, bracing himself for a continuation of their prior argument, but Tristan shook his head.

"I'm not here to have a row," he said. "You're right, of course. I know you're right."

Callum looked warily unconvinced. "Is that supposed to be concession or a compliment?"

"Neither. A fact. Or rather, a white flag."

"So this is a truce?"

"Or an apology," Tristan said. "Whichever you prefer."

Callum arched a brow. "I don't suppose I need either."

"Perhaps not." Tristan folded his arms over his chest, leaning against the frame of the reading room. "Drink?"

Callum regarded him another moment, then nodded, shutting the book before him and rising uncomplicatedly to his feet.

The two of them walked in practiced cohesion to the painted room. Callum summoned a pair of glasses from the corner, glancing over his shoulder to Tristan. "Whisky?"

"Sure."

Callum poured with a wave of his hand, leaking magic as he always did, and beside him, Tristan took his usual seat. Their motions were practiced, frequently rehearsed, and Callum set a glass in Tristan's hand, taking hold of the other. For several moments they were silent, each savoring the drink. It was a smoky, hollow blend, silken with amber and caramel in the light, with the smooth finish they both tended to prefer.

"It doesn't have to be Rhodes," Callum said eventually. "But you have to admit she's unpopular."

Tristan sipped his whisky. "I know."

"Unpopular doesn't mean valueless."

"I know."

"And if your attachment to her is…"

"It isn't." Again, Tristan sipped his glass. "I don't think."

"Ah." Callum turned his head, looking at him. "For the record, she has been trying to research her dead sister."

Tristan blinked. "What?"

"Her sister died of a degenerative disease. I suppose I might have mentioned that before."

He hadn't, though Tristan remained undecided as to whether or not he should have.

"How do you know that?"

"Because I know," said Callum simply. "Someone who has seen another person waste away is easy to spot. They are haunted differently." He paused, and then added, "And she is also requesting books on human degeneration, which the library is currently denying her."

"And *that* you know because of...?"

"Coincidence. We do live in the same house."

"Ah." Tristan cleared his throat. "How do I know you're being honest with me?"

"What reason would I have to lie?"

"Well, it's not as if it doesn't benefit you. Having someone."

"Having someone, or having you?"

"You tell me." Tristan slid him a glance, and Callum sighed.

"You are not accustomed to being desired, are you?" Callum prompted, and before Tristan could manage his surely uncomfortable reply, Callum clarified, "As a friend, I mean. As a person." A pause. "As anything."

"Please don't psychoanalyze me today," Tristan said.

"Fine, fine." Callum's smile quirked. "Daddy issues."

Tristan glared at him, and Callum laughed.

"Well, the whisky's good, and so is the company," said Callum. "Astoundingly, that is the primary extent of your worth to me, Tristan. Ample conversation, at the very least."

"I don't know about ample."

"That," Callum said, "is the best part. The silences are particularly engaging."

Aptly, they sat in silence for a moment, saturating themselves in the relief of conflict resolution.

After a few minutes of quiet coexistence, Callum glanced at the clock.

"Well," he said. "I suppose I'm for bed, then." He rose to his feet, setting his empty glass on the table. "Are you staying up?"

"For a bit," Tristan said, and Callum nodded.

"For what it's worth," he said, clapping a hand on Tristan's shoulder, "the parts of you that you seem to loathe are hardly abhorrent at all."

"Thanks," said Tristan pithily, and Callum let out another hearty laugh. He strode through the doors and disappeared, the warmth of his magic swallowed up by the dark and gone with him.

Tristan, left alone in the light of the painted room's fireplace, set his glass on the table, reaching into his pocket. He removed the note he'd scrawled to himself earlier, unfurling it to read the script written inside.

A glass of wine. Vintage. Old World.

Tristan looked up at the sweat on his glass of whisky, watching it fall to the table below.

"Fuck," he swore aloud, crumpling the piece of paper in his hands.

LIBBY

"Miss Rhodes," said Atlas pleasantly, "what a surprise."

She paused in the doorway, frowning.

"It's not actually a surprise, though," she determined aloud, "is it?"

Atlas glanced up, half-smiling. "What gave it away?"

A lack of disturbance, mostly. There was no magic to that, aside from observation.

"Just a hunch," she said, and Atlas beckoned for her to take a seat.

"How did you know I was here?"

Surveillance wards. "I heard Dalton mention it."

"Mm," said Atlas. "I take it you have further questions about initiation?"

If you could call them questions.

"Yes," said Libby, "*several.*"

So many, in fact, that she hardly knew where to start.

Libby had been doing a variety of things over the past couple of days. Research, as always. Following her visit from the Forum, she had been looking primarily for anything to do with Kitty, to no particular results. All the library would give her—or, in any case, all the library was programmed by someone else to give her—were subjects pertinent to their task at hand: degenerative curses, longevity and its opposites. The decay that was a process of natural entropy was currently off limits unless it had something to do with the study of intentional corruption.

Libby had just begun to wonder who was actually keeping them from the contents of the library when Nico had pulled her aside for another conversation entirely, looking unusually distressed.

"I have to tell you something," he said. "You're not going to like it."

"Apropos of nothing? I assume not." Libby had never liked anything Nico had to say to her uninvited and certainly wasn't expecting to start now. She opened her mouth to tell him she had other things on her mind, but hastily he stopped her.

"Just… try not to Rhodes this," he said. "Okay?"

"Once again, my name is not a *verb*, Varona."

"Whatever." He rubbed his temple. "Look, definitely don't tell Fowler—"

"I don't tell Ezra anything," she snapped, preemptively irritated. "Certainly not anymore."

Nico blinked. "What does that mean?"

"Nothing." Nothing she wanted to say to him, anyway. "I don't want to talk about it."

"Fine, just—" Nico exhaled, dropping his voice. "I think," he murmured, "when they say we have to eliminate someone, they mean it… literally."

That wasn't what Libby had been expecting at all. "What?"

"The sixth person, the person who doesn't get initiated. I think they get—" An agitated pause.

"Get what?"

"Jesus." Nico tousled his hair with one hand. "Killed."

"No," said Libby. "That's ridiculous. That's impossible."

"I mean, I'm sure it is," said Nico reflexively. "But also, is it?"

"That's nonsensical."

She glared at him, frowning. "Who told you that?"

"Parisa, but—"

That was slightly more troubling, given the mind-reading. "Then she must have misinterpreted or something. Or maybe she's lying."

Nico was surprisingly hesitant. "I don't think so, Rhodes."

"Well, it's outrageous," said Libby caustically. "There's no way we're part of… of some kind of…" She fumbled, flustered. "Some sort of *murder* competition—"

"Maybe we're not," Nico agreed. "Maybe it's a trick or something. Or maybe it's the whole intent thing Dalton was going on about," he said, waving a hand in reference to the lesson he had probably only half-listened to. "Maybe we just have to be *willing* to do it in order for it to work, but—"

"What do you mean 'work'?"

"Well, Parisa says—"

"Parisa doesn't know shit," said Libby staunchly.

"Okay, great, maybe not, but that's the information I have, so that's what I'm giving you. Christ," Nico suddenly swore loudly, "you're fucking impossible."

"Me?" She glared at him. "Who else knows, then?"

He winced. "Everyone, I think."

"Everyone '*you think*'?"

"I—" He faltered. "Fine, I know."

"Seriously. Everyone?"

"Yes, Rhodes, everyone."

"That's impossible."

She was aware she was repeating herself, but it seemed unlikely she could bring herself to respond another way.

"Has anyone bothered to ask Atlas?" she demanded, suddenly infuriated. "Is any of this even remotely confirmed?"

"I don't know, but—"

"You don't *know*?"

"Elizabeth, would you listen to me?"

"Of course not, this is absurd."

"Fine," said Nico, throwing his hands up. "For what it's worth, I hate it too, but—"

"But what?" Libby demanded. "What could possibly be the *but*, Varona? What about this would you kill for?"

"Jesus, Rhodes, which part of this *wouldn't* you kill for?"

He had shouted it at her, his mouth snapping shut with alarm. She blinked, taken aback.

"I only meant," Nico began hastily, and then shook his head, grimacing. "No, never mind. Talk to me when you're ready, when you've processed. I can't explain this right now."

"Varona," Libby growled, but he was already walking away, shaking her off like a chill.

So Libby had checked the surveillance wards to discover that Atlas Blakely, who had offered them a position beyond their wildest imaginations without ever mentioning the cost, was alone in the reading room.

"You must have known there would be something," Atlas said, jarring her from her momentary stumble.

She didn't bother asking how he knew what she was thinking about. "So it's true?"

"It's not as gruesome as it sounds," said Atlas placidly. "But yes, one of you will have to die."

Part of her was convinced she was imagining this. Was it a dream? Surely not, and yet not a thread of her had ever believed, even for a moment, that Atlas would ever confirm Nico's suspicions as truth.

"But—"

"Sometimes it is a conspiracy," Atlas admitted, mercifully keeping her from spluttering any further. "On occasion it bears some resemblance to the Ides of March. But often it is a sacrifice, and therefore beholden to great sorrow."

"But," Libby attempted again, and hesitated, finding herself unable to begin. "But how—"

"How can we ask it of you? Not easily," said Atlas. "It is, I'm afraid, an ancient practice. As old as the Library itself. With each generation of initiates we learn more, we expand the breadth and use of our knowledge, but the primary principle of magic remains unfailingly true: It always comes at a cost."

"But we were not informed," Libby said flatly, and Atlas nodded.

"No one ever is, Miss Rhodes."

"Would you have told us?"

"Yes, of course, eventually. Secrets are difficult to keep, and the Forum often interferes."

Libby gritted her teeth. "How do they know about it?"

"The Society is ancient, Miss Rhodes, and therefore so are its enemies. Humans are fallible creatures. Better the Forum's interference than the Wessex Corporation, at least. Capitalism has a terrible tendency to abandon its principles altogether."

"And somehow your principles remain?"

"If there were another way," Atlas said simply, "we would use it."

Libby fidgeted a moment, both wanting and not wanting to ask.

"You want to know how," Atlas guessed, and she glanced up, resentful of his sympathy. "It's a reasonable question, Miss Rhodes. You may ask it."

"Is it—?" She broke off. "Is it... some sort of full moon sacrifice, some customary ritual? Each year on the solstice or the equinox or something?"

"No, nothing like that. It is a sacrifice, the sliver of a whole."

"That's it?"

"It?" he echoed, and she blinked. "There is no small matter of *it*, Miss Rhodes. You are all bound to each other by your experience here, whether you like it or not," Atlas informed her, suddenly more adamant than she had ever heard him. "There is nothing forgettable or small about the way you have all embedded yourselves in each other. Without exception, you become more deeply inextricable from each other with every passing day. The purpose of the elimination is not to rid yourself of something you can lose, but rather to remove something which makes you what you are."

"So we just have to kill someone," Libby summarized bitterly. "That's it? No particular method, no ceremony, no specific day?"

Atlas shook his head.

"And every few years you simply stand there and watch someone die?"

"Yes," said Atlas.

"But—"

"Consider, Miss Rhodes, the scope of power," Atlas cut in gently. "Which specialties benefit the world, and which do not. This is not always a matter of personal allegiances."

"Why would an unbeneficial specialty be chosen to begin with?" Libby demanded. "Didn't you say yourself that each initiate is the best the world has to offer?"

"Of course. However, each initiation cycle, there is one member who will not return, and the Society is cognizant of this," Atlas said. "This must always be a factor in discussion among the board's members when nominating which candidates to submit for consideration."

"Are you saying someone is… *intentionally* chosen for death?"

The idea itself was astounding. Libby could hear her blood rushing in opposition, a deafening tide of disbelief.

"Of course not." Atlas smiled. "Just something to think about."

They sat there in a long, unwavering silence until Libby rose clumsily to her feet. She stopped, halfway to the door, and pivoted around.

"The archives," she said, belatedly remembering her sister once again. "Who controls what we can see?"

Atlas glanced up, fixing her with a long moment of scrutiny. "The library itself."

"Why should I believe that?" she asked, and then, frustration igniting, she pushed him more vehemently. "Why should I believe anything you say?"

His expression didn't change. "I do not control the archives, Miss Rhodes, if that is your question. There are numerous subjects denied to me as well."

"But this is your Society!"

"No," Atlas corrected. "I am one of this Society's Caretakers. I do not own it, I do not control it."

"Then who does?" she demanded.

He gave her a small, impassive shrug.

"Does the arrow aim itself?" he asked.

Libby, rather than answer, turned frustratedly on her heel, launching herself toward the stairs and making her way back to her room.

On the landing of the gallery she collided with someone who'd been turning the corner simultaneously, the two of them barreling into one another. Had she been more able to focus on anything outside her thoughts, she might have heard him coming. As it was, though—

Tristan steadied her, hands around her shoulders.

"Have you seen Parisa?" he asked her, and because Libby was distraught—because she was fucking *human*—she glared up at him.

"Fuck you," she said venomously.

Tristan blinked, taken aback. "What?"

"You knew." Ah, so that was why. In a fit of delayed recognition, Libby suddenly understood the force of her resentment. "You knew this whole time, didn't you? And you didn't tell me."

"Knew—" He stopped, contemplating her face. "You mean—?"

"Yes. The death. The fucking *murder*."

He flinched, and for a moment, she hated him. She *loathed* him.

"I can't—" She broke off, agonized or anguished, unable to tell the difference and unwilling to locate the divide. "I can't, I won't—"

"Rhodes." Tristan's hands were still tight around her shoulders. "I should have told you, I know. I know you're angry—"

"Angry?" She wasn't not, though that hardly seemed the proper word for it. She was feeling something that festered, true, and it could easily have been rage. She had learned long ago to control her magical impulses, restraining them, but at the moment she could feel it spark, smelling smoke.

"Believe me, Tristan, *angry*," she seethed, "doesn't even begin to describe it—"

"None of us actually knows how much this Society controls," Tristan reminded her, dropping his voice to a conspiratorial hush. "Do you really think anyone can walk away from this? Believe me, I know recruitment, I know the difference between institutions and cults, and there is no innocence to this one. You do not get to walk away."

He may have quieted, but she refused. "Then why? Why do it?"

"You know why." His mouth tightened.

"No." The thought sickened her. "Tell me why anyone would do this, tell me *why*—"

"Rhodes—"

"No. No." She wasn't entirely sure what had inflamed her so maniacally, but she beat a fist against his chest, letting her delirium take over. "No, you're one of them, aren't you?" Her lips felt cold, impassive, the words tumbling out like debris, retching from her unfeeling mouth. "It means nothing to you, because of course it doesn't. Sex is nothing to you, this is all a game— Everything is just a game!—so what's murder? What is a *life*, compared to all of this? This Society is just a poison," she spat, her fury so rapidly spent her head fell heavily against Tristan's chest, fearful and exhausted.

"They dose us," she muttered, "a little at a time with it, a little more each round, until we can't feel anything anymore—until we're blind and deaf and *numb* to everything—"

Tristan took her hand and tugged her around the corner, pulling her wordlessly into his room. She nearly flung herself inside, swaying unbalanced beside the hearth, and he sealed the door shut behind them, staring at the handle.

"What's really going on, Rhodes?"

She shut her eyes.

Ask yourself where power comes from, Ezra said in her head. *If you can't see the source, don't trust it—*

Don't tell me who to trust!

"Rhodes."

Tristan came no closer, and she couldn't decide whether she wanted him to.

"Why would we have done this?" Her voice sounded thin, girlish. "Why?"

"Because, Rhodes. Because look around you."

"At who? At what?"

He didn't answer. Bitterly, she conceded that he didn't need to.

She had more power now than she had ever possessed. It wasn't a matter of what she was born with or what she was given; being here, among them, with access to the library's materials, she had every opportunity to travel miles beyond herself. She could feel the outer edges of her power more distantly than ever, further than the tips of her fingers or the soles of her shoes. She could feel herself in waves, pulsing. She could feel herself expanding, and there was no end to it, no beginning. Who she had been once was as distant and unrecognizable as what she would, inevitably, become.

"Whose side are you on, Tristan?" Libby choked from the depths of her remorse. She was dismayed with herself for even asking, but it was making her nauseated, flooding her with bile. The not knowing was making her physically unstable, and she shivered, suddenly sick with it.

"I don't know." Tristan's voice, by contrast, was mechanical and measured. "Yours, maybe. I don't know." He gave a little off-color laugh, sounding precisely as unhinged as she felt. "Did you know Callum's been influencing me? I don't know how much, or how strongly, or how lingering its effects have been, but he has. Did you know that?"

Yes. It was obvious. "No."

"I thought I had control of myself but I don't." He turned to look at her. "Do you?"

No. Even now she didn't.

Tristan's lips parted and she swallowed.

Especially not now.

"I'm not being influenced by Callum, if that's the question," she managed to snap at him, incensed by the desperation of her longing. It wasn't what he'd asked, but selfishly she couldn't bear to tell him the truth, not even a sliver of it. There were only so many pieces of herself she was willing to lose.

Tristan faced away from her again, turning his back.

Libby wanted to sob, or to vomit.

Fine. "I want it." Her voice was small when she confessed it to his spine. "This life, this power, Tristan, I want it. I want it so badly it hurts me. I'm in such terrible, disgusting pain."

He brought one hand up, leaning his forearm against the door and sagging against it.

"When Atlas was telling me about it," she continued slowly, "it almost made sense: Of course there is a cost. Of course we all have to pay a price.

And maybe there is one person I could stand to lose."

She inhaled deeply; exhaled.

"And for a moment, I thought… maybe I could kill him. Maybe I could do it. Maybe he shouldn't even exist; maybe the world would be better without him. But my god," she gasped, "who am I to decide that?"

Silence.

"Who am I to place value on someone else's life, Tristan? This isn't self-defense, this is greed! This is… it's *wrong*, and—"

Before she could continue, dissolving into a puddle of her own incoherent babbling, Tristan had turned away from the door, pivoting to face her.

"Do you worry much about your soul, Rhodes?"

In another world he might have touched her.

In another world, she would have welcomed it.

"Always." All it would take was a step. "Constantly." His hands could be on her jeans, stroking a line down her navel, tucking her hair behind one ear. She recalled the sting of his sigh on her skin, the tremors of his wanting. "It terrifies me how easily I can watch it corrupt."

Whatever was in motion—whether Parisa had started it willfully or if it had always been Libby, if she had manifested this somehow after viewing herself in projections, in visions, in daydreams disguised as phantoms—it was already too late to stop. Still they hung in idle paralysis, precariously balanced.

One more step could break it. She could have him, this, all of it, in one fatal swoop. Whatever corruption of herself she might become next, it was all within arm's reach. It pulsed in her head, throbbed in her chest, static and blistering,

this

could

all

be

"I should go," said Libby, exhaling.

—mine.

Tristan didn't move until after she was gone.

PARISA

"You're avoiding me," murmured Dalton.

"Yes," Parisa agreed, not bothering to stiffen performatively at his approach. Anyone who sat too calmly—like, say, a highly skilled telepath— had an eeriness to them that instinctively set the teeth of others on edge. Callum was a perfect example of off-putting magical peculiarity, which Parisa typically took care not to be. Normality, and its necessary imitation, was king.

But as Dalton hadn't prevented any indication of his approach, she discarded the reflexes people usually wanted to see from her.

"For what it's worth, it's not for lack of interest." She simply had other things on the mind, like whether the collision that was Tristan Caine and Libby Rhodes was about to finally come to fruition.

Dalton shifted to lean against her table in the reading room, folding his arms over his chest.

"Ask," said Parisa, flipping the page in her book. Blood curses. Not very complex in the end, except for the costs to the caster. Those who cast a blood curse almost always went mad, and those who received them almost always broke them eventually, or at least bore progeny who would. Nature craved balance that way: with destruction always came rebirth.

"We knew about your husband," said Dalton, evidently speaking for the Society on high. "Not your brother or your sister."

That wasn't the question in his head, but Parisa wasn't surprised he had to work up to it. There were clouds of discomfort hovering around in Dalton's mind, thick layers of stratosphere to reach through.

"That," said Parisa, "is because nothing happened with my brother." She flipped another page, scanning it. "There would have been nothing worthwhile to discover."

Dalton sat in silence a moment. "Callum seemed to find quite a bit."

In Parisa's mind, which thankfully Dalton could not read, Amin was always soft, Mehr always hard.

You are the jewel of the family; so precious to me, to us.

Kindness that was actually weakness: *I admire you enough to want to possess you, control you.*

You are a whore, a bitch, you corrupted this family!

Cruelty that was actually pain: *I despise you for making me see my own ugliness, the value I lack.*

Parisa closed her book, glancing up.

"Warfare is like compromise. Both parties must lose a little in order to win," she said impatiently. "If Callum gained access to my secrets, it is only because I saw the purpose in him doing so."

Dalton frowned. "You think I blame you?"

"I think you think me weak and now hope to comfort me, yes."

"Weak? No, never. But would I be wrong to try for comfort?"

When Parisa didn't answer, Dalton remarked, "He killed you with those secrets."

"No," Parisa said. "He didn't. I did."

Dalton cast a glance to his hands, his folded arms. A tacit *if you say so.*

"Ask," Parisa said again, impatiently this time, and Dalton's attention slid to hers. Every now and then she saw glimpses of his insidious fractures, the memory of him she'd found locked away. She always found them in the most interesting places. Never academia; Dalton never resembled his spectral self when discussing books or thoughts. It was only ever in moments like this, when he looked at her with an intensity he didn't realize was hunger. When he was searching for something blindly in the dark.

"You told me not to interfere," he began, and Parisa stopped him with a shake of her head.

"Yes, and it was a good thing you didn't. Someone—Callum, for example—might have noticed where we were if you had, and then I might have lost."

Dalton applied a manufactured tone of amusement. "I thought you said he won?"

"He did. But I did not lose."

"Ah."

He turned to stare straight ahead, and Parisa paused to look at him.

"Why stay here?" she asked him. "You had the world at your feet."

"I have the world here," he said without looking at her. "More than."

"You have only that which the library chooses to give you," she corrected him.

"Better that than what I must take from the world."

"Is it better?"

At that he finally met her eye, casting his attention to hers like a weight.

"What did you find in my head?"

Finally. The real question.

"Something very interesting," she said.

"How interesting?"

"Enough to compel me to stay, don't you think?"

"Would you have left otherwise?"

"Would I? Maybe. It is barbaric, this Society." If it required death purely for entry, it would surely require more. Even if this was the extent of their sacrifice, they were contributing to something incomprehensibly vast; a tradition that had lasted centuries, millennia. Principles of magic bound them to *someone's* intent, and there was no telling if those origins were the philosophers of Alexandria or the administrators of the library itself. Perhaps it was the same someone who determined which pieces of the library they were able to receive; perhaps they were all indebted to the magic which bound them.

Gods demanded blood in almost every culture. Was magic any different?

If it was, Dalton wouldn't tell her.

Not *this* Dalton, anyway.

"Let me go back in," Parisa suggested, and Dalton's brow furrowed. "I would understand better what's there if you let me."

"You say that like it's a minotaur," Dalton said wryly. "Some monster inside a labyrinth."

"A princess in a tower," Parisa corrected, reaching up to brush the fabric of his collar. An intimate gesture, to remind him of their intimacy. "But princesses can be monstrous at times."

"You say that like a compliment."

He leaned into her touch, perhaps instinctively.

"Of course." She offered up a delicate smile. "I want you to let me in again."

"So you're seducing me?"

"Always." Her smile broadened. "There are times when I think I may enjoy your seduction most of all."

"Mine, among so many others?" He sounded languid, unbeguiled.

She arched a brow. "Is that jealousy?"

"No. Disbelief." His smile in reply was thin. "There is only so much to gain from me."

"Nonsense, I have plenty. But I wouldn't say no to more," she said, rising to her feet.

She stepped in front of him, pairing their feet like corresponding pieces and matching her hips to his. He set his hands on her waist, gingerly. With the sense that he could retract them if necessary, only she doubted he would.

"Everyone has blind spots," she said. "Things others can see that they can't."

She slid his dark hair from his forehead, brushing his temples, and he closed his eyes.

"Five minutes," he finally said.

She leaned forward, touching her lips lightly to his in compensation.

"Five minutes," she agreed, and his hands tightened on her hips, anchoring her in place.

Entering his mind with permission was both easier and more difficult than before. She opened her eyes to a lobby, somewhere sterile and glassily white. There was an empty receptionist desk, a lift. She pushed the button, waiting. The doors opened with a ding, revealing nothing. Parisa watched her own reflection from the elevator walls as she stepped inside, facing the buttons.

There were countless. She grimaced; unfortunate. She could guess a numeric floor (and then another and another and several into perpetuity, rapidly deteriorating her frothy five minutes) but this was not the way to find herself back where Dalton's subconscious had brought her before.

Here he was neatly organized, which meant these were his accessible thoughts. He was the usual occupant in the lift, hitting buttons to access various levels of memory and thought.

She hit a random floor—2,037—and felt the lift lurch to use.

Then she pried the doors brutishly open, slipping through the narrowest possible crevice. Magic could keep her from falling, but she didn't bother to secure her footing. The construction of this part of him was deliberate, the result of survival techniques and psychological coping mechanisms, like anyone's mind. Cognitive thought looked different from person to person; Dalton's was more organized than most, but it was still nothing more than a carefully manufactured illusion. If she intended to get where she was going, she would invariably have to fall.

She tipped backwards from the lift, closing her eyes to collapse into empty air. It would only feel like falling to her, registering more like a headache to Dalton. She would pulse somewhere behind his brow, mounting pressure below his sinuses. With his permission she would be met with fewer guards, less opposition, but as to whether she would find her destination—

She slowed suddenly, paralyzed mid-fall, and opened her eyes.

"You're back," said the younger version of Dalton, rising greedily to his feet at the sight of her. She was suspended midair, Snow White in her invisible coffin, and he stroked two fingers over her cheeks, her lips. "I knew you would be."

Parisa jerked out of stillness, falling onto the hard wooden floors of the castle where she had been before, and turned her head to find Dalton's shoes beside her. He wore motorcycle boots with black jeans, like a caricature of his external academic, and she looked up, cataloguing him piece by piece. The crown jewel was a fitted t-shirt, so white and crisp it gleamed.

He knelt down beside her, observing her through narrowed eyes.

"What's he doing?" asked Dalton.

"Nothing," she said. "Research."

"Not him," Dalton said, waving a hand. "I know what he does. I meant *him*."

She braced herself. "Atlas?"

Dalton rose to his feet, suddenly irritable. He was prickly, agitated by something.

"He's coming," he said. "I can feel him getting closer."

"Who?"

Dalton glared at her. "You're here for the wrong reasons."

Parisa sat up on her elbows, watching him pace.

"What are the right reasons?"

"You want answers. I don't have answers. I have questions, I have research unfinished, I WANT OUT," Dalton's spectral self suddenly shouted, pivoting to slam a fist into the castle wall.

Parisa winced, expecting stone, but the appearance of it only warped; revealing cool, finished steel before smoothing over, the castle image rippling back into view.

She blinked, wondering if she'd imagined it, but then Dalton was at her side again, crouching down to take her face in one hand.

"I made the castle for you," Dalton said, eyes wide and manic, his voice soft.

Then she felt a lurch, something dragging her backwards until she was in the reading room again, the real Dalton's fingers painfully tight on her waist.

Beads of sweat had formed on his forehead, condensation around the surface of his temples. "You were difficult to remove."

She was panting a little herself, drained by the effort. "Painful?"

"Very. Like a barb."

"I'm sorry." She stroked his brow, soothing it, and he leaned gratefully against her shoulder.

Their breaths syncopated, pulses gradually finding common ground. It took a few moments to slow, to loosen the magic coursing through both their veins, finally allowing their separate parts to settle. Easier to exist in reality, corporeal among the usual dimensions. Nothing to fight with her in his arms, her fingers coiled in his hair.

Eventually the effort at being other faded away, settling into stillness.

Dalton's voice, when he spoke, was coarse with confession. "What did you find?"

Nothing.

No, not nothing. Nothing she could explain, which was worse. Always difficult to admit when something remained out of reach.

"What does the library show you?" asked Parisa instead, easing away to look at him. "There's something here that only you can access."

She could see immediately that he wasn't going to tell her.

"Dalton," she began, but was promptly interrupted.

"Miss Kamali," came Atlas' buttery baritone. "I was hoping to find you."

Dalton moved to release her, stepping away with an averted glance as Parisa revolved in place, finding Atlas in the doorway of the reading room. He beckoned her with a barely perceptible motion, not bothering to acknowledge Dalton.

"Come," he said. "Let's take a walk."

There was a tug to her thoughts, lassoed like a command. She would clearly be walking whether she wished to or not.

She pursed her lips, displeased.

"Fine," she said, glancing over her shoulder at Dalton, who stood with his arms folded again. Lacking any reaction from him, she plucked her book from the table and followed Atlas, who led her into the corridor.

"Am I being scolded for my misbehavior?"

"No," Atlas said. "You're free to pursue whatever recreation you wish."

She glanced up at him, suspicious. "Is that supposed to feel like freedom?"

"I know where you were, what you were doing." He slid a pointed look at her. "You can't use that much magic and expect me not to notice."

"Is your surveillance a personal favor, or do you watch all of us equally?"

"Miss Kamali." Atlas slowed to a halt, pausing before they reached the door to the garden. "Surely you don't need me to tell you the uniqueness of your gift. You will have observed several times by now, I'm sure, that your skills far exceed those of other telepaths."

"I have observed it, yes." She wasn't Libby. She did not need to be informed of her talent. She was clever enough to sort it out for herself.

"But surely you must also understand that you are not the first to possess such ability."

He left the remainder of his intentions unspoken.

"So I should consider you my equal?" she prompted him, half-daring him to argue.

"I had thought us kindred spirits. Or rather, I suppose I'd hoped it." Atlas lingered in the doorframe, casting a glance over the greenery outside.

"Do you think me an enemy?" he asked her, directing the question outward.

"I think your presence much too reliable to be coincidence," she replied, adding, "You pulled me out of Dalton's head once before."

"You shouldn't have been there."

She bristled. "But *your* presence in his thoughts is acceptable?"

"Miss Kamali, there is no point pretending we are not the same," Atlas told her, finally conceding to arrive at his point. "We are both telepaths, talented ones. Rarities." A pause. "What we do is not unlawful surveillance so much as unwilling access. I feel disruptions in thought, just as you must feel them yourself."

Surely there was more to it. "And?"

"And," he confirmed, "you are a frequent disruption."

"Is that what being a Caretaker means?" she mused. "Quieting disruptions?"

Atlas faced her fully now, his effort at languor cast aside.

"I care for the Society," he said. "Of which you are not currently a member."

"Not until I conspire to kill someone," Parisa said.

"Yes." Atlas' confirmation was stony, unflinching. "Not until then."

She felt her mouth tighten, curiosity warring with her more mutinous impulses.

"You interfered with the outcome of Dalton's class, didn't you?" she asked. "You intervened to save him."

"Dalton has also intervened," Atlas pointed out. "It's human nature."

"Yes, but your intervention was purposeful, intentional. His was—"

"His was no less intentional."

She thought of Atlas' desperation and compared it to Dalton's, measuring them against each other.

"Why Dalton?"

"Why you?"

They were squared off defensively, which was unwise. A seductress by nature, Parisa understood the fruitlessness of combat compared to subtler methods of resolution. She eased her posture, leaning against the wall behind her to relieve the tension between them.

"You don't like me," Parisa guessed aloud, and Atlas' mouth tightened.

"I neither like nor dislike any of you. I know nothing of who you are," he said with a rare glimpse of impatience, "only of that which you are capable."

"Do my capabilities threaten yours?"

"You do not threaten me," he assured her.

She eyed him for a moment, transitioning to thought.

What is this Society?

His reply was perfunctory and clipped. *Defenders of all human knowledge.*

Do you really believe that?

It was difficult to lie via telepathy. Thoughts consisted of various materials, and lies were flimsy, easy to see through. The flaws in them were always tactile, either like gauze for the inept or like glass from the proficient:

unnaturally still.

"No one who takes the initiation oath does so in vain," said Atlas.

Answer the question.

He fixed her with a glance, mouth twisting. Not a smile, but wry enough.

I would not have spilled blood except for something I believed unquestionably.

It was not the answer she expected, though she had little time to consider it.

"Go to the library," Atlas said, unsteadying her for a moment.

"What, now?" she asked, taken aback.

"Yes, now." Atlas ducked his head in something half-bow, half-tip of a hat.

He turned, retreating to the corridor that served as the house's primary artery, but paused after a step, turning over his shoulder.

"Whatever you hope to find in Dalton, Miss Kamali, it will only be to your detriment," he said. "Seek it if you wish, but as with all knowledge, whatever follows will be yours to bear alone."

Then he departed, leaving her to take to the stairs, still buried in her thoughts.

It wasn't a long walk. By now it was one she took frequently. She paused to brush the walls, strumming the wards like harp strings. Nothing amiss.

She stepped into the library, unsure what she would find, and discovered upon entry...

Nothing.

Certainly nothing terribly out of the ordinary. Tristan sat at the table, sipping tea. Libby was on the sofa, staring into the flames in the hearth. Nico and Reina were standing near the window, glancing outside. The roses were beginning to bloom.

Parisa paused to reconsider the contents of the room, and then conjured thoughts of its opposite: what the room did *not* contain. Perhaps it was clear after all, if one merely grasped that Atlas was not the neutral party he pretended to be.

Parisa waved the doors closed behind her, prompting the others to look up.

"Someone has to die," she said, and added in silence: *I nominate Callum.*

Reina didn't even turn. *If the others agree,* she thought in reply, glancing irritably at a fern across the room.

Libby lifted her head, slate eyes darting around apprehensively. "Where is he?"

"Wherever he is, he won't be gone long," Parisa said with a shrug, impassive. "He'll feel the discussion and come soon, within minutes."

At the window, Nico was fidgeting, his fingers tapping relentlessly at his sides. "Are we sure this has to be done?"

"It will be done," Parisa reminded him. "And we can either decide on someone as a group or wait to see who comes for each of us in the night."

They all exchanged mistrusting glances at that, though a small sensation of distaste was reserved for her specifically.

"I merely said it aloud," Parisa told Reina. "Everyone would have come to the same conclusion eventually."

"You think we'll turn on each other?" asked Nico, disbelieving.

"We could be easily split into factions," Parisa confirmed, "in which case it would become a race."

That seemed to ring true without exception. Already, none of them trusted the others enough to believe they wouldn't turn assassin once things got dire.

"Who would do it? If we actually chose someone." Nico cleared his throat, clarifying, "If we were all in agreement on… him."

"I will," Parisa said, shrugging. "If that's what's necessary and I have your support, I'm perfectly capable of doing it."

"No."

Libby's interruption both surprised Parisa and didn't. The others turned, equally wary and braced for the argument to come—*murder is wrong, morality and virtue,* so on and so forth—but it never arrived.

At least, not the argument Parisa anticipated.

"It has to be sacrifice, not retribution," Libby said. "Isn't that the purpose of studying intent, unluck?"

There was no answer for a moment.

Then Reina said, "Yes."

That, apparently, was enough to spur Libby onward. "The texts make it clear that spells cast in vengeance or retaliation will only corrupt over time. If this is for the purpose of moving forward in the library—if it's even going to have any value *at all*," she amended firmly, "then it can't be someone who'd be happy to see him go, and certainly not someone indifferent to him. It can't be someone whose soul won't suffer from the cost of it. The arrow is most lethal only when it is most righteous, and that means one thing."

She rose to her feet, turning to where Tristan sat alone at the table, eyes locked on his tea.

"It will have to be you," Libby said.

It was clear at once that Reina agreed, and Nico, too. Parisa, out of habit, slid unobtrusively into Tristan's thoughts, testing them.

Inside Tristan's head were a meld of memories and visions, a monster of many parts. Callum's voice, Parisa's lips, Libby's hands. They blurred together, inconstant, inarticulate. Libby was right about one thing, at least: It would be a sacrifice indeed from Tristan. There was love in him, too much and still insufficient, twisted and anguished and equal in consequence to fear. It was a type of love Parisa had seen before: easily corruptible. The love of something uncontrollable, invulnerable. A love enamored with its own isolation, too frail to love in return.

Tristan wasn't thinking about anything, but was instead suffering it all acutely, intensely. Intensely enough that Callum would feel his distress soon.

Parisa threw the library doors open quickly, anticipating Callum's appearance, when sharply the agony from Tristan broke, colliding with some internal ceiling. A little slip of parchment from his head ignited suddenly in flames; curling edges that fell to smoldering pieces, crumbling to ash.

"Fine," he said.

One word for eventuality to surface.

AN INTERLUDE

"Most people don't know how to starve," said Ezra.

Silence.

"I guess that's a weird thing to say, but it's true. It's something you learn. People think they have to be born one way, with resilience built in or some incapacity to burn or whatever. Either you are or you aren't, that sort of thing. Like some people want naturally and others want nothing, but it's not true. You can be taught to want. You can be taught to crave. You can learn to starve."

Silence.

"The issue is when you eventually get fed," Ezra continued. "You've heard about the stomach pains and shit when vegetarians eat meat for the first time? It feels like dying. Prosperity is anguish. And of course the body adjusts, doesn't it? But the mind doesn't. You can't erase history. You can't just excise the wanting, and worse—you forget the pain. Eventually you grow accustomed to excess and you can't go back, because all you remember are the aches of starvation, which you took so long to learn. How to give yourself only as much as you need to continue—that's a lesson. For some people it's lifelong, for others it's developmental if they're lucky and eventually it fades. But still you never forget it, how to starve. How to watch others with envy. How to silence the ache in your soul. Starvation is dormancy, isn't it? The mind still hungers even when the body adjusts. There's tension, always. Survival only requires so much but existence, completion, that becomes insatiable. The longer you starve the more haunting the ghost of starvation. After learning to starve, when someone finally gives you something you become a hoarder. You *hoard*. And technically that's the same as having, but it isn't, not really. Starvation continues. You still want, and wanting is the hard part. You can learn to starve but you can't learn how to have. Nobody can. It's the flaw in being mortal."

Silence.

"Being magic is even worse," said Ezra. "Your body doesn't want to die, it has too much inside it. So you want more powerfully. You starve more quickly. Your capacity to have nothing is abysmal, cataclysmic. There isn't a medeian on earth capable of casting themselves down to ordinariness, much less to dust. We're all starving, but not everyone is doing it correctly. Some people are taking too much, making themselves sick, and it kills them. The excess is poison; even food is a poison to someone who's been deprived. Everything has the capacity to turn toxic. It's easy, so fucking easy to die, so the ones who make themselves something are the same ones who learn to starve correctly. They take in small amounts, in survivable doses. We're immunizing ourselves to something—*against* something. Everything we manage to have successfully becomes a vaccine over time, but the illness is always much larger. We're still naturally susceptible. We fight it, trying to starve well or starve cleverly, but it comes for us eventually. We all have different reasons for wanting, but inevitably it comes."

"What does?" asked Atlas.

Ezra smiled, closing his eyes in the sun.

"Power," he said. "A little at a time until we break."

CALLUM

As a child Callum never sympathized much with storybook villains, who were always clinging to some sort of broad, unspecific drive. It wasn't the depravity that unnerved him, but the desperation to it all; the need, the compulsion, which always destroyed them in the end. That was the distasteful thing about villains, really. Not the manner in which they went about their business, which was certainly gruesome and morally corrupt, but the fact that they desired things so *intensely*.

The heroes were always reluctant, always pushed into their roles, martyring themselves. Callum didn't like that either, but at least it made sense. Villains were far too proactive. Why the drudgery of it, being despised for the purpose of some interminable crusade, when it would be so much easier to simply let things happen? Taking over the world was a mostly nonsensical agenda. Have control of these puppets, with their empty heads and their pitchforked mobs? Why? The world didn't even love a hero for long. Wanting anything—beauty, omnipotence, absolution—was a natural flaw in being human, but the elective tirelessness of villainy made it indigestibly worse.

Simple choices were what registered to Callum most honestly, the truest truths: fairytale peasant needs money for dying child, accepts whatever consequences follow. The rest of the story was always too lofty, about choosing good or the inevitable collapse of desperation and vice; recordings of human nature, prescriptions to rectify its ills. They were the lying truths, ideologically grand but implausible on the whole. In his view, human nature wasn't an artful curation of morality, but merely cyclical patterns of behavior. Self-correcting; leaning one way only to balance it out with the other over time.

Callum had always tended towards the assassins in the stories, the dutiful soldiers, those driven by reaction rather than a cause. Perhaps it was a small role to serve on the whole but at least it was rational, explainable by even biological terms. A person had to have a foothold somewhere; a role in the ecosystem, like any species. Callum admired that, the ability to choose a side and behave as it dictated. Take the huntsman who failed to kill Snow White, for example. An assassin acting on his own internal compass. Whether he lived or died as a result of his choice? Unimportant. He didn't raise an army, didn't fight for good, didn't interfere much with the queen's other evils. It wasn't the whole world at stake; it was never about destiny. It was whether or not he could live with his own decision, because life was the only thing that truly mattered.

The truest truths: Mortal lifetimes were short, inconsequential. Convictions were death sentences. Money couldn't buy happiness, but nothing could buy happiness, so at least money could buy everything else. In terms of finding satisfaction, all a person was capable of controlling was himself.

Libby was a hero. Parisa was a villain. Their goals were overarching, appositional.

Nico and Reina were so impartial and self-interested as to be wholly negligible.

Tristan was a soldier. He would follow wherever he was most persuasively led.

It was Callum who was an assassin. It was the same as a soldier, but when he worked, he worked alone.

"Do you worry about dying?" Tristan asked him after dinner one evening, the two of them left behind beside the dining room fire. Unnecessary warmth, given the spring breeze outside, but the Society was nothing if not committed to aesthetics. "That someone might choose you to die, I mean."

"I will die someday," Callum said. "I've come to terms with it. People are free to choose me if they wish." He permitted half a smile as he raised his glass to his lips, glancing at Tristan. "I am equally free to disagree."

"So it doesn't bother you that the rest of the group might elect—"
Tristan stopped.

"Elect what? To kill me?" Callum prompted. "If I feared elimination I would not have come."

"Why *did* you come?"

Reaction. Tristan would not understand that, of course, even if his reasons were precisely the same. He was a soldier who wanted a principled king, though he seemed unaware what his own principles were.

How pitiful, really.

"You keep asking me that," commented Callum. "Why should it matter?"

"Doesn't it? The point of the current subject is intention."

"So you're asking my intentions?"

Callum took another sip while he considered his answer, allowing his thoughts to steep.

His life at the Society was not uninteresting. It was methodical, habitual, but that was a consequence of life in any collective. Self-interest was more exciting—sleeping through the afternoon one day, climbing Olympus to threaten the gods the next—but it scared people, upset them. Tending to every whim made others unnecessarily combative, mistrustful. They preferred the reassurance of customs, little traditions, the more inconsequential the better. Breakfast in the morning, supper at the sound of the gong. It soothed them, normality. Everyone wanted most desperately to be unafraid and numb.

Humans were mostly sensible animals. They knew the dangers of erratic behavior. It was a chronic condition, survival. "My intentions are the same as anyone's," said Callum after a few moments. "Stand taller. Think smarter. Be better."

"Better than what?"

Callum shrugged. "Anyone. Everyone. Does it matter?"

He glanced at Tristan over his glass and registered a vibration of malcontent.

"Ah," Callum said. "You'd prefer me to lie to you."

Tristan bristled. "I don't want you to *lie*—"

"No, you want my truths to be different, which you know they won't be. The more of my true intentions you know, the guiltier you feel. That's good, you know," Callum assured him. "You want so terribly to dissociate, but the truth is you feel more than anyone in this house."

"More?" Tristan echoed doubtfully, recoiling from the prospect.

"More," Callum confirmed. "At higher volumes. At broader spectrums."

"I would have guessed you'd say Rhodes."

"Rhodes hasn't the faintest idea who she is," said Callum. "She feels nothing."

Tristan's brow furrowed. "A bit harsh, isn't it?"

"Not in the slightest." Libby Rhodes was an anxious impending meltdown whose decisions were based entirely on what she allowed the world to shape her into. She was more powerful than all of them except for Nico, and of course she was. Because she would not misuse it. She was too small-minded, too un-hungry for that. Too trapped within the cage of her own fears, her desires to be liked. The day she woke up and realized she could make her own world would be a dangerous one, but it was so unlikely it hardly kept Callum up at night.

"It is for her own safety that she feels nothing," Callum said. "It is something she does to survive."

He had not told Tristan the truth, which was that Tristan was asking the wrong questions. For example, Tristan had never asked Callum what books the library gave him access to. It was a grave error, and perhaps even fatal.

"Tell me about your father," Callum said, and Tristan blinked, taken aback.

"What? Why?"

"Indulge me," Callum said. "Call it bonding."

Tristan gave him a hawk-eyed glare. "I hate it when you do that."

"What?"

"Act like everything is some sort of performance. Like you're a machine replicating human behaviors. 'Call it bonding,' honestly." Tristan glanced moodily at his glass. "Sometimes I wonder if you even understand what it means to care about someone else, or if you're just imitating the motions of whatever it's meant to look like."

"You wonder that constantly," Callum said.

"What?"

"You said you sometimes wonder. You don't. It's constant."

"So?"

"So nothing. I'm just telling you, since you seem to like it when I do that."

Tristan glared at him again, which was at least an improvement. "You do realize what I know, don't you?"

"The betrayal, you mean?"

Tristan blinked.

Blinked again.

"You feel betrayed by me," Callum clarified. "Because you think I have influenced you."

"*Manipulated* me." The words left Tristan's mouth with a snarl.

It had certainly been a mistake. Callum couldn't think how Tristan had suddenly conjured up a method to test him, but now that it had happened it couldn't be undone. People hated to lose autonomy, free will. It revulsed them, the controls of another. Tristan would not trust him again, and it would only get worse. The difficulty of it was the festering, the ongoing sickness. Tristan would wonder forever whether his feelings were his own, no matter what Callum did to reassure him.

"Can you really blame me? I preferred the libation of my choice," said Callum, suddenly finding the whole thing rather exhausting. "Anyone given a talent has a tendency to use it."

"What else have you done to me?"

"Nothing worse than Parisa has done to you," Callum said. "Or do you really think she cares about you more sincerely than I do?"

Tristan's expression was anguished, curiosity warring with suspicion. That was the trouble with possessing too many feelings, Callum thought. So difficult to choose one.

"What does Parisa have to do with it?"

"Everything," Callum said. "She controls you and you don't even see it."

"Do you even hear the irony of what you just said?"

"Oh, it is exceptionally ironic," Callum assured him. "Petrifyingly so. Tell me about your father," he added tangentially, and Tristan scowled.

"My father is not at issue."

"Why not? You discuss him at length, you know, but you never actually say anything when you do it."

"Ridiculous." A scoff.

"Is it? Speaking of ironies," Callum mused. "Upfront but never true."

"Why would I be honest with you?" Tristan retorted. "Why would anyone, ever, be honest with you?"

The question fell like an axe over them both, clumsily surprising them. A shift, then.

For a moment, Callum said nothing.

Then, "When Elizabeth Rhodes was a child, she discovered she could fly," Callum said. "She didn't know at the time that she was altering the molecular structure within the room while shifting the force of gravity. She already had a predilection for fire, always reaching for candle flames, but that was normal for a child her age, and her parents were devoted, attentive. They kept her from burning, so she has never actually discovered that she cannot, as a rule, burn. Her understanding is that she can only alter physical forces without disturbing natural elements," Callum added, "but she is wrong. The amount of energy it would require for her to change molecular composition is simply more than she possesses on her own."

Tristan said nothing, so Callum continued, "It startled her sister, or so Libby thought. In reality her sister was suffering the early symptoms of her degenerative illness: weight loss, loss of hearing, loss of vision, weakening bones. Her sister fainted, which was purely coincidence. Lacking an explanation, Libby blamed herself and did not use her powers for close to a decade, not until after her sister passed away. Now she thinks of it only as she would think of a recurring dream."

"Why are you telling me this?" Tristan attempted brusquely, but Callum pressed on.

"Nicolás Ferrer de Varona is the only child of two deeply average medeians who made a considerable profit on good investments, despite what talent they lacked themselves. He is, of course, their *most* profitable investment, being more aware of his talents than Libby, but not by much."

At Tristan's arched brow, Callum shrugged. "He can transform his own shape as well as the things around him." Few medeians who were not naturally shifters could do so, and shifters could not perform Nico's magic in reverse: shifters could transform themselves, but nothing else.

Tristan, already familiar with the difficulty of the magic involved, furrowed his brow into the obvious question of *why*.

"I don't know if he's in love with his roommate and unaware of it, or simply careless with his life," Callum commented with a roll of his eyes, "but unbeknownst to him, Nico de Varona died briefly in the process of transforming the first time. Now he can do it easily," Callum assured Tristan, "having trained his body to recognize the muscle memory of being forced into its alternate shape, but if not for the magic in his veins restarting his heart, he would not still be breathing. Now he is quicker, more intuitive, his senses keener because they have to be, for survival. Because his body understands that by trying to keep up with him, it might die again."

"What animal?" Tristan asked. An irrelevant question, but interesting enough.

"A falcon," said Callum.

"Why?"

"Unclear," Callum said, and moved on. "Reina Mori is an illegitimate daughter belonging to an influential mortal clan, the primary branch of which are members of the Japanese nobility. Her father is unknown and she was raised in secret, albeit in wealth and privilege, by her grandmother. The control she has over nature is nearly that of a necromancer. Why she resists it so much is incomprehensible—why she refuses to use it, even more so—but it has something to do with resentment. She resents it."

"Because it makes her too powerful?"

"Because it weakens her," Callum corrected. "She is a universal donor for some life source she cannot use herself, and there is nothing available to strengthen her in return. Her own magic is essentially non-existent. Everything she possesses can be used to whatever excess it wishes by anyone but her."

"So she refuses to use it out of," Tristan began, and frowned. "Self-interest?"

"Perhaps," Callum said. When Tristan paused in thought, he added, "As for Parisa, you know her story. She is the most aware of her talents. *All* of her talents," Callum qualified with half a smile, "but the magical ones in particular."

When Tristan was quiet again, Callum glanced at him. "Ask."

"Ask what?"

"What you always ask me. Why is she here?"

"Who, Parisa?"

"Yes. Ask me why Parisa is here."

"Boredom, I assume," Tristan muttered, which proved how little he knew.

"Perhaps a bit," Callum acknowledged, "but in fact, Parisa is dangerous. She is angry," he clarified. "She is furious, vindictive, spiteful, naturally misanthropic. If she had Libby's power, or Nico's, she would have destroyed what remains of society by now."

Tristan looked doubtful. "So then why is she here, according to you?"

"To find a way to do it," he said.

"Do what?"

"Destroy things. Or take control of them. Whatever suits her when she finds it."

"That's absurd," said Tristan.

"Is it?" countered Callum. "She knows what people are. With very few exceptions, she hates them."

"Are you saying you don't?"

"I can't afford hatred," said Callum. "I've told you this, as you may recall."

"So you are capable of feeling nothing when it's convenient for you," Tristan muttered.

Callum slid him a grim smile.

"Did it hurt?" he asked.

Tristan braced for something. Rightfully. "Did what hurt?"

"The things your father did, the things he said," Callum said. "Was it painful, or just humiliating?"

Tristan looked away. "How do you know all of this about us? Surely not just by sensing our emotions."

"No, not just that," Callum confirmed, adding, "Why wouldn't you leave?"

"What?"

"Well, that's the story, isn't it? If it was so bad, why didn't they leave. Why didn't Cinderella leave the home of her wicked stepmother, why didn't Snow White flee the evil queen's kingdom. Why didn't Rapunzel leave her tower?"

Tristan curled a fist. "I'm not a—"

"Not what? A victim? You are," Callum interrupted, "but of course you can't allow the world to call you that."

"Is that judgment? An accusation?"

"Not at all. Your father is a violent man," Callum said. "Ruthless and cruel. Demanding, exacting. But the worst of it is that you love him."

"I hate my father. You know this."

"It's not hate," Callum said. "It's corrupted love, twisted love. Love with a sickness, a parasite. You need him in order to survive."

"I am a medeian," Tristan snapped. "He's a witch."

"You are only anything because you came from him," Callum said. "Had you been raised in a loving home, you would not have been forced to see a different reality. Your magic might have accumulated in some other way, taking some other form. But you needed to see through things, because seeing them as they were was far too painful. Because seeing your father for the whole of what he was—a violent, cruel man whose approval you still need more than anything on earth," Callum clarified, and Tristan flinched. "That would have killed you."

"You're lying. You're—" Tristan turned away. "You're doing something to me."

"Yes, I am," Callum said, setting aside his glass as he rose to his feet, coming closer. "This is what you would feel if I were manipulating you. I'm doing it now. Do you feel this?" he asked, closing a hand around the back of Tristan's neck and turning the dials up on Tristan's sorrow, his emptiness. "Nothing hurts like shame," Callum murmured, finding the ridges of Tristan's love, riddled with holes and brittle with corrosion. His many pockets of envy, desire; his madness equating to want.

"You want his approval, Tristan, but he will never give it to you. And you can't let him die—not the real him, not even the *idea* of him—because without him, you still have nothing. You are seeing everything as it truly is and still, do you know what you see?"

Tristan's eyes shut.

"Nothing," Callum said, as a sound left Tristan's mouth, bitterly wounded. "You see nothing. Your ability to understand your power requires accepting the world as it is, but you refuse to do it. You gravitate to Parisa because she cannot love you, because her contempt for you and everyone feels familiar, feels like home. You gravitate to me because I remind you of your father, and truthfully, Tristan, you *want* me to be cruel. You like my cruelty, because you don't understand what it is, but it entices you, it soothes you to be close to it, just like Rhodes and her proclivity for flame."

Tristan's cheeks were moist, probably with torment. Callum did not enjoy this, the destruction of a human psyche. It was ashy, like rubble. Wreckage was so empty and unalluring, even when suffering was overripe. A sense of cusp; not salty, not sweet, but not neither. It was the peril of tilting one way or another, falling too heavily—irreversibly and irreparably—to one unsurvivable side.

"I am the father you didn't get to have," Callum observed aloud. "I love you. That's why you can't turn your back on me, even if you want to. You know my flaws but crave them; you lust for them. The worse I am, the more desperately you are willing to forgive me."

"No." It was no small amount of admirable that Tristan could speak, given what he was going through. "No."

"The truth is I don't want to hurt you," Callum told him softly. "This, what I'm doing to you, I would never have done it if not to save you. To save us. You no longer wish to trust me," he acknowledged, "I understand that, but I cannot let you keep your distance. You need to know what my magic tastes like, how it feels, so that you will recognize the absence of it. You need to know pain from my hands, Tristan. You need me to hurt you so that you can finally learn the difference between torture and love."

Whatever remained in Tristan's chest brought him to his knees, and Callum followed, sinking with him to the floor. He rested his forehead against Tristan's, holding him upright.

"I won't break you," Callum said. "The secret is people want to break. It's a climax, the breaking point, and everything after that is easier. But when it becomes too easy, people crave it more, they chase it. I won't do that to you. You would never come back."

He eased his touch, taking his magic along with him. Tristan shuddered, but it wouldn't be immediate relief. He would have no release, and the fade was like a muscle cramp. Like a limb gone numb and then waking, pins and needles. Nerves twitching to life again, resurrecting. Pressure finding a place to fill.

"How," Tristan began, and Callum shrugged.

"Someone in the Society has books on us," he said. "Predictions."

Tristan couldn't lift his head.

"Not like an oracle," Callum clarified. "More like… probabilities. Likelihood of one behavior or another. Charts and graphs of data, plus volumes of personal history, what drives us. What follows is a narrative arc of our lives, a projection. Most likely outcome."

Tristan sank against his chest, and Callum pulled him closer, letting him rest his head there, feverishly returning to the stasis of his own soul.

"Yours isn't the most interesting," Callum told him regretfully, "but it does have some relevant details. Obviously I paid more attention to it than the others."

"Why," Tristan attempted hoarsely.

"Why me? I don't know. I requested it on a whim, to be honest. To see what the library would give me. I wrote down Parisa's name first, for obvious reasons." Callum chuckled. "I should have known she would recruit people to her cause against me, and Rhodes was such an obvious choice. So hideously moral, so tragically insecure. Surprisingly acrobatic, though," he offered as an afterthought. "Or so I can only assume, given your... encounters."

Tristan said nothing.

"Her book predicts she'll never come into the full scope of her power. Odds of 1/1, actually. Frustrating thought, isn't it? She nearly wasn't chosen for the Society because they couldn't agree on whether she would, but in the end Atlas Blakely convinced them."

He felt Tristan shift.

"Blakely hates me, of course. Wants me dead. Wiped out like the plague. Loves you," he added, shifting to look at Tristan. "If I were you, I'd start wondering why."

"What did it say—" Tristan swallowed. He could speak normally by then, but probably didn't want to. "What did it say about—"

"This? The elimination?"

No answer.

"I know we've only been left alone this long because they are waiting for you to do it," Callum said. "I know you chose the dining room because, not long ago, you slid a knife into your pocket. I even know," he added, glancing down to where Tristan's hand had disappeared from sight, "that your fingers have wrapped themselves around the handle of that knife right now, and that the distance from there to my ribs is premeditated, carefully measured."

Tristan stiffened. The hand around the knife was strained, though it had paused.

"I also know it's insurmountable," Callum said.

Silence.

"Put the knife down," Callum told him. "You won't kill me. It was a good idea," he added. "Whoever decided it would have to be you—Rhodes, probably," he answered himself on second thought, and when Tristan didn't deny it, he shrugged. "It was a good idea," he said again. "But so deeply unlikely."

Tristan braced, and Callum waited.

"I could kill you," Tristan said. "You might deserve to die."

"Oh, surely," Callum said. "But will I?"

Silence.

Elsewhere, a clock ticked.

Tristan swallowed.

Then he shoved Callum away and slid the knife from where he'd concealed it in his pocket, tossing it into the space between them.

"You can't kill Rhodes," said Tristan hoarsely.

"Fine," Callum agreed.

"Or Parisa."

"Fine."

Tristan's mouth tightened. "And you're wrong."

"About what?" It didn't matter. He wasn't wrong.

"Everything."

Things fell silent between them again. Exhausted, emptied, and probably in need of more healing than he realized, Tristan summoned his glass from the table, draining it in one motion of his head. Callum watched the sheen of wine lingering on Tristan's lips, slick when they parted.

"So who dies?" Tristan asked.

Finally. For once, he was asking the right questions. Callum reached over to pick up the knife with one hand, observing it in silence. The flicker of the dining room flames danced along its edge.

"As it turns out," he said quietly, and glanced up, meeting Tristan's eye. "I kill you."

Within moments, the silence was punctured by a scream.

VIII: DEATH

LIBBY

"Men, conceptually, are canceled," Libby said to her knees. "This Society? Founded by men, I guarantee it. Kill someone for initiation? A man's idea. Totally male." She pursed her lips. "Theoretically, men are a disaster. As a concept, I unequivocally reject them."

"If only you meant that," drawled Nico, who was blindfolded for the moment. He grew easily bored, which Libby had already known, though it was different to have to actually live with it. She was starting to feel a bit of sympathy for Gideon, who had always looked exhausted during their four years at NYUMA. He must have had his hands full having a roommate who wouldn't stop for anything, least of all the sun.

At present, Nico was throwing knives. Something about being prepared for any possible invasion, which Libby reminded him they already were. More likely he felt agitated about having a situation he couldn't control, and therefore felt the need to stab it.

He held out a hand, feeling around the forces in the room.

"Levitate it," he said. "The lamp."

"Don't break the lamp, Varona."

"I'll fix it."

"Will you?"

"*Yes*," he said impatiently.

Libby rolled her eyes, then focused on the forces of gravity surrounding it. She wished, not for the first time, that she could see things as Tristan saw them. She had never wondered before whether she should question what her eyes were promising her, but now it was all she ever did. She could feel Nico's magic now like waves, invisible. He was stretching out his range, uncoiling it. He could tell where things were in the room just by filling it, taking up the volume of what he and Libby only saw as emptiness.

Relativity. In reality, there were pieces there, little particles of something that made up all that nothing. Tristan could see them. Libby couldn't.

She hated that.

"Stop," said Nico. "You're changing the air again."

"I'm not changing the air," Libby said. "I can't do that."

Tristan probably could.

"Stop," said Nico again, and the vase shattered. The knife remained in his hand.

"Congratulations," Libby muttered, and Nico tore off his blindfold, giving her a look of total agitation.

"What happened with Fowler?"

She bristled. "Why does everything have to be about Ezra?"

Nico's shrugged. "I don't like him."

"Oh *no*," Libby lamented facetiously. "Whatever will I do without your approval?"

"Rhodes. For fuck's sake." Nico tossed the knife aside, beckoning her to her feet. "Come on. It'll be like the NYUMA game."

"Stop," she said. "I don't want to play with you. Go find another toy."

"What happened?" he asked again.

Nothing. "We broke up."

"Okay, and…?"

"That's it." Like she said. Nothing.

"Uh," said Nico. He had a particular gift for making one sound mimic an entire musical performance about the interminable nature of suffering.

"What do you want me to say? That you were right?"

"Yes, Rhodes, of course. Always."

Fair. She had walked into that one.

Libby rose to her feet on the basis of her own agitated desire to stand. The significance of it being a response to her own volition and not Nico's command felt especially relevant at the moment.

"You weren't *right*," she corrected him sharply, though she was pretty sure it didn't matter what she said. Nico de Varona lived in his own reality; one that even Tristan couldn't make sense of, probably. "Ezra's not… unremarkable. Or whatever it is you always say about him."

"He's average," said Nico bluntly. "You're not."

"He's not av-"

She stopped, realizing she was focusing on the wrong thing.

"You make that sound like a compliment," she muttered under her breath, and Nico made a face that was equal parts *shut up* and also, *I said what I said*.

"The problem with you, Rhodes, is that you refuse to see yourself as dangerous," he told her. "You want to prove yourself, fine, but this really isn't the uphill battle you think it is. You're already on top. And somehow, you don't seem to see the unfiltered idiocy of choosing someone who makes you…" He paused, considering it. "Duller."

"Are you finally admitting I'm better than you?"

"You're not better than me," Nico replied perfunctorily. "But you're looking for the wrong things. You're looking for, I don't know. The other pieces."

She made a face. "Other pieces of what?"

"How should I know? Yourself, maybe." He scoffed under his breath before oppressing her with, "Anyway, there aren't any other pieces, Rhodes. There's nothing else. It's just you."

"What's that supposed to mean?"

"Either you're complete or you're not. Stop looking. It's right fucking there," he informed her, snatching impatiently at her hand and half-throwing it back into her chest. She glared at him and pulled out of his reach, vandalized. "Either it's enough for you or nothing ever will be."

"What is this, a lecture?"

"You're a fire hazard, Rhodes," he said. "So stop apologizing for the damage and just let the fucker burn."

Part of her was annoyed beyond recognition.

The other part of her didn't want to walk into the trap of taking Nico de Varona at his word.

So, lacking a conceivable response, Libby glanced askance at the broken lamp and reconstructed it, replacing it on the desk.

Nico, in answer, turned the desk into a box.

Whenever Nico did any magic, it always unsettled her. He was vast, somehow. She never saw the details of what he was doing; if the world's materials were strings with Nico as the puppeteer, they were unidentifiable. Things simply were and then they weren't, just like that. She never remembered it happening, even if she stared. It was a desk, now it was a box, soon it might be a chair or a swamp. Probably the desk didn't even know what it had once been.

"What are you, then?" she asked him. "If I'm a fire hazard."

"Does it matter?"

"Maybe." She returned the box to the form of a desk.

"It's funny," Nico said. "I wouldn't have done any of this if they hadn't come for both of us."

"Why's that funny?"

"Because of this place I'm a murderer," he said. "Complicitly," he amended after another moment's consideration. "Soon to be." The last was a conclusive mutter.

"Get to the funny part," Libby suggested drily.

"Well there's a stain on me now, isn't there? A mark. 'Would kill for _____,' followed by a blank space." Nico summoned the knife back to his palm, only of course it didn't register that way. One moment the knife was cast aside, the next it was in his hand. "I wouldn't have that if I hadn't come here. And I wouldn't have come here at all if it weren't for you."

She wondered if he blamed her. He didn't sound accusatory, but it was hard not to assume that he was. "You were going to do it regardless, remember?"

"Yeah, but only because they asked you."

He glanced down at the knife in his hand, turning it over to inspect the blade.

"Inseverable," he said, neither to himself nor to her.

"What?"

"Inseverable," he repeated, louder this time. He glanced up at her, shrugging. "One of those if-then calculations, right? We met, so now we can't detach. We're just going to always play a weird game of… what's the word? The thing, espejo, the game. The mirror game."

"Mirror game?"

"Yeah, you do one thing, I do it too. Mirror."

"But who does it first?"

"Doesn't matter."

"Do you resent it?"

He looked down at the knife, and then back up at her.

"Apparently I'd kill to protect it," he said, "so yeah."

Libby summoned the knife from his palm, which in practice was more like it had always been hers.

"Same," she said quietly.

She set the knife down on his desk that had briefly been something else.

"We could stop," she suggested. "Stop playing the game."

"Stop where? Stop here? No," Nico said with a shake of his head, fingers tapping at his side. "This isn't far enough."

"But what if it's too far?"

"It is," he agreed. "Too far to stop."

"Paradox," Libby observed aloud, and Nico's mouth twisted with wry acknowledgement.

"Isn't it? The day you are not a fire," he said, "is the day the earth will fall still for me."

They stood there a few seconds longer until Libby plucked the knife from his desk, stabbing it into the wood. The beams of the desk grew around it, securing it in place.

"We broke up," she said. "Ezra and me. It's over. The end."

"Tragic." Nico looked smug. "So sad."

"You could at least pretend to be sorry."

"Could," he agreed. "Won't, though."

She rolled her eyes and turned to the door, throwing it open and crossing the hallway to her room. She paused beside Tristan's door, contemplating it, and wondered how he was doing downstairs. She didn't expect it to be easy. Truthfully, she didn't even expect it to work. The whole point of choosing Tristan to kill Callum was that Tristan was the least likely to do it, and therefore the whole thing was a gamble.

She thought of Tristan's mouth, his eyes. The way it had felt to master something with his hand steady on the stillness of her pulse.

Do you worry much about your soul, Rhodes?

A pity she was so terribly risk averse.

Libby slid into her room and shut the door behind her, falling backwards onto her bed. She considered picking up one of the books on her nightstand but gave up before she even started. Nico was probably onto something, what with giving himself a task to preclude falling into a full-bodied state of waiting, but for Libby, there could be no distraction. Her mind only bounced from Tristan to Callum back to Tristan, and then briefly to herself, which gave her fleeting moments of Ezra.

So it's over? You're done?

He had sounded more exhausted than anything.

It's over, she confirmed. *I'm done.*

It wasn't a matter of anything changing between them so much as Libby no longer being the person she had once been. She was so fundamentally altered that she couldn't remember what version of her had put herself into that relationship, into that life, or somehow into this shape, which still looked and felt as it always had but wasn't anymore.

She hardly even suffered guilt for what she'd done with Tristan and Parisa, because whoever Libby had been that night, she was different from that, too. That was some transitional Libby who'd been searching for a cataclysm, seeking something to shatter her a little. Something to wipe the slate clean and start over. Ashes to ashes, dust to dust. She'd found it, decomposed, and moved on.

Whatever Libby was now, she was powerful with possibility. Helpless, too, with the knowledge of her own exceptionalism. Ambition was such a dirty word, so tainted, but she had it. She was enslaved by it. There was so much ego to the concept of fate, but she needed to cling to it. She needed to believe she was meant for enormity; that the fulfillment of a destiny could make for the privilege of salvation, even if it didn't feel that way right now.

The library still refused her books. The subject of longevity in particular was denied; the question of whether her sister could have lived had Libby been better or more talented was repeatedly denied. It was like the whole structure of the library's archives feared her in some way, or was repulsed by her. She could sense intangible waves of nausea at the thought that she wanted some knowledge she wasn't meant to have.

She could feel it breaking, too. She could feel the way it would soon give way beneath her weight. It was just waiting for something, or someone. Waiting for whoever Libby Rhodes would be next.

Conservation of energy meant there must be dozens of people in the world who didn't exist because she did. Maybe her sister had died because she lived. Maybe her sister had died because Nico lived. Maybe the world had a finite amount of power and therefore the more of it Libby had, the less of it others could reach.

Was it worth it to let that go to waste?

She could feel herself rationalizing. Half of her was full of answers, the other half full of questions, the whole thing subject to the immensity of her guilt. Killing is wrong, it's immoral, death is unnatural, even if it is the only plausible result of being born. The need to soothe herself with reason buzzed around her head, flies to honey.

What would happen when Callum was gone? It was strange to think the wards around the house were imprints of past Society initiates, and therefore, in a sense, ghosts. One-sixth of the house's magic belonged to people who had been selected to die.

When Callum had gone, would his influence remain?

It was Callum who had built the most integral defense into their wards. Libby and Nico had been the architects of the spherical shield, of course, but it was Callum who had created what he called the vacuum within the interior fabric of them. A layer of insulation, wherein all human feeling was suspended.

What replaced feelings when there were none to be had? The absence of something was never as effective as the presence of something, or so Libby had thought until then. She had suggested they fill the space with something; a trap of some kind, or possibly something nightmarish if Callum really wanted to build some sort of existential trap, but he disagreed. To be suspended in nothing, he said, was to lack all motivation, all desire. It was not numbness, which was pleasurable in fits, but functional paralysis. Neither to want to live nor to die, but to never exist. Impossible to fight.

Libby sat up with sudden discomfort, a little prick of worry. It wasn't as if Tristan was powerless by any means, but maybe there was a reason Atlas had implied that Callum himself was something that should not exist. Callum's power was always hazy, indefinable, but the effect of its use was unquestionable. He had taken a piece of Parisa's mind and driven it to such anguish that she had destroyed herself rather than live with what he'd done.

Suddenly, Libby was aware of the chance they'd taken when they left Tristan and Callum alone together. It was a fight to the death, where only one would come out alive. If Tristan failed, then Callum would know. There was no going backwards, no halting what would come next. Callum would know they had come for him, marked him expendable in their ledgers of who deserved what, and for that there would be consequences. This, the two of them downstairs, was no different from two gladiators meeting in the ring, one of them doomed to failure.

She should not have let Tristan do this alone.

Libby sprang up from her bed and ran for the door, about to jerk it open, when something in the room shifted. The air changed. The molecules rearranged themselves, becoming cool somehow, slowing to a crawl. There was a foreignness to the room now, amnestic. It was as if the room itself no longer recognized her, and therefore hoped to crush her like a malignant tumor.

Was it fear? It wasn't *not* fear, but she had been right about one thing in her conversation with Nico.

The air itself was different, and she wasn't the one who had changed it.

Libby spun, or tried to. She felt her pulse suspend again, a thing that didn't belong. Just to exist in the room was terrible enough, because she wasn't meant to be there. There was no way to explain the sensation; only to feel it as a lack, an absence. She suffered it, her alienness, with the way her own lungs didn't want to expand.

If she had caught it sooner she could have stopped it. If she knew where to find its source now, she could drag it to a halt. This was the trouble with her, a weakness she would never have known she had if she had never met Tristan. She could have all the power in the world, enough to rid the global population twice over, and still, she couldn't fight something if she couldn't see clearly what it was.

But it wasn't total emptiness. Distantly, she could hear something.

Do you really even know what you've said yes to?

An arm wrapped around her waist, dragging her backwards, and the air in the room rushed back into her lungs at the moment she finally found the voice to scream.

TRISTAN

HE ALMOST DIDN'T HEAR HER over the sound of his blood rushing, but it had been enough to make Callum blink. Enough for him to glance down at the knife in his hand and toss it away after looking at Tristan with visible disgust.

"I wouldn't have done it," he said, but Tristan's adrenaline said otherwise. The knowledge of Callum's face unmasked said otherwise. The reality of their circumstances said, quite firmly, otherwise. Tristan's muscles ached, his entire body slow to reconvene its usual rituals of survival.

How would Caesar have made Brutus pay if he had lived?

"I'm sorry." The words left Tristan's mouth numbly, unevenly.

"Apology accepted," said Callum, his voice cool and unaltered. "Forgiveness, however, declined."

The red light in the corner flashed, attracting both their attention.

"No one could have gotten through the vacuum," said Callum. "It's nothing."

"Is it?" Tristan's breath had yet to slow. "That's not what it sounds like."

"No." Callum's brow furrowed slightly. "No," he agreed, "it doesn't sound like that."

He rose to his feet, exiting the dining room, and Tristan glanced at the discarded knife before shuddering, stumbling upright in Callum's wake.

Callum's stride was long and surprisingly urgent as Tristan followed him up the stairs.

"What is it?"

"Someone's here," said Callum without pausing. "Someone's in the house."

"No shit," came Parisa's voice around the corner. She was hurrying after them from somewhere else in the house, lovely and disorderly and wearing a man's shirt over bare legs.

Tristan arched a brow in response to her appearance, and she gave him a silencing glare.

"I don't understand how it happened," she said. "The house's sentience usually alerts me when someone tries to enter. I see he's still alive."

It took Tristan a moment to register that the last line had been said in his thoughts.

"Obviously," he mumbled, and Callum's eyes slid to his. Tristan didn't have to look to know that Callum had understood perfectly well what Parisa had asked him, even without words. Even without magic, Callum knew.

He knew they had agreed on him to die, and now none of them would ever be forgiven.

They rounded the gallery corner to the rooms. Nico was forcing open the door to Libby's bedroom, Reina at his heels.

"Did you—"

"No," Reina answered Parisa blandly. "I heard nothing."

"Who could have—"

There was a blast of something inconceivable from Nico's palm as Tristan thought for the thousandth time, *my god*—marveling at the power they had, Libby and Nico; individually and apart.

Imagine having something so wild in your bloodstream. Imagine feeling something, anything, and seeing it manifest without the blink of an eye. Even at Tristan's angriest he was nothing, only of any use to anyone when he was thinking clearly, seeing sense. No bombs exploded at the whims of his frustration, which made him ordinary. It made him normal; something he had tried his whole life not to be.

It was Nico who entered the room first, letting out a sound like a wounded dog in answer to the fading sound of Libby's scream. The bitterness on Tristan's tongue at the sound, however mystifying and incongruous it was to feel, was envy, because of course. Of course one pseudo-twin would suffer the other's pain, the two of them in orbit to something Tristan would never grasp or understand. It was the same reaction as always: brittle unsurprise.

But what startled him properly were the others.

The sound from Parisa's tongue had to be Farsi, though it was the first time Tristan had ever heard her use it. It morphed rapidly into French, but by the time her color had fully drained, she had fallen silent again. Reina, too, was speechless and pale, though she was often speechless. More alarmingly, it was the first time Tristan had ever observed her forcing her gaze away from something rather than boring holes in it, unrelenting.

Callum stared loudly. His expression was vocal, even if his mouth was not. He was saying things like *how could this be happening* and also, somehow, *I told you*. It was as if the hard look in his eyes was saying something to all of them that the rest of him could not: *See? I was never your enemy after all.*

Nico fell to his knees, shoulders folding in around his torso like he'd lost an organ.

"This can't be real," he said, and swore softly under his breath. "No. No."

The four of them, one by one, had turned to Tristan, expectant. His brow furrowed, lips tight.

"Do we think it was the Forum?" asked Parisa after a moment, her voice like sandpaper. "They got in and out last time, didn't they?"

"Could have been someone like Wessex Corp," said Reina darkly.

"Someone should tell Atlas. Or Dalton."

"Whoever did this, are they still here? In the house?"

"No." Parisa glanced at Callum, who shook his head. "No. Not anymore."

"I want answers." The words, when they left Nico's mouth, were explosive, juvenile with demand. "I want an explanation."

"Does it count?"

To that, the others glared at Reina, who sighed loudly.

"Look, we were all thinking it," she said. "Rhodes is gone. So that means—"

"The elimination is about sacrifice," Tristan spat. "*Death.*"

The room fell silent.

"Is this not death enough for you?" Nico's voice shook with outrage. The ground beneath them rumbled with it, but in answer, there was little Tristan could do but stare.

"How dare you," Nico suddenly snarled at Tristan from the floor, leaking with toxicity that sparked mid-air. "How *dare* you—"

"Wait," Tristan said. "What are you seeing?"

The others froze, stiffening.

For several seconds, no one spoke.

"It's Rhodes," Callum supplied, and the others flinched at her name, revulsed. "Her body on the ground."

"What?" Tristan's pulse quickened. "No. No, it can't be—"

He felt the cool traces of Parisa's presence in his head and shivered.

"He doesn't see it," Parisa said, sounding bewildered at first, and then astounded. "He doesn't see anything."

"Wait." Nico scrambled to his feet, taking Tristan brusquely by the shoulder. "What's there, then?"

"Nothing." Not entirely true. There was an excess of magic in the room— volumes of it, impossibly swollen—but the air was empty of her. It was vacant of Libby herself, and that was the only thing Tristan could see or feel: her absence.

Libby was gone, clearly. Even her magic was gone from the room.

"She's not there."

"But she's *here*," Nico insisted raggedly, while Parisa, the first to manage a response, hastily bent down, brushing her fingers over nothing.

"This is... uncanny." She stared down in awe. "The blood, it's—" *real.*

Blood. No wonder they were all repulsed.

"There's no blood," Tristan said.

"No blood?"

He could feel their eyes on him, waiting.

"I told you, nothing." Only emptiness. Only absence. Magic unrecognizable, belonging to no one. "But she's definitely not here."

"So it's an illusion," Parisa said, as Nico's expression turned to a ghastly mix of concern and relief. "A really excellent one."

"Professionally done," Reina said, glancing at Callum.

It took a moment for Callum to process what she'd said.

"You honestly think I would abduct Rhodes and leave an illusion in her place?" he demanded.

"Your family is famous for their illusions," Reina said. "Aren't they?"

"I also know Tristan would see through it," Callum snapped. "I'm not an idiot."

"So someone outside the Society must have done it," Parisa inserted quickly, rising to her feet again. She was barefoot, Tristan registered, and still thoroughly unconcerned with her appearance. "Only someone who wouldn't know what Tristan's specialty is could have done it."

"Does anyone know—?"

"No," Tristan said. Only Atlas had ever guessed the details, though he must have had to discuss it with the Society's board. "I mean, maybe. But I don't think so."

"Could still be the Forum," Reina said. "Or one of the other groups." She glanced at Nico, whose face was pale.

"But why?" he asked, swallowing. "Why Rhodes?"

Reina glanced at Parisa. "Victim of circumstance?"

"No. This was planned," said Parisa with abject certainty, just as Atlas entered the room behind them, Dalton trailing in his wake.

"What's this? Wh-" Atlas broke off, staring. "Miss Kamali, your hands—"

Parisa glanced down, scrubbing them with disgust onto the shirt that was clearly not her own. It was comical, really, how Tristan wanted so desperately to see the carnage the others were seeing, even if they obviously wished to put it out of their minds.

For him there were only the traces left behind, which was oppressive. There were no fingerprints, no clear signature. Only the enormity of what was missing.

"It's an illusion," said Tristan. "It's not real."

Atlas frowned, glancing at him without conviction. "An illusion that powerful would take—"

"I know what it would take," Tristan snarled, rapidly losing his patience with repetition, "and I promise you, *it's not there*."

It was the harshest tone any of them had ever taken with Atlas, though at the moment Tristan didn't much care. That someone who could break into this house and take something inside it did not mean Libby Rhodes was still alive. The fact that she had not been killed in this room, or that this was not her body, was not, for Tristan, a comforting piece of information. Particularly not if whoever had taken her had the resources to do it in a way that could successfully trick all but one of the most talented medeians alive.

The look on Atlas' face in response was carefully measured.

"I will have to contact the board," he said. "They will need to know about this immediately."

Then he disappeared, leaving Dalton standing alone in the doorway.

None of them particularly expected him to speak, though he did. "It's not an illusion," Dalton said, his tone blank and perfunctory, and Tristan gave a loud growl.

"For fuck's sake, I'm telling you, it's not r-"

"It's not real, no," Dalton confirmed quickly, "but it's not an illusion."

He waved a hand and whatever the others saw, they leapt back from the sight of it, Parisa stifling a scream as the traces of magic rose up in a thick blur, like heavy fog. Nico looked like he was going to be sick.

"It's an animation," Dalton said, and then he turned and left.

In his absence, the others stood speechless again.

"We should go," Callum said in a measured voice, at the same time Reina said, "It's his specialty."

Parisa glanced up. "What?"

"Dalton. He's an animator. I don't know what that means," Reina added. "But that's what he does."

"What's the difference between an illusion and an animation?" The question sounded bitter from Nico, though it might not have been. His anger or his loss or whatever it was that was ailing him at Libby's loss was bleeding, uncontained, into everything he said.

To Tristan's immense surprise, Parisa turned to Callum for confirmation of something.

"Sentience?" she asked. She was asking him alone.

"Sort of," Callum said. Nobody but Parisa seemed willing to meet his eye. "Illusions have no sentience, but animations have... some. It's not strictly sentience," he corrected himself, "but it's an approximation of life. A sort of... naturalistic spirit. Not to any level of consciousness, but to the extent of being, arguably, alive."

"There are myths about that." Reina's tone was cerebral. "And writings from antiquity."

"Yes," Callum said. "Spectral things, certain creatures. They're animated but not sentient."

"It's not in our heads," Parisa said. "Tristan can't see it."

"No," Callum confirmed. "It's still just magic. Manufactured somehow and put here deliberately for us to find."

"But why would someone want us to think Rhodes was dead?" (Nico.)

"Is the question why Rhodes, or why us?" (Parisa.)

"Either. Both."

Their collective silence suggested a confounding lack of answer. Tristan's sore muscles ached, throbbing with pain.

"Let's get out of here," Parisa said eventually, turning her face away with another flinch. "I'm done looking at this."

She turned and left, followed by a hesitant Nico. A less hesitant Reina glanced at Tristan, then at Callum. Then she, too, turned and left.

When only Callum and Tristan remained in the room, the briefly forgotten intensity of the evening returned. It occurred to Tristan that he should be prepared for something, anything, but acknowledging so to himself already seemed like the beginning of an end.

"There was something else in the scream," Callum remarked without looking up from whatever animation had been left in Libby's place. "It wasn't fear. It was closer to rage."

After another beat of silence, Callum clarified, "Betrayal."

It took a while for Tristan to find his voice.

"Meaning what?"

"Meaning she knew the person who did this to her," Callum said, perfunctory in his certainty. "It wasn't a stranger. And—"

He stopped. Tristan waited.

"…and?"

Callum shrugged.

"And," he said. "That means something."

Clearly more remained unsaid than not from Callum, but considering that Tristan was expected to have killed him by now, he didn't particularly feel the need to press the issue. The magic left in the room, whatever it was and whoever it belonged to, was already starting to rot. The whole room was off-color, tainted, like the magic itself was corroding the further its creator went from them. Whatever form of intent had cast it, that was poisoned now.

Along with other things in the room.

"Why didn't you tell the others?" Tristan asked, and now Callum's mouth morphed into some misbegotten smile, like a laugh he meant to indulge earlier but remained somewhere deep in his throat, awaiting a more spontaneous delivery.

"I may have to kill one of them," Callum said. "Tactically speaking, I'd rather they not know everything I know."

So Tristan had been correct: They would not be forgiven. None of them.

Nor, he realized, would they get a second shot at Callum.

"Why tell me?" Tristan asked, clearing his throat.

The thin line of Callum's mouth told him he already knew the answer.

"Because you deserve to wonder whether it might be you."

Tristan forced himself not to flinch when Callum raised a hand, touching his thumb to the center of Tristan's forehead. A blessing, or the mockery of one.

"Truthfully, I respect you more for this," Callum remarked, withdrawing his hand. "I always hoped you'd make someone a worthy adversary."

In his mind, Tristan manifested a new talisman; a new scroll to recount his new truths.

Part one: *Your value is not negotiable.*

Part two: *You will kill him before he kills you.*

"Sleep well," Tristan said.

Callum spared him a nod before turning to the door, passing irreversibly through it.

NICO

No one could find her.

If they had not understood the Society's scope of power before, they did now. Representatives from countless foreign governments were contacted for information from any and all forms of magical and mortal surveillance. Medeians with advanced tracking abilities were summoned. A team of the Society's own specialized task force was called upon to search.

Nico, of course, offered to help them. "I know exactly what shape she takes up in the universe," he pleaded in explanation. "If anyone can recognize her, it's me."

Atlas didn't stop him.

"As I told the six of you once," Atlas said, "anything taken from the Society must eventually be recovered."

Still, there was nothing Nico could do that was any better than even the Society's most generic efforts. There were no traces of Libby Rhodes anywhere. She had been wiped clean the moment she disappeared. No explanations were provided for why measures existed to track magical output—it was, as it turned out, a bit like tracking credit card purchases—or why each of their movements seemed to be mined for someone's observation like medeian points of data, but Nico didn't ask. That was a future Nico problem. Right now, it was about doing whatever it took to find her.

"A lot of work for someone you claim to hate," remarked Gideon.

Nico had been spending a lot of time fitfully asleep for the purposes of these conversations. When Reina asked him one night about his groggy arrival to dinner, he lied. And he lied and he lied and he lied, but then eventually he couldn't take it anymore and confessed. "I know someone. A friend, my roommate. He can travel through dreams."

It was the most forthcoming Nico had ever been on the subject of Gideon aside from his conversation with Parisa, but as he might have predicted, Reina said almost nothing in response.

"Oh," she said, "interesting," and wandered away.

The frequent overuse of Nico's magic was starting to show, even in the manifestation of his dreams. The atmosphere of his subconscious felt thinner, and remaining purposefully inside it was more difficult than usual. He had to wrestle between his need to sleep soundly and the importance of clinging to his conscious thoughts, vacillating between his waking self and his dream self. He could feel himself wavering in some in-between place, ready to snap awake, prepared to slumber more deeply, depending how much energy he exhausted containing Gideon within his consciousness.

At least it was easier the longer the days got, the warmer the weather became. Body temperature was easier to regulate, and even groggy half-sleep was sufficient to remain where he was. The only thing that refused to lessen was his guilt.

"Was it Eilif?" he asked hoarsely.

"No," Gideon said.

"But how do you know?"

"Because I know."

"But it could it have been—"

"It wasn't."

"But—"

"Sleep," Gideon advised, and Nico shook his head, forcing himself not to manifest any dancing lollipops or sheep into the ambiance of his dream space.

"Not until I understand this. Not until it makes sense."

"What doesn't make sense? You have enemies," Gideon pointed out. "Libby could have easily been a target for one of the other agencies like yours. Or for anyone."

"But she's not a hostage," Nico said, frustrated. "I could understand it if she were, but—"

He broke off, blinking, and frowned.

One of the other agencies like yours.

"Wait," he said, and Gideon turned away. "Wait. *Wait*—"

"Cálmate," said Gideon, not looking at him.

"Absolutely not," snapped Nico, rising sharply to his feet. "How long have you known? And *how* do you know?"

Gideon glanced through the bars at the spare inches between them and then set his mouth grimly, suggesting that Nico should not ask.

"Fuck." Nico shook his head, furious. "Que cojones hiciste? Tell me you didn't," he answered himself, cognizant enough now to indulge the heat of his frustration. "Not after everything I did to keep her out! After every precaution I took, Gideon, *fuck*—!"

"I didn't break any wards to meet her," Gideon countered blandly. "I stayed in here."

"Jesus," Nico exhaled, letting his forehead fall against the bars. "Gideon."

He could feel the twist of Gideon's tension, the tightening of his knuckles from the other side.

"Listen to me, Nico." A low warning. "Libby's gone. You think I'm going to sit back and wonder if you're next?"

Nico didn't look up.

"I agreed to meet with my mother on the condition that she would tell me *exactly* where you were, what you were doing. Which, by the way, I should have known. You should have told me from the start this was more than a—"

Nico winced.

"A fellowship," Gideon finished with obvious resentment.

"Gideon—"

"There was a catch, obviously. The usual strings. She wants me for a job, and I knew she would." He paused. "But it was worth it to finally have an answer."

Nico shut his eyes, warring with his dream self's need to float away like a balloon.

"What's the job?"

"I told you, the usual."

"Meaning what? Theft?"

Gideon shook his head. "Break someone out. For a fee."

"Break them out of what? Their subconscious?"

"Their conscious mind, actually."

Nico glanced up with confusion, finding Gideon's eyes on him. "How is that possible?"

"You really should have taken more electives," Gideon sighed, but at a pursed look of impatience from Nico, he shrugged. "The mind has mechanisms, Nicky, levers. It is possible to trap certain functions inside it, or to prevent the pieces of a person's mind from working as intended."

"So then how would you break in?"

"I wouldn't," Gideon said firmly, which Nico did not find particularly reassuring. "I'll tell my mother it's impossible. Or I'll find her the money some other way, she won't care about the details. Whatever it takes. But I knew she'd tell me where you were."

"Eilif is a real piece of work," Nico reminded him gruffly. "She's basically just a mermaid with a gambling problem."

"It's not a gambling problem—"

"It's close enough," Nico snapped, though immediately, his head hurt. Worse, Gideon gave him a look that said *don't snap*, which he loathed. Mostly because it was effective.

"This Society of yours is not a secret," Gideon told him. "Not enough of one, anyway. And I wouldn't be surprised if it's corporately funded."

"So?"

"So money is important, Nico. Don't you care to know whose pocket you're in?"

Nico tipped his head back with a groan. "Gideon. Basta."

"Libby is gone."

Nico shut his eyes again.

"She's *gone*, Nico. But you will not disappear."

"I won't, I told you—"

"No, you won't," Gideon said flatly. "And you know why? Because I won't let you. Because I'll do whatever my mother asks of me, *for you*. Because I'll hunt you down if you even try."

"Gideon—"

"You're not safe there. Not as safe as you think you are."

"What are you talking about? You've seen the wards." He had repaired them himself. He and Libby.

"Yes, I know, but you're not prepared."

"For what?" He was. He had checked everything. Libby had checked everything.

Impenetrable. They should have been impenetrable.

Libby is gone.

Impossible.

"Dimensions, Nicolás, dimensions. Don't just think big, think shapeless.

Think infinite."

"Gideon basta, infinity is false, it's a false conception." Even Nico could hear himself mumbling. "Grains of sand and atoms could all be counted if we really tried—"

"Listen to me Nicky, your wards have a hole. A big one."

"That's—"

"Don't say impossible."

Blearily, he watched Gideon's feet step closer to the bars.

"Watch this," said Gideon, and before Nico could look up, it was already happening.

It was a touch against his cheek, spectral and bodiless.

It was *Gideon's* touch; gentle, soothing. Impossible.

Nico closed his eyes and felt relief again. Impossible.

Libby was gone. Libby was gone. Libby was gone.

Impossible.

"It's a memory," Gideon explained, and the little spurts of dreamscape shook Nico a bit, rocking him somewhere less stable. He could feel the earth beneath him shaking, the smell of fire, the sound of the scream.

She had left his room moments before she disappeared. She had been gone what, five minutes? Ten at the most? He had been drifting off, not quite awake, and it had been the warp in the atmosphere that called him. Waves were Libby's method of interference. Nico was reliant on her ability to sense them—*too* reliant—but for that moment, she had been the wave. He only understood the danger after he'd already smelled smoke.

The loss of his usual grasp of reality—the box of limitations he used in order to function, in order to exist—came over him with a flood of sudden nausea.

Dimensions, Nicolás, dimensions.

Nico lifted a hand to his face, trying to understand it through the low doldrum of restless slumber.

"What is it," he asked, "a memory?"

"Time," said Gideon, shrugging. "I told you. Another dimension."

Time. Fuck. Fuckballs. Fucking balls. Nico felt the sharp pins of opposition bursting in through the numbing wave of sleep.

"The amount of energy it would require to break a time ward is… impossible, unfathomable," Nico mumbled, trying to sift through his thoughts.

"And easily combated by other wards. Too much magic." His wards, Libby's wards. They would have been enough to keep it out.

"Okay, but what if it wasn't?"

"What if it wasn't? Gideon, it *is*. Rules of conservation apply. No one could possibly restore that amount of energy and power themselves unless—"

"Unless they could," Gideon answered for him, and then, "Unless someone exists who can."

The idea that someone could possibly be so powerful was beyond disconcerting. It was well outside the scope of Nico's understanding. He had never met anyone more powerful than he was, or more powerful than Libby was, so for this to have been the work of some unknown medeian who wasn't even in this Society was—

"They wouldn't have to be more powerful than you," Gideon said. "It could be a very specific ability. Something very niche, possibly even limited."

"Stop," grumbled Nico, because Gideon was reading his mind. It wasn't the same as Parisa reading his mind, because Parisa didn't care and she did it by magic, but Gideon was doing it because he *did* care and it wasn't magical at all. It was because Gideon knew Nico too well, and all the caring Gideon was doing about Nico was starting to make Nico feel slightly sick, or at least unsteady. It was wrapping around Nico like a blanketed embrace, making him drowsy, serving a gratifying warmth to the aching in his chest.

"Help me," Nico said. He was suddenly tired, too tired to stand, and he sank backwards. "Help me find her, Gideon, please."

"Yeah, Nico. Okay."

"Help me."

"I will."

"You promise?"

"Yes. I promise."

Nico felt it again, the touch that had been against his cheek before, only now it was full-bodied, whole. He remembered it from years ago, suddenly reapplying itself like a fine layer of gauze over the person he'd once been.

You don't need to help me, Nico. You have a life, plans, a future—

You should have all those things!

Face it, a ticking clock isn't the same as a future.

You and your ticking clock, Gideon, that's my future. That's mine.

Gideon's voice was apparitional, in two places at once.

"Sleep well, Nicky." Distant. Safe.

Comforted, Nico finally closed his eyes and drifted, the warmth of his memories slowly fading into the precipice of rest.

PARISA

IN LIBBY'S ABSENCE, THE FIVE remaining members were offered initiation. When asked whether there would be magical consequences for not fulfilling the traditional ritual, Dalton was unflappable as usual.

"Something," he evasively explained, "has come up."

They had taken a week to look for Libby with no results. Parisa had been among the first to give up, as she could no longer feel or sense Libby's thoughts and therefore did not want to know what had happened to her. Whatever it was, it was enough to effectively kill her, and that was all Parisa needed to know. If the Society had enemies who could wipe a person's consciousness from the face of the earth, clearly it was worth it to lay claim to whatever else it had to show them.

The five remaining candidates had settled uncomfortably into the painted room for the introduction of their next subject, leaving Libby's chair empty out of habit. Not that they sat in any particular order, but disorder was hardly preferred. Libby usually sat near Nico, on his left. Nico refused to look at the empty seat beside him, and Parisa could hear the same buzzing from his mind that she heard from everyone else's. The acknowledgement of a missing piece, like a dismembered limb.

She wondered if it would have been the same if it was Callum's seat that had emptied.

"This," Dalton said, "is Viviana Absalon."

The others tensed as he waved in a cadaver, neatly preserved, the facial expression limp and non-committal, as if death had been something she'd preferred not to do but had gone ahead with anyway. Nothing gory had been done to the body, aside from a gaping incision that had been tastefully resewn. Obviously an autopsy had been performed somewhat recently, but outside of that, in death Viviana Absalon lay as still and tranquil as if she'd fallen asleep.

Briefly, Parisa's stomach churned with the memory of Libby's animation; the way Libby had been broken and contorted, her eyes vacant and wide. That, unlike this, had been gruesome, Parisa's hands sweltering with the blood her mind had refused to grasp was actually nothing. The idea that it was all magic, none of it real, had unnerved her deeply, reminding her what was at stake in the world.

Mortality was one thing; power was another. It was a lesson she would have to remember not to forget.

"Viviana is a forty-five-year-old female of French and Italian descent. She was misclassified as a mortal," said Dalton, "in more ways than one."

He pulled up a projection of pictures. Not unlike the preservation of the body, there was a clinical nature to the slides. Handwritten notes were scribbled unobtrusively next to arrows, annotative observations from the cadaver's incisions.

"By the age of eighteen, which is when most medeians have already shown signs of magical prowess, Viviana had revealed nothing out of the ordinary. She lacked any conceivable talent for witchcraft, and by age twenty-one, the alarms she had begun to set off were formally dismissed. 99% of medeians are identified correctly," Dalton reminded them, "but when it comes to a population of nearly ten billion people, there is a lot of room for error in the remaining 1%."

He waved a hand to move to the next slide. "At the time of her death, Viviana was in excellent physical health. She had already given birth to four children by the time she was thirty, while many in her village of Uzès still regarded her as the town beauty, even more lovely than the young women seeking husbands in their twenties. Unfortunately," Dalton said, "Viviana was hit by an automobile a matter of weeks ago. She died instantly."

Another wave, another slide, this one showing the accident before moving onto the details of Viviana's peculiarities. "As you can see," Dalton said, pulling up a side by side comparison with two sets of similar cadavers, "Viviana's internal organs stopped aging around twenty-one."

He swept through quickly, comparing incomprehensible (to Parisa) portions of her body first to those of a twenty-one-year-old, then a comparable forty-five-year-old.

"Her skin had not lost any elasticity. The features of her face were unchanged. Her hair did not turn grey. Most of her village simply believed she had exercised and eaten well, and perhaps dyed her hair. As for whether Viviana herself noticed anything suspicious, it appears not. She seems to have merely considered herself lucky—inordinately so, but not extraordinarily."

The slides concluded as Dalton turned to face them.

"As far as we can surmise, Viviana would not have died of natural causes if not for her accident," Dalton said, clarifying what had already been heavily implied. "Her death was not the result of any form of degeneration. What we do *not* know," he emphasized, "is how long she would have lived had she not met an untimely end, nor how frequently this occurs in other undiagnosed medeians."

"Did she show any signs of regeneration?" Tristan asked.

"Damage that repaired itself magically, you mean? No," Dalton said. "She simply didn't degenerate as a mortal should."

"Would she have been more or less susceptible to disease?" (Reina.)

"Unclear. Her village was particularly homogenous."

"Did she contract any significant illnesses?" (Tristan again.)

"No, but she was regularly vaccinated, so that would not be out of the ordinary."

"The common cold," Callum suggested drily, and Dalton shrugged.

"Most people do not take note of commonalities," he said, "hence the inadequacy of our existing research."

"What exactly are we supposed to do with this?" Nico asked, his fingers tapping impatiently at his sides. "Her magical specialty was… life?"

"Somewhere in her genetics is the ability to not decay," Dalton replied, which appeared to be confirmation. "We have no way of knowing how common this ability is, which is part of the purpose for research. Is Viviana the only one?" he posed to the group. "Have there been, historically, others? If none have lived long enough to become remarkable, then do people blessed with longevity typically *attract* fatalities? Is it possible they habitually die young, and if so, is this a result of magic?"

"Or," Dalton asked after a moment of silence, "is it somehow proof of fate?"

Parisa felt her eyes narrow, at odds with Dalton's offhanded remark. Magic the way they typically studied it was narrow, predictable, scientific in its results. Fate was inherently not. The magnetic quality of being drawn to a particular end was to remove the option of choice, which was so displeasing as to prick her slightly. Parisa did not care for the sensation of not being in control; it filled her mouth with bitterness, like excess salivation.

"You said something had come up," Reina said in her low voice. "Is this not what was planned for our next subject?"

Dalton tilted his head, reconciling with what appeared to be his own thoughts. "Yes and no. The unit of study following the initiation rites is always death," he said. "Most often we perform the traditional rituals on the eliminated member."

Tristan twitched with discomfort. Callum, solemnly, did not move.

"This particular case is, contrary to its appearance, fortuitous timing," Dalton flippantly remarked. "The Society's work remains uninterrupted, in a sense."

"Does it?" said Nico blisteringly, and Dalton slid a glance to him.

"For all intents and purposes, yes," he said. "Initiation will move forward as scheduled. You will also find that the units on life and death will allow you to access far more of the library's resources."

"And in exchange?" Parisa prompted.

Dalton's shoulders gave his customary indication of tension at the sound of her voice. It was a reflex born from a need to not look so quickly, fighting eagerness, which ultimately manifested like a tic of hesitation.

"You are beholden to the Society as it is beholden to you," he said without expression, before returning his attention to the details of Viviana's undiagnosed medeian status.

Parisa left the remainder of her questions for when they were alone. When she found him, Dalton was sitting in the reading room over a single book, toying with something out of her sight; invisible. Whatever it was he was doing, it was causing him intense strain. She watched the fight go out of him at the realization of her presence and stepped forward to reach him, smoothing a bead of sweat from his brow.

"What is it?" she murmured.

He glanced blearily up at her from a distance, traversing miles of thought.

"Do you know why he wants you?" he asked.

It was a question that had been plaguing Parisa since Libby's disappearance, if not earlier.

"No," she said.

"I do." He leaned his cheek against her hand, closing his eyes. "It's because you know how to starve."

They sat in silence as Parisa considered the implications of this. After all, was there a way to starve properly?

Yes. Conservation done well was to survive when others would perish.

Longevity, she thought in silence.

Then she stroked the back of Dalton's neck, smoothing the tension from his vertebrae.

"You saw something," she said. "In Libby's... in that thing."

It had been haunting her a bit from night to night. First the image of Libby on the floor, bleeding out, contorted. Then what Dalton had done, launching the corpse upright, making it dance.

An animation, he said. For which he was briefly the puppeteer.

"What is it?" she asked him again, and in the moment Dalton's eyes met hers, she thought she caught a glimpse of the familiar. Not the man in her bed from time to time, but the one she sought like firelight, drawn to him like a flame.

"Only one person could have made that animation," Dalton said.

"Who?"

She knew the answer before he said it.

"Me."

There was no point asking what he remembered. If that animation had ever been his creation, he clearly didn't know. Whether Dalton was indeed some god descending from machines was outside his existing mind's jurisdiction, and now he was pleading with her in silence. Begging for her to take away the guilt unearned.

Parisa slid the contents of the desk aside, replacing them with herself, and Dalton leaned forward to breathe her in, a wrench from his throat like a silent sob to bury in the fabric of her dress.

This was the difference between life and longevity; somewhere between a car crash and a splintered soul.

"I'll get you out," Parisa whispered to him. To some distant him, to his little fractures. The solution dawned like clarity in her mind.

If he was in pieces, she would take whatever rubble remained for herself.

REINA

"HELP ME with something."

Nico looked up from a long distance. As far as Reina could tell, the introduction of a new subject hadn't distracted him or eased his guilt, but something had. He was less aimless now, more determined, properly sleeping again. Impatiently waiting, but waiting nonetheless.

"Help you with what?" he asked.

"I have a theory."

She sat across from him in the grass, which protested as it always did. For once, she was glad to hear it. It served as a confirmation of sorts.

"Okay. About what?"

"I was thinking about what Callum said about sentience. Naturalism," Reina said, gesturing wordlessly to the whispers of *MotherMotherMother* that ached below her palms in tiny, willowy blades. "And about that medeian, her specialty of longevity."

"What about it?" Nico wasn't leaping to curiosity, but he was interested enough.

"Life," Reina posited, "must be an element. I can't use it, but maybe someone could." She fixed him with a careful glance. "You could."

"Could what?" He looked startled.

She sighed, "Use it."

"Use it?" he echoed.

"Yes." Maybe there was a better way to explain it. Maybe not. "Maybe you could manipulate it, shape it, like any other force. Like gravity." She paused. "Possibly you could even create it."

"You think I could create life?" Nico sat up slightly, frowning. "If it were a physical element then yes, theoretically speaking. Maybe." His brow furrowed. "But even if I *could*—"

"Energy doesn't come from nothing, I know." She'd already thought about it at length. "That's where I come in."

"But—"

"The theory is a quite straightforward. Suppose life is its own element. What if Viviana Absalon's magical specialty really *was* life—the ability to be alive and stay that way?" she said, waiting to see if he followed. "Life and sentience are not the same, but there are microorganisms that live without sentience, so if magic like an animation can *live*, in some sense—"

Nico was staring at her, brows still furrowed, and Reina reached out with a sigh, gruffly placing a hand on his shoulder.

"Just try it," she said, and he balked.

"Try... what, exactly?"

Ha ha ha, laughed the grass, rustling with amusement. *Mother is much too clever, much more clever, she seesandseesandsees ha haaaaa—*

"Just try," Reina repeated.

She felt Nico's shoulder stiffen beneath her touch, bracing for an argument, but then it settled gradually into place as he must have conceded, either willingly giving in or responding against his own volition to something she was offering him. Reina wondered, not for the first time, if he could now hear what she could hear, or if that was still reserved for her personal annoyance. At least when Nico was using it she was permitted moments of reprieve, the rush of channeling it into something. It was indistinct from the sensation of allowing nature itself to take from her, as she had when Atlas had first entered her cafe.

Grow, Reina had told the seed then, and it had grown.

Now she told Nico *try*, and she could feel the way his power had accepted hers gratefully, willingly, hungrily. There was a sense of both relief and release, and when he lifted his palm, the response was a staggered lurch, like a full-bodied gasp.

There was no other way to describe it outside of a *spark*. Whether they saw it or felt it or merely intuited its presence was grossly indeterminable. Reina knew only that something which had not existed previously had existed briefly for a time, and she knew that Nico knew it too, his dark eyes widening with astonishment and the aftershocks of belated apprehension.

He had expected nothing; if she had expected anything more, it was only for having been the one to own the theory, to make use of the thought.

It really was a simple idea, almost laughable in its lack of complexity. If life could come from nothing—if it could be born at all, created like the universe itself—then why should it not come from her?

Mother, sighed the sweep of a nearby branch.

She and Nico both seemed to know what they'd done without consulting the other for evidence.

"What does it mean?" asked Nico.

"I don't know." She didn't. Not yet.

"What could you do with it?"

"Me?" Reina turned to him with surprise. "Nothing."

He frowned back at her, not understanding. "What?"

"I can't do anything with it."

"But—"

"*You* used it," she said.

"But you gave it to me!"

"So? What's electricity without a lightbulb? Useless."

"That's—"

But then he shook his head, seeming to see no point in furthering the argument.

"If Rhodes were here," he said deflatingly, "then maybe I could do something with it. But as it is, it's just… that." A spark. "Whatever that was."

"So you need more power?"

"More than that. More than *more*." He drummed his fingers in the grass, a brief return to his usual state of fidgeting. "It's not a matter of how much, it's how… good. How pure."

"So if Libby were here it would be something?"

"Yes." He sounded certain. He always sounded certain, but that particular certainty was more persuasive than smug. "I don't know what, but something."

"Well." Reina paused to shield her eyes as the sun broke through the cloud cover overhead, enveloping them in a harsh wave of brightness. "We'll have to find her, then."

There was a pulse of tension as Nico braced himself again.

"We?"

"If I can help, yes." She glanced at him. "I assumed you were doing something already."

"Well—" He stopped. "I'm not. I'm out of options, but—"

"Your friend," she guessed. "The one who can move through dreams?"

He said nothing.

"You never mentioned that about him," Reina observed aloud. "His name, yes, but never what it was he could do."

Nico seemed retroactively guilty, kicking out his feet in the grass. "I never planned to tell anyone."

"Because he is… secretive?"

"Him? Not so much. But what he can do…" Nico sighed. "It's just best if people don't know."

To her displeasure, Reina found herself more annoyed by that than usual.

"You should trust us." She was surprised by how adamant she was. "Don't you think?"

Nico's expression in reply was one of total, incomprehensible openness. Parisa had been right that he was scarcely capable of guile.

"Why?" he said.

Reina considered it. Nico would want a good answer, a thorough one, and for possibly selfish reasons, she needed him to be persuaded.

"Do you understand," she said slowly, "how alone we are one thing, but together we are another?"

A beat of silence.

Then, "Yes."

"So it is a waste, then. Not to use the resources you have." Another simple concept.

"You would trust Callum? Or Parisa?"

Nico sounded skeptical, for good reason.

"I trust that they are talented," Reina confirmed slowly. "I trust their skill. I trust that when their interests align with mine, they are useful."

"And if they don't align?"

"Then make them." To Reina it was logical, sequential, if-this-then-that. "Why are we part of this if not to be great? I could be good alone, as could you," she reminded him. "We would not still be here if we wished to settle only for goodness."

"Are you—" Nico faltered. "Are you really so certain about this?"

About the Society, he meant.

"Yes," she said.

It wasn't true at the time, but she had plans to make it so. She intended to *become* that certain, and to do so would only require a few answers.

Only one man could satisfactorily provide her with those.

She could see she hadn't startled him with her presence. Perhaps he'd been expecting her. His office had always held little interest for any of them, largely because the space itself contained nothing worth inspection. Only he was interesting, in his unobtrusive way. There had always been an air of eternal patience about him.

"What is initiation?" Reina asked without preamble, and Atlas, who had been rifling through some of the books on his shelf, slowed his motions to a halt.

"A ritual. As everything is." He looked tired, as he often looked when they caught glimpses of him lately. He was dressed in a bespoke suit as he always was, this one a slate grey that somehow reflected his state of academic mourning. "Binding oaths are not particularly complex. I imagine you must have studied them at one point."

She had. "Will it work without a death?"

"Yes."

Atlas took a seat at his desk and gestured for her to do the same, removing a pen from his pocket and setting it carefully just to the right of his hand. "There may be fractures. But after two millennia of oaths to reinforce the binding, I can assure you," he said with something close to irony, "it will hold."

She didn't bother asking why they didn't simply do away with the elimination process, then, if it would hold without it. It seemed fairly obvious there were no more reasons to support it than there were to support the divine right of kings. Tradition, ritual, the general fear of chaos.

It didn't matter. She was alive, and that was the only factor of relevance.

"I doubt you came to ask me about the logistics of the ceremony," Atlas remarked. He was regarding her with a certain wary interest; guarded.

"I wanted to ask you something else."

"Then ask."

"Will you answer?"

"Perhaps. Perhaps not."

Comforting, Reina thought.

"You told me in the cafe that my invitation to join the Society had come down to me and someone else," she reminded him.

"Yes, I did say that." He didn't look as if he planned to deny anything. "Has it bothered you much?"

"In a sense."

"Because you doubt your place here?"

"No," Reina said, and she didn't. "I knew it was mine if I wanted it."

Atlas leaned back in his chair, contemplating her with a glance. "Then what's to think about?"

"The fact that there are others." It wasn't a threat so much as a curiosity. "People who nearly make the cut, but don't."

"There's no reason to worry about them, if that's what you mean," Atlas said. "There are plenty of other pursuits, noble ones. Not everyone merits an invitation to the Society."

"Do they work for the Forum?"

"The Forum is not the same, structurally," Atlas said. "It is closer to a corporation."

"What's the difference?"

"Its members stand to profit."

"From what?"

"Our loss," Atlas said simply, waving a hand over an empty mug. Within moments there was tea inside it, the smell of lavender and bergamot wafting in the air between them. "But such is the nature of things. Balance," he said, bringing the cup to his lips. "There cannot be success without failure. No luck without unluck."

"No life without death?" asked Reina.

Atlas inclined his head in agreement. "So you see the purpose of the ritual," he said.

She wondered if perhaps she wanted this too much. She was willing to make excuses for it, to believe its lies. A toxic love, born of starvation.

Too late now. "Do you know what happened to Libby Rhodes?"

"No." It came without hesitation, but not too quickly. She could see the formulation of concern in his brow, which seemed real enough. "And I'm sorry to say I would have readily believed her dead if not for Mr. Caine."

"Do you believe it was the Forum?"

"I think it's a possibility."

"What are the other possibilities?"

She could see his tongue catching, a mechanism sliding shut.

"Innumerable," he said.

So he would not be sharing his theories with her.

"Should we trust you?" Reina asked him.

Atlas gave her a paternal half-smile.

"I will tell you this," he said. "If I could retrieve Elizabeth Rhodes myself, I would do everything in my power to do so. There would be no reason for me to abandon her pursuit. I reap no benefit from her loss."

Reina did believe that, grudgingly. She supposed there was no reason to doubt him. Anyone could see Libby's value.

"But none of this is why you came here," Atlas observed.

Reina glanced down at her hands, wondering for a moment what felt so strange about them here. She realized eventually it was the lack of tension within them, because unlike other rooms in the house, this one did not contain any life. There were no plants, only books and dead wood.

Interesting, she thought.

"You said there was a traveler," she said. "I wanted to know if it was Nico's friend."

"Ah yes, Gideon Drake," said Atlas. "He was a finalist, albeit not in the final ten."

"Is it true that his friend can travel through dream realms?"

"Realms of the subconscious," Atlas clarified with a nod. "A fascinating ability, without question, but the Society's board was ultimately unconvinced of Mr. Drake's control over his abilities. I believe even Miss Rhodes knew only of his incurable narcolepsy, which could not be successfully prevented," he added with a small inward chuckle. "Very few of NYUMA's professors knew what to do with him. He is quite close to untrained, in some senses. And his mother is highly dangerous and likely to interfere."

"Who is she?"

"No one in particular," Atlas said. "Something of a spy. No telling why or how she fell into it, but she appears to have a debt, or at least a fondness for earning new ones."

Reina frowned. "So she does... what, exactly?"

"She's a criminal, but a forgettable one. Not unlike Mr. Caine's father."

"Oh." For some reason, that information made Reina deeply sad. Perhaps it was the way that, in calling Gideon Drake's mother forgettable, Atlas was so quick to suggest that memory was a luxury not to be wasted on the unworthy.

"And Gideon?"

"I suspect that if Mr. Drake had never met Nico de Varona, his life would look quite different," Atlas said. "If indeed he were still living without Nico's help."

Reina shifted in her chair. "So that's it?"

"What is?"

"The unremarkable are punished for their unremarkability," she said.

Atlas set down his cup of tea, steeping the moment in silence.

"No," he said at last, adjusting his tie. "It is the remarkable who suffer. The unremarkable are passed over, yes, but greatness is not without its pains." He fixed her with a solemn glance, adding, "I know very few medeians who would not ultimately choose to be unremarkable and happy, were they able to do so."

"But you do know some who wouldn't choose that," Reina pointed out.

Atlas' mouth twisted upwards.

"Yes," he said. "I do know some."

He seemed ready to let her go, his episode of candor coming to a close, but Reina lingered a moment longer, contemplating her lack of satisfaction. She supposed she had thought the confirmation of Nico's friend would solve her puzzle, but it hadn't. The initial satisfaction of having questions answered was a cheap high, and now she was unfulfilled again.

"The traveler," she said. "The one you rejected to choose me instead. Who was it?"

She knew without a doubt this would be the last question she was permitted to ask.

"He was not rejected," said Atlas, before inclining his head in dismissal, rising to his feet and leading her conclusively to the door.

EZRA

EZRA MIKHAIL FOWLER WAS BORN as the earth was dying. There had been an entire fuss of it on the news that year, about the carbon crisis and how little time the ozone had left, leaving an entire generation to turn to their therapists and proclaim a collective, widespread existential disengagement. The United States had been awash in fires and floods for months, with only half the country believing they had any hand in its demolishment. Even the ones who still believed in a vengeful God had failed to see the signs.

Still, things would have to get much worse before they got better. Only when time and breathable air and potable water were running out did someone, somewhere, decide to change their stance. Magical technology that had once been bought and sold by governments in secret transitioned to private hands, allowing it to be bought and sold via trade secret instead. It healed some of the earth's viruses, provided some renewable energy, repairing enough of the damage caused by industrialization and globalization and all the other -ations that the world could successfully go on a bit longer without any drastic change in attitude or behaviors. Politicians politicked as usual, which meant that for every incremental step forward there was still a looming end in sight. But it was delayed, and that was what was important. Any senator could tell you that.

Ezra, meanwhile, grew up in an unfortunate corner of Los Angeles. The sort that was too far east to have ever laid eyes on the ocean, and that also believed unquestionably that a river was nothing more than a slow trickle above cement. His was a generally fatherless nation, a community of misfortune for which mothers were primary caregivers and breadwinners as well, albeit for very little bread. Ezra had been a tribesman of his local multigenerational matriarchy until the age of twelve, when his mother died as the result of a shooting while at worship inside her temple. Ezra had been there, but also not there. He remembered the details of the event clearly for multiple reasons, her death notwithstanding: One, he and his mother had had an argument that morning about him running off somewhere the day before, which he assured her he hadn't done. Two, it had been his first experience with a door.

Perhaps if he'd been braver or more aware of what he was doing he might have held his mother's hand more tightly. As it was, the sound of the automatic rifle had sent him careening backwards in space, to the point where he wondered if he had actually been shot. He was familiar with the idea of a live shooter, having been made to run drills for it in school, but death itself remained a foreign concept. In Ezra's mind, the idea of a bullet piercing any part of him was just like this had been: a collapse, his ears ringing, the entirety of the world tilting sideways for a moment. When the sensation cleared, though, Ezra realized he was either dead or very, very much alive.

When he opened his eyes the temple was quiet, eerily so. He walked around to the spot where his mother had been, feeling at the edges of the wood for evidence of bullets. There were none, and he thought perhaps he had made it happen by magic. Perhaps he had fixed everything, done it over, and now everything would be fine? He went home to find his mother asleep on the sofa, still in her nurse's uniform. He went to bed. He woke up. The sun shone.

Then things began to happen oddly. The same burnt toast for breakfast as yesterday, the same terrible jokes on the daily morning news. His mother yelled at him for running off the day before, disappearing and coming home after she'd been asleep. She dragged him to the bathroom, shouting for him to wash his hair and get dressed for temple. No, no, he said instantly, no we can't go there, Mom listen to me it's important, but she was insistent. Put your good shoes on Ezra Mikhail, wash your hair and let's go.

When the shooter appeared again, Ezra finally confirmed with certainty his suspicion that he had somehow gone into the past, which at first he took as a blessing. He tried several times to save his mother, thinking it his divinely appointed task. Each time things repeated as they had before, the situation altering like puzzle pieces to form the prophetic picture on the box. Exhausted, he eventually fell through the little vacancy in time for the thirteenth round and stayed there, and then, for the first time, he tried to open a new crevice for himself, something to lead him elsewhere. When he stepped out, he was three weeks beyond his mother's funeral—the furthest he could take himself at the time.

Social services soon arrived to gather him into custody. Perhaps because he had already watched his mother die twelve times, Ezra numbly went.

It's not a secret that the foster care system leaves much to be desired. Ezra had vowed never to run away again, never to tell a soul about what he'd seen and done, but life has a way of breaking its promises to children. Within a year, he was learning to use the doors with some regularity, securing control over their outcome. He did not age as time passed if he didn't choose to, moving fluidly through it instead, and by his sixteenth birthday he was only fifteen and one day, having skipped through any instances of the time he couldn't otherwise abide.

At seventeen (or so), Ezra was offered a scholarship to the New York University of Magical Arts, which was the first time he fully understood that he was not alone in what he could do. True, he was the only one who had access to the doors specifically, but for the first time, he understood that he was not the only magician in the world—no, *medeian*, they told him. It was a new word, unfamiliar on his tongue.

So what was he? Not a physicist, not exactly. He was definitely opening and closing tiny, Ezra-sized wormholes to navigate through time, that much seemed clear, but his magic was limited and self-concentrated. It was a unique power, dangerous.

Keep it quiet, his professors advised. You never know what sort of people will try to mess with time. Never the kind with good intentions.

Dutifully, Ezra kept his abilities a secret, or tried to. Eventually, though, the Alexandrian Society found him out.

It was a tempting offer. (It was always tempting; power always is.) What was particularly interesting to Ezra, though, were the others, his fellow initiates, or the four who would become his fellow initiates after one of them had been eliminated. Ezra was introverted by nature—a combination of poverty, inexplicable power, and his mother's untimely death had combined to make him relatively standoffish—but there was one other initiate with whom he instantly shared a bond.

Atlas Blakely was a rakish vagrant with wild natural hair and an insuppressible grin. A "bi' o' London rough," as he called himself, who laughed so loudly it regularly frightened pigeons. He was wolfish and lively and so sharp it sometimes made others uneasy, but Ezra warmed to him immediately, and Atlas to him. They shared something they gradually deduced was hunger, though for what was initially unclear. Ezra's theory was that they were merely cut from the same indigent cloth, the easy cast-offs of a dying earth. The other four candidates were educated, well-born, and therefore bred with a comfortable cynicism, a posh sort of gloom. Ezra and Atlas, on the other hand were sunspots. They were stars who refused to die out.

It was Atlas who first sorted out the death clause of the Society's initiation, reading it somewhere in someone's thoughts or whatever he did that Atlas insisted was not actually mind reading. "It's good and rightly fucked, innit?" he said to Ezra, his accent thickly unintelligible at times. "We're supposed to kill someone? Thanks, mate, no thanks." (*No fanks*, as it sounded to Ezra.)

"The books, though," Ezra said, quietly buzzing. The two of them shared a fondness for intoxicants, mortal drugs when they could get it. It made the doors easier to access for Ezra, and Atlas got tired of hearing the sound of other people's thoughts. Gave him a bleedin' migraine, he said.

"The damn books. A whole library. All those books."

"Books ain't enough, bruv," grunted Atlas sagely.

But fundamentally, Ezra disagreed. "This Society is something," he said. "It's not just the books, it's the questions, the answers. It's all something more than nothing." (Drugs made this theory difficult to communicate.) "What we need is to get ourselves in, but then get on top somehow. Power begets power and all that."

It was clear that Atlas did not understand him, so he went on.

"Most people don't know how to starve," said Ezra, going on to describe how few people were capable of actually understanding time and how much of it there was, and how much a person could gain if they could just hold on a little longer. If they could starve long enough to get by on almost nothing, if they fed themselves only little by little, in the end they would be the ones to last. The patient shall inherit the earth, or something like that. Killing was bad, sure, but worse it was unnecessary, inefficient. What had Ezra's existence ever been aside from a recurring loophole to the nature of life itself?

And besides, they still wanted the damn books, so from there they made a plan: it was Atlas who would do the waiting, Ezra who would disappear. They could fake his death, Ezra suggested, and thus with one person out of the running, there would be no need for either of them to kill anyone. The other initiates didn't like Ezra, anyway. He was too secretive, they didn't trust him. They also didn't know what he could do, and in the end, that was clearly for the best.

So Ezra opened a door and went forward five years, meeting Atlas in the cafe they'd agreed on before he left. In what felt like a matter of hours to Ezra, Atlas had advanced to twenty-eight and lost the accent, but not the swagger. He slid into the chair opposite Ezra and grinned. "I'm in," he said.

"They bought it?" The Society knew what Ezra could do, but still. Who were they to say he wasn't dead?

"Yes."

"So what'd they do with... you know. Me?"

"Same thing they do to every eliminated candidate. Erased you," Atlas said. "Like you never existed."

Perfect. "And even without the ritual...?"

Atlas raised a glass. "The Society is dead; long live the Society."

Continuity into perpetuity. Time, as ever, went on.

"So what next?" asked Ezra, blazing with the prospects yet to come.

They kept their meetings up sparingly, a year at a time. Neither of them wanted Ezra to age unnecessarily; for him, time passed differently, but it was still passing. They were waiting for the six, Atlas said. The *right* six, the perfect collection, including Ezra. Atlas, meanwhile, would have to work his way up, to ensure he would be the next Caretaker of the archives (theirs had been quite old already, which aside from wealth beyond measure made an excellent qualification for impending retirement), and then once Atlas managed it, he would be able to start hand-selecting the candidates himself. He would choose the perfect team of five—one to die, of course, at the initiates' choosing, though even that unlucky soul would be someone carefully and thoughtfully selected—and then Ezra, the sixth, would be at the helm of it.

The perfect team for what?

"For anything," Atlas said. "For everything."

He meant: *Let's take this bloody mess and all its damn books and do something that's never been done.*

They drafted imaginary plans for it at length: a physicist who could approximate what Ezra could do, but bigger. Wormholes, black holes, space travel, time travel. Someone who could see quanta, manipulate it, understand it, use it. (Was that possible? Surely it must be, said Atlas.) Someone to help them power it, like a battery. Another telepath to be Atlas' right hand, to be his eyes and ears so he could finally rest his own. What were they building? Neither of them were entirely sure, but they knew they had the instincts, the guts, the painstaking deliberation.

"I found something," Atlas said, earlier than anticipated. Just the one, an animator.

(Animator?)

"Just trust me," said Atlas, who was entering his late thirties now and beginning to dress in suits, concealing his true origins behind a posher accent and better clothes. "I've got a feeling about this one, bruv."

It was around this time when the initial euphoria of the plan had begun to wane, and Ezra was starting to question his usefulness. The plan relied mostly on Atlas' gut, which was certainly something Ezra trusted, but all the darting in and out of time and meeting wherever Atlas happened to be in the world wasn't exactly the same as being present. Ezra wasn't contributing anything, wasn't part of it, not really. Go back to NYUMA, Atlas suggested, see what you can find, you're only twenty-three now (or something) and you still look young. Besides, Atlas said with a laugh, you're too American to blend in anywhere else.

So Ezra went.

Unfortunately, in order for Ezra to see anything worth finding, time had to slow down. He had to experience time linearly again, remaining in one chronological place and putting down the half-hearted roots of a passably unthreatening persona. He resented it, finding existence slightly dull without the one thing that had always felt natural to him, but before he could abandon his efforts and move on, the banality of his existence led to a position as a resident advisor in a freshman dorm and then, unexpectedly, he had found something.

"You need them both," Ezra told Atlas after seeing Libby Rhodes and Nico de Varona face off in the row of the century. "When the time comes, you absolutely must take them both."

"But they have the same specialty," Atlas pointed out, looking doubtful. His hair had started to grey at the temples a few years before, so by then he had opted to shave it off. "Don't you want to be initiated? You were always meant to be the sixth."

Ezra paused to consider it. He had always intended to be initiated someday, but suddenly the formality seemed unimportant.

"You'll have to have both," he repeated, adding, "Nor do I think you could conceivably get one without the other."

Atlas mulled it over, considering the idea from all angles.

"They're… physicists, you said?"

"They're mutants," Ezra said. (High praise, in his opinion.) "Absolute mutants."

"Well, keep an eye on them," said Atlas thoughtfully. "I've got something else I'm working on right now."

Easy enough to do. Assuming the unremarkable role of a student two years above them despite being born nearly twenty-five years before meant that Libby in particular proved herself to be intriguing to Ezra. That wasn't an interesting story, particularly after knowing it would eventually sour.

As for Nico, they never quite got on. Ezra already knew he was giving up his spot for Nico, or for whomever Atlas found to serve one of the more necessary roles among the six. (A naturalist, Atlas said. What did they need plants for? scoffed Ezra, only to be met with Never mind about the plants, I've got a feeling, you'll see.) At least Nico made things easier by rendering the offer impossible for Libby to refuse.

It was the year leading up to their initiation that finally opened Ezra's eyes to the possibility that he may not have been starving so much as fasting. Now that Libby and Nico were gone, Ezra was left performing his cultivated mundanity for a fleet of empty seats. Worse, he had underestimated the discomfort of no longer being integral to Atlas' plan.

"Nonsense, of course you are," said Atlas. "In fact, I suspect you can do the ritual this year after all."

"How?" Ezra asked irritably. Boredom stung, it itched somewhere intangibly, like a cramp in his calf. "Five are initiated, not six."

"Yes, but I suspect I was wrong about Parisa," Atlas said.

Ezra frowned. "Is she not as good as you thought?"

"No, in terms of ability she's precisely what I'd hoped." A pause. "But I suspect she's a problem."

"What sort of problem?" Ezra was unaware Atlas had any of those. As far as he knew, everything was going swimmingly without him. Hence the boredom.

"A problem." Atlas sipped his tea. "I can convince her to get the others to kill Callum, at least."

"Which one, the empath?"

"Yes." That was always the one meant to die; even the perfect group of candidates would have to lose a member, after all. In Atlas' eyes—and Ezra agreed—Callum was the equivalent of a nuclear code, and ridding the world of him was a favor to humanity. "Then you can have Parisa's spot."

"Oh yes of course, just kill her and take her spot, everything all neat and tidy," Ezra said, waiting for a laugh that didn't come.

Atlas sipped his tea again, and Ezra blinked.

"What?"

No reply.

"Atlas," he growled. "Why on earth would I do that?"

"She slept with your girlfriend, for one thing," Atlas offered with a misbegotten smile.

Which was not an answer, so Ezra rolled his eyes.

"Libby doesn't know a thing about me. Bit hypocritical, don't you think, if I held that particular blemish against her?"

"Regardless, you know there's a bonding aspect to initiation. You'll have to become part of them somehow if you plan to take their initiation oath. Sacrifice will do the trick."

"And if I don't want to be initiated?"

Atlas' cup paused partway to his lips. "What?"

"I don't see the point," Ezra said restlessly. "You're here, aren't you, with me? What do I need to be part of the Society for? I've been on your side since the beginning."

"Yes, and it's been exceedingly helpful," said Atlas, setting his cup to the side.

There was something about the foreignness of the motion—Atlas had never liked tea, preferring extreme intoxication instead—that made Ezra wonder whether he really knew Atlas Blakely at all. He certainly had at one point, but over two decades had passed since then, and Ezra had missed them. What might have happened to Atlas' mind, to his convictions, to his soul? What had initiation into the Society done to him?

So Ezra decided to do something he had never bothered with doing before.

He opened a door to the distant future.

This was not as exciting a thing as it sounded, because the future could always be changed. True, there were some unalterable events, but in general Ezra had learned to take his distant doors as a pseudo-reliable astrological reading: likely to happen, but not guaranteed. So long as he did not remain there, he wasn't bound to the consequences of anything he saw. His presence, if he did not disrupt anything, was as forgettable as the motion of a single grain of sand.

But what he discovered discomfited him intensely. Because what Ezra saw—the conclusion of his and Atlas Blakely's plan—was almost certainly the end of the world.

"Let's make a new one," Atlas had said once. Not long ago, in Ezra's memory. Twenty years in Atlas Blakely's, and therefore perhaps long enough for him to believe Ezra might have forgotten what he said. "This one's shitty, mate, it's gone and lost the plot completely. No more fixing, no more tinkering around with broken parts. When one ecosystem fails, nature makes a new one. Nature, or whoever's in charge. That's how the species survives."

He had turned his head, locking his dark gaze on Ezra's.

"Let's be gods, bruv," Atlas said.

At the time, Ezra had blamed it on the drugs. But then he saw Tristan Caine inside one of his doors, traversing time itself on the wards Ezra had helped put in place, and he understood for the first time that Atlas Blakely had already built the perfect team without him.

"What is it Tristan can do?" Ezra asked casually on their next meeting. "You never told me."

"Did I not?" said Atlas, lifting his cup to his lips.

Ezra, irritated, knocked the tea out of his hands. "You know you didn't, Atlas—"

"Getting cold feet, old friend?" Atlas murmured, giving Ezra a thin smile as he waved a hand, returning the cup to its original state. "I imagine you may find yourself less devoted to our goals than you once were. Perhaps," he said, in English so falsely aristocratic he might as well have fucked the queen, "because you've made no sacrifices to get here."

"Me? *Atlas*," Ezra snapped. "This was always part of the plan—"

"Yes," Atlas agreed, "but while I've spent the last quarter of a century getting older, you've remained a child, haven't you, Ezra? We erased you, remade you, to the point where your stakes don't exist. You," he said with accusation, or possibly disappointment, "can't see the way the game has changed."

"I'm a *child*?" Ezra echoed, astounded. "Have you forgotten that I did your dirty work for you?"

"I believe I thanked you for that several times over," Atlas reminded him. "And I offered you a seat at the table, did I not?"

"Only because you want me to take out another obstacle to you—and what's wrong with Parisa, anyway?" Ezra demanded, bristling. "What threat is she to you?"

"No threat," Atlas said. "Just… not the ally I'd hoped she'd be."

The inadequacy of his response pricked like a needle, and Ezra stared at him.

"We started all this because we agreed this Society was fucked," he said flatly.

"Yes," Atlas agreed.

"And now?"

"Still fucked, as you put it," said Atlas. "But this time, I can fix it. We," he amended. "We can fix it, if you're willing to see things as I see them."

When one ecosystem fails, nature makes a new one.

That's how the species survives.

The silence between them hollowed out and refilled with a new, tactile wave of doubt.

"The archives would never give you what you want," Ezra said to Atlas in a low voice. "You can't hide your intentions from the library itself."

Silence.

"Are you using someone else to do it?"

"Either you're in, Ezra, or you're not," Atlas told him, grimly exasperated.

"Of course I'm in," Ezra said. "I've never not been in."

And he hadn't.

Not before then.

"So then it's simple, isn't it? You'll see what they're all capable of," Atlas told him. "Open up a space for yourself among the six and it's yours, all of it. I wouldn't deny you any of it."

Ezra knew better than to question him, even inside his own head.

"Fine," he said. "Fine, get Parisa to kill Callum and I'll deal with the rest."

"Does Libby suspect anything?" asked Atlas.

No. No, he would make sure of it.

"I'll keep her close," Ezra said, having once mistaken that for something that could be done.

But truthfully he knew it couldn't. The more Ezra had pushed her, coaxed her, worshipfully tried to persuade her of his devotion the way he assumed she would want to be loved—the more he hoped to remain inside Atlas' confidence by maintaining Libby's—the further she got from him, growing more distant each time they spoke. Ezra had wanted an alliance of sorts, anticipating that Libby would trust him enough to allow insight to Atlas' plans even if Society rules precluded them. He clung to their years of companionship, their one-sided trust, and set himself to the task of distant espionage, hoping to rely on the one person whose morality he had always assumed would persist, even if their relationship did not. But Libby had pushed back, fruitlessly mistrusting, aimlessly angry.

"I'm not yours," she said, and drew a line between them, closing the door on his access to her life.

So now, without Libby or even the promise of her, Ezra had no choice but to do something drastic. If he wanted to make sure Atlas Blakely's plans never came to pass, then he would have to neutralize the Society on his own.

What he needed first was a way to take one of Atlas' pieces off the board.

Breaking in would be the easy part. Twenty years ago, Ezra had quietly built a failsafe into the wards, precisely his own size and shape, for which no succeeding class of initiates would know to prevent. He could slip easily through it, falling through a dimension no one else could see, but what to do upon arrival was another matter; a troubling one.

Ezra knew, to some extent, which of the six mattered to Atlas and which ones didn't. Libby, Nico, and Reina were part of the same triumvirate of power, and therefore Atlas would need all three. Tristan... there was something about Tristan that Atlas wasn't telling him, which made Tristan possibly the lynchpin of Atlas' plan.

Whichever candidate Ezra chose, Atlas would need to believe they were dead.

An illusion?

No, something better. Something convincing.

Something *expensive*.

"I know someone who can help you," came back once Ezra sent feelers around, reaching out to whatever he could find among less law-abiding circles. A mermaid, they said, though the term was slung around with a derogatory aftertaste. "It'll cost you, but if you can pay…"

"I can pay," Ezra said.

(He could easily rob a bank in the past and come back to the future scot-free.)

It was someone known only as the Prince who, via the mermaid, gave Ezra the animation. It was sickening and faceless, expressionless and limp. Just a generic, unremarkable diorama of a corpse that had encountered a violent end.

"You'll have to give it a face," the mermaid said, her voice shrill and high, like glass breaking. The sound of it set off something in Ezra's inner ear, leaving him temporarily straining for balance. "It will have to replicate someone you know well enough to complete the animation. Someone whose every expression and motion you know intimately enough to reproduce."

That, Ezra realized with a momentary stiffening, narrowed his options considerably. But if he were going to take one of Atlas' prizes, he may as well take the one he knew for a fact that Atlas could not do without. She and Nico were a key and a lock, and Ezra, a person who trafficked in doors, knew one was no good without the other.

Libby had intuited his presence in the room before seeing him. She had keen hearing, and something had always alerted her to his presence. Echolocation, almost. She had known his entry to the house, had felt the disruption of time that he'd caused. For a moment, seeing her eyes change, Ezra suffered a twinge of remorse.

Only for a moment.

Taking her with him was an effort, one which was only narrowly possible given the limitations of his ability to travel. Convenient that she was so small, and so taken unawares. The only sound as they went through the door was her scream, which echoed from the place they'd left until they arrived where he'd intended, and then it ended with a spark, like a match flaring.

Libby spun from his grip and glared at him.

"Ezra, what the *fuck*—"

"It isn't what you think," he said quickly, because it wasn't. If he could have taken one of the others, he would have. This wasn't about her.

"Then tell me what to think!"

"I don't have time to tell you everything," he said, and summarized for her the basics: Atlas Blakely bad, Society bad, everything mostly bad, Libby gone for her own good.

She took it badly. "My *own good*? I told you not to decide that for me when we were together," she snarled at him. "You certainly don't get to decide it now!"

Appealing as it was to spend his time having another fight with his ex-girlfriend, Ezra didn't currently have a lot of patience for a heart-to-heart. "Admittedly, there's a lot of things about our relationship I'd like to change," he told her briskly. "Most notably its inception. But seeing as I can't—"

"It was all a lie." Libby lifted a hand to her mouth. "My god, I believed you, I *defended* you—"

"It wasn't a lie. It just wasn't—" Ezra paused, clearing his throat. "Entirely true."

She stared at him, dumbfounded. In her defense, Ezra conceded, it was indeed a terrible answer. He had not improved much since their breakup at telling her things she wanted to hear—but in *his* defense, he'd never actually known the right things to say to begin with.

Gradually, Libby found her voice again.

"But you…" A pause. "You know everything about me. *Everything*."

He had hoped it wouldn't come to this. "Yes."

"You know about my fears, my dreams, my regrets." Her face paled. "My sister."

"Yes."

"I trusted you."

"Libby—"

"It was real for me!"

"It was real for me, too."

Most of it.

Some of it.

"Jesus, Ezra, did I even—?"

He watched Libby stop herself from asking if she had ever mattered to him, which was a brilliant idea as far as he was concerned. Even if she could have been satisfied with his answer (likely not), being made to question it at all would cause her irreparable harm. Libby Rhodes, whatever emotional insufficiencies she may have struggled with intrinsically, knew her limits, and she regarded them with abject tenderness, like fresh bruises.

"So why did you *abduct* me?" she demanded, half-stammering.

"Because of Atlas," Ezra sighed. Now they were going in circles. "I told you. This isn't about you."

"But then—" Another pause. "Where did you take me?"

It was starting to settle in now, he suspected. The sensation of being held captive. The initial shock of being taken was starting to wear off, and soon she would start to consider the plausibility of escape.

"It isn't," Ezra began, "entirely a matter of *where*."

He stopped before explaining himself any further. She was too clever, after all, and certainly too powerful not to find her way out unless it remained a labyrinth, part of a maze she couldn't see. People generally only knew how to look at the world one way: in three dimensions. For them, time was exclusively linear, moving in a single direction never to be disrupted or stopped.

Imagine looking for someone and knowing only that they were somewhere on earth. Now imagine looking for someone knowing only that they were on earth during a time with indoor plumbing. In short, nobody would find her. Ideally, Libby Rhodes would even struggle to find herself.

"You can't keep me here," she said. It was flat, unfaceted, deadly. "You don't understand what I am. You never have."

"I know exactly what you are, Libby. I've known for some time. Is the empath dead yet?"

She gaped at him.

"Is that a yes?" Ezra prompted.

"I don't—how—" She was blinking rapidly. "You know about Callum?"

He set his jaw, taking it for a rhetorical question. Obviously he had already made his answer plenty clear. "Yes or no, Libby."

"I don't know," she snapped, restless. "Yes, maybe—"

He was running late now, though punctuality was never a primary concern for him. He was often late to things, finding time to be such an arbitrary measure of motion. Even in his youth, which was admittedly both enormous and a mere sliver of things, he had never felt tasked by the prospect of arriving anywhere on time. His mother had wasted countless hours haranguing him about it, even on her very last day.

Though, perhaps that was what had drawn him to Atlas, in the end. Ezra knew how to starve, and Atlas knew how to wait.

"I'll be back," Ezra told Libby. "Don't go anywhere." Not that she could, even if she tried it. He'd built the wards specifically for her, made them molecular, soluble, water-based. She would have to alter the state of her environment in order to break them; to change the elements themselves individually, draining herself more with each step of progress. One step forward, two steps back.

Keys and locks.

"You're keeping me here?" She sounded numbly disbelieving, though that would change. Numbness would pass, and pain would surely follow.

He lamented it. "It's for your own safety," he reminded her.

"From Atlas?"

"Yes, from Atlas," he said, feeling a rush of urgency. He was running late, but again, that wasn't the problem; it was what awaited him if he stayed.

Eventually the truth would sink in for Libby, and when it did, it was best to remove any flammable objects from the room, such as Ezra's limbs and clothing.

"What," Libby spat, "does *Atlas Blakely* need me for?"

Yes, there it was. The rage was settling in.

"You'd better hope you don't find out," Ezra said, and then he departed for his meeting through a door, the sound of his careful stride echoing from the floors the moment they hit familiar marble.

He already knew who the room would contain when he entered it. Much like Atlas, Ezra had chosen its occupants carefully, using the contacts he had procured beneath the meticulous cover of his unremarkable face, his eradicated name. They all *wanted* to be found—were easily lured by the right price—and so the primary leaders from every enemy the Society had ever possessed would not have hesitated to reply to Ezra's summons. They had been lured here by the promise of a single prize: the Society itself, which no one but Ezra had ever turned down.

Provided the animation worked, Ezra doubted Atlas would suspect him. But even if he did, it was Atlas who had made him invisible, and therefore impossible to find.

"My friends," Ezra said, striding in to address the room without preamble. "Welcome."

If they were surprised to discover he was so young, they hid it well. They would not have known, after all, what to make of the summons they had received, each of which contained secrets from their youth as irreconcilable leverage. (Only people who exist in three dimensions ever believe history to be sacred. Keep that to yourself.)

"The six most dangerous human beings alive," Ezra said to the room, "are, as you all know, currently in Atlas Blakely's care. One has been neutralized, which should buy us some time, and another has been eliminated by the Society itself. But the other four will bear the enormity of either our extinction or survival—the chosen of a despotic Society for which we are little more than pawns. We have one year until they emerge again from its protection."

The members of the room exchanged glances. Six of them, as Ezra found beautifully ironic. The synchronicity was so crisp that even Atlas would have appreciated it, had he known.

"What do you want us to do about them?" asked Nothazai, the first to speak.

Ezra smiled as Atlas would have shrugged.

"What else? Our world is dying," he said, and took a seat, ready to put himself to work. "It's up to us to set it right."

END.

AND SO FIVE STOOD where there had once been six.

"I won't do it," said Nico de Varona, breaking the silence. "Not unless I have some assurances moving forward."

Parisa Kamali was first to reply. "Assurances of what?"

"I want Rhodes back. And I want your word you'll help me find her." Nico's expression was determined and grim, his voice steady and unflinching. "I refuse to be part of this Society unless I know I have your support."

Dalton opted not to contribute things like *there is no refusal*, because it did not seem relevant.

Instead he sat quietly, waiting for what would come.

"I'm with Nico." That was Reina Mori.

"As am I." Callum Nova's voice was smooth with confidence. Presumably he possessed the cleverness to know that for him, only one answer would be sufficient.

"You?" Nico asked Tristan Caine, who didn't look up from his hands.

"Of course." His voice was thin with derision. "Of course."

"Which leaves you," Reina observed, turning to Parisa, who glanced askance with irritation.

"Would I really be stupid enough to refuse?"

"Don't," Nico cut in before anyone could respond. "This isn't a fight. It's not a threat, it's a fact. Either you're with me or you're not."

Either they were with him or he was not with them, Dalton interpreted in silence. But this was the point of the binding, wasn't it? They had not suffered this year for nothing.

"Fine," Parisa said. "If Rhodes can be found—"

"She will be," Nico said brusquely. "That's the point."

"Fine."

Parisa slid a glance around the room, to the five candidates present alongside the absence that none could ignore. She dared them to contradict her, but when, as predicted, they did not, she said, "You have our word, Varona."

And so where there had once been six were now, irreversibly, one.

WHEN AN ECOSYSTEM DIES, nature makes a new one. Simple rules for a simple concept, for which the Society was proof itself. It existed on the ashes of its former selves, atop the bones of things abandoned or destroyed. It was a secret buried within a labyrinth, inside a maze. To reach it was only to find a tumor that grew insidiously within itself.

The Society was built upon itself, higher and higher, like Babel reaching for the sky. Invention, progression, the building up of everything had no option but to continue; something put in motion did not, of its own volition, stop. The trouble with knowledge, the idiosyncrasy of its particular addiction, was that it was not the same as other types of vice. Because knowledge was not chemical, was not physical or hormonal or easily within reach, someone given a taste of omniscience could never be satisfied by the contents of a bare reality without it. Life and death as once prescribed would carry no weight, and even the usual temptations of excess would taste unsavory. The lives they might have had would only feel ill-fitting, poorly worn. Someday, perhaps quite soon, they might be able to create entire worlds; to not only reach, but to *become* like gods.

Dalton Ellery stood before the five initiates of the Alexandrian Society and watched them take their vows, marrying themselves to the inevitability of change and inseverable alteration. Henceforth, things would only be more difficult. Barriers would fall away; the world belonging to those who had not merited entry through the Society's doors would no longer exist, and the only walls left to contain these five would be the ones they managed to build themselves. What they did not realize yet, Dalton thought in silence, was the safety of a cage, the security of containment. Given a task, even a lab rat could be capable of satisfaction; from a prescribed morality, contentment; from the fulfillment of a purpose, the discovery of a cause. Endless choices, by contrast, would only leave the rat to chase itself in circles, unable to rest or be fulfilled.

For a moment it occurred to Dalton like a seedling of something half-remembered that perhaps he should say something along those lines. That perhaps he should warn them how the access they were soon to have would be too much to allow for any weakness, too little to accommodate for pre-existing strengths. He thought: You are entering the cycle of your own destruction, the wheel of your own fortune, which will rise and fall and so will you. You will deconstruct and resurrect in some other form, and the ashes of yourself will be the rubble from the fall.

Rome falls, he wanted to say. Everything collapses. You will, too.

You will, soon.

But before Dalton could bring himself to speak, he looked up at the mirrored surface of the reading room's glass and saw, behind him, the face of Atlas Blakely, who was the reason he still existed in any form. He had needed walls, an addict, and Atlas had given them to him in the form of a purpose. It was Atlas who had promised him that there would be an end, a conclusion to the hunger, completion of the cycle. He had taken away the chains of Dalton's invulnerability and given him what he needed most; the one thing the others might not find on their own: an answer.

Was there such a thing as too much power?

In the glass, a little manic glimmer flashed behind Dalton's eyes; a glimpse of who he'd once been. Past lives, ill-fitting. But this answer Dalton Ellery knew, as the initiates would soon learn, because it was the only answer even if it was the worst one, the least comforting, the most limitless:

Yes.

But as the world itself will tell you, something put in motion will not stop.

ACKNOWLEDGMENTS

I can't believe I keep writing things and you keep reading them. Miraculous.

This book in particular was a long time coming; these characters existed in an entirely different world amid a vastly unrelated plot before I dismantled the whole thing, used the remains for kindling, and rebuilt the story before you from the ashes of its former self. A special outpouring of thanks to Aurora and Mr Blake, who read all of this book's different versions and persuaded me to keep going. I say this every time, but every time, I mean it: if not for them, the book you hold in your hands would not exist.

Many thanks to the usual suspects: my editors, Aurora and Cyndi; my science consultant, Mr Blake; my fight consultant, Nacho; my beloved illustrator, Little Chmura. Will I ever be able to thank you enough? Distressingly no, but I'll keep trying. For my parents, who cheerfully back away when I'm writing and don't ask me too often how things are going. Thank you for putting up with my artistic temperament and my deep, disturbing love of my work. For my sisters, KMS. To all of my family, my friends who continuously support me: Allie, Ana, Bella, Cara, Carrie, David, Elena, Garrett, Kayla, Lauren, Mackenzie, Megan, Stacie. To the Boxing Book Club. To my therapist, who let me use an entire hour for an incoherent stream of consciousness to work out a plot point I couldn't untangle. To all the people who say you're not crazy, keep going, this is good. I wish gratitude were easier to package.

To my mom, since I know she reads these: I love and am very indebted to you. (Just generally.)

To Mr Blake: thank you for telling me that my construction of magic proves I understand basic principles of physics. I worry you will eventually discover this is not correct; when that day arrives, my condolences. Thank you for considering me the good kind of crazy. Thank you for teaching everyone,

CPSIA information can be obtained
at www.ICGtesting.com
Printed in the USA
LVHW031023070921
697190LV00004B/349

ACKNOWLEDGMENTS

I can't believe I keep writing things and you keep reading them. Miraculous.

This book in particular was a long time coming; these characters existed in an entirely different world amid a vastly unrelated plot before I dismantled the whole thing, used the remains for kindling, and rebuilt the story before you from the ashes of its former self. A special outpouring of thanks to Aurora and Mr Blake, who read all of this book's different versions and persuaded me to keep going. I say this every time, but every time, I mean it: if not for them, the book you hold in your hands would not exist.

Many thanks to the usual suspects: my editors, Aurora and Cyndi; my science consultant, Mr Blake; my fight consultant, Nacho; my beloved illustrator, Little Chmura. Will I ever be able to thank you enough? Distressingly no, but I'll keep trying. For my parents, who cheerfully back away when I'm writing and don't ask me too often how things are going. Thank you for putting up with my artistic temperament and my deep, disturbing love of my work. For my sisters, KMS. To all of my family, my friends who continuously support me: Allie, Ana, Bella, Cara, Carrie, David, Elena, Garrett, Kayla, Lauren, Mackenzie, Megan, Stacie. To the Boxing Book Club. To my therapist, who let me use an entire hour for an incoherent stream of consciousness to work out a plot point I couldn't untangle. To all the people who say you're not crazy, keep going, this is good. I wish gratitude were easier to package.

To my mom, since I know she reads these: I love and am very indebted to you. (Just generally.)

To Mr Blake: thank you for telling me that my construction of magic proves I understand basic principles of physics. I worry you will eventually discover this is not correct; when that day arrives, my condolences. Thank you for considering me the good kind of crazy. Thank you for teaching everyone, me most of all. I tire of everything, always, but never you.

To you: writing is my excruciating joy, my feast of hope, my method of survival. Ipso facto, so are you. As always, it has been an honor to put these words down for you. I sincerely hope you enjoyed the story.

xx, Olivie

record

CPSIA information can be obtained
at www.ICGtesting.com
Printed in the USA
LVHW031023070921
697190LV00004B/349

9 781679 910999